MOSES

❧

JOSHUA

TWO BOOKS IN ONE SPECIAL VOLUME

ELLEN GUNDERSON TRAYLOR'S

MOSES

❧

JOSHUA

HARVEST HOUSE PUBLISHERS
Eugene, Oregon 97402

MOSES-- THE DELIVERER

Copyright© 1990 by Harvest House Publishers, Inc.
Eugene, Oregon 97402

Library of Congress Cataloging- in- Publication Data

Traylor, Ellen Gunderson.
    Moses the deliverer / Ellen Gunderson Traylor.
    ISBN 0-89081-781-2
    1. Moses (Biblical leader)----Fiction. 2. Bible.
  O.T.--History of Biblical events----Fiction. 1. Title.
  PS3570.R357M6 1990
813'.54--dc20   90-35980
                                                    CIP

Printed in the United States of America.

First combined edition for Christian Herald Family Bookshelf: 1991

ELLEN GUNDERSON
TRAYLOR

MOSES

THE DELIVERER

HARVEST HOUSE PUBLISHERS
Eugene, Oregon 97402

To
Dr. Don Gilmore
—my pastor—
who has the gift of prophecy

Other Books by
Ellen Gunderson Traylor

Song of Abraham

John—Son of Thunder

Mary Magdalene

Noah

Ruth—A Love Story

Jonah

Mark—Eyewitness

Esther—The Story of a Woman Who Saved a Nation

Joseph—Dreamer of Dreams

Contents

A Note to the Reader

The story of Moses is one of the grandest of all time. No single volume can do justice to its importance. When I set out to capture some of its glory on paper, I was confronted immediately with its overwhelming scope.

Early into the project I saw that the period of Moses's life that prepared him to lead Israel was of massive dimension. Likewise, the period following the exodus of the Israelites from Egypt is epical.

For this reason, *Moses: the Deliverer* culminates in the highly dramatic confrontations between Moses and Pharaoh that signal the Israelites' release from bondage. Following the exodus, the story of Moses becomes so intertwined with that of Joshua as to be one great adventure, deserving of its own volume. *Joshua: God's Warrior,* captures the wilderness experiences of the chosen people as they make their way into the Promised Land.

The adventure of writing this first installment has taught me much regarding the intricacy of God's plan for his people, its sure fulfillment, and his pressing demands for holiness. Most of all, however, I sensed the Lord's fatherly heart toward those who know him best and toward those who have only begun to seek him.

Ellen Traylor
Spokane, Washington

When Israel was a child,
then I loved him,
and called my son out of Egypt.
Hosea 11:1

PROLOGUE

White moonlight spilled through the only window of Jochebed's one-room house. Leaning close to the opening, she sat with her face upturned, a rare look of peace and fulfillment caressing her dark features.

Though it was midnight, the silver glow of the moon was so bright it cast her shadow in graceful silhouette against the far wall.

As she glimpsed it, she sighed and smiled deep within herself. The gentle swell of her abdomen dominated the shadow, and she caressed her stomach fondly.

In a few weeks she would feel the first pangs of labor, and one night soon she would be sitting at this window in the silence, nursing her newborn son.

Jochebed knew this child would be a boy. Some instinct told her so, some primal understanding she could not explain.

Softly she hummed one of the native lullabies of her ancestral homeland, believing that the child within would hear it, would perceive her mother love and feel secure.

As she did so, she wove a row of woolen yarn onto a small swatch of fabric, the start of a blanket for her baby. The pattern of stripes which she had chosen was the hallmark of her husband's tribe, the same pattern which marked her identifying headband. When her son became a man, he would use the blanket as his sacred mantle, wearing it whenever he prayed to his father's God.

Just now her husband, Amram, snored as he slept on the couple's thin pallet. Too bad he could not know the womanly luxury of such a night, the young mother thought. But women deserved some private delight when their lot was so hard on earth.

Not that Amram's life had been easy. No slave, male or female, Semite or black, led a pleasant existence in this cruel country.

Jochebed had always lived in Egypt. But she was an alien here, and Nubia, the land of her mother and her mother's people, haunted her from happy tales heard at her mother's knee. To be sure, moments of joy had pressed through the years of bondage that defined her existence. Overall, however, life had been a sad thing, full of arduous labor and emptiness of soul.

She knew Amram loved her. As she fondly studied his sleepy countenance, she remembered the first time she had ever seen him. His presence now was as reassuring as it had been from the beginning.

That long-ago day had begun as a nightmare, when Egyptian troops had invaded her village on the plain of Goshen. Pharaoh's soldiers had every right to enter the slave town. But even a prison cell feels like home to one who spends a lifetime in it. And when the Egyptians swept through the only streets Jochebed claimed as her own, they violated the single safe place she knew.

The fields of Egyptian flax in which she toiled each day were not safe. More than once she had felt the sting of a slavedriver's whip upon her back. Even as a small girl, she had seen her father and mother endure the abuse of the overlord's rod, and once she had seen a comely girlfriend hauled behind a baling wagon, the victim of whatever lust the foreman would satisfy.

The ghetto to which the slave families retired at sunset was sanctuary. Miserable sanctuary to be sure, with its dirt-floored hovels and free-running sewage. But here no Egyptian would lightly set foot, keeping a clear distance from the unsavory place.

When the troops had come, therefore, from the city of Raamses to raid the peasant villages, they were a sight never to be forgotten.

Jochebed was used to the sun-darkened faces of the Semite slaves who inhabited her little town. Her father, Gershom, was one of these—a Levite Hebrew, intelligent and proud, whose spirit the rigors of bondage had never defeated. And she was accustomed to the black, shining faces of the Negros: the Nubians, Libyans, the Ethiopians who lived beside the others. Her mother, tall like a mustard tree and sleek as ebony, was one of these, bearing in her veins a princely African blood and proud as Gershom, whom she loved ardently.

But Jochebed had never seen Egyptians in great number. Had she been a city slave, and not a fieldworker, she would have seen them every day. As it was, the only Egyptians she encountered were the overlords, and even these rarely made appearances. The men who commanded her people's workparties were more often former slaves themselves, promoted for their size and strength, and hated by their fellow captives whom they had betrayed.

Tall and slender, the Egyptians, with their clean-shaven faces, their pale olive complexions and straight, thin noses, were an awesome host. Like swift spears at morning they shot into town, taking the drowsy villagers by surprise, shouting and forcing them into queues. Without explanation, the soldiers herded them from their houses and with whips and poised bows marched them toward the pink-dawn walls of Raamses, Pharaoh's delta treasure city.

As quickly as that, life in the fields was exchanged for labor on the many ego-inspired projects of Pharaoh Thutmose, whose grandiose dream was to experience immortality in this present world. Jochebed would no longer harvest the grains of Goshen, but would spend her days treading the straw of the fields into yellow mud, which would be cast into bricks for the temples, mansions, and spas of Pharaoh's insatiable mania.

Dreadful as that day had been, however, it had brought with it a spark of hope. For when Jochebed and her villagers were taken to the capital, they were commingled with other captives, and upon that day, she first saw Amram.

Actually, Amram saw her before she saw him. As he would later tell her, he lost his heart to her at first glance. When to his great joy he learned that she was, like himself, a Levite, his soul surged with delight. From that moment he determined to make her his own.

When Jochebed's people were thrust to the dirt within the city ghetto, left to weep and to sort out what had happened, a long-lost relative recognized Gershom.

"Jehovah be praised!" a venerable Hebrew cried. Tears streaming down his face, he clutched Jochebed's father to his chest. Soon names were being passed about as Levite greeted Levite and introductions were made between folks who had been torn asunder years before.

Gershom proudly showed his wife to his family, and shy Jochebed met her father's people for the first time.

Rejoicing swelled through the crowd as others found loved ones and families separated by the slave system were reunited. In the midst of what had begun as the saddest of hours, music and celebration broke loose. The few Egyptians left in charge of the merged parties looked on with aloof disdain as the captives, black and white, danced and sang. The city slaves, whose village now must make room for the field slaves, sparked in chorus, folks running for their huts and bringing out instruments of music. Soon the rich, rhythmic sounds of Nubian tambourines, drums, and pipes blended with the hand harps and timbrels of the Hebrews. Black women in pink and white veils spun and clapped, and Hebrew maidens with vivid striped skirts and curly black tresses swayed and skipped beside them.

While a slave town was a miserable place, whether inside or outside the city walls, it could be a lively site when occasion allowed.

The city slaves were somewhat better off than those of the fields. Jochebed's mother had often told her of the whitewashed huts of Nubia, with their colorful wall paintings of stylized gazelles, antelope, and water buffalo. Now for the first time the girl was privileged to see replicas of them, since many of the little houses in this village sported such designs.

The captive girl's fears began to subside, overswept by the revelry of the moment. But it was not until Amram's smile caught her eye that they vanished altogether.

From that instant, she would be a captive of another sort—a captive to the love of a Hebrew man. And like her mother, she would from that day forward live on the cultural line dividing Semites and blacks.

Jochebed smiled at the memory of that distant day and stroked her abdomen tenderly. She observed her sleeping husband with fond gratitude for his always-gentle way with her.

Though she had been reared in the faith of Jehovah and in the traditions of her Hebrew father, those traditions were still as mysterious to her as they had been to her mother. She honored them, but stood in awe of them, as though they could never be wholly her own.

What was her own was the family she and Amram had together. Wistfully she peered through the firelight at the center of the room. On pallets slept her two elder children, a tall nine-year-old girl named Miriam and her spirited brother, three-year-old Aaron.

Amram had shown his love for Jochebed in a most poignant manner when he had allowed her to give her firstborn son a Nubian name. And both children took after her in appearance, their sharp Hebrew features set off by skin darker and ruddier than most of their companions'.

Jochebed hoped that her kind husband would allow her to bestow an African name upon the new baby as well, when he received the Hebrew mark of circumcision eight days after his birth. Even now, as she continued to work on the child's striped blanket, the young mother rehearsed a list of popular tribal designations, trying to choose between them.

As she pondered possibilities, the tiny one beneath her heart gave a little kick. Cupping her hand over her swollen belly, she could feel the wee, round head. Yes, the position was right. He would be healthy and bright.

But once more, memories of the invading Egyptians colored the peaceful moment, unbidden, unsettling. Why they should crowd into this precious, private time, Jochebed could not imagine. With a shake of her shoulders, she tried to obliterate them.

Still they persisted, and she pressed her hand against the her taut belly as if for reassurance.

Leaning her head toward the child's silent sanctuary, she whispered, believing again that he would hear her.

"Jehovah protect you," she prayed. "God of your father, protect you."

PART I
Child of Prophecy

1

Jannes, grand wizard of Raamses, passed through the halls of Pharaoh's pleasure palace with a resolute stride. Arms crossed over his chest, he lifted his chin high and counted the wall torches through half-closed eyes.

"Five, six, seven..."

The seventh marked the entry of Pharaoh's private suite. With a firm grip, Jannes lifted the door handle and announced himself.

Of all the people of Egypt, Jannes, priest of the palace, was the only one granted admission to Pharaoh's chamber without prior notice.

To the wizard's dismay, but not to his surprise, King Thutmose was still asleep.

"It is nearly noon!" the priest growled.

Walking to the balcony arch, he flung back the heavy drapery, sending a sheet of midday sun across the king's ornate bed.

"Another night of folly!" the priest muttered. "How shall the nation survive?"

Thutmose, rousing from slumber, heard the objection through a besotted haze. But he was used to the old fellow's ravings. Pulling his pillow over his head, he snuggled down for more rest.

"'Yet a little sleep, a little slumber,'" the wiseman entoned, quoting a proverb, "'a little folding of the hands to sleep. So shall your poverty come as a robber, and your want as an armed man!'"

"Now, now, Jannes," Thutmose laughed, "go away! I have heard it all before!"

"And you shall hear it again," the priest warned, "not by my voice alone, but by your own experience. Every morning, thousands of your people trek to their temples and shrines, in the smallest villages and the largest cities of this land. They await word that the great god Ra has risen to start his day; they await assurance that he has washed his face and donned his royal garb, so that their own day may begin. And every morning, I must send forth your proxy to stand in for you as the incarnate deity, to wash his face in the holy basin and announce the rising of the sun! But this cannot go on forever!"

Sitting up at last, Thutmose stretched his arms and yawned deliciously. "All the people need do is look to the sky," he said with a laugh. "Each dawn, Ra shines bright and warm, sending rays of divine guidance throughout the earth. They need not see Pharaoh rise from his bed to know I am with them." Propping himself against a mound of plump, round pillows, he winked at the old priest.

Most Egyptians slept on thin pallets, their heads supported by rigid neckstands, their bodies straight as pokers. Not so Thutmose. His chamber was lined with bolsters, and everywhere he reclined, whether upon a couch, within his chariot, or upon his private barge, pillows cradled his royal frame.

This luxury Jannes had often decried, saying that the lap of ease into which the nobility had fallen betrayed a lazy spirit and heralded the demise of the culture.

Jannes had ably served two administrations and would, Thutmose confessed, likely live another century, but the king wearied of his doomcrying. He was an old man, and it seemed the special province of old men, particularly priests, to see the dark side of life.

As for Thutmose, though he was middle-aged, he considered himself eternally youthful and refused to let Jannes ruin his day.

The New Empire, as his line of rulers had styled themselves, was half-a-century old and showed no sign of weakening. Egypt, in fact, had never been stronger, basking in glory and wealth unparalleled in its long chronicle.

With the sunlight spilling across his bed came the sounds of building and commerce from the streets beyond. Egypt had always owed its success to the toil of slaves, and never more than now, when its heyday was mounted upon the sweating backs of its bondsmen.

The every-morning sound of picks and hammers, the chant of chain gangs, the obedient clatter of a thousand-thousand captives was music to Thutmose's ears. And the scene was repeated across the empire, every day, in a dozen cities where workers, predominately Hebrew, gave their lives in service to Egyptian overlords.

Jannes knew Thutmose reveled in unconditional power. But the priest watched the streets with a worried look, taking no satisfaction in the suffering before him. Feeling the king's prideful sneer against his back, he shuddered.

"Ever since the expulsion of the Hyksos, the throne has expected slavery to weaken the enemy," the priest reminded him. "Is this not true?"

Thutmose was in no mood for a history lesson. It was indeed true that when the legendary Ahmose had felled the last regime of the "shepherd kings"—the Hyksos to whom Jannes referred—he had taken their followers as slaves. Since that day the empire had thrived on Hebrew labor as the cornerstone of its economy. But Thutmose saw no threat in such utilitarian policy.

"'Never question the wisdom of the ancestors,'" the emperor quipped, rehearsing one of Jannes's favorite maxims.

But the priest still sadly surveyed the city and the many projects up and down the boulevard, works executed by forced labor.

Not the least of the slave-assignments was the construction of yet another obelisk, one among a bevy of ancient monoliths erected by devout pharaohs. This, like all the rest, would be dedicated to Ra, god of the sun, but would bear the name of the present emperor.

The city of Raamses would forever bear the mark of Thutmose. Determined to leave an impression grander than all his predecessors, he had commissioned his obelisk to dwarf the others and to reflect the light of heaven off slabs of granite, black and shiny.

Yet as Jannes studied the growing monument, he seemed only burdened by it.

Thutmose, following Jannes's gaze, shrugged absently, not relating to the priest's mood.

"So tell me, friend," he spurred him, "to what do I owe the pleasure of your company?"

The king was about to indulge in another mouth-stretching yawn when the old man suddenly pronounced, "I have had a dream, Your Majesty."

Nothing else Jannes could have said or done would have grabbed the king's attention. Thutmose had witnessed the old man's sorcery. He had seen him conjure up spirits, move objects without touching them, bring thunder and lightning into a room. But no such act would have intrigued him like the mention of a dream.

A dream, at least a priestly one, was no light thing, no frivolous interlude of slumber. Rather it was a highly sacred matter, an issue of omen and warning, a herald of the divine word, and an indicator of the future.

"A...dream?" Thutmose stammered. "A vision?"

"Nothing less," the priest asserted.

Thutmose had left his pillows and had thrown his legs over the side of the bed. Clutching a blanket about his shoulders, he ran a hand across his face and tried to clear his foggy eyes.

"And what does this vision portend?" he managed, almost afraid of his own voice.

"I and my brother, Jambres, have tried to warn you before," the elder rebuked him. "Our fathers tried to warn your fathers, but never would any of you listen."

Thutmose bristled, but humbled himself, anxious to hear a prophecy. He knew that such moments as this were very rare, coming in any pharaoh's career once or twice at most. His own father had often told the story of how the priests had warned of attack from the west, just in time for him to alert his forces and successfully prepare. And then there was the most famous tale of the strange prophet who had served the first Hyksos king, the Hebrew seer named Joseph, who had warned of famine and saved the nation from starvation.

Could Thutmose do any less than listen reverently to this, the first prophecy of his administration?

"Speak, Father," the king pleaded. "I may not be religious, but I have humbled my heart, this moment, in this place."

Head bowed, Thutmose sat with his hands folded in his lap. His demeanor was persuasive, and for the instant Jannes softened. He recalled the king's more innocent years, the days of unsullied youth when he had held the elder's heart and had seemed to promise hope for the empire's moral fiber.

"Come," Jannes called, motioning the king toward the balcony. "Look with me; see with my eyes."

Obediently Thutmose joined the priest at the arch, and following his gesture, watched the workers in the street.

"The Hebrews do not languish beneath your oppression, O King," Jannes asserted. "Far from it. No, they grow stronger with each generation. Their bodies are hardened by the very toil with which you would break them. In number they surpass our own people, and for energy and wit, they have no equal."

Thutmose studied the sun-darkened men who easily carried loads two times the weight which would bow an Egyptian to the ground. Tensely he watched their steadfast endurance under the African sun and their heroic spirit beneath the onslaught of their slavedrivers.

Yet he resisted. "If they are so strong," he argued, "why have they never risen up? In 350 years, they have never rebelled!"

"Only one thing have they lacked, Your Highness," Jannes explained, tracing a crooked finger through the air. "They have been bred, these generations, to mindlessly follow. They have the instinct of the herd. But give them a leader, and all that will change. It is a leader they need, and nothing more. For they are still people of the desert, wild and free in their deepest hearts. A mere hint of unity, and they will rise above any obstacle."

Thutmose stared into Jannes's eyes, incredulous. It was inconceivable that chattle should so easily become noble. And the Hebrews were chattle, plain and simple. No reasonable Egyptian saw them as anything more.

Still, Jannes made no idle observation. He was a priest, no small achievement in Egypt; and he was the highest of the priests, Grand Wizard, Chief Magus, Sovereign Seer of the select caste. He and his brother, Jambres, who filled the post in the ceremonial capital of Thebes, never made idle observations.

"The vision," Thutmose pleaded. "Share it with me."

Jannes closed his eyes, recapturing the mood and essence of the dream, which he had worn into the room like a cloak.

"I see a child," he whispered, "a Hebrew child. And now, he is no child, but a prince, a man garbed in Egyptian gold, like the sun's wisdom. From his dark brow go forth the rays of divine ordination. Through his hair trickles the oil of anointing, and his tongue is like a sword."

Thutmose was riveted by Jannes's words, and when he at last took a breath, he nervously glanced out the window, almost expecting the visionary leader to pass beneath his gaze.

The scene outside had not changed. Incompatible with the priest's dream were the ongoing sounds of slave industry, the dust-raising work of hammers and chisels, and the scrape of man-hauled pallets, laden with sun-dried bricks.

Speechless, he listened as the seer concluded.

"In my dream, the prince is adored by thousands. His believers slough off the chains of bondage and follow him to freedom beyond Egypt's gates!"

Thutmose trembled, and with sudden dread, clutched at the priest's sleeve.

"Impossible!" he objected. "They are greater than we in number. But they have no means to defeat us!"

He hoped Jannes would concede to his objection. But the priest only closed his eyes again, and Thutmose saw the glimmer of a tear upon his cheek.

"There is more, O King," he added. "But you cannot bear it now."

Thutmose tightened his grip on the old man's arm, but the priest only shook his head. "Enough for now," he insisted.

The emperor stepped away, looking helplessly about his chamber.

"Surely, Wise Man, you do not tell me all this to no purpose. Surely it is a warning only, and with this warning I can act to deflect this evil."

Jannes made no reply, and Thutmose grew more adamant.

"But, Your Holiness," he argued, "did not Emperor Salatis take warning from the Hebrew seer Joseph's prophecy? Did he not store up grain against the famine

Joseph predicted? Surely your prophecy warns me, and I will prepare against it."

Jannes was turning to leave. In panic, Thutmose called him to a halt.

"This child," he cried, "is he yet born? Or is he only a phantom of the future?"

The priest stopped and faced the frantic ruler.

"I cannot say with certainty. But the dream left the impression that he will be born shortly."

"He is yet unborn!" Thutmose concluded. "And is he Hebrew?"

"Hebrew." Jannes nodded.

Pacing the room, the king rubbed his nervous hands together. Casting about for some defense, he muttered anxiously beneath his breath. Suddenly he stopped and wheeled about. Inspiration, black and wicked, colored his face.

"There is a quick solution," he leered. "Call in the midwives. I wish to speak with them."

"The midwives?" Jannes shuddered.

"Certainly, my good man," the king plotted. "I shall command that all Hebrew boys born from this day forth be killed!"

The priest marveled at the hideous ease with which Thutmose wielded his power.

"But, sir," Jannes pleaded, "no god or goddess would condone such atrocity. This is evil...evil..."

Thutmose glanced at the holy man carelessly. "The defense of Egypt is never evil," he asserted, flicking a casual hand. "Summon the midwives, now!"

As Jannes turned, white-faced, for the door, Thutmose turned again for his bed and, climbing in, settled against his pillows.

2

The irrigation ditch ran cold and swift with spring-time water, coursing through the ghetto in rhythm with the laughter of children. The sun, raging against the slave village, raised sweat on their young bodies.

But these children were used to the sun, used to the heat of the African sky. Because they did not worship the searing orb as did their Egyptian overlords, they paid it no mind. Besides, the rapid water of the little canal was a welcome reprieve from the fever of noontime.

Today the children played a game of war, mimicking adult battles with loud enthusiasm. The two sides had been chosen by the drawing of straws, the lucky participants taking the side of the Hebrews, and the unlucky, the side of their oppressors.

The captain of the Hebrew team was Jochebed's daughter, Miriam. Tall and authoritative, she was stationed where the canal entered the village, so that she could keep watch for real Egyptians in order to warn her daring companions to cease their seditious play.

Presently Miriam was fending off a volley of fruity artillery, a barrage of rotten pomegranates and splattering grapes aimed at her contingency by their heartless captors. Grasping a long stick, she held it horizontally before her and advanced against the "Egyptian" host with combative stride.

Soon enough, the tables were turned, and the slave-masters were duly repaid. To the cheers of the restive slaves, the overlords were dispossessed and herded into the communal chicken pen, which served as the insurgents' stockade.

Tomorrow the very ones who had taken the role of the antagonists would be the triumphant Hebrews. For these little wars always ended happily; only the players changed sides.

One actor alone maintained her role day after day: Miriam, stalwart commander of the Hebrew force.

Miriam was a natural leader. Though her father, Amram, was no better off materially than any other slave, he was honored by the Hebrews for his ancestral ties to Levi, the revered patriarch of the Israelite teachers. Being Amram's firstborn set Miriam in a position of responsibility among her peers, and this, added to her striking stature and commanding looks, had assured her a place of prominence among her people from birth.

Therefore, despite the fact that she was female, Miriam was rarely challenged regarding her permanent assignment in these childish games. Any youngster who had ever dared to dispute her right to the role had been forced to concede to her stronger personality.

Sturdy as a young mare, Miriam had never shied away from playing with the village boys. While the other girls were loathe to mix in the mud with the local rowdies, this young woman eagerly donned the "armor" of a tough leather vest, and proudly carried a hickory spear in her hand. She took the added role of lookout very seriously, for it was the only one that connected their world of play with the real world, feeding the protective, matriarchal bent of her heart.

These war games were the single respite from the children's arduous days, for they, like the adult slaves, were obliged to work long, hard hours for their masters. It was only as they awaited their noon and evening meals that they were given opportunity for recreation.

Downtrodden though they were, the Israelites had never lost a sense of cultural solidarity. Though it often lacked direction and purpose, their ethnic pride had managed to survive three and one-half centuries of bondage in this alien land. And ever since Father Jacob had been compelled to seek refuge from famine within the borders of this country, his descendants had maintained their cultural integrity.

When playtime was done, and when each family was gathered about its own stewpot in its own hovel, the fathers would speak of The One True God, and of his love for Israel. Tales of the patriarchs punctuated the time about the table, and though the children might have grown weary of the repetition, the pride with which the fathers spoke buoyed their spirits and reinforced their heritage.

It was this secret, and not their enslavement alone, which had always set the Hebrews apart. There were many enslaved groups in Egypt: captive Ethiopians, Cushites, Nubians, and others. But over time, their racial identities had been blurred by intermarriage, by a spirit of subservience, and by forgetfulness.

While many Israelites had married across racial lines, the "foreign" wives and husbands generally adopted the Hebrew faith.

Thus it was that bondage had strengthened rather than weakened this strange group. Thus it was that, though Thutmose preferred to deny it, the Hebrews had flourished under his oppression.

And thus is was that as Miriam, stood guarding the canal this day at the village entrance, she was a formidable sentry.

Only one thing could have distracted her from her duty. She knew that her mother was due to give birth within a few weeks. Though Jochebed was preparing the noon time meal inside the house, she was heavy with child and could require Miriam's assistance at any time. Therefore, while the girl watched the village gate, she also kept an eye on the door of the house and an ear cocked for her mother's voice.

Should Jochebed cry out, Miriam would not hesitate to abandon the war game and rush to her side. And if the woman should be ready to deliver, Miriam had been drilled in just how to respond. She would hasten first to fetch the midwives, and then to find Amram in the city.

Since all had been well when last she checked, it came as a surprise when the very midwives she would enlist were seen entering the village gate. Shiphrah and Puah were their names, and as they entered they leaned against one another, deep in anxious conversation.

These ladies were well known in the slave community. They and their many employees were the official attendants at all slave births, assigned by Pharaoh himself to oversee the management of pregnant captives. These two had in fact been present at the births of Aaron and Miriam.

Without even greeting the young guard, the glorious, lanky Shiphrah fluttered by in a flurry of veils and scarves, her many necklaces jangling against her flat chest like a worried chorus. Puah, the exact opposite in shape, bounced beside her like a plump, round ball, her ample body also decked in the veils that their monied positions afforded. Together they shook their heads and sighed over and over, Shiphrah weaving and unweaving her slender fingers and Puah clinging to her arm like a heavy purse.

When Miriam overheard their first words, she was alarmed. "First we will check on Jochebed," they said. "Jehovah preserve us!"

Forgetting her hickory staff, the sentinel hurried after the two women. The next snatches she caught of their conversation were a puzzle.

"Pharaoh...cruel...the babies...God help us!" the women whispered.

"Ladies!" Miriam cried, running up behind them. "What is the trouble?"

Shiphrah and Puah, according to their profession, had a great love for children. When Miriam hailed them, they turned about.

"Where is your mother?" Puah asked, her round face flushed as a desert rose.

"In the house," the girl replied. "But why..."

"Never mind now," Shiphrah said, shaking a long finger before Miriam's nose. "You stay outside!"

With this, the tall woman bent her head and entered through Jochebed's door, followed closely by Puah.

By now Miriam was worried indeed. Not only were the midwives seeking her mother, but they did not come with their normal, confident bearing, ready to assist at a simple birth.

Gazing after the newcomers, the girl clung to the doorpost. Yes, Jochebed was still in the kitchen, little Aaron playing at her ankles. Far from being in prenatal trouble, the woman bustled energetically about her dinner-making.

"Welcome!" she greeted the surprise visitors.

Shiphrah surveyed her carefully. "You are well, I see."

"Yes," Jochebed laughed. "I think you have come much too early." When this was received with only somber silence, the hostess wiped her floury hands on her skirt and shrugged. "Is there some problem?"

"We are on an urgent mission," Puah replied, her chubby face dotted with perspiration. "We are visiting all our mothers-to-be, to warn you..."

At this, Shiphrah nudged the speaker in the ribs.

"...to give you some advice..." Puah quickly rephrased.

"What Puah is trying to say," Shiphrah interrupted, "is that it will be best for if you are as private as possible when this child is born."

The women's awkwardness with this "mission" was quite evident. Bewildered, Jochebed objected, "You have been with me through two other births. What is so different about this one?"

"It is simply imperative that you do as we say," Shiphrah asserted. "When your labor begins, you must not cry out. We will be with you as soon as possible. But throughout your travail, you must try to be quiet."

When the two women turned to leave, Jochebed clutched at their sleeves.

"You hide some terrible news!" she cried. "You cannot keep it from us all!"

"We have others to see," Shiphrah answered. "We have said what we came to say."

As the woman exited through the low door, Puah patted Jochebed on the cheek. "There, there, dear," she consoled. "Do as we say, and all will be well."

"Puah!" Shiphrah called. "Come!"

With a sigh, the plump midwife bustled out the door, following her friend to the next appointed house.

As Miriam watched them depart, her mother joined her on the step. Neither could imagine the cause of the peculiar visit. But the joy of the approaching birth would be henceforth tinged with anxiety.

3

Pharaoh Thutmose paced the platform of his stateroom, his bare-chested image reflecting in the sheen of his gilded throne.

Jannes watched him from a claw-footed stool, glancing up from a long scroll draped across his lap. And he shook his head, his tendriled beard wisping across the papyrus.

"Did I not warn you?" the old priest muttered. "Your schemes cannot undo a prophecy!"

"We shall see; we shall see," Thutmose snarled, fidgeting with the broad, striped collar that graced his shoulders. "There is surely some conspiracy!"

Just then, at the far end of the hall, a stateroom page appeared, announcing the arrival of two summoned subjects. Pharaoh gave an anxious nod and took his seat, calling them forward.

Shiphrah and Puah, the Hebrew midwives, could have feared for their lives. If they fumbled during this inquisition, they might not live another day. Weeks ago they had been given orders by Pharaoh himself, and they had rebelled. If they should give themselves away by expression or faltering speech, they would not only forfeit their own safety but also the future of their race.

But it was with chins lifted high and eyes clear with purpose that they came before the king.

When he had first called for them, giving his grisly command for the extermination of the Hebrews, they had returned home in hopeless dread. But they had rallied, agreeing between themselves to put personal interests aside, to violate his order, and to do so secretly.

That the king was furious with them was evident. But he had no proof against them, and so, as they bowed before his livid face, they did not flinch.

Thutmose glared down on them and snapped his fingers, calling for the scroll that Jannes pondered.

When the old man brought it to him, he snatched it as though he were equally angry at the priest.

"See here!" the king raved, pointing to a list of figures stretching down the scroll. "In the last month, since I gave you my orders, 40 Hebrew boys have been born in Raamses alone! The sand fleas multiply more rapidly than ever!"

He spoke to the women as though they were in sympathy with his cause. It was true that they had been employees of the king for years, overseeing all births among his slave families. But had he forgotten that they were Hebrews?

"We have tried to do as you ask," Shiphrah replied, folding her hands calmly before her. "But the Hebrew women are fit and strong. They have delivered before we reach their houses, and the babies are already safe upon their mothers' laps before we can lay hands on them."

Her heart pounded as she spoke this lie. But she had rehearsed it well, and Pharaoh did not detect her uneasiness.

"You were to see to it that every Hebrew man-child dies at birth!" the emperor cried, pointing at them sternly. "You were to instruct your nurses to snap the necks, or cut the cords too closely, or by any means kill the sheepticks!"

Puah, shaken by his tone, swallowed hard. "Amazing, isn't it, Your Majesty," she managed. "We are just as surprised as you, but every one of our nurses gives the same report. The slave women are simply too lively. It is always too late to act on your command."

If Pharaoh believed them, it would be a miracle. Jannes studied them knowingly, trying to suppress a grin. Looking away, he raised a hand, as if to yawn, and covered his stubborn lips.

It seemed the miracle was inevitable, as inevitable as the prophecy's fulfillment.

Thutmose turned to the priest, seeking support. But Jannes gazed absently across the room, offering none.

For a long while, the king stammered over silence, and the women watched him pace to and fro.

"I have tried to be patient!" he shouted, putting his hands on his hips. "I have tried to make this as easy on the poor beggars as possible! But, it seems my best intentions and my kind heart have been thwarted."

Jannes knew the king well enough to read the revenge in his tone. But he would never have dreamed him capable of a worse horror than the aborted plan.

"Because you have failed in your duty," he ranted, "you leave me no choice but to turn the mission over to my own people."

Even the stalwart Shiphrah was frightened now, her ears burning.

"Write this upon the scroll, Jannes!" the king cried. "Tell my people to closely watch all women who are with child among the Hebrews. Every daughter that is born among them shall be saved alive. But every son shall be cast into the Nile! So shall the gods of Egypt save us, and so shall our enemies come to nothing!"

4

Amram awoke with a shudder. He had not slept well for nights, ever since Pharaoh's dreadful command had been broadcast to the nation. Every dream was fitful, every sleeping thought a nightmare. And his rest was interrupted by any sound outside, and any movement on the part of his pregnant wife.

Already, according to the king's will, hundreds of Hebrew children had been slain, and every slave village in Egypt was a din of mourning and fear.

Several families in nearby compounds had already been divested of newborn sons, the wee ones torn from their mothers upon birth by a league of spying citizens. Squalling and hungry, the babes had not even known the warmth of an embrace before they were taken from their parents, taken from the helpless nurses, and greeted by the cold waters of the Nile.

Paralyzed by shock, the Hebrews had hardly been able to react in emotion or word before the vengeance was upon them. Now, several days into the holocaust, they still did not know how to respond.

Chattel they were, and so they behaved, unarmed, impotent, and incapable of retaliation.

Certainly there were those who had tried to save their children. Some families had attempted to hide the women when they entered labor, and some parents had tried to secret their newborns away.

But already, men and women had forfeited their own lives in the process, and their children had not been spared.

Therefore, it was with a trembling heart that Amram lay beside his wife each night. It was with a lump in his throat that he tried to reassure Aaron and Miriam each evening when bedtime came. For he had no reason to think his family's case could be different.

Still, he did not know if it was fear or awe that roused him just now.

Down the narrow path that ran through his village, lights and voices could be heard. And he thought a woman had screamed. But another impression, equally vivid, throbbed in his head. Was it a vision? Or was it a figment born of desire, the stress of days and nights of dread?

Turning, he saw that Jochebed was also awake, her eyes white and wide against her dusky skin. Furtively she reached out and clutched at his nightshirt.

"I am afraid," she whispered. "Did you hear a cry?"

"I did," Amram admitted. Standing, he drew back a corner of the window blind.

The lights were more active now, bobbing at the doorway of a neighbor's house. They were small torches held by Egyptians, commoners who had been seen earlier in the day lurking about the edge of the village.

"There is trouble at Misnah's house," Amram whispered.

"Misnah?" Jochebed choked. "She is due to deliver any day!"

Amram interpreted the activity down the way. "I fear she does so now," he sighed, watching the anxious shadows against her blind. "They have come for the child."

Even as he spoke, he could see silhouettes in the covered window, the shadow of a tiny baby held high in grasping hands.

"Pharaoh's henchmen!" the woman cried.

"Hush, Jochebed," Amram warned, rejoining her upon the bed. "We must not draw their attention."

With this, he stroked her swollen belly, and she lay her head upon his shoulder. The feel of his beard against her cheek was always a comfort, but tonight she was rigid in his arms.

Pulling her tight to his chest, Amram breathed into her ear. "I have had a dream," he said. "It was the dream that woke me."

"Oh," Jochebed wept, "I have dreadful dreams every night! I cannot sleep for fear of them. What will become of us, Amram?"

The man pressed his fingers gently to her lips. "Hush," he said again. "This was not a dreadful dream. This was different, Jochebed, a vision...a promise..."

Incredulous, the woman pulled back, studying him doubtfully.

"I saw our newborn son," he whispered. "The child shall be a boy."

Under the circumstances, this should have evoked the greatest fear. But Amram's tone suggested hope.

Still, Jochebed had known for some time that she would bear a man-child.

"Yes," she replied. "It is as I have feared."

"But," Amram went on, "that is just the point. There is no reason to fear. The child will survive the king's decree."

Now Jochebed was curious indeed. But just as she would respond, the cry of the bereft mother down the way quivered through the night air, and the shuffle of feet could be heard as the kidnappers hastened back toward the village gate.

"How can you speak of hope?" Jochebed shuddered. Tears filled her eyes, and she speared him with an accusing look.

"I do not understand my dream," he replied. "Least of all do I understand why a slave like me should be privileged to bear a prince for Israel. But I know here in my heart that the vision portends the future, and that our child shall save our people!"

Jochebed followed his insistent finger, where it pressed against his chest. Tenderly she reached for it and drew it to her lips, her mind a muddle of resistance. Shaking her head, she pleaded with him, "Speak no more of the child. He stirs even now within me, filling me with fear. If you say there is hope, I shall try to believe. But your God is a mystery to me, as mysterious as life and death."

5

Amram hastened through the streets of Raamses, sweat streaking his brow. He had put in a full day of labor under the Egyptian sun, but urgency chased him home.

Only moments ago Miriam had come for him at the site where he pushed mud-laden barrows for Pharaoh's brick masons. Because it was the close of the work day, he was able to leave without being questioned. If all went well this evening, no Egyptian would know that Jochebed's child was on its way.

The dream that had encouraged Amram a few days previous had stayed with him ever since. How the child of a bondman could rise to greatness in Egypt, he could not imagine. But the hope was sacred, a certain trust.

As the man and his daughter arrived at the house, low voices could be heard within. Rhythmic and even, they were the promptings of the midwives, Shiphrah and Puah, who sat beside Jochebed in her labor.

Dusk was coming on. Inside the house, a small lamp burned in a corner of the ceiling. The midwives greeted Amram with a nod, keeping the rhythm of their chant. Quickly he knelt beside the birthing chair.

Like other women, Egyptian or slave, Jochebed would give birth while sitting upright. To her back was Puah, bracing her as she heaved with each throe. To her front was Shiphrah, who watched as Jochebed stradled a narrow stool, ready to report as the infant emerged, ready to catch the child upon her own lap, where he would be swaddled in linen.

The scene in this delivery room was not unlike that in any other. Eagerness and anxiety filled the air. But fear infused the mood with extra tension, and while the focus was on Jochebed, eyes often traveled to the door, and ears were attuned to any sound outside.

Even little Aaron, who clung to Miriam's skirt, was somber and silent. Normally a young child would not have been privy to such a scene. But tonight the entire family was sequestered in the hut, ready to defend Jochebed and her baby.

On the two previous occasions when Jochebed had given birth, her delivery had been difficult. Narrow of hip and delicate, the half-Nubian woman had been at risk in both cases. But tonight her pain seemed lighter than before, her breathing more controlled.

As her labor quickened, her body was slick with sweat, and her tunic clung to her abdomen like a second skin. Miriam passed a cold, wet cloth over her mother's forehead, and the midwives poised themselves for action.

Somehow, the woman was able to restrain her cries. Amram bent close, reminding her that all would be well.

"A son," he said, "a prince. Remember the dream, the promise."

His voice blended with those of the midwives, and his encouraging whispers pulsed through Jochebed's heart.

Within moments, the long-awaited babe found the light, and his strong and lusty cry pierced the air.

Shiphrah, efficient and adept, received him. Puah, reaching around Jochebed, clipped the cord and placed her gentle hand over the squalling infant's mouth.

They held him for only an instant, inspecting him and pronouncing him healthy.

"A boy," Shiphrah affirmed, placing him on Jochebed's stomach.

Speechless for joy, the woman cradled the baby against her breast. With tears streaming down their cheeks, she and her husband admired him.

Aaron and Miriam drew near and studied their brother. Nursing hungrily, the child was quiet now, his cries replaced by anxious feeding.

Little Aaron reached out a dimpled hand and touched the newborn. Like him, the baby was ruddy and dark, with a shock of fine black hair.

Turning to Miriam, Jochebed instructed, "Fetch the satchel."

Obediently, the girl went to a corner and returned with a thick tapestry bag, one which had taken Jochebed hours of nighttime labor to create.

Well-padded, it was furnished with a pillow in the bottom and lined with the striped blanket Jochebed had made. The top was made of net, to admit air. It resembled a cradle inside, but could pass as a shoulder bag. It would serve as the baby's hiding place for as long as possible.

"He is a fine child," Amram said, stroking his wife's forehead.

Drawing his family to him, he reminded them of their well-rehearsed plan.

"Miriam, you know your duty," he said.

"Yes, Papa. I will look after the satchel when mother is in the fields. When she cannot carry it, I will do so."

"Aaron, stay close beside your mother when she is at work," Amram insisted. "Help Miriam guard her when she must nurse the child."

Shiphrah and Puah listened in wonder to the determined family.

"You mean to hide the infant night and day?" Puah marveled.

Her doubts were obvious. She considered the many others who had tried in vain to conceal their newborn sons.

Jochebed clutched the wriggling baby in a protective embrace. "Is he not a beautiful boy?" she said. "Would you do any less, if he were yours?"

Puah smiled wistfully. "The God of Abraham be with you," she said.

"He is with us," Amram replied. "He has promised always to be."

6

Jochebed stood straight, lifting her face to the persistent sun and rubbing the small of her back.

Many times during the last months of her pregnancy, this same gesture had been necessary, as the weight of her front-heavy form strained the tender muscles.

Of course, she no longer carried an unborn child. Her baby was asleep inside its concealing cradle, and the big purse sat in the shade of a palm grove near the brick pit where she labored.

Still her spine was strained by the bag of barley chaff with which she padded herself, to appear yet-with-child.

The baby was now three days old. No one suspected Jochebed's duplicity. As though nothing had changed, she worked at the task that had occupied her days for so long, the tredding of straw into the mud that would be fired for the king's monuments.

As usual, Miriam labored beside her, but now they both had the added burden of tending to the bag, of listening for the child's least stir, and of diverting others away from their secret.

It was confirmation of Amram's vision that the newborn was unusually quiet. Rarely did the little one so much as whimper, and he slept for longer periods than most infants.

Jochebed knew it might not stay this way, however. She dreaded the possibility that her private times with the child, for nursing and diaper changes, would eventually be detected.

To this point, she had managed to slip away quietly when the baby needed her, to station herself just long enough behind some tree or wagon to feed and tend to him.

But this was only the third day of her trial. Within hours of his birth, she had returned to work. The least slip could bring the disaster they all feared, putting not only the child in jeopardy, but the entire family.

Then too, she could not masquerade as a pregnant woman forever. Already her supervisor eyed her often, wondering how long she could carry on. But he was a busy man. He could not trouble himself with an over-interest in her condition.

Likewise it was to her benefit that she was dark-skinned. Rarely, except in the slave village, was she seen in the company of her Hebrew husband. Being only one among hundreds of people who labored in the pit, her Israelite connections were rarely considered.

Jochebed and Amram had decided that their baby would not be circumcised until he was out of danger. By Hebrew tradition, the child should receive the mark in his flesh upon the eighth day, and not until this rite was performed should he receive his name. In order to conceal his identity as a Hebrew, he would have neither until he could do so without jeopardy.

One hour of reprieve was allowed the slaves each day, at noon, when the sun burned hottest.

When the watchman announced the break, Miriam and Jochebed grabbed the bag and scurried home.

"If we hurry, we should have time to bathe him," the mother whispered.

Once inside their hut, they hastily opened the bag. On cue, the baby roused from his long nap and began to cry.

"God of Israel!" Jochebed groaned. "See here, Miriam. The baby is covered with a rash!"

Peering into the cradle, the girl sighed. "He gets too hot, staying in there all day. Mama, what shall we do?"

Fretfully Jochebed soothed his skin with a cool rag. Then, with liberal strokes, she smoothed corn flour over his body.

"There is no other way to hide him!" she cried. "And soon he will be far too big to hide."

Miriam bent over her little brother, brushing his forehead with a kiss. As he grew calmer, she slipped a finger into his palm and gave a tug.

"He is a strong one, Mama!" she exclaimed. "Strong and beautiful! Surely the Lord is his keeper, and not we alone."

7

Although few in the slave village had held out much hope for Jochebed's child, the faith and determination of Amram's family eventually inspired the people to rally around their mission.

After all, perhaps there could be strength in unity. Perhaps if this child could be saved, so could others.

A popular conspiracy took hold. For the next three months the safety of this little one became the village's secret project. Women who were home when Jochebed was at work volunteered to care for the baby in her absence. He was posed as a girl-child, dressed in garments befitting someone's daughter; he was slipped to Jochebed at the worksite, where others stood in for her as she nursed him in secret. When the young mother could no longer pass herself off as pregnant, the rumor was created that she had lost her child in labor.

Joining in the collusion were the midwives, Shiphrah and Puah. They had risked deceiving Pharaoh before and would not hesitate to help this cause. Between their efforts and those of the neighbors, the child was never alone.

The time came, however, when the risks were just too great.

Today Shiphrah sat on Jochebed's doorstep, holding the sturdy boy upon her lap. Stretched to his full length, his tiptoes pressed into her knees, he kicked his strong legs over and over, bouncing up and down. His giggle was lusty and jubilant, his ruddy face glowing with health.

Together the two of them laughed, enjoying the afternoon sun. But suddenly it seemed a cloud passed overhead, and Shiphrah turned her eyes to the sky.

It was no cloud that cast her in shadow. An Egyptian slavemaster towered over her, eyeing the baby with a suspicious leer. In his fist was a leather whip, and it seemed he would just as soon strike the woman as speak to her.

From between gritted teeth, he spat, "Whose child is this?"

Shiphrah, who was used to dealing with Egyptians, did not cower beneath his demanding gaze. Standing to her feet, she threw her slender shoulders back and confronted him squarely.

"Do you address a servant of Pharaoh in such a tone?" she barked. "I should have you reported!"

Taken aback, the man cleared his throat, wondering whom he challenged. "It is my duty to oversee this compound," he stammered.

"And it is my duty, as chief of Pharaoh's midwives, to oversee the mothers and children of this place," she countered.

Redfaced, the slavemaster bowed his head. The office of midwife was a noble one, assigned like any high government post by the king himself.

"Very well, madam," he conceded, "but you know the law. I am within my bounds to inquire about this child."

Shiphrah breathed shallowly, her heart fluttery as a bird's. "This is Misnah's daughter," she said.

If the master had ever known of Misnah's tragedy, of the fact that she had borne a son, only to lose him to the kidnappers, he did not recall it now. Vaguely he remembered that the female slave named Misnah had been pregnant.

"Daughter?" he muttered, leaning down for a closer look.

"Yes. And she is due for a diaper change," she added. "Would you hold her while I fetch one?"

Suddenly the slavemaster was more than willing to let the matter go. Shielding his nose, an Egyptian's most cherished feature, he refused the offer. And turning on his heel he hastened for the gate.

Holding the baby close to her chest, Shiphrah grinned triumphantly.

Still it had been a close call, and one she did not care to endure again.

8

The lantern burned low in Amram's house that evening, and the little family, as they gathered about the
dinner table, spoke in hushed voices.

Shiphrah's story of the brush with disaster still burned
in their ears, and they huddled together, trying to bolster
their courage.

"God has spared us so far," Amram whispered. "Three
months...it is a miracle! He will surely give us wisdom to
carry on."

Aaron and Miriam listened quietly. The past weeks
had been a time of deep lessons for the two youngsters,
lessons in the faith of Israel and the strength of their
God. They knew their father spoke the truth, though
they could not imagine how the Lord would continue to
intervene.

But Jochebed, for whom the past three months had
been the most tense and nerve-racking, reflected on
today's near-exposure in somber silence.

Clutching the baby to her bosom, she rocked to and
fro. Tears rose to her eyes but did not spill over.

"We cannot ask our neighbors and our friends to continue with this charade!" she sighed at last. "Every day
they risk their own safety in our defense. Every time
someone covers the truth, the entire village is put in
jeopardy."

The family did not like to hear reality so plainly spoken, but they knew it must be faced.

"I have given much thought to our predicament," Jochebed went on. "I cannot leave the baby home another day. He must be my responsibility, regardless of the dangers."

Amram's brow furrowed. "But the purse-cradle is too small now," he objected. "You cannot carry him to work as you did before. You cannot hide him from the overseers."

"My work team is being moved tomorrow," she replied. "We are being sent to haul mud from the river bank. For the next few weeks, Miriam and I will be working beside the Nile."

As Amram listened, his wife reached under the table and brought forth a large, reed basket. Placing it before her family, she said, "I purchased this at market today. Tomorrow I am going to gather some river slime with which to seal it over. It will be a fine vessel for our little one!"

"A vessel?" Amram said with a start. "What do you mean?"

"A boat," Jochebed replied matter-of-factly.

"You mean to set our child adrift?" the father cried.

The woman, still pressing the baby to her chest, lifted determined eyes to her husband.

"You have taught me to have faith in the God of Abraham," she said. "The time has come to let the child go."

Amram studied his wife in amazement. Never had he seen this side of her.

"I am not sure..." he faltered.

But even as he spoke, his words accused him.

Had he not said the child would rise to glory? Had the Lord not shown him this?

Reaching out, he stroked the baby's chin. And in his heart, at that moment, he released him.

9

Jochebed and Miriam crept through the dusky lowland of the Nile, casting fretful glances over their shoulders. Thick mud invaded their sandals, caking the creases between their toes. Spiny cattails clung to their homespun skirts.

The sun would be rising soon. As yet it had not touched the sky, and only a gray pallor promised the light of day. But the two raced against time, and against the tug of the marshy ooze sucking at their feet.

Their journey toward the river was awkward and uneasy, not only because of the darkness and the swampy terrain, but because they carried between them the boat-cradle that the family had made.

Amram had helped his wife seal the little vessel with river slime. They had seen Egyptians treat the bottoms of their barges with the pitch-like substance, and they spent several evenings working the preservative between the reeds of the basket, drying it over the fire and applying layer after layer. Whether or not the boat was watertight remained to be seen. At least it was a sturdy craft, maintaining its shape despite being tugged between the jostling travelers and strained by the weight of a three-month-old child.

No words passed between the mother and daughter. Grief had tightened itself about their hearts, choking them with silence. But an indelible faith moved them forward.

One question dominated Jochebed's thoughts. Why, she wondered, had she never been privileged to name the child? Why must this one, of all her children, go nameless into that mystery which lay ahead?

If only he had received a proper rite of passage, the initiation into Israelite society that went with circumcision, he would have more claim in the earth.

But even this she must release, this yearning for the child's identity.

And with it, she must let go her hold on the child.

PART II
Child of Egypt

10

Sunlight filtered in comforting strips through the basket lid. It was early morning and the heat of day did not yet pelt the river.

The wee one dozed, lulled by the gentle rocking of the little vessel. The fear he had known an hour ago had subsided as the chanting of the slave gang reached him from the shore.

He could not know that Jochebed was far away, working on the mud line, working with her hands in the clay bank yards from him. The womb that enclosed him felt secure. Its latticed cover prevented him from knowing that he floated yet further from his mother, and that his sister followed him anxiously along the bank, trying to keep track of the boat as it drifted with the current.

The girl would be in grave trouble if she were caught shirking her work, and so would the mother who had told her to watch over him. But the baby could not know this.

Nor did he know that the long papyrus reeds that had held his boat for a time had loosened their grip, and that he was at the river's mercy.

The Egyptians believed that papyrus rushes had power to protect against evil river spirits. The tiny vessel was made of such, but the ones who had set it adrift trusted a higher power. Someday the baby would learn of spirits and of powers, great and small. But for the moment he was content to wake and sleep, to play with the lazy shadows within his cocoon, moving his dimpled hand through them as they flirted across his face.

As for Miriam, she had run along the bank for a good while now. She was weary from the early morning trek from home and from the stress of worry. But she was a strong girl, boyish in her stamina.

There were few buildings along this stretch of the Nile. But ahead, where the current carried the basket, there was one palacial structure. Miriam was not familiar with the group of prestigious apartments that marked the resort of Tanis. She could see, however, that they were residences of nobility.

Nervously she watched as the basket moved toward them.

Her mother had said that if the basket remained in the bulrushes all day, the girl must sit nearby. But she had clearly instructed her not to intervene if it was swept away. "We must trust the child to Jehovah," she had said.

Still, as the little ark drew near the populated bank, she feared not only for the baby, but for her own safety. Were she seen wandering free down the river, her poor clothing and work-hardened hands would betray her as a slave. She could be branded a runaway!

Miriam had seen what became of runaways. Once she had seen such a man in the city, hobbling on crutches and minus a foot.

The cluster of buildings was hemmed by a high wall. But Miriam could see their many terraces and balconies, adorned with gold and turquoise, reflecting the morning sun. As she came closer, she also saw that porches and promenades led down from the resort directly into the river.

The gate was open. Taking a deep breath, the girl tiptoed through. Inside, running the length of the wall, were flower bushes. Between these and the wall she crept until she came upon a quiet bower.

This riverside retreat afforded a scene of such opulence that the slave girl was stunned. Here the Nile was captured in languid pools, and from the shaded site rose music and laughter.

From her hiding place behind the bushes, Miriam watched the bathers in the pools—women and girls of the leisure class, garbed in white linen sarongs and bedecked with golden bracelets, jeweled neckchains, and feathered headpieces. Some of them must be members of the royal household, for on the deck overlooking the spa was a gilded couch, shaded by a huge umbrella, and on the umbrella was the insignia of a poised cobra.

No one occupied the couch at the moment. But Miriam surveyed the swimmers in awe, wondering if Princess Hatshepsut, Pharaoh's daughter, might be among them.

All her life, Miriam had heard of the princess and the pride Pharaoh took in her. Though she had a half-brother by one of Thutmose's concubines, there were rumors that Hatshepsut had been groomed to succeed to the throne.

Starstruck by the regal group, Miriam almost forgot her mission. But suddenly she saw that the basket was floating directly toward the lagoon. While the current should have carried it farther toward the center of the river, it was instead pushing it into the captive pond!

What happened next was unaccountable. Not only did it transpire quickly, but as though it were orchestrated by an unseen hand.

As the basket drifted into the quiet pool, it caught the attention of the women. Like a flock of swans, they pushed through the water toward it, the nearest woman reaching out and drawing it close.

"Open it! Open it!" the others giggled.

But someone wisely counseled caution. "Careful! It could be a trap."

The advice was not unwarranted. The present administration was not popular, and some enemy could have filled the basket with poisonous vipers or some lethal device. The royal household was well advised to be wary.

Suddenly the flock parted, leaving the basket bobbing on the water's surface. Eyeing the vessel fearfully, they huddled together until one woman emerged from their midst. Seemingly without fear, she approached the basket.

"Princess!" the others gasped. "Watch out!"

Scarcely could Miriam believe her ears. Was this daring lady Pharaoh's daughter? Breathless, she watched as the young woman reached for the basket, lifted the lid, and admitted sunlight to the interior. Just as soon, the baby began to cry.

Astonished, the women pressed in on the bobbing cradle until Miriam feared it would be crushed.

"Stand back!" the princess commanded, lifting the child out of the little ark. Holding him aloft, she turned him this way and that, her eyes wide with wonder.

The women squealed with delight. "How precious! How beautiful! Did you ever see such a pretty baby?"

Miriam could not mistake the royal lady's transparent adoration of the child. No longer was she holding the baby in the air. Instead she clutched him close to her breast, pressing her head to his round cheek as though she would keep him forever.

"Surely he belongs to someone up the river," one of the women suggested. "Perhaps they set him on the shore, and the basket fell into the Nile..."

"Hush!" said the princess. "He belongs to no one up the river or down the river!"

Bewildered, the attendants looked at one another. "What do you mean?" someone asked. "Surely you will not keep the child!"

But it seemed this was precisely the royal lady's intention.

"We will bathe him and anoint him," the princess announced. Cuddling the infant to her chest again, she crooned into his ear, "Quiet now," for he still cried loudly, his pudgy hands raised to his eyes against the brilliant sun. "Quick," she ordered one of her maids, "bring me a blanket."

The woman who had first spied the basket reached inside and drew out the striped mantle upon which the baby had slept.

"Will this do?" she asked, holding it gingerly above the rippled water.

Again the women were astonished, for they recognized the design.

"He is one of the Hebrew children, the princess gasped, her hands trembling as she held him. She, like all her maids, flashed instantly to the royal edict, knowing that the baby should not be alive.

But for only a moment did the princess hesitate. When cool determination lit her eyes, and she lifted her chin in resolve, her friends were amazed.

"You cannot mean to keep him!" they cried.

The princess, being of royal blood, had a royal temper. To this point she had exhibited marvelous patience with her contrary maidens. But she had had enough of their nay-saying.

"I shall do as I please!" she barked, grabbing the blanket and wrapping the child in it.

Instant silence overcame the group. No one said a word as the princess hummed an Egyptian lullaby and surveyed the baby's pouting face.

"There, there," she soothed him. "No more basket for my darling. A fine golden cradle shall be yours...and a tunic of finest linen."

But as she began to head for shore, gently carrying the little one close to her heart, someone dared to question one more time.

"What about your father?" the brave maid asked. "If he learns of this, he will surely have the child's life."

"Yes," another joined in, "if he learns the child is Hebrew..."

Wheeling around, the princess faced them squarely.

"Does he look Hebrew?" she challenged. "He is too dark. And see here," she bragged, pulling back his blanket so that all could observe, "he is not circumcised. Don't all Hebrews circumcise their sons on the eighth day?"

When no one could refute her, she raised her chin again and turned haughtily from them.

Miriam stood quivering in the shadows. Desperate, she watched as the Egyptian woman carried her little brother toward the shade of the royal umbrella.

Her parents would never have countenanced this. What worse fate could befall the child than to be hauled away to a pagan palace and raised in the manner of the Egyptians? But she barely had time to take the matter in, before a door of salvation was thrown open.

"How shall the child be fed?" yet another maid inquired. "There is no fit nurse in the palace."

This was a true observation, and one which must give the princess pause. For not just any nurse would do.

A nurse, the Egyptians believed, must be of the same race as the infant. Any other match would be unseemly.

But the princess would not be dissuaded. "We shall simply send for a Hebrew woman," she announced. Then, shaking her head sadly, "It should not be difficult to find a new mother among them who has recently lost a child."

At this, the women murmured, wondering at the princess's sympathatic tone and perplexed by her fond attachment for the foundling.

As for Miriam, however, the opportunity was golden. Forgetting her precarious position, she crept forth from the bushes.

"Majesty," she hailed the princess, "pardon your servant, but I could not help but notice what you have found there."

When the women turned to the girl, and saw that she was a slave, they were amazed at her daring. Miriam bowed low, showing as much humility as possible.

"Shall I go and fetch you a nurse of the Hebrew women?" she asked. "I know of one who has just lost a son."

11

Jochebed sat on a balcony in the servants' quarters in the palace of Raamses. A smile of joy and contentment such as she had never known brightened her face. That smile had impressed itself upon her features months before and had rarely faded.

At her feet, rocking to and fro upon his chubby knees, his hands gripping the marble floor, was her little son. Soon he would be crawling, and then she would see him take his first step. The son she had given up to God, and to the river, had been miraculously returned to her. If all continued as the princess had commanded, Jochebed would be the baby's nurse and governess until he was weaned.

It seemed the princess never suspected Jochebed might actually be the child's mother. Although the little one was darker of skin than most Hebrews, the royal lady never made the connection with Jochebed's even darker color.

Jochebed attributed all of this to divine providence.

The only difficulty involved in the arrangement had come during the first few months, for at that point the child had still required nursing during the night hours. Because of this, Jochebed had been obliged to stay at the palace day and night, and had been unable to go home except for brief visits.

Now that time had passed, however, and the baby slept well at bedtime, Jochebed was free to spend evenings with her family.

Her good fortune had fallen out in other ways as well, for the princess paid her handsomely for her service, and she was able to send her wages home to Amram and the children.

One sorrow alone was Jochebed's. Not since the day she had been brought to the palace had she been able to share her baby with her husband. Not since the day she had released him to the river had Miriam, Aaron, or Amram beheld him. All the little milestones in his development were hers alone to enjoy. Every time he made a new sound or achieved some new feat, she must revel in it privately.

As she considered this, feeling a twinge of unhappiness, the baby crawled toward her. Reaching for her skirt, he clutched at it with a hard grip. Suddenly, his face red with exertion, he managed to pull himself upright.

When Jochebed gave an approving cry, the babe squealed with pride, and the mother lifted him to her lap, cuddling him lavishly.

"Moses!" she sighed. "Such a champion you are!"

The child responded with gay laughter. Though his name was foreign to Jochebed's tongue, bestowed upon him by the princess, the mother always pronounced it with love.

She would have given him a Nubian name. A Hebrew name, at least, was his rightful due. But this Egyptian name troubled her, meaning nothing more than "child." Sometimes she played with the sound of it, altering it slightly when no one was around. The Hebrew "Moseh," meaning "drawn out," was close enough and certainly meant more to her.

"Moseh," she whispered, pressing her lips to the baby's ear, "you were drawn out of the river just for me, drawn out by the hand of God."

* * *

Princess Hatshepsut believed, as did Jochebed, in the hand of providence. But for her, the god who had brought little Moses into her life was the god of the Nile.

Just as surely as Jochebed believed Moses had been spared to serve Israel, so the princess believed that the river-god had ordained him to be a future leader in Egypt.

Pharaoh Thutmose had once had two sons, elder brothers of Hatshepsut. At an early age, death had claimed them both, leaving the girl-child heiress of his empire.

There were those who said his heir should be Thutmose II, the son of his concubine. But Pharaoh had always insisted that the only way such a son would wear a crown would be as husband and coregent to Hatshepsut.

Because Thutmose II was her half-brother, a marriage between them would, according to royal tradition, help keep the sacred bloodline undiluted.

But in Hatshepsut's estimation, Thutmose II, with his low brow and dull eyes, looked moronic. She would sooner die than be his wife. The line of Pharaoh would end with her barrenness before she embraced the imposter.

This afternoon, as she waited in her opulent parlor for a visit with Moses, she considered how gracious was the guidance of the gods.

To this point Pharaoh had not deigned to lay eyes on the foundling. But someday he would. In a couple of years the babe would be weaned. He would be free to live with Hatshepsut and would be raised in the manner befitting royalty.

When that time came, the princess knew, her father would love Moses just as she did. Never would he guess that the uncircumcised child with the dusky skin and the dark nursemaid was Hebrew.

He would receive him just as his daughter had. And once he did, there would be no limit to Moses's future. He would be heir to the throne—son of Pharaoh returned from the grave.

Hatshepsut thrilled to the idea. Glancing out her window at the Nile's deep current, she felt she had received a revelation.

Was not water a type of the grave, a symbol of death? Perhaps, indeed, the river-god had returned the spirit of Pharaoh's departed heir in the being of this little babe.

The shimmer of afternoon sun across the rapid river seemed to confirm her thoughts.

"Ra," she whispered, speaking to the light. "Thank you."

Just then the sound of Jochebed's footsteps in the hall recalled her to the moment.

As the nurse stood waiting in the doorway, the baby in her arms, Hatshepsut summoned her forth.

"Thank you," she said again, taking the child to her bosom. Laughter tumbled from her lips like a song. "Moses," she sighed. "My child."

Suddenly Jochebed understood that the simple name was no insult, no indication of worthlessness. As the princess spoke it, she invested it with great meaning.

For Hatshepsut, this was "the child," the child of lost dreams and withered hopes, the one ray of light in a vacant heart.

Jochebed's own heart was a muddle as she observed the woman's tender gestures. Did the God of Israel truly mean for this Egyptian to take her place?

Bowing low, she backed out of the room, her face burning. As she hastened down the hall, she wrapped her arms about herself, trying to soothe the ache within her soul.

12

Shiphrah and Puah, the Hebrew midwives, hurried breathlessly through the palace corridor. They should not be in this wing of the royal house, but they knew that Jochebed was here, and they had promised Amram they would find her.

Just this week, construction had begun on a dormitory that would house many of Pharoah's slaves and employees. Attached to the royal compound, it would be a luxurious place, and already Shiphrah and Puah had been provided spacious apartments.

It was ironical that the very women who had deceived the king should be catered to in this way. But Pharaoh's army had recently taken hundreds of captives during a foray into Ethiopia, and the services of the midwives would be more valuable than ever as the new slaves populated his work force.

Pharaoh's focus on the Hebrews had thereby been diverted. Presuming that his purge against them had eliminated any possibility of the wizard's prophecy coming true, he had turned his attention to other exploits.

Nonetheless, the two Hebrew women should not venture into other parts of the palace. Tiptoeing past the many rooms bordering the hall, they anxiously glanced into each, hoping to glimpse Jochebed.

When she suddenly appeared directly before them, leading her child by the hand as he toddled on wobbly legs, Puah stifled a cry of surprise.

Little Moses was over a year old, and the women had not seen him or his mother since he had been brought to the king's house.

"Jochebed!" Shiprah exclaimed. "Is it really you?"

Amazed at the sight of her friends, Jochebed stopped still, tears of loneliness and joy welling in her eyes.

"Ladies!" she cried. "What are you doing here?"

"We have come to see the miracle child and his mother," Puah replied. "How beautiful he is!"

Smiling broadly, Jochebed lifted Moses in her arms, displaying him with pride.

"The prettiest on earth!" Shiprah sighed. "His father misses him terribly."

"You have seen my husband?" Jochebed guessed.

"We have," Puah enthused. "And we promised to help him see the baby."

"Is such a thing possible?" Jochebed pleaded. "How I have prayed for this!"

"We believe it can be done if we are very cautious," Shiprah whispered, glancing over her shoulder. "The king is building a great house for us and all our women on these very grounds. From our quarters there is a view over the palace wall. If you stand just so, you can see into the street."

"Come this very evening after supper," Puah went on. "Amram will be waiting beyond the wall to catch a glimpse of the child."

* * *

It was with a heart near breaking that Jochebed stood two years later at the high window of the midwives' apartment. The quick view to the street had become a daily ritual for the mother and little Moses. It was the only contact the child had with his father, his young brother, Aaron, and his sister, Miriam. But today would be the last time the family would have this privilege.

This would, in fact, be Jochebed's last night in the palace. For tomorrow was the official day of the baby's weaning.

By tradition, a child was to leave the breast by his third birthday. Though tomorrow was not Moses's actual date of birth, it was the third anniversary of his rescue from the river. The princess had always considered that the beginning of his life.

Jochebed knew that his true birthday had come and gone three months before. But she had clung to him, nursing him and tending him as long as possible. Tonight she would stay very close to the child, clutching him to her through the dark hours. She would not sleep, for sleep would rob her of the few precious moments left in his presence.

Even now as she stood at the window, awaiting the arrival of her husband and children, she hummed an Israelite lullaby softly into his ear. Though she often sang him songs of her mother's Nubian homeland, this night she hoped to impress upon his tender soul the spirit of his holier heritage—a heritage soon to be silenced. "Milk and honey," she sang,

> We shall have milk and honey.
> In the land of Father Jacob,
> In the valley of Jehovah,
> We shall rest ourselves.

And she would pray for him in the dark hours. She would pray that whatever lay ahead, he would be protected as surely as when he was set adrift on the river—protected by the hand of God.

Jochebed had never forgotten Amram's insistence that this child had a special purpose, that he would someday save their people. Had that promise not been confirmed by the babe's miraculous salvation from Pharaoh's purge?

Had it not been ratified by God's returning him to her, even for this short time?

Shiphrah and Puah stood with Jochebed, watchful as always against her being discovered off-limits. As anxious as she, they watched the street, feeling her sadness with her.

But when Amram at last appeared, flanked by Aaron and Miriam, the two midwives stepped aside.

"No," Jochebed pleaded. "Do not leave me. Shiphrah, Puah, come close. I need you."

Obediently they drew near, and Jochebed spoke again, her throat tight.

"Reach into my satchel," she said. "The breeze is cool tonight, and I have brought a blanket."

Puah complied, opening the bag that Jochebed carried on her arm. When she pulled forth the little mantle, she gasped. "It is the Hebrew blanket! The one you wove for him."

"I put it in his river-basket," Jochebed said. "He was wrapped in it when the princess gave him to me."

Proudly the mother wrapped him in it again, and lifted him to her shoulder that Amram might see him from below.

"Moseh," she whispered into his ear, "wave to Papa. Wave long and hard."

Gaily the little boy obeyed, his soft giggle belying the fact that he might never see any of them again.

As he did, the father waved in return, smiling a sad, longing smile. At his side, Miriam and Aaron stood silent, wondering what fate had taken their brother from them.

13

Princess Hatshepsut sat with her maidens in the porch of the harem at Raamses. Warm spring air wafted over the veranda, and the sound of merry singing rose from the shore of the river below.

It was spring, time of the annual rise of the Nile's waters. The Taniatic branch along which the singers walked and danced was one of several that pushed through Lower Egypt toward the Great Sea, fingers of the sacred Nile that left a rich deposit of fertile earth in this lush region.

So lush, in fact, was this delta of land that for centuries it had been the most prized real estate in the empire. Many kings had lived here, owning this city as their favorite. Under the numerous administrations that had come and gone, the city had gone by various names.

The shepherd land that bordered it, called Goshen, had been given to the Israelites by their brother Joseph when Jacob first settled in Egypt. For a time the city was called Avaris, so named by the Hyksos during the time of Joseph's rule. Grand were its obelisks and its edifices, broad were its streets.

But Princess Hatshepsut loved the porch of the harem best.

The sound of singing lifted her spirits, for it was a hymn, a song of gratitude to the river for blessing the land again, for preparing the way for spring planting.

Not that Hatshepsut's spirits were in any way low. For the past two hours she had observed young Moses at his lessons, something that always made her proud.

The lad was a strapping ten-year-old, handsome as a cedar tree, ruddy as sun-baked clay. So dearly did the princess love him, she rarely remembered that he was not bone of her bone.

Jannes, the old priest, sat with the boy at a low ebony table, studying him as keenly as Moses studied a papyrus scroll spread on the tabletop. The princess could see in the priest's eyes a pride almost as intense as her own, and she smiled in private delight.

Yes, she thought, the elder should be proud. His student was surely the brightest of his career, with an uncanny memory and amazing insights.

Just this morning, the teacher had taken the boy through seven dynasties of Egyptian history, reviewing with him months of intensive study into the decline of the Old Kingdom, the Delta revolution, and the rise of the kings of Middle Egypt. The boy's memory for detail was flawless, as was his copious note-taking. Anything he could not remember, he could easily recall by a glance at his own records.

But Jannes's interest in Moses was more than academic. Always dutifully aware that those who sat at his feet were being groomed for high office, he took his teaching task as seriously as his priestly role.

Never did he forget that Moses was Pharaoh's adopted grandson, and that he was thus in line for the throne itself. After Hatshepsut, Moses could one day lay claim to the grandest empire on earth.

Therefore, as Jannes took the lad through his history lessons, it was with respect to the future. Since the old man was a philosopher as well as a teacher, he never rehearsed historical facts only, but enjoined his students to analyze the events of the past, using them as models of administrative failure and success.

"Moses," he said, leaning across the table, "we have come to the Eleventh Dynasty. The scroll you have been reading is the Festal Dirge of King Antuf."

"Yes," the boy replied, his brow knit. "It is very sad."

"I agree," the priest said. "So are many of the writings of that period. What passage, in particular, is sad?"

Perusing the dirge again, Moses shook his head. "There is no hope here. Listen to this," he said, quoting from the papyrus. "'The body is fated to pass away; they who build houses, and they who have no houses, see what becomes of them! Their fenced walls are dilapidated. Their houses are as that which has never existed. No man comes from thence who tells of their sayings, who tells of their affairs, who encourages our hearts. Ye go to the place whence they return not. Strengthen thy heart to forget how thou hast enjoyed thyself, fulfill thy desire whilst thou livest. Yield to thy desire whilst thou art upon earth, according to the dictation of thy heart. The day will come to thee, when one hears not the voice, when the one who is at rest hears not their voices. Lamentations deliver not him who is in the tomb. Yea, behold, none who goes thither comes back again.'"

Hatshepsut stirred uneasily upon her claw-footed couch. She did not like these words, so counter to the mindset of the day. She was used to merriment and parties. Why, she wondered, would the ancients have preferred such heaviness?

Stiffly, she watched as Jannes presented another scroll, spreading it alongside the first.

"See, here is a hymn of our own," he said. "You have likely heard it sung in the temple court from time to time. How does it compare with the dirge of Antuf?"

Respectfully lifting the manuscript to the light, Moses began to read.

"'Men pass away since the time of Ra; every nostril inhaleth once the breezes of dawn, but all born of women go down to their places. Make a good day, O holy father!

Let song and music be before thy face, and leave behind thee all evil cares! Mind thee of joy, till cometh the day of pilgrimage, when we draw near the land which loveth silence. They in the shades are sitting on the bank of the river...drinking its sacred water, following thy heart, at peace...'"

The young reader broke off. "Why," he marveled, "this is much happier!"

Hatshepsut sighed, her mood reviving. "Certainly," she laughed. "Jannes, must you subject the child to such dreary matters? No one thinks those old, unhappy thoughts today."

But the priest gazed upon her with somber eyes. "There is a reason why Moses must see the past for what it was," he answered. "If we do not see the past, we cannot clearly see our own time. And if we do not see our own time clearly, there is no hope for the future."

The princess leaned back with a shrug and, picking up her ivory- handled mirror, tried to distract herself as the teacher continued.

"Now, Moses," he went on, "you see how differently people think at different times. The writings of an era reflect the soul of that era. What inspired the people of Antuf's time to write such morbid things? What have you learned from all your studies?"

The youngster thought for a long time, not because he did not know the answer, but because he wished to formulate it exactly. At last, taking a deep breath, he proceeded.

"Well, Master, the Old Kingdom had passed away with all its splendor and prosperity. Four centuries of glory had been replaced by upheaval and revolution. Pharaoh had not been the absolute ruler for generations, and foreigners were weakening the social order."

Jannes repressed an approving grin. He would test the boy further.

"But, son," he argued, "by the eleventh dynasty, order had been restored. The princes of Thebes had reunited Egypt under one strong scepter, vanquishing all their rivals. Should it not have been a time of rejoicing?"

Again Moses was thoughtful. When he was ready to answer, he glanced at the princess. Though her face was hidden behind her hand mirror, he knew it was dour.

"Sir, it is likely that the common people were rejoicing. Perhaps even the kings were at ease. But philosophers are not easily pleased. They have long memories."

Jannes could not have received a more fitting answer had he spoken the words himself. Swallowing a cry of praise, he sat back, folding his arms across his chest.

"So, my bright young man, what did the philosophers remember? Of what were they afraid?"

The reply came so swiftly, it was more like light than speech.

"Consequences," he said. "They feared consequences."

Jannes made not a sound. He understood the lad's reasoning without an explanation. And when Moses went on to elucidate, the elder quivered with awe.

"The kings of Middle Egypt established themselves on blood, and the princes of Thebes on insurrection. When they created order, they maintained it with military might and carried it on the backs of Asiatic slaves. The arts and the sciences were owned by the court. While the glory of the Old Kingdom had been the product of freemen, only propaganda, dictatorship, and forced labor sufficed to keep the new state in tact."

The mirror jerked in the princess's grip, and Moses detected a twitch at the corner of her mouth. Sometimes it seemed her son spoke too freely in her presence.

Still, he was not drawing any analogies. Perhaps she only imagined he saw any similarities between those cruel times and the present administration. If he did, he kept his thoughts discreetly to himself.

As for Jannes, he did not hesitate to draw more insights from the boy.

"You mention propaganda," he spurred him. "Of what do you speak?"

"Why, the precedent for deceit and treachery was so entrenched that the king of the twelfth dynasty went so far as to proclaim himself 'savior of Egypt,'" Moses replied. "And his priests spent their time formulating elaborate curses against all his enemies. This is the literature of the time."

Jannes, stunned by the lad's sagacity, was speechless. At last, rising from his seat, he rolled up the scroll.

"As always, you have proved yourself a worthy scholar," he confessed. "I learn from you, as much as you from me."

Moses smiled broadly, his boyish heart thrilled at the praise of his teacher.

"It is only because you are such a fine example, Master," he said.

But the princess was not so pleased. She had heard enough of entombed pharaohs and long-past sins.

Putting her handmirror aside she called her son to her.

"Moses," she cooed, pulling him to her lap, "when I was Jannes's student, years ago, he told me merry tales from the time of those ancient kings. Not everything about them was so bad."

"Truly, Mother?" Moses inquired. "I would like to hear such stories."

"Well, then, so you shall," she agreed. "Jannes, fetch the scroll of the 'The Shipwrecked Sailor,' or 'The Adventures of Sanehat.' Enough of these doldrums. Turn my boy's mind to happy things."

14

It was a day of great merrymaking throughout the land of Egypt.

Merrymaking was not rare in this pragmatic and materialistic society. In fact, if one had the stamina and the resources, one could find a festival in some part of the country almost any day of the year.

Just as religion was infused into and inseparable from the events of everyday life, so was the joviality which Egyptian theology inspired.

Today was a national holiday, an especially rollicking one. Pharaoh's army had just returned from a triumphant campaign in Syria, reinforcing Thutmose's reputation as one of the mightiest warrior kings in history. Thutmose had proclaimed this day of revelry, not only as a victory celebration, but as a fortuitous time to establish his daughter upon the throne beside him. Likely he reasoned that he would never be more popular than he was just now, and the controversial coronation of Hatshepsut would never have a better chance of going undisputed.

The people had been given ample warning. As soon as word was received that the army fared victoriously, the king announced his decision to elevate the princess. A week of feverish preparation ensued as every citizen, great and small, planned for the event.

At dawn of the glorious day, Moses stood in the courtyard of Pharaoh's private chapel, the House of the Morning. Jannes, chief lector-priest, stood beside him, awaiting the emergence of Thutmose from his chamber.

There had been no need for Jannes to awaken the king this morning. There would be no proxy standing in for the daybreak ritual. Thutmose would take today's opening ceremonies very personally.

It was believed that a day in Egypt could not begin until the ruler, the incarnation of the sun-god, entered his chapel for the ritual washing of his limbs. Just as the great god Ra bathed each morning in the primordial ocean of heaven, so Pharaoh must bathe his body in order to restore the vital force that flowed from it, energizing the realm.

Though Jannes had often been frustrated by Thutmose's casual approach to these traditions, the king could be quite zealous of formality when occasion demanded. The inauguration of his daughter was such an occasion.

Nor had anyone needed to rouse Moses this morning. He had barely slept during the night. At 12 years of age, he was imbued with the teachings and theology of the priests.

All week long he had anticipated the moment when his mother would parade forth with Grandfather Thutmose, to be led for the first time through the dawn ritual. All week he had awaited the honor of entering the sun god's private sanctuary with his beloved mentor, Jannes.

Now that moment had arrived, and it was as delicious as he had imagined. Had he been younger and smaller, he would have reached for the priest's hand as the trumpets heralded the approach of the royal couple. But he must not be so foolish.

Jannes was garbed in his most holy vestment, a long, pleated gown with a panther-skin draped over one shoulder. Upon his head was the mask of Horus, an enormous, concealing hawk-head, its long feathers flowing down his back. Atop this was perched the tall, white helmet of royalty, and in his hand was a golden dipper for use in the ritual laver. No one, not even the young prince, should touch him now.

It was essential that Moses be present at this auspicious event. One day he would follow in his mother's footsteps, and he must be prepared for the solemnity of his future duties.

Pride infused the young prince as dawn light spilled through the golden lattice overhead. He had seen Thutmose only a few times in his life, and those occasions had always been so hedged about with state ritual and the dogma of Ra that, to his circumscribed mind, Grandfather and the deity were inseparable. The knowledge that the incarnate god would any moment pass before him filled him with awe.

As the trumpets blared, the rhythm of drums marked the steps of a whole processional of bald scholar-priests from the House of Life, who bore upon their shoulders the replica of a long riverboat. Within the boat was a huge golden orb, the image of the deity. Following the priests, a retinue of dancing girls with feathered fans and stylized wigs swayed sensuously in submissive adoration.

The drums, tambourines, and castanets spurred Moses's heart in sympathetic cadence. By the time his grandfather and his mother appeared in the wake of the flashing spectacle, he was nearly giddy with religious passion.

He was too well trained to give way to emotion. But when Hatshepsut passed by, the room spun about his head.

His mother was no longer only Hatshepsut. She was robed in the garb of Isis, supreme daughter of earth and sky; she was sister-wife of Osiris; beloved mother of Horus; wife of Ra, the Mighty.

Her long, tight dress clung to her shapely body. Upon her head was the serpent crown, and above this, another golden orb, the diadem of the Chief Wife of State.

Yet Hatshepsut was no one's wife. All her loving energies she had poured into "the child"—into Moses. And though he had from time to time realized his privileged position, that position suddenly took on new meaning.

While Thutmose was unreachable, Hatshepsut was not. The queen was his mother, and he needed no father.

As the sacred parade passed by, to be repeated again in even grander fashion upon the river Nile in the life-sized boat of Ra, Moses felt that his soul had left his body.

If Hatshepsut was his mother, and Pharaoh his grandfather, he must himself be divine. If he would one day reign over Egypt, he must be the incarnate god himself!

What moved him to reach out at that moment to take Jannes's hand, he could not have said. But before he knew it, his fingers were intertwined in the grip of the chief wizard.

As it dawned upon him just how dangerous this gesture was, he tried to withdraw it. But Jannes held on tight.

Glancing up, Moses found that the priest's eyes were locked upon him, peering through the slits of the bird-mask.

Always he had loved Jannes. Always he had been proud of his approval. And he would have been proud this moment, had a haunting eeriness not accompanied the wizard's gaze.

"You have received it," the priest whispered. "You have received what is rightfully yours. Well done, my son."

15

Raucous music, hilarity, and dancing filled the streets of Raamses. Through the winding bazaar, between swarms of staggering tavern-hoppers and klatches of soliciting streetwalkers, an elegant carriage followed the cobblestones.

At the owner's command, the driver stopped every now and then, always a safe distance from any danger, but close enough to the ribald activities that the passengers might easily view them.

It was a royal carriage, by the insignia on its canopy. Not only royal, but priestly. Yet those who rode in it observed the night's orgiastic follies uncritically.

It was Jannes who owned the vehicle. His guests were sons of noblemen and sons of the highest harem. Beside Jannes on the foremost seat was Moses, enjoying an evening out with his closest companions.

For most of Moses's life, his time had been divided between rigorous study under the priest's instruction and carefree play with the boys of the royal house. As he approached his thirteenth birthday, Jannes must introduce him to the larger world.

This was no mere concession on the priest's part. The ways of the world and the ways of the flesh were a highly practiced art in Egypt. In fact, they were not separate from the world of spirit, but were considered of equal value and must be part of any worthwhile education.

Beneath the stylized sophistication of the royal house beat a primitive heart. Never in any line of rulers had enough generations passed to kill the primal urges, the ways that worked in the desert and the ever-encroaching jungle. Lust and violence, rather than being overcome, had merely been recast into ceremony and festival, bearing the stamp of priestly endorsement.

Such was the Festival of Bast, the cat-goddess.

Taking their cue from the nocturnal beast, men and women prowled through the torchlit streets, wearing cat-masks and indulging freely in physical pleasures.

So encouraged was liberty and license on this night that even slaves were allowed to party. When enough wine had been drunk, it did not matter who took up with whom. If a monied merchant passed the night with a comely slave-girl, no one cared. If the local tinsmith awoke next morning beside the nobleman's wife, there was no retribution.

The mood in Jannes's carriage was no less liberal. Whereas the priest usually required perfect etiquette from his pupils, this night they were allowed great freedom of expression. At first, they had ridden in tense silence, witnessing the follies about them with guarded reactions. It helped, however, that Jannes had brought a wineskin, and that he passed it from hand to hand.

This was a night of "coming out," a rite of passage for the adolescents, all of whom would approach manhood within the next year.

As every corner and byway revealed some new licentious scene, and as their young heads succumbed to the slippery seduction of drink, laughter filled the cab. For Moses, no less than for the others, it was a night of emergence. Never had he been spectator to such sports as he watched tonight; never had his ears heard such language as was spoken in the streets or his eyes beheld what hands and arms and bodies could do.

Jannes would not permit the boys to participate in the spectacle. For such they were not ready. But, according to tradition, this was an evening of revelation, a stepping stone to manhood.

In honor of the occasion, Moses had worn his most festive garb, a long, pleated loincloth, gathered between his legs, its ends draped in another cascade of pleats from the waist. About his upper arms were sleeves of the same crimped material, but his torso was bare. Only a wide collar of laminated strips, colorful and gem-studded, graced his chest. His wavy black hair, while touching his shoulders, was cut in a perfect frame about his face, revealing his ears and a face that did not yet need a razor. Except for a slim diadem about his forehead, he wore no other adornment.

Though he was lightly clad, he was sweating. It was a warm night, but more than this raised his temperature. As a child of the palace, he was used to seeing gorgeous women, the most beautiful in the empire. But always their activities had been quite circumscribed. What they did when they were alone with Pharaoh, he had rarely considered. And when he had considered it, he had no experience on which to base a guess.

Tonight, however, the freedom of the streets spurred his pulse, and the whispers of his companions drew him into wild speculation.

Though they were all equally uninitiated, they did not wish to appear so to one another. Teetering on the line between innocence and sophistication, they wished to impress each other with their daring.

And so they pointed, they hooted, they rolled their eyes. The wine freed their tongues, and they tried profanity. When some passing female returned a flirtatious glance, they pretended to be easy with it.

Still it was a warm night, and Moses pulled back the curtain, seeking a breeze. As he leaned his head outside, yet one more fantastic sight greeted him.

It was fantastic, not because it was supremely vile, but because it was out of keeping with the surroundings. As the young prince beheld it, his heart was strangely moved.

A tiny group of slaves stood on a street corner, their arms locked about each other. In this alone, there would have been nothing peculiar. All about town, people who barely knew each other shared intimate embraces. But this huddle was self-protective, as other people stood about the slaves, taunting and reviling them.

Again, in this particular, there was nothing unusual, for the folly and the libations of the festival easily induced cruelty and even violence. Racial differences could flare into street war, and animosity between classes could spark revolution if the city were not heavily patrolled.

What caught Moses's attention, however, went beyond the obvious.

He could see by their tribal headbands that these slaves were Israelite Hebrews. As they stood on the corner, they raised their eyes to the dark night as if seeking help from beyond the torchlit sky. And their persecutors seemed held at bay, unable to wield any harm.

"Who are they?" the prince asked his friends.

The boys scanned the street, but saw nothing noteworthy in the corner gathering.

"Just a bunch of sand fleas," one answered. And the others laughed at his free use of the racial slur.

"I know they are Hebrew," Moses replied. "I mean, why are they so strange?"

At this, the others snickered. "Israelites are always strange, Moses! Everyone knows this!"

It was true that of all the ethnic groups in Egypt, Israelites were unique, guarding their racial heritage as though it were gold and maintaining a peculiar form of worship about which Moses knew nothing.

"They have not come for the party," Moses marveled. "Why would they be standing here, staring at the sky?"

"Most likely their master brought them to the festival," suggested another. "No one should ignore a holiday."

Jannes made no comment, but clearing his throat, called to the driver. "Move on!" he commanded, and suddenly the carriage lurched down the street.

"Teacher," Moses said, still craning his neck to glimpse the oddity, "tell me about these folk. Why were they staring at the sky?"

Jannes gave no quick reply, piquing Moses's curiosity all the more.

"Were they at prayer, Master?" he prodded. "Who is their god?"

At last, the priest quipped, "I do not know, my boy. I do not know their god."

Now silence again filled the cab. Never in all their years of study at the feet of Jannes had any of these youngsters heard him claim ignorance on a point of theology. The idea that he did not know any single god, though thousands were worshiped in Egypt, was beyond belief.

As the cab passed down the street, the quiet within seemed to drown out all sounds beyond, until the priest fidgeted nervously with his sarong.

Finally, seeking relief from their inquisitive gazes, the priest turned to his students.

"What I mean to say," he muttered, "is that I do not know the name of their god. The god of Israel has no name."

16

That night, Moses could not sleep.

Never in his life had he found sleep hard to come by, having known nothing but luxury, privilege, and ease. But the witness of the Hebrews and their peculiar prayer haunted him without mercy.

As he lay restless upon his bed, he wondered if the hounding memory was only the result of too much drink. Perhaps when his head cleared, he would forget. Perhaps the witness would not seem so mysterious, so important.

Rising, he quietly paced his chamber, not wishing to alarm the guards who stood all night beyond his door. He did not want to speak with anyone, for he would not know how to explain his troubled heart.

There were millions of slaves in Egypt, descendants of countless tribes and nations. Never had it been of interest to Moses what any slave thought, or what his heritage might be. He had been reared to give them as little mind as he would a beast of burden—an ox, a donkey, or a mule. It was the irony of the Egyptian system to attribute divinity to the dung beetle while regarding slaves as less than human.

But this night, as the wine cleared from his head, he did not find himself forgetting. He could not consider those people on the street corner irrelevant.

As he fretted back and forth before his window, he tried to analyze just what it was that troubled him.

He knew nothing of the Israelites or their faith. It could not be a question of theology that kept him awake.

He knew none of them personally, never having noticed if the one who groomed his mount was Syrian or Ethiopian, never having cared if the one who fetched his shoes was Midianite or Phoenician. It was not sympathy for their plight that tormented him.

As the night wore on, trailed by pale gray light, he determined that some evil spirit had entered his head. Yes, surely this was it! Some enemy had cursed him with a nameless distress.

Standing before his window, he wrung his hands in tight fists, trying to imagine who would wish him ill.

As he furtively surveyed the waking streets, his eyes were caught by a figure standing just beyond the wall. It was a woman, dark and slight of build, and bearing upon her head a waterpot. She was a slave, perhaps Nubian, and she was likely on her morning walk to the nearest well to fetch water for her household.

There was nothing unusual in her appearance except that she seemed fixated upon his window. When Moses leaned out for a closer look, she took a jolting breath, and her hand flew to her throat.

Suddenly she was running, fleeing from the palace and from the sight of the royal prince.

Moses would have dismissed the incident, had he not recognized her identifying headband. While she was dark of skin, even darker than himself, her headband was that of an Israelite.

17

Over the next few days, Moses's anxieties did not abate. Thoughts of the Israelites and questions regarding them filled his mind every waking hour.

During the night he was haunted by strange dreams that roused him from sleep, and left his head buzzing. Upon waking, fragments of the dreams still lingered like a soft song drifting through his soul.

These nightly episodes were not unpleasant. They were perplexing, but full of warmth and tenderness, like some long-lost memory which he could not quite revive.

The woman whom he had seen from his bedroom window was part of those dreams. He did not know why she should be, or who she was. But now and then she entered his sleeping vision, reaching out to him and calling him with her sweet song.

At first he had believed all this would pass—that it was only residual emotion inspired by the trip through the festive streets on his night of "coming out." But the feelings were not fading. They were stronger each day. And they were taking a strange twist.

While he was convinced some conjurer must have toyed with his mind, he could not resist the peculiar sympathies that had been sparked in his heart, burning sympathies for the oppressed of earth.

A palace education did not encourage such feelings. Condescension and mercy were qualities rarely practiced, and certainly not extended to slaves.

But for some perverse reason, Moses found himself keenly aware of every harsh word spoken, every whip wielded against an underling. He especially felt the plight of the Israelites, the most despised captives of the realm.

If an enemy had planted these perversions in his head, he was a clever enemy indeed. For the fulcrum strength of Egypt, the Egypt which would one day belong to Moses, derived from the labor of slaves. Sympathy for them was counter to the welfare of the state, traitorous to all that had made the empire great.

This afternoon Moses was obliged to tour the many work projects in Thebes, the ceremonial capital city several days' journey from Raamses. Often during his life he had ridden with Hatshepsut on such an outing. But this day he observed the spectacles with new eyes.

For the first time he was appalled by the burden of the workers. Though their strength was amazing, he cringed at the sight of the loads they carried and at the toil they endured beneath a blistering sun. All of their hauling, pushing, pulling, and lifting was done under threat of the whip, rewarded by biting curse.

It did not matter whether a slave was male or female, sick or well, young or old. The feeble were only driven more cruelly, the infirm forced to the point of death.

Hatshepsut, who rode beside him, may have wondered at his silence throughout the tour. But Moses had always been a quiet child, contemplative by nature. He was enthralled by the vastness of his grandfather's projects, she guessed, and was caught away in dreams of his own empire.

However, as they drew near the grandest work site of all, she sensed that Moses was anything but enthralled. Anger clouded his face as he studied the pillared temple being erected to Ammon at Deir el-Bahri. While he should have been enraptured by its beauty, which was unrivaled by any other edifice in the world, he seemed instead to focus on the thousands of laborers who swarmed like ants up and down its steps.

"Stop the carriage!" he suddenly called, hailing the driver. "Let me out here!"

Without explanation, Moses leaped from the cab and began to wander through the bustling project. Confounded, Hatshepsut watched as her son made a staggering path through the workplace, as though searching for something.

She could not know the contents of Moses's heart, for he had shared with no one the misery of recent days. Nor did she realize that it was a sound he followed and not a sight.

He had heard singing, the minor chords of some lament. And it had stirred the deepest currents of his buried spirit.

It was a song of slaves, the voice of a people who could endure their labor only as they sang. Though he did not comprehend the song's meaning, he had to find the ones who called to him, whether they knew him or not.

At last he rounded a corner of the temple square, and he stopped short. Before him were the singers, hauling barrows of mud for the making of bricks. They worked in community, and they all wore the same bands about their heads—striped bands . . . like the one worn by the dusky stranger of his dreams.

As he came upon them, his heart burned within him. Pieces of a mystery began to fall in place.

For the song they sang was the same one which drifted through his night visions, the one sung by the dark woman. He had been unable to reconstruct it until now. For upon his waking, the song had always fled him, leaving only its haunting impression and nothing more. "Milk and honey," they chanted,

We shall have milk and honey.
In the land of Father Jacob,

In the valley of Jehovah,
We shall rest ourselves.

Now Moses knew it was a song of Israel. And it filled him with inexplicable yearning.

* * *

Moses could hardly wait to return to Raamses. When he arrived back at the palace, he hastened down the corridor of the priests, his short robe slapping his thighs. He must find Jannes, and quickly.

When he reached the door of the old man's chamber, he barged in without an announcement, pushing past the guards who bowed as he entered.

"Holy man!" he cried. "We must talk!"

Jannes sat up from the table where he had stooped all day over a papyrus of prayers to Horus. Lately one of the temple scribes had faltered over a translation from archaic Egyptian and had brought it to Jannes for assistance.

"Put the manuscript aside, Master!" Moses demanded. "Why pray for spiritual light when you have hidden it from your students!"

The old wizard looked at Moses in astonishment. Never had a pupil spoken to him in anger.

"What troubles you, lad?" he asked, rising from his seat.

Confronting him boldly, Moses declared, "I am troubled that my teacher of religion has hidden a doctrine from me. Who, Master, is Jehovah? You claim to have taught me about the gods, and yet you have never mentioned him to me."

At the question, the priest's face became drawn and white. "Where have you heard this name?" he inquired, his voice quivering.

"I heard it in a song," Moses replied, "a song of the Israelites at the temple of Deir el-Bahri."

"Ah, well," the priest laughed, rolling his eyes, "there you have it. I am sure there are a hundred obscure gods and goddesses revered by foreigners, of whom I have not told you. Do not trouble your head with such things."

"Obscure?" Moses cried. "This Jehovah is adored by millions in this country, millions who have lived here for centuries and who have built the empire with their own sweat and blood!"

The priest was stunned. When Moses continued to demand an explanation, the old man's tongue became leaden.

"Have you not taught me that the spark of the divine is in all things?" the prince asked. "You have told me that we must worship all matter and all life from the Nile to the buzzing fly, for a sacred spirit invests all things."

Jannes nodded numbly, wondering at the direction of the boy's logic. It was true that in the animistic teaching of Egypt, divinity pervaded all existence, taking its ultimate form in the person of Pharaoh.

"Yes, son," the priest replied. "I have taught you this."

"Then how is it that the Israelites and their god are ignored?" Moses demanded. "Can it be that Jehovah frightens you, Master?"

Suddenly Jannes's tongue was loosed. His eyes gray and steely, he laughed again.

"Afraid?" he countered. "Do you think the magic of Jannes and the oracles of Egypt are cowed by some tribal god? Why, Moses, I am ashamed of you! Have I taught you nothing in all these years, that you should belittle my powers this way?"

Moses had great respect for this wise man. He had witnessed priestly magic and had soaked in priestly teachings. Never had he questioned Jannes. But the past days had been a torment, and he could not blindly accept what his mentor said.

"*Your* powers, Master?" Moses objected. "So this is

what matters most? Is there no right and wrong? Is religion only a matter of manipulating forces?"

"All things are holy..." Jannes stammered.

"It is convenient to believe so," Moses argued, "for this makes no god higher than yourself—no god higher than your power to control."

The priest's eyes flickered with anger. "You tread on sacred ground," he muttered. "Be careful."

"Or what?" the boy challenged. "Shall your wizardry turn me into a dung beetle? Shall the son of Pharaoh crawl on the dirt at your feet?"

"You are not yourself today," Jannes crooned. "Sit down, my son."

Pulling a chair from his table, he offered it to Moses, but the young prince refused.

"Perhaps I am only beginning to find myself," he suggested.

Jannes could have taken offense, but wisely tried conciliation.

"Any gifted student will eventually question his teacher," he said. "In this there is nothing wrong."

"Exactly," Moses asserted, "for just as you have taught me, there is no such thing as right or wrong. If all things are divine, where can evil exist? Yet I recall when you admitted there were such things as *consequences*."

How well Jannes remembered the day his brilliant student had analyzed the corrupt administrations of the past.

"Yes..." the old man faltered. "I did admit that much." Running a cold hand over his bald, perspiring head, he sighed. "But what does all this have to do with Jehovah?"

"This empire, like the dynasties of the past, has risen on the sweat and toil of conquered enemies. Injustice is as strong today as it was in the days of Middle Egypt. The squelching of Jehovah's name will not prevent the consequences," Moses warned. "I think it is this you fear. I think you fear what the god of the Israelites may do!"

PART III
Child of Israel

18

Paper lanterns swung in the evening breeze above Hatshepsut's courtyard. Their colors, bright and bold, announced that a celebration was under way.

The gay lanterns were rivaled by the costumes of a thousand partiers: dignitaries and dancing girls; statesmen wearing plumed hats; servants bearing food-laden trays; and noblemen's wives garbed in slinky gowns, valets trailing them with ostrich-feather fans and fawning faces.

It was Moses's thirteenth birthday. Tonight he would be ushered into manhood, his princely status no longer a matter of childish privilege, but a mark of authority.

Many of the guests were from far corners of the empire. Because this was an event of imperial importance, administrators from throughout the realm had been invited. And because it was an honor to be listed on the guest roster, no expense had been spared in dress or coiffure. Aristocrats had arrived in the capital with entourages numbering hundreds of servants, and wagonloads of accoutrements.

Much of what they brought was for the prince. No one wished to be outdone for conspicuous generosity. The most lavish presents imaginable would be bestowed throughout the week-long affair.

The streets outside the palace had begun to fill with caravans days ago, and were now a veritable sideshow of giving. It would take Moses weeks to look through the accumulation of gifts. In fact, he would never even see most of it before it was hauled away for storage in his private treasure house.

Among the gifts were many animals—Asian camels and donkeys, chimpanzees from Ethiopia, elegant birds from Nubia and Cush, prancing horses from Arabia. These would be housed in the palace zoo or in the stables of the king. Meanwhile they made the bazaar and nearby alleyways raucous with screeching, braying, and chittering.

Of course, all the executives and head servants of the palace had been invited. This was a command performance, one eagerly awaited all year. For Moses was well loved by those who worked in his house. His reputation for kindness and humility had earned him uncommon devotion.

The gifts of the household servants would be received this first night. Already presents lined the foot of the head table where the prince sat, awaiting his inspection.

Across the room two women were making an inspection of their own. Shiphrah and Puah, the Hebrew midwives, were among the palace officials invited to the party, and they watched the regal youngster with special interest.

Rarely had they seen him since he had been taken from their friend, Jochebed, and relegated to his palace upbringing. Of all those present at tonight's affair, the midwives were the only ones who knew the full truth about him.

Of course Hatshepsut, and the handmaids who had been with her the day of his rescue from the river, knew that he was an Israelite. But not even they knew who Moses's parents were or how he had been spared from the wrath of Pharaoh from the beginning.

All this was hidden in the midwives' hearts, along with their original deception of the king and their refusal to accommodate his cruel command.

As they observed the prince this evening, they were impressed again by his good looks and noble features. He had always been a beautiful child, and he would certainly grow to be the handsomest man in Egypt.

But they also noted his wistful expression. He tried to enjoy the festivities, talking amiably with his companions, smiling through a magic show, and partaking of the food and wine. But there was a sadness behind his eyes. Sometimes his gaze wandered to the veranda, as though he wished to be alone.

"Perhaps he will step out for some fresh air," Puah whispered, nudging her friend. "If he does, perhaps we can give him our present."

"He will have guards," Shiphrah replied. "We won't have a chance."

Puah sighed and tucked a package tightly under her arm. The women had not left their gift at the head table, but carried it with them, fearing to part with it. For it was in truth a gift from Jochebed, put into their safekeeping when last they visited her. If the prince were to have it, it would be on their terms—and those terms were that they should give it to him directly.

"Isn't he marvelous?" Puah sighed again. "Jochebed would be so proud!"

"Yes," the other agreed. "We will give her a detailed account of this evening."

"She will want to know what he wore," Puah guessed. "We shall not tell her that he was dressed in the sarong of Horus. Nor shall we tell her that he was crowned with the cobra."

"No, not at all," Shiphrah agreed. "Her heart would break."

"Nor shall we tell her how the princess sits so close to him," Puah grumbled. "Oh, to think that he was taken from his real mother..."

Suddenly, however, the prince rose and headed for the porch. It seemed he wished not to be followed. To the midwives' surprise, even his bodyguards lingered behind.

This was the chance the midwives had hoped for. Maybe, if they were discreet enough, they could saunter out for a bit of air. And if they were lucky, maybe they could speak with the prince.

Glancing around, they made a circuitous path for the veranda. They knew they took their lives in their hands, but they had always been daring ladies and once again felt their mission was of divine importance.

With great caution they managed to slip outside. A cool breeze swept in off the Nile, and the women drew their shawls close to their shoulders.

The veranda was not so brightly lit as the interior. Scanning the dark, they sought their objective. Yes, there he was, young Moses, standing at the railing, his gaze drifting with the river's current.

Easing toward him, Shiphrah cleared her throat and bowed low.

"Take mercy on your servants, Your Highness," she said. "We would speak with Your Highness."

Such boldness in two underlings was not only daring, but disarming. As Moses watched them draw near, and saw that they bowed all the way, he was more amused than angry.

"I came out here to be alone," he said. "What is it you wish of me?"

He had not rejected them! Quivering, the women kept their heads down but drew a little closer.

"We are the palace midwives," Puah explained, "servants to His Majesty. We have a gift for Your Highness."

"You may leave it at the table," he directed. "Did the headwaiter not tell you so?"

Puah nodded, her face coloring. "Pardon us, Your Highness. We know this, but begging your patience, it would do us great honor if you would receive our humble gift from our own hands."

As the ladies continued to bow before him, Moses saw by their dress that they were Israelites. Suddenly his interest was piqued.

"I shall be happy to take your gift," he replied, bowing in return.

Such indulgence was very rare. Slowly the women stood up, fearing to look him in the eye. Puah drew the little bundle from under her arm, passing it to him with shaky hands.

Moses could have been very skeptical of this breach of etiquette. His advisers would have told him to beware of opening such a package. After all, did he not have bodyguards for such a purpose? Let them risk whatever danger might be contained in the pretty wrapper.

But Moses had a soft heart, and these women appealed to him as worthy of his trust.

"What is it?" he asked, turning it over in his hands.

To explain the contents was the greatest danger of all for the bold women. But they had a well-rehearsed answer.

"Sir," Shiphrah said, "it was left in our charge years ago. It belonged to you when you were but a baby, and was made by someone who was once very dear to you."

"When I was a baby?" he marveled. "But who..."

"She was your nursemaid, sir, a friend of ours. She asked that we would give it back to you when you reached your Bar Mitzvah..."

At this, Shiphrah's face went white. She had not meant to use this phrase and feared she had made an irreversible mistake.

"My what?" the prince asked quizzically.

"I...I mean, your thirteenth birthday," Shiphrah stammered. "'Bar Mitzvah' is a term used among our people for a young man's emergence into manhood. I did not mean to offend you."

Moses studied the midwives with a bemused twinkle in his eye. Their straightforward manner and the words they spoke touched him deeply.

"An interesting phrase," he said. "What does it mean?"

Shiphrah hesitated. "'Son of the divine law,'" she choked.

The women had no idea that Moses had been obsessed of late with their people and their ways. When he jumped at the opportunity to talk further, they became uneasier yet.

"Ah, yes," he enthused, "you are Israelites! I have wondered what you folks believe. 'Divine law,' eh? So what god do you worship, and what is his law?"

That an Egyptian prince should take an interest in such matters was incredible. The women were not prepared for this, but they answered him as best they could.

"We speak the name of our God most cautiously," Puah began. "In fact no one knows his true name, and so we call him Jehovah, 'The Lord.'"

"This is curious," Moses observed, being used to gods who loved to hear the sounds of their names. "And what does he look like, this god of yours?"

Again the women were flattered. "No one knows," Shiphrah admitted. "No one has ever seen the Lord."

"But...but," Puah interjected, "there have been those who were very close to him. Our patriarchs talked with him on many occasions!"

Moses almost laughed, but out of kindness toward the women, tried to be respectful. "Do you mean to say that your god hides himself? How can it be that some have spoken with him, but have never seen him?"

For a long moment the midwives were silent, looking uncomfortably at the floor.

"Sir," Shiphrah confessed, "we are not learned in these matters. If you desire counsel regarding our faith, we have many wise men..."

"Yes...yes..." Moses sighed, remembering his argument with Jannes. "It does seem your god is quite elusive. So then, what of this 'divine law'? Is it much different than ours?"

Shiphrah looked at Puah sideways. Surely she could not answer this without offending the prince.

"We are not scholars, Your Highness," she offered. "But our teachers tell us that our patriarchs were chosen for a high purpose—to reveal the truth to all men."

Moses turned the package over again, his hands strangely clammy.

"What truth is that?" he rasped.

"Perhaps you should ask our teachers..." Puah pleaded.

But Moses would not be put off.

"What is the truth?" he insisted, piercing her with his dark eyes.

Shiphrah intervened, courage rising as he pressed them.

"Sir, our law is quite simple, really. We have no great books, but seek the path of humility. If our law were put in words, it consists in the prayer we recite every morning, and every evening."

"Yes, go on," the prince spurred her.

Looking at Puah, Shiphrah nodded, and the two spoke in unison: "The Lord our God, The Lord is One. There is no other god beside him."

19

Moses sat alone in his room, the sounds of his birthday party flooding up from the court toward his window. Though it neared dawn, he had not returned to the party since speaking with the Hebrew women.

Several times Hatshepsut had come seeking him, pleading with him to consider his guests and the auspicious occasion. But he had excused himself, saying that he did not feel well and that he would return for the second day of festivities.

It seemed, by the sound of laughter and gaiety rising from the party site, that the guests were doing well on their own. Moses was glad to be free of the crushing crowd.

It was true that he did not feel well. His head was fuzzy and his stomach tight as a fist.

He had gone to be alone in his chamber, so that he might open the package the midwives had given him. Somehow he knew that whatever it contained, it would hold great meaning for him. But he was apprehensive as to what that meaning might be.

For hours he had held the unopened gift, fearful to look inside. As a rosy dawn tinted the river, he knew he must not hesitate any longer.

Tugging at the colorful string that bound the linen wrapper, his stiff fingers at last worked the cord free. Gingerly he pulled back the cover.

The gift was a blanket of some sort. Quickly he unfurled it, holding it up to the light.

At first there was nothing remarkable about the shawl-like piece. Apparently his nursemaid had made it as a baby blanket when he was very small, and being sentimental, wished for him to have it on this significant occasion.

In this there was nothing strange. Spreading the thick fabric across his lap, Moses shook his head. Why had he been so afraid of this simple gift? Surely he was losing his mind to sneak away from his guests and his party for some nameless superstition.

Standing, he paced the floor, rebuking himself. He did not even remember the nursemaid. The gift of a nameless, faceless servant, should not have merited a moment of his time.

Quickly he returned to his chair and snatched up the blanket. He would fold it, put it away, and rejoin his partiers. But as he looked at the gift one last time, his breath caught in his throat.

The design was familiar. He had seen this configuration of stripes and zigzags before. As the interpretation dawned on him, his knees grew weak.

Sitting down again, he turned the blanket over and over. This was an Israelite design, the same he had seen on the headbands of the temple workers...the same worn by the strange woman in his dreams.

But why would his nursemaid select such a weave for the royal swaddling cloth? Surely she was not, herself... Israelite!

Suddenly the implications formed an eerie picture. Nursemaids were matched with babies on the basis of race, Egyptian with Egyptian, Cushite with Cushite...Hebrew with Hebrew.

Moses's hands went numb, and the blanket slipped to the floor.

He had been a foundling. Hatshepsut had never denied this. Yes, she had told him he was a gift of the gods, the reincarnation of Pharaoh's lost heir, borne upon the waters of the sacred Nile and presented to her to be her son.

Beyond this she had never said more. And he had accepted, with the trusting innocence of a child, that this information was sufficient.

But he was no longer a child. He had entered manhood. And overnight the mysteries of the past had taken on vital importance.

For a long while he sat staring into space, the pieces of the puzzle linking into a formidable pattern in his mind.

If the nursemaid was Israelite...was he?

He barely felt himself rise and begin again to pace the room. As the grisly speculation seared his brain, he tried desperately to fight it.

But suddenly, as the chamber grew brighter with morning light, he caught his reflection in his polished wall-mirror, and for a moment his fears subsided.

A laugh, deep and hearty, swelled from his throat. What could he be thinking? Was any Hebrew so dark of skin as he? Hadn't Hatshepsut told him he must be of princely Nubian blood, or a descendant of Ethiopian royalty? The gods had chosen a noble specimen for the throne of Egypt!

Then, as quickly as his fears subsided, they rose again.

He had seen a dark Hebrew once. He had seen her outside his window. And she had returned to haunt him in his dreams, over and over.

Even now her sweet lullaby cursed him, its Hebrew strains tormenting his soul.

Half crazed, he raced to his balcony, his eyes flashing angrily to the street which bordered the palace wall. To his horror, he found that she was there!

Yes, she was searching his window, searching for a glimpse of him, her waterpot upon her head, her headband catching the sweat of her forehead.

"Ho there!" he cried, waving at her. "Wait! Wait there!"

But the woman was terrified. Never had she expected him to call out. Surely she was in grave danger, lurking so near his royal house.

Turning, she fled, her waterpot falling to the street in a shattering crash.

20

A small Egyptian chariot careened through the bazaar of Raamses. Though the morning market had just opened, it was already full of shoppers and merchants who cleared a path for the speeding vehicle.

For weeks the focus of the entire city had been on the royal birthday and its accompanying festivities. Now that the celebration was underway, no one would have expected to see the prince on a chase through the marketplace.

Yet the passenger was easily recognized as young Moses. Gasping, the onlookers bowed low as he came near and whispered together in amazement as the chariot went by.

Moses was heedless of their adoration. Standing close to his driver's back, he wore an intent, almost frantic expression as he sought desperately for someone in the crowd.

"She is not here," he said. "Head for the slave village!"

At the far side of the bazaar, alongside Pharaoh's monumental work site, spread the slave town. Never had any royal person entered the pathetic place. That the prince should make it his destination was unfathomable.

As the chariot reached the ghetto, the driver pulled to a stop before the low gate.

"Go ahead," Moses directed. "Do not stop here."

"You wish me to enter?" the driver marveled.

"Do as I say!" the prince insisted. "Pass through the gate!"

His face white, the driver obeyed, inching the chariot through the humble door as though he approached the underworld.

The slave village was nearly vacant, its occupants having left for work before dawn. Only a few families who worked a later shift were emerging from their hovels.

If the early shoppers in the bazaar were surprised at Moses's venture into public, the lowly villagers were even more dumbfounded.

Peering out from their houses, or standing frozen in their paths, they hardly thought to bow as the prince suddenly leaped from his chariot and scanned their faces, his brow furrowed and his fists taut.

"His Highness, Prince Moses!" the charioteer announced. "Son of Hatshepsut, son of Pharaoh, Prince of the Nile! All bow!"

As though felled by arrows, the crowd complied, lying prostrate before the royal master. Normally, a prince, whatever his errand in this unhappy place, would have been as heedless of these subjects as a great bull is heedless of the ants beneath his hooves. Prince Moses was used to being obeyed, used to people bowing before him. But for some reason, when these slaves fell down at his feet, he was moved to pity.

For a long, uneasy moment, Moses did nothing. He only stood silent, surveying the pathetic crowd: elderly men and women, bent and crippled by a lifetime of cruel service; young women, leather-faced by years in the relentless sun; able-bodied men, hardened and muscular, but bitter-eyed and hopeless; and tattered children, prepared for nothing but the miseries into which they had been born.

The prince was not aware of how much time passed before his driver whispered in his ear. "Master, shall I ask them to rise?"

"Yes, yes," Moses stammered. "Of course."

"All rise!" the chauffeur cried. And the people obeyed, fearing to breathe.

"The Master is looking for a certain slave woman!" he shouted. "A dark Hebrew who once served in the palace of his mother!"

This was specific enough. Surely there was only one who could fit such a description.

Still the slaves of this village were loyal to one another. Never would any of them play traitor, and surely the prince's quest could not bode well for the one he was after.

Therefore, Jochebed's whereabouts was kept secret. If she had somehow displeased the royal house, she would not be delivered up at the hands of her own friends.

Not a word came from the crowd. Everyone looked at the ground, hoping to avoid interrogation.

"Very well!" the driver called. "You know what befalls those who defy the court. Your rations shall be cut in half until the woman is found!"

Usually the driver had authority to make such a pronouncement. On behalf of the prince, he could wield punishment against any who offended him when he was on an outing. But Moses was not amenable to his decision.

"I don't think that will be necessary," the prince interjected. Then turning to the crowd, he lifted his hands in a beseeching manner.

"Is the entire village represented here?" he asked.

When the people again made no reply, he stepped closer and began to pass between them.

"Make way!" the driver commanded. "The prince will go through!"

A rush of whispers followed, and all watched in amazement as the mighty son of Egypt condescended to visit the ghetto.

From hut to hut he searched, calling at the door of each and commanding anyone inside to come out.

Intrigued, the crowd followed, swelling through the narrow streets and murmuring together.

At last he came to a house where a young man stood guard. He looked to be about 16, only a few years older than Moses, but much taller. And he shielded the place as though he would die rather than let it be invaded.

Standing with his arms crossed over his chest, he silently dared Moses to step closer.

"Move aside!" the driver shouted as they came upon the house. "The prince will speak with those who dwell here."

"*I* dwell here!" the young man replied. "He may speak with *me*."

"Do you use that tone with the royal prince?" the man retorted, raising his whip above his head. "Bow, or die!"

"Enough!" Moses cried, grasping the whip. "I will talk with him."

Dumbfounded, the driver moved aside, and Moses studied his steely-eyed challenger.

"Sir," he said, with unthinkable patience, "are you the master of this house?"

The older boy glared down upon the visitor. "My father is the master," he replied.

The crowd observed this exchange with a thrill of wonder. Everything about the meeting was topsy-turvy, as though the roles of prince and slave had been reversed.

But for Moses, there was something more important than protocol or the lack of it. He had known the moment he laid eyes on the teenager that this was the right house, for its young guard was ruddy and dark of skin like the woman in the street, like the woman in his dreams...like himself.

"And what of your mother?" the prince asked, his voice thin. "Is she here?"

Before the guard could say no, a shuffle inside the house belied him.

"Aaron," a woman called, "it will do no good. I am coming."

With this, a slight, dark woman at last appeared, poking her face into the sunshine. Behind came her husband, a white man. Crowding in beside them both was a young woman, dark like the guard.

Aaron stepped in front of them protectively, but the father corrected him. "Do as your mother says," he commanded. "She will meet the prince."

Slowly Jochebed came forward and greeted Moses with a quick bow, fearing to look at him. As the prince gazed upon her, she shook as though she would break.

"Woman, why were you standing outside my window?" Moses asked.

"I . . . I was merely passing in the street," she hedged. "Is it unlawful, Master, to gaze upon your lovely palace?"

"Why do you tremble so, my lady?" the prince inquired.

That a person of royalty should speak tenderly to one who was less than a dog was unheard of in Egypt. Jochebed only quivered more, and her husband reached for her.

"Do not fear," Moses said, his throat so tight he could barely breathe. "You knew me once, my lady, did you not?"

At this, Jochebed was overcome with feeling. Tears began to trickle down her cheeks, and she tried to wipe them away.

But Moses caught her hand in his own, and lifting her chin with his fingertips, forced her to look into his eyes.

"You knew me once, my lady, did you not?" he repeated.

At last, the woman surrendered. "Yes, my lord," she confessed. "I knew you before anyone else ever knew you, and better than anyone else ever has."

21

Moses never returned to his birthday party. The week-long festivities continued without him while he spent his time between lonely bouts of heart-searching in his palace chamber and secret treks to the house of Amram and Jochebed.

From the moment he met his long-lost family, he became a soul divided. Outwardly he was an Egyptian, and part of him loved the power, glory, and comforts of his position. But inwardly he was drawn to the simple people who were teaching him great truths.

Moses's attraction to the Hebrews was more than a coming-home, more than a solving of the mystery of his roots. Ever since he had first seen them praying on the streetcorner and had heard their voices lifted in song, he had yearned for the spirit they expressed.

He was catching that spirit now, soaking it in, as though making up for lost time, as he sat night after night at the feet of his Hebrew father.

It was not easy to escape the palace as often as he did. His dreadful breach of etiquette in abandoning his party guests had created no small ripple of resentment in the household, making it risky for him to disregard protocol.

A prince's activities were meticulously ordered, every moment proscribed, so that the independent and head-strong nature which was highly prized once an heir took the throne could be exhibited only with great caution.

Still he managed to be with the family many times—at odd hours, by way of night, and in disguise.

Two years passed in this way, two years of midnight rendezvous, of whispering and dark streets, of collusion with the midwives, of secret arrangements, of quiet reentries, of tiptoeing past Hatshepsut's suite and hoping she never suspected.

He could not have counted how many times he reached his bedroom door just before dawn, breathing a sigh of relief for one more success.

Tonight as he put his hand on the door lever, he repeated an Israelite prayer of thanks learned in Amram's house.

But when he opened the door, he found he was not alone.

Sitting in the halo of a low lamp, her face drawn with misery, was the princess, his Egyptian mother.

Across her lap, like a scroll of revelation, lay Moses's baby blanket, the one Jochebed had made.

Quickly the prince interpreted the scene. He knew that Hatshepsut knew. And he stood numb before her.

"Is this where you go when you sneak away?" the woman asked, not so much accusing as full of hurt. "You go to visit slaves?"

Moses gave no answer. Heartsick, he pretended to be angry and stalked across the room, throwing his cloak upon the bed.

"Why didn't you tell me?" the woman cried. "You could have told me!"

"Ha!" Moses laughed, turning on her. "I should be the one asking you that question. Why didn't *you* tell *me* the truth? You kept my identity a secret, lying to me from the first!"

"There were reasons," the princess choked. "It was best that way."

Moses's harsh face softened. He knew she referred to Pharaoh's edict, the one that would have had him drowned along with all the other Israelite babies. Jochebed and Amram had told him all about it the first time they talked. And they had also told him of Hatshepsut's compassion, so rare and so miraculous.

"You speak of Grandfather and his cruel command," he said.

"Yes, son," the woman replied. "But that was long ago and best forgotten. Have you been so unhappy with me?"

Moses could not stay angry. Gazing upon the hands that had so often soothed him and the face that had always smiled upon him, he shook his head.

"Dear woman," he said, "you know I love you. Had it not been for you, I would not have lived. The God of my fathers brought you to me."

Incredulous, the princess received these words with mixed feelings. "'God of your fathers'?" she repeated. "You mean Osiris."

"Osiris is the god of the Egyptians. Not the God of my fathers."

Hatshepsut's lips trembled. "Jannes said you were dabbling in strange matters. Oh, Moses," she beseeched him, "return to us. Remember who you are!"

Kneeling before her, the prince took her hands in his, much as he had done with Jochebed the morning they met. The irony of his predicament, his attachment to two cultures and two families, tore at his heart.

"I am only now finding myself, Mother," he whispered.

Hatshepsut bent close and stroked his face. The beginnings of a man's beard tickled her fingers, and she contemplated his future with fear.

"Do what you must," she sighed. "But be careful. Pharaoh does not know that your life defies his command. Whatever caused him, years ago, to make his dreadful decree, he is bound by it. His anger has a long memory."

22

The shadow of a royal cab fell across the door of the marble mason's shop on the Boulevard of the Gods.

Ineni, the most prestigious craftsman in Egypt and the shop's owner, was renowned for the precise cuttings and handcarved embellishments of his stonework. Contracted to do the detailing on Pharaoh's grandest projects, he hired only the most talented masons, and whether they were of the slave or freeman class, all who worked for him received handsome wages.

The men inside looked up from their exacting labor to see who approached. As the cab was lowered to the ground, they bowed in homage.

Moses, now a strapping man in his early twenties, entered the shop with an eager step. By virtue of his authority, he had found slots for his brother and father, Aaron and Amram, in the stonecutter's employ. At the same time, Jochebed and Miriam had been sent to work in the house of the midwives, and the prince delighted in the fact that his family was more comfortably situated.

Although Amram and Aaron had no experience in stonecutting, having spent their lives in the brick pits, they confirmed Moses's word to the marble mason that they would learn quickly and could be artisans if given the chance.

Over the years since he had met his Hebrew family, Moses had seen to it that they were well provided for.

Gifts of money and food were often delivered to the door of their humble home, and they always knew the source. In time they had risen from the status of bondslaves to that of indentured servants with the potential of freedom should they prove themselves worthy.

Of course, if Moses were pharaoh, he would have freed them years ago. But he must, for their sake and his, make his moves with caution.

Though his generosity was an unspeakable boon to Amram and his household, Moses had often felt that Aaron harbored resentment toward him.

Today as he entered the shop, he sensed it once again. Though Aaron bowed before him, he stood up more quickly than the others, and he avoided Moses's smile.

As Aaron picked up his chisel to continue his work, Moses admired his carving.

"The mason is highly pleased with you," the prince said, trying to draw him out. "I can see why."

Aaron made no reply, keeping his eyes to the project. Moses glanced up at Amram, who only shrugged his shoulders.

"May I speak with you, Aaron?" Moses asked. "Outside?"

This was said in a whisper, but it caught the attention of all present. They watched inquisitively as Aaron silently complied.

"I understand there is a party in the village tonight," Moses began once they had reached the street. "A Bar Mitzvah."

"Yes," Aaron said. "The son of a Levite."

"Did you know I learned of my ancestry on the night I turned 13?" the prince reminded him.

Again Aaron was sullen.

"I would like to attend the ceremony," Moses went on.

"Why would an Egyptian attend a Hebrew party?" Aaron sneered.

Moses was offended. "Have I been with you so long, only to have you hate me?" he marveled.

Aaron sniffed, rolling his eyes. "Why should you care?" he laughed. "Oh, you have been good to us. Mother and Father have received your gifts and your promotions with gratitude. But you do not need to lower yourself to eat from our trough!"

"You know my interest goes deeper!" Moses objected. "You know I want to learn all I can of your ways. Why, one day I shall rise to power! I shall sit upon the throne! Think what I can do for you then!"

"Just so," Aaron muttered. "That is just the point."

"What do you mean?" Moses sighed.

Suddenly Aaron could restrain his tongue no longer. Suddenly a decade of pent-up anger came spilling forth.

"Always you are condescending! Always you are reaching down to us from your lofty palace," he cried.

Stammering, Moses countered, "Wouldn't you do the same? If you had the power to help your people, wouldn't you do just as I have done?"

"But we are not your people!" Aaron argued, his voice rising more than it should. "You can give us gifts and lift us up, but you will never know what it is to be Israelite!"

Moses's heart was pricked. "Who are you to speak to me this way!" he growled. "Someday, I shall be pharaoh, and when that day comes I shall have power to free the Israelites from bondage!"

People were passing on the street, observing this confrontation with interest. So far the dialogue had been private, but Moses must not risk further conversation. Turning for his cab, he used the back of a bowed slave as his stepping stool, entered, and took his seat beneath the canopy.

Clapping his hands, he ordered the pole bearers to take him away.

As the cab moved down the street, however, Aaron's voice rang out behind him.

"Enjoy your comforts, Prince!" he mocked. "And remember, they are the comforts of an Egyptian! You have never been anything more."

23

It was a sad time for Egypt. A pharaoh's death always precipitated the most intense period of mourning imaginable.

No matter how popular or unpopular a pharaoh might be, his passing was the loss of the nation's father, the death of an incarnate deity. And Thutmose was dead.

Ever since he had taken ill and suddenly died more than two months before, the country had been paralyzed with grief. There was limited commerce, and most daily activities were suspended as citizens made pilgrimages to their local temples or bowed before their household gods, offering up prayers for the king's safe passage through the underworld.

As the common folk lent their united efforts to invoke happiness for the departed, the priests in the necropolis spent weeks preparing the body, chanting intricate spells and inscribing within the tomb and the sarcophagus magical formulas designed to protect and aid the deceased. Guidebooks and maps of infernal geography were placed within the mausoleum so that Thutmose would find his way to the Celestial Fields.

Today, as 40-year-old Moses walked with his Egyptian mother in his grandfather's funeral processional, his feelings and his thoughts were a jumble.

For four decades he had been trained for ascension to the throne of Egypt. Now, with the end of Thutmose's rule, the dream of his ultimate reign came into sharper focus than ever.

Thutmose had left his kingdom to his daughter, Hatshepsut, with Moses as her immediate successor. But so much of what the prince should have felt eluded him. While he, too, mourned the king's passing, he found tears hard to come by. And while the prospect of his own eventual power should have been glorious, thoughts of the throne filled him with dread.

An hour ago a lengthy march through the city of Thebes had brought the royal family and its many attendants to the Nile. In the past, the coffin of the king would have been carried across the river, symbolizing the crossing of the River of Death, and would have been placed within a mammoth pyramid. The tomb of Thutmose, however, would not be so clearly visible.

Upon passing over the river, the family proceeded alone toward the mountains that bordered the Nile's west bank. Behind that range, within a narrow valley, the coffin would find its resting place.

Thutmose had been one of the mightiest pharaohs in the history of the land. His military exploits had thoroughly subdued Ethiopia, and he was the first king to push the power of Egypt to the border of the Euphrates, over 700 miles away. He had executed so many architectural projects that the memory of former kings paled by comparison.

Yet he had spent a good part of his career preparing for the afterlife. As a young man he had broken with tradition, deciding against a pyramid as his eternal home, and selecting, instead, to be buried in a hollowed-out tomb in a cliff of the obscure valley.

He would be the first monarch to be buried in the Valley of the Tombs of the Kings, his gravesite inaccessible to all but his most intimate associates.

When the family crossed the river, they left behind them the thousands of mourners who had observed the funeral march. They now traversed the floor of the fissure-like valley and ascended a lonely fold within the westward cliff.

Ineni, the marble mason, had served as architect for the hidden grave. Pledging his devotion as the most favored craftsman in Egypt, he had sworn to construct the sepulcher in secrecy, with no one to see or hear.

It had been Thutmose's deepest desire that his tomb never be pillaged by grave robbers. While the grand pyramids, with their many baffles and dead-end chambers, had served for a time to preserve the sanctity of ancestral remains, they had eventually been mastered by ghoulish thieves. Perhaps a secret resting place, approachable only by a steep ascent, then by a precipitous, descending stairway, and finally by a series of maze-like anterooms, would be safe from desecration.

Such precautions reflected the Egyptian belief that the soul could be destroyed if its mummy were defiled. Since the survival of Egypt supposedly depended on the guidance of its departed kings, protection of the royal mummies became a matter of national interest.

Still, as Moses and his mother crossed the valley floor and followed Ineni, Jannes, and a dozen priests to the foot of the western cliff, the prince had little heart for the undertaking.

When they at last came to the narrow, sandstone stairway marking the ascent to the tomb, an eerie blast of desert wind whipped toward them. Moses tried to pray for his grandfather, but found his inward thoughts as confusing as the maze that had been chiseled step-by-step into the mountainside.

Up, up he went, holding Hatshepsut's hand. But her tears shamed him, for he could not feel as she did.

Though Moses had lived all his life in the palace and had been called before the king many times, though he had been pulled onto the pharaoh's lap as a child and had been told he was the favored son of Egypt, he could not recall ever loving Thutmose.

Behind the little entourage came the court musicians, the pounding of their drums and the shrillness of their flutes intensifying Moses's discomfort.

When the company had picked their way along the twisting stairs, and at last stood before the door of the vault, Hatshepsut clung to Moses's arm like a vine. Jannes stood with his head bowed for a long time, chanting a final eulogy. Then he pushed against the great stone slab that was the tomb's entrance.

With a whoosh the door swung back, sucking desert dust into the interior. Several temple slaves ran ahead with lighted tapers, setting ablaze the many wall torches that lined the first anteroom.

Sighing, Hatshepsut tightened her grip on her son's arm. They were being ushered into the very house of death, following the priests and the tomb-maker like lambs.

Once the countless cells of the baffles were behind them, the approachway broadened out upon a colossal, pillared hall, already lit by a hundred colorful lanterns.

All about the walls were the embellishments and hieroglyphs of temple artists, each symbol intended to elicit good for the passing soul. And upon the floor, arranged in neat rows, were the king's death treasures—furnishings, food, clothing, and luxuries that would attend him for eternity.

As Moses surveyed the room, the angst of his spirit was suddenly clarified. Within this sanctuary would lie forever the bones of his enemy, the remains of the one who would have had him dead at birth, and who had received him only under the deception of Hatshepsut.

It was this, this irony of his life, that troubled him today. As he stood here in the droning silence, viewing the mummy of his predecessor stretched out upon a marble slab, he knew at once the meaning of his soul's shadow.

The twisted destiny of his rescue from the river had brought him to walk in his enemy's path, to rise to power in a land that would hate him if only it knew his true identity.

Suddenly he did not know right from wrong. He did not know whether to follow the deception, or break with it. He did not know the will of any god, neither the gods of Pharaoh nor the God of Amram.

Like a swelling fist, conflict rose within him. He could almost taste it as it pushed up from his heart, threatening to spew forth blasphemy.

Whether that blasphemy should be against Osiris, against Horus, against Isis, or against Jehovah, he knew not. He was the product of some heavenly collusion, and just now he hated all that was divine.

No longer able to endure his drumming pulse, certain that it must thunder through the halls of this desolate mountain like the fretting of the damned, Moses suddenly turned away.

Pushing Hatshepsut from him, he tore back through the entrapping maze, blindly seeking the light of day. And when, by some miracle, he at last found the outer staircase, he fell back against the cliff with a heaving groan.

"Lord God," he cried, his voice echoing pathetically through the gorge, "who are you? Lord God, who am *I*?"

24

That night Moses sat alone in his room, haunted by thoughts of his grandfather.

He remembered the tales told to him as a child of what became of a soul after death. Jannes had said that when a king died, he entered the boat of the sun-god, Ra, and sailed away to the easternmost part of the sky to dwell forever among the immortals.

But he had also described a more fearful journey, and Moses had never been clear regarding whether or not a member of the royal family must endure such a thing.

In this account, Jannes had taught that the soul must travel beneath the cities of Egypt on a subterranean Nile, in quest of the Celestial Fields. When the soul crossed the mountain range of death, it could not reach the abode of bliss until it traversed a region inhabited by fiends and monsters. If the soul shrank back, it would be subjected to the most miserable tortures and ultimately be devoured or cremated.

If the departed one managed to safely pass through this fearful domain, it must face the gravest test of all, a trial in the Hall of Maat, goddess of truth. Here the heart would be placed in a scale and weighed against the sacred feather of righteousness. The dog-headed god, Anubis, would adjust the balance as the ibis-headed Thoth recorded the results. A jury of 42 Assessors, one for each disqualifying sin, would look on.

If the soul passed the test, Horus would conduct it to Osiris, Prince of the West, who rested patiently in his shrine, wrapped in a winding sheet.

But if the soul failed, the Devourer—an obscene creature with the head of a crocodile, the forepart of a lion, and the hindquarters of a hippopotamus—would chew the bones, tear the flesh, and drink the blood of the sinner.

The more Moses dwelt on these stories, the more uneasy he became. Images of Thutmose being clawed and torn in shreds, or worse yet, floating forever in helpless confusion in quest of eternal rest, filled the prince's head with morbid fear.

What the Hebrews taught about the afterlife, he was not certain. They rarely mentioned it, and when one of them passed away, the ceremonies were simple. They spoke of some place called Abraham's bosom, a resting place. But they did not specify just how one achieved this paradise.

Far more elaborate and precise were the Egyptian descriptions. And therefore, far more potent. Except for the mention of the national deities, they might have been closer to the truth than the nebulous concepts of the Hebrews.

But how could Moses know? Who could tell him?

He would have gone to see Amram, to fill his father's ears with questions, had he not been obliged to stay in the palace until the time of mourning was fulfilled.

Instead he must content himself with meager prayers, hoping they would reach through the gloom of the underworld, or somehow touch the ears of God. Though he had never loved Thutmose, he had been taught to respect him and wished him no ill on whatever journey he experienced.

Rising from his bed, he crossed the room to a low table on which were a few small candlestands. Though all sorts of prayers had been said to all sorts of Egyptian gods and goddesses since the king had died, Moses doubted whether any soul in the land had raised petition to Jehovah on his behalf. Perhaps the prince should do this. Perhaps it would ease his own mind, whether it spared Thutmose anything or not.

Lighting the candles, Moses watched as they cast light and shadow across the room. Then, going to his private closet, he pulled out the blanket which the midwives had given him.

Reverently he returned to the table. With shaky hands, he pulled the little shawl over his head, just as he had seen Amram do with his own mantle whenever he spoke with the Lord.

But words did not come. Moses did not know how to pray for the soul of the king, for the soul of the one who had slain thousands of his infant brethren. Indeed he wondered if he should pray for Thutmose at all. Was it wicked to do so?

As he wavered, a knock on his door broke the silence.

Tearing the mantle from his head, he called, "Who is it?"

"It is I, Jannes," the old priest replied.

Quickly hiding the shawl behind his back, Moses croaked, "Come in."

Light from the hallway spilled into the room, and Jannes squinted, trying to adjust his eyes to the dark interior.

Like an aged moth, he was drawn to the candles. With curious gaze he studied Moses's pensive face in the yellow glow.

"I see you have been at prayer," the elder observed.

"Yes."

"That is good. That is what we all must do."

Moses stood rigid before him, still gripping the mantle behind his back.

"I came to say goodnight," the priest explained. "It has been a difficult day for those I love most."

As he turned to leave, Moses tried not to show his relief. When the elder reached the door, the prince nodded to him. But suddenly Jannes was crossing the room once again.

"Let me embrace you, my son," he pleaded, his voice tight with feeling. "While this is a sad day, it is also a happy one, for tomorrow your mother will ascend the throne!"

"Yes," Moses nodded. "That will be good."

Jannes was surprised at the simplistic response. But shrugging, he reached out, drawing the prince close.

When Moses embraced him with only one arm, keeping the other still to his back, the old man pulled away.

"What have you there?" he inquired, turning Moses about.

Jannes was a highly knowledgeable theologian. He was versed in the faiths of all the people of Egypt. When he beheld the mantle, his eyes grew wide.

Adrenalin raced through Moses's veins. "It is a gift," he said. "I don't know much about it."

Jannes knew he lied. "It is a Levite shawl," he hissed, taking the blanket and turning it this way and that. "You use a Hebrew shawl when you pray?"

Moses said nothing. The blood drained from his face as he sensed the discovery of all his dark secrets.

25

Hatshepsut's rise to the throne was heralded with joy among most of her subjects, but met with reservation and even bitter anger among others.

A female pharaoh? Such a thing was against tradition. In many circles it was considered a blasphemy against Egypt, against all that was holy.

When Thutmose had placed his daughter beside him as co-regent, the country had accepted her as they would accept a queen. But never had they anticipated that she would rule independent of a man.

So it fell out that her day of inauguration was also her wedding day.

Though Hatshepsut had sworn all her life that she would rather die or go to her grave childless than marry her half-brother, Thutmose II, she was ultimately forced to bow to political and social precedent. Indeed, she *would* risk her life if she defied tradition, for assassination would, to some, be preferable to the autocratic rule of a female.

Let her take the throne, but let it be in the shadow of her brother. Let her retain her virginity if she wished, but let her reign as his wife or not at all.

Six months into the new administration, Thutmose II used his new power to wield a devastating blow to Hatshepsut. Seeing that she was determined to be his wife on paper only—that she would never be his bedmate or bear him a child—he took matters into his own hands and announced that the son of a concubine would be his heir.

Overnight the morale in the palace, which had been none too high since the king's death, plummeted to dangerous depths. It became a house divided, one faction supporting the rule of Hatshepsut and her adopted heir, Moses, the other the male domination of Thutmose II and his illegitimate son.

Though Moses's loyalties had long been confused, he deeply resented the mistreatment of his Egyptian mother, and his readiness to defend his own right to the throne surprised him greatly.

His cousin, the would-be heir, was 20 years his junior. Though bright and headstrong, he had always impressed Moses as selfishly crafty. A favored pet of the harem, the concubine's son took after Thutmose II, having a low, slanting brow, and simian eyes. Moses had always marveled at the attentions the strange creature received and had written it off as the result of his monkey-like cuteness.

But to pass the rule of Egypt to such a character seemed utter folly. So thought all those who preferred Hatshepsut and her son.

Moses was not certain where Jannes stood in all this. He knew that the priest had deciphered his secret. He knew that Jannes now realized he was Israelite, that his rescue from the river had been the rescue of an infant against Pharaoh's edict.

The fact that the secret had come to light after Thutmose's death was a saving grace. If Jannes loved Moses at all, he would honor the fact that Hatshepsut had taken him as her heir. He would keep the secret of his birth from Thutmose II, or he would see Moses dead.

It was in this context that Moses's life became a constant tension, a drama of looking over his shoulder, of fearing every whisper, every sideways glance.

He did not know what Jannes would do, and it seemed that the priest was now the master of his fate.

This night, dark spilled through the streets of Raamses on the wake of a heavy fog. It was winter, as close to winter as was ever experienced in this perfect climate. Moses had left the palace without a cab tonight, without chariot or chauffeur. He wished to wander the streets in silence, to be alone in the thick, wet black that rose from the river.

He did not wear his customary disguise. He would be cloaked by the foggy blanket. Besides, he wished to be free of imposture.

In fact, if he could have his way, he would be free of all the insanity of his existence. Perhaps Grandfather Thutmose, whatever his present plight, was the fortunate one, free of responsibility and sham. Thutmose had only his own soul to be concerned with. He need not hide his identity or worry over the welfare of two disparate peoples.

Surely, Moses thought, no man on earth had ever been so lonely or so out of harmony with the universe as himself.

A man without a place, he was. A man without a country and without true friends. For no one, even those who believed they loved him, knew him as the torn and double-hearted fellow he really was.

Had they known, he reasoned, they could not have loved him. Hatshepsut would resent his ongoing duplicity. Amram and Jochebed would wish they had never reclaimed him.

As Moses stumbled through the dark streets, hugging self-pity to his chest, he thought of Aaron. Yes, Aaron alone had read his heart. He had known from the beginning that Moses was weak and spineless.

"Why, God?" Moses breathed. "Why did you choose me instead of my elder brother? Why wasn't Aaron raised up in power instead of me?"

Fists taut, he pulled his striped cloak tight and fought

back the tears that rose hot behind his eyes.

"Surely Aaron would have been a better choice! Strong, confident Aaron! I am but a liar, a man of faltering and unclean lips, afraid to speak the truth, and dying from a lie!"

Moses had come to a bend in the river, many city blocks from the palace. How long he had wandered through the streets he did not know. But as he stood upon the bank, gray sunlight pushed through the fog and touched the swollen current.

It seemed the holy river and the dawn sun beckoned to him, as though the great god Ra whispered in his ear: "I saved you once from death-by-drowning. But now I repent that folly. Jump, Moses! Jump!"

Suddenly the prince's feet slipped on the clay soil. His pulse tripping, he teetered above the wintry waters, barely catching himself.

Turning about, he scrambled up the bank and lay for a long time weeping on the shore.

With the dawn came the sounds of movement and industry upon the riverside highway. As the fog lifted, Moses rose, returned to the water, and reached his muddy hands into the Nile. Trembling, he splashed the waters of death upon his face and straightened his disheveled hair.

No one must see him like this.

How he wished, now, that he had worn his disguise! People were filling the streets with their daytime activities. Knowing he would be recognized, Moses tried to appear casual. Perhaps the gawking onlookers would think he had only partied all night, an undignified but forgivable indulgence.

It was a long way back to the palace. He found congested areas unavoidable, and at last was obliged to traverse the Boulevard of the Gods.

Here the familiar sounds of hammer and chisel, the

shout and cry of master and slave, the groan of burden-bearers and the grating rasp of man-hauled pallets met his ears.

All about him were his agonized Hebrew brothers. Pharaoh's fabulous projects required relentless taskmasters and superhuman laborers. But there were no superhumans. Though the images of the kings carved into the sandstone buildings were gigantic, symbolizing the titanic rule of the dynasties, the ones who created them were only mortal. Their fingers bled, their skin blistered in the sun, and they fainted as their energies ran dry.

All this Moses had seen before. All his life he had witnessed the humiliation and abuse of slaves. For years it had troubled him, but today he had no stomach for it.

Dizzy from exhaustion, he sought refuge from the grisly scene. Down a narrow side street he wandered until he came upon a vacant sand patch. Sitting down, he held his drumming forehead in his hands.

But all too soon his retreat was invaded. Shouts and angry epithets issued from the back gate of a nearby house.

"I am sorry, Master!" someone cried in the broken accent of an Israelite. "I meant no harm!"

"Stupid, lazy sand flea!" an Egyptian replied. "Worthless as the day you were born!"

Suddenly the door flew back, and the Israelite was cast face first into the alley. Smoke from the kitchen's clay oven poured out behind him, and the master appeared, waving a whip above his head.

"Black as the muddy Nile! My bread is burned black, you silly swine! You couldn't boil water without a tutor!"

The helpless slave raised himself from the dirt and bowed repeatedly, begging for mercy.

"I am not a cook, Master. I have never worked in the kitchen until today!" he cried.

"You haven't the brain of a sage hen!" the Egyptian hollered, his face bloated with rage.

Moses watched as the slaveowner wielded his whip, and he cringed as the torturous instrument ripped at the bondslave's back.

Hardly knowing it, the prince was suddenly on his feet, flying across the sandlot toward the alley. In one instant, all the frustration, rage, and helplessness of his own life coalesced, surging through his veins in an urge for revenge.

Looking madly about him and seeing that they were alone, Moses seized a rock in spasmed fingers and lifted it in the air. With one flash of movement, he brought the rock broadside the slaveowner's forehead, sending him to the ground with a thudding groan.

The ugly whip, already bloody from tearing into the Hebrew's back, grew bloodier still as it lay beside the slaveowner's head. A puddle of red seeped toward it, trickling from the man's temple and soaking the sandy ground like spilled paint.

Numbly, Moses observed the widening pool while the slave, beaten and bent, struggled to rise up. Seeing his owner's crumpled body, his eyes grew wide.

"Master!" he cried, crawling toward the limp form. "Master! Speak to me!"

Pressing his ear to the man's lips, he found no sound there, no breath. Falling back, he studied Moses in astonishment.

The prince, still charged with adrenalin, reached for the slave, eager to lift him up. But to his bewilderment he was rebuffed.

The slave, shrinking back, only cried, "What have you done, Majesty? See what you have done!"

"I...I wanted to help," Moses limply replied.

But the Hebrew, the one who had been flogged, found strength to stand, and without a word of thanks, fled down the alley from the face of the one who had saved him.

26

All that day and the next night, Moses lived in mortal fear that his crime would be discovered. His only solace lay in the hope that the slave would keep the secret. Surely he would not want his own involvement in the incident to become known, but would play dumb regarding the matter.

Though Moses kept close within the palace, he fought the urge to return to the sandlot, where he had hastily buried the corpse.

When the Israelite had run away, Moses had pulled the heavy body to a corner of the site, behind a clump of sage, and had frantically dug a pit in the sand. With bare hands, raw and blistered by the cutting granules, he managed to form a shallow grave. Because the rotund body more than filled it, he had simply heaped the extra sand over him, piling it higher with brush against the persistent desert wind.

But he had feared ever since that the sifting breezes would reveal the makeshift tomb.

On the second day, he was obliged to leave the royal house on an accounting errand. He was to oversee the removal of his personal treasury from the House of the Harem to the House of the Queen, where his mother now resided.

Before she was officially inaugurated on the throne, all his personal effects had been considered princely goods and had been under the auspices of the harem guards, along with the treasures of all the sons of concubines and secondary wives. Today, as the heir-apparent of Hatshepsut, his cache of goods would be kept under her authority.

He had never seen most of his treasure. The first installment had come upon his thirteenth birthday, and the collection of gifts, tribute, and taxes had grown so enormous over the years that it required a warehouse of its own upon the queen's grounds.

But Moses cared not for such things today. He wished to cloister himself away until the sands of Egypt and the winds of time eroded the bones of his victim, until there could be no implication of his name with the death of the cruel Egyptian.

As he made his way to the first warehouse, his face shaven and scrubbed, he wondered if the stress of past hours was apparent. His brain was foggy from sleeplessness and he felt the duties of this day were beyond him. But straightening his shoulders, he climbed the broad ramp that led to the storeroom door and greeted his accountants with a smile.

Already palace servants were hauling his treasures from the musty interior, piling crates of Phoenician glassware, rolls of gaudy Arabian carpet, and urns of rare ointment on the runway.

Hovering over the accountants, Moses tried to concentrate on the figures they tabulated as the goods were loaded on carts and carried away. But images of the slain corpse, echoes of its thudding fall, and the memory of the slave's accusing face tormented him.

Reaching for an accounting tablet, he began to make his own entries, hoping that focusing on numbers and measures would clear his head. But he could not manage his own hands, which grew shakier with each notation.

As he sensed his co-workers' inquisitive glances, he fought for self-control. But it was no use. The tremors were only more pronounced, and his face was flushed with color.

Suddenly one of the carts wobbled on the ramp, sending an urn of pungent herbs and spices to the pavement. A heady aroma filled the court as little flasks of turmeric, cinnamon, cloves, and mustard mingled together.

Coughing and covering their noses, his accountants avoided the pungent potpourri. But the odor was too much for Moses. His stomach, already churning from stress, threatened to revolt. With a nod of apology, he quickly left the site.

Seeking refuge, he fled the palace grounds and hastened again through the streets. Driven by anxiety, he went straight for the sandlot.

He must assure himself that the grave was still intact.

He did not get far before he found it necessary to rest. Leaning against a building, he closed his eyes and took several deep breaths, allowing his pulse to ease.

Once again, however, the sound of a scuffle roused him. Glancing down the avenue he saw that two men quarreled, this time both of them slaves, both Israelite.

As they fought, they attracted a small crowd that moved with them along the sidewalk. Without knowing it, they were coming toward the prince, who watched them in amazement.

"Ho there!" he called to them. "Come here!"

Stopping in their tracks, the company looked at the royal figure in surprise and quickly bowed before him.

Disapproval clouded his face as Moses challenged the bigger of the two squabblers. "Why are you striking your companion?" he asked. "How can you people hope to rise above your enemies when you fight among yourselves?"

Such a question coming from an Egyptian would have been strange enough. But it so happened that these men knew who Moses was, knew who his parents were. And indeed, they knew more than that.

Boldly the confronted slave threw back his shoulders, staring Moses directly in the eye.

"Who made you a prince and a judge over us?" he spat. "Shall you kill me as you killed the Egyptian?"

PART IV
Man of Midian

27

Strange partners they were—Moses, an Egyptian prince, and Aaron, a Hebrew slave—scurrying through the night, scurrying in a wobbly cart toward the wilderness border. But for the first time in their lives, they were truly brothers.

It was an irony that the very act which compelled Moses to flee Egypt was evidence to the skeptical Aaron of his loyalty to Israel. For what greater proof could there be than the murder of an Egyptian slaveowner in defense of an Israelite?

When Moses discovered that his crime was known, that the slave whom he had rescued had spread the word among his own companions, he knew it would not be long before the news reached Pharaoh's ears. He also knew he could never again return to the palace. For no amount of love on Hatshepsut's part, no loyalty on the part of Jannes, would spare him the wrath which was his rightful due.

And how could he know that Jannes *would* defend him? Perhaps, once learning of his crime, the priest would utterly turn against him. Likely he would reveal the circumstances of his birth, the fact that the prince was Hebrew and that his life had been spared years ago by the whim of Hatshepsut.

Thutmose II would not hesitate to hunt Moses down, to seek his death and strike the final blow against the queen and her appointed heir.

No, Moses could never again return to the palace.

The moment he realized his desperate deed had been uncovered, he fled to the only safe place he knew: the house of Amram. Confessing all, he fell on the mercy of his true family.

As for Aaron, while the story Moses told was dreadful, it sparked into flame the long-dead embers of love he had once felt for his younger brother. He vowed then and there to aid in his escape.

Thus it came to be that a slave cart carried a prince through dark of night southeast from Raamses, skirting the lush region of Goshen, where Israel had made its fateful entrance into Egypt four centuries earlier.

Hobbling across the open plains, the cart would meet with no waystation, no inspectors, before it reached Great Bitter Lake at the edge of the vast Sinai wasteland.

The single stop the men had been obliged to make was at the gate of Raamses. But the prince, whose crime was still not widely broadcast, had demanded passage. And the bewildered guards had let him leave the city.

The Nile's wintry fog did not reach to the eastward slope of the plains. An hour into the desert, the sky was clear. No street torches diluted the blackness, but overhead a thousand stars pierced the dark canopy with fingertips of light.

This was shepherd country, land of the nomads and of wandering African tribes who had never been enslaved.

It was country such as the patriarch Jacob had known when he traversed Palestine in freedom so many years ago. It was the kind of country, and this was the kind of sky, which young Joseph had loved before he was sold into Pharaoh's hands.

Though Moses was Israelite, he had never been privileged to see such a night. Neither had Aaron, though he had heard songs at his father's knee that lauded the shepherd life, songs passed down through generations of bondage and sung by people who had never known liberty.

The two brothers, though they had led the most disparate of lives, were tonight experiencing identical emotions. Aaron, slave of Pharaoh, and Moses, slave of Pharaoh's palace—each frozen in his own distinct prison—had never known such a night.

Thus they found themselves huddling together under the sky's blanket in the unity of newfound kinship.

The desert wind licked at their faces, pushing Moses's coiffed hair back from cleancut cheeks and tossing Aaron's mop of dark curls back from a bearded jaw.

Beneath the coiffure and behind the beard, the faces were much alike: ruddy, noble, Hebro-Nubian—faces of the sons of one man and one woman.

"When you reach Bitter Lake, which way will you turn?" Aaron asked, breaking the silence.

"I could take the Way to Shur," Moses answered, "but I do not think it would be safe. Too much traffic."

Aaron was thoughtful, listening to the crunch of the wagon wheels upon the desert floor.

"The way south would lead to Suez. There you could get supplies," he suggested.

To this point, they had not spoken of Moses's further plans. Aaron felt a lump in his throat as he considered his brother's lost condition.

"How far do you mean to go?" he managed.

Moses breathed deeply of the sage-spiced air. "As far as necessary."

"Into Sinai?" Aaron marveled. "But you are not... prepared."

Moses knew he choked on the word. There was so much more he could have said about the prince's pampered past, about the fact that he had never toiled in his life and had no experience with sheer survival.

"I have no choice," Moses muttered. "But what of you? You risk your life to help me. When you return to Raamses, you will be a wanted man."

Aaron surprised him with a smile. "God is with me," he said, "as he is with you."

The fugitive prince swallowed hard. Tears of remorse and anger flooded his eyes.

"How can you say that?" he groaned. "I am a sinner in the eyes of God and man!"

As he looked at his lap, at the knotted fists that rested there, Moses felt Aaron's arm about his shoulders.

"You are destined for greatness far beyond the greatness of Pharaoh," Aaron whispered. "Don't you see? God rescued you from the Nile, and he will rescue you from exile. He will return you to us, in power beyond anything you have ever known."

28

Moses leaned against the trunk of a palm tree in the oasis of Migdol, and watched as an Arabian trader wound a linen cloth into a sausage-like coil. At the little bazaar of the nearby fortress, the last outpost of the Bitter Lake region, he had purchased a length of similar fabric and must now learn to fashion it into the type of headwrap which had for centuries protected nomads from the desert sun.

Against his protest, Aaron had left him with the donkey that had pulled their cart from Raamses. Knowing that Moses would never make much distance without transportation, the elder brother had refused to take the beast. He, being stronger and having a shorter way to go, had left the wagon and returned home on foot once they reached Lake Timsah, to the north of Suez.

That had been two days ago. Since then, Moses had surprised himself by making it all the way to the southern tip of Bitter Lake, nearly 40 miles of travel.

As he had told Aaron, he would not take the Way to Shur, the road which led directly east of Goshen. That road was heavily traveled and led to the "shur" or "wall" of Egypt, the snake-like chain of border fortresses separating Palestine from the Land of Pharaoh. News of his crime and of his fugitive status preceding him, he would doubtless be arrested at the terminal checkpoint, which was garrisoned by Egyptian troops.

Instead he must take the Way of the Wilderness, which

led from the Gulf of Suez to the Gulf of Aqaba, or the Red Sea. But even here he would need to be careful.

With his Egyptian clothes and stilted palace dialect, he was out of place in this setting. His only means of barter were the few jewels he had worn the day he went to his treasure warehouse. With a small ring he had purchased food at Timsah, and here at Migdol he had purchased the linen cloth with a single, slender bracelet. Although the nomad traders had accepted his story that he had stumbled across the rare pieces in a Theban market, suspicion was in their eyes.

Just now, as he watched the Arab merchant making the turban, he must not appear too curious. As soon as the man finished coiling the linen sausage about his head, Moses ducked behind his donkey, and proceeded to fashion his own headpiece.

"There," he whispered, addressing his flop-eared companion. "What do you think?"

The donkey stared at the turban, passing no judgment. Munching on the shaded grass that grew beside the oasis pond, he turned vacant eyes to his master and snorted.

"Right," Moses shrugged, looking at the uneven coil. "I am not good at this."

Pulling a dried fig from the donkey's pack, Moses sat down against the palm tree and observed the busy stop-off with growing interest. It was a colorful company who came and went from this place. Though he had seen many merchant trains in his life, he had never mingled with them. Today he observed their activities with new eyes.

Egyptians were here, to be sure, traders who traveled the routes between Asia and the west, and who knew the southland of incense, myrrh, gum, and ivory like they knew the necks and arms of their wives.

But the majority of those who stopped here were from the east: Ishmaelites, Edomites, Midianites, and other Arab tribesmen. Moses tried not to grin as he listened to their mingled gibberish.

He was amazed by their parti-striped garments, the clash of colors, the flashing glint of their gold ornaments and silver bangles. No people loved adornment more than these, and they lavished it on themselves whether they could afford it or not. Tinkling bells rang on the upturned toes of their shoes, brass and copper bracelets clattered upon their wrists, and myriad chains and necklaces graced their torsos.

The smell of the Arab camp was equally intriguing. From its campfire arose the aroma of thick coffee, and wooden bowls swam with acidic yogurt, warm and ripe from the sun. The Arabs' wavy hair, thick as rope, was anointed with so much oil, and their bodies with so much heady perfume, that the air about them fairly steamed with syrupy fragrance.

Not so sweet was the odor of their camels. The foul creatures, whose welfare was crucial to the Arab way of life, were a smelly lot, their frothy sweat having dried to a crust, their breath the essence of well-worked cud.

Their owners doted on them, outfitting them with elaborate harnesses and saddles, embroidered and studded. Nonetheless, camels were offensive, spitting when angered and bleating like collicky children.

It was nearing sunset. Moses gazed across the southern desert, which spread like a vast, red sandlot toward Suez. The Egyptians had always called the Nile Valley the "Black Country," for the ground that bordered the river was rich and dark, and the fertile land was abundant with shady vegetation. All adjoining regions, they called the "Red Country," and today Moses understood why.

As he watched the descending sun, the earth deepened from a dusky rose to lingering vermillion, and at last took on a maroon tinge.

The site where he had left his murdered victim came to mind, and despite the desert heat he was chilled by memories of the deeper red which had saturated that ground.

He did not like to think that the night would soon be upon him. In the dark, the face of the dead Egyptian, the sound of his fall and of his body being dragged toward the pit, more easily haunted him.

As Moses fought the memory, he sensed the presence of an onlooker. Glancing up, he found the smiling face of an Arab who greeted him with a broad, yellow grin.

"I see you travel alone," the man observed.

"Yes," Moses admitted.

"We have plenty to eat," the stranger said. "Won't you join us?"

Moses had heard that Arabs were very gracious to other travelers, being compelled to hospitality and expecting the same in return.

Emerging through the less pleasant odors of the caravan was the smell of a savory stew, bubbling above the Arabs' fire.

Pressing his fist against his growling stomach, however, Moses declined. "Thank you, no," he said, returning the man's smile. Fearing to speak further, he hoped the fellow would leave, and he looked away uneasily.

But the Arab's compulsory etiquette would not allow rejection.

"You come!" he insisted, bowing low. "I will be offended if you do not join us."

Seeing that further reticence might only invite unwanted scrutiny, Moses stood up and followed the man to his camp.

"Where are you headed?" the Arab inquired, his small, black eyes shining with genuine interest.

What should he say? He must say something. Devising a quick answer, Moses simply replied, "East."

But far from satisfying the host, this seemed to spark his interest more. Knowing there was only one route from this point east, this eyes grew even brighter. "Here, here, sit!" he exclaimed, pulling a large pillow toward the fire. "You will be going toward my homeland, then?"

"I don't know," Moses shrugged.

"Yes, yes, if you follow the Way of the Pilgrim, you will come to Midian."

Moses knew that the wilderness road across Sinai led to Ezion-geber, at the top of the Red Sea. And he knew Migdol was indeed the last outpost before the land of Midian. But he had not thought whether to go that far or not.

Intrigued, he forgot his reticence. "The Way of the Pilgrim?" he repeated. "Why do you call it this?"

The Arab handed him a bowl of fragrant stew and sighed wistfully. "Because it is the way to the land of Abraham's children, don't you know? Fortunate are those who make that pilgrimage."

Moses saw his zeal for the topic, but shook his head. "You speak of Abraham just as the Israelites do," he marveled.

Suddenly the man sat up, rigid. "Israelties?" he spat. "Half-breeds! Israelites are not true sons of Abraham!"

Moses was stunned. "Why do you say this?" he managed.

Spitting again, the host looked at his companions, who gathered about the dinner fire, laughing with him.

"Egyptian," he said, nodding to them. "He is Egyptian. Forgive him."

Again laughter followed, but it was kind laughter, taking into account the ignorance of a foreigner.

Turning to Moses, the Arab sighed, "It is a long story. Do not trouble yourself with it."

Moses swallowed hard and studied his stew bowl. Silence fell across the company, and everyone ate in tense peaceableness.

Had it not been for the fugitive's fear of exposure, he would have pursued the subject.

Never had he heard that Israelites were not sons of the Patriarchs.

29

Moses was not so much a pilgrim as a runaway. He was not heading toward something so much as he was fleeing from it.

But as he ventured into the Sinai, following the Way of the Pilgrim, he began to wonder what lay ahead as much as he feared what lay behind.

Midian was his present objective. The evening he had sat with the Arab and his companions about the dinner fire, they had spoken so lovingly of their homeland that he thought he could do worse than go there.

Of course, he kept from them the fact that he was Israelite. Surely it was hard enough for them to befriend an Egyptian. Had they known he was a "half-breed," as they put it, they would not have treated him so kindly.

As it was, the Arab, sensing his lost condition, had been more than generous. Following the meal, he had supplied him and his donkey with enough food to take them many miles into the desert, and had given him a blanket.

This blanket, no mere bedtime cover, could be transformed by means of pegs and poles into a shelter against the perpetual wind. For over a week, Moses had used it to set up camp wherever he stopped to rest.

Though there were very few oases along the Sinai route, the road followed the path of the Nile-Red Sea Canal. Built nearly five centuries before under Pharaoh Sesostris, the canal was one of the wonders of the world, a masonry work slicing through the sands to a depth of 16 feet, and wide enough for two war galleys to travel abreast.

Therefore, water was abundant, and the major considerations of travel were safety from the sun and from bandits.

Highwaymen gave no respect to a man's background. It would not matter to a thief that Moses was a royal prince, or that he now traveled in poverty. A highwayman and his roving band would strike without asking questions.

So while a glimmer of anticipation pushed through Moses's depression, fear was still his companion.

Just last night he had stayed at Ezion-geber, the last outpost of the Sinai Peninsula. While it was little more than a collection of wells and palm groves, leaving it represented his final break with the palace and all that life there had offered.

This morning, as he strapped his pack on the back of his long-eared donkey, he cast a wistful look westward. Back through the gray haze not yet touched by the rising sun, lay the land of his youth, the comforts of the court, the love of Hatshepsut, and the hopes of glory on which he had been raised.

That way, also, dwelt his truer family—the mother and father he had come to cherish, the sister who had once risked her life to protect him, and the brother whose respect he had finally won.

Tears stung his eyes as he studied the twilight plains. Perhaps, he suddenly thought, perhaps it was not too late. He was still a prince after all. If he were to return, he might be surprised at the ease of his defense. He might find that Hatshepsut and his advisers could influence the despotic king.

But with a resigned sigh he cinched the saddlebags tight on the donkey's back. No, he must never go back. Whatever lay ahead, it had to be better than the double life he had lived so long.

At least in a new land he might be himself. No one need know he had once been "son of Pharaoh." No one need know he had once been "divine."

As for his Israelite lineage, he might need to cover that for a time. But each step away from Egypt was a step in the right direction.

"Come," he said. Giving a jerk on the donkey's tether, he set out to cross the last boundary between himself and freedom.

Midian lay ahead. And Midian was a new beginning.

* * *

The whisper of a breeze awoke Moses the following day. Sunrise revealed a pastoral setting of rolling hills and small oaks, the beauty of which he had not seen when he had selected his campsite in the dark.

The route out of Sinai had turned north once Moses reached the Arab country. The ancient King's Highway, along which a dozen cultures had risen and fallen, and along which a hundred armies had marched in their time, stretched through TransJordan all the way to Lebanon and Syria.

Moses had avoided that road. His secret and his new life would best be protected by the quiet retreat of the beckoning highlands and quiet wadis to the east.

Rising from his bedroll, he indulged in a delicious yawn and stretched his arms to the sky. For the first time since his flight from Egypt, he knew peace.

He did not know how far he had wandered from the highway in quest of a campsite the night before. A full moon had allowed him to pick his way well into the outback, however. As he surveyed his surroundings, he realized he was in isolated country indeed.

Even in the desert, morning could be chilly. Pulling his cloak over his shoulders, he rose and splashed his face with water from his waterskin, shocking himself alert.

He must gather kindling for a breakfast fire. Surveying the hillside, he saw that the ground beneath a hugging cluster of oaks was littered with twigs and dry leaves.

No sooner had he collected a small pile in the lap of his cloak, than he was startled by the sound of laughter.

Frozen in place, he held the bundle of twigs close and cocked his head. Yes—there it came again, the sound of laughter rising on the desert air from the far side of the hill.

Gently he lay the pile of kindling on the ground and crept up the incline, peering over the ridge. What met his eyes stopped his heart.

Moses had seen countless beautiful women in his day. The courts of Pharaoh were graced with the loveliest creatures in the realm. But just now, below him, walking through the narrow vale of an Arab countryside, were females far lovelier.

There were seven of them, the number of perfection—just as they were, themselves, perfection. Stunned, Moses watched them with delight.

Their lilting laughter was mingled with the enchanting song of fingerbells and bracelets, ankle chains and earrings. Some wore glistening gold rings through their noses. Black hair, wooly and thick, hung to their narrow waists like horses' manes. Their skin, naturally dark, had been darkened further by the sun. And their bodies, the outlines obvious beneath their light tunics, were hardened by years in the outdoors.

Moses wondered if he were still asleep, if he had not at all awakened. Perhaps, heady with exhaustion, he only dreamed, and what he thought he saw was sheer fantasy.

But, no. The hills were real, the sound of the breeze behind him was real, the feel of the sun upon his face was growing warmer. This was no dream. Sitting down on the hilltop, he took in the scene with pleasure.

A little rill, fed by a living spring, or "well," flowed through the niche where the girls walked. Beyond this lay several wooden troughs. As Moses watched, a dust-raising flock of sheep descended the little wadi behind the young women, bleeting happily at the smell of the water.

"Come, come!" the girls called. "This way, lambies!"

Some of the ladies carried buckets, and with these they began to draw water from the spring, passing them up to the troughs where others dumped them out. Slowly the troughs were filled, and the flock, which skittishly avoided the rill's moving water, gathered eagerly about the captive pools.

The women's task was not easy. They had a large flock, cumbersome to manage, although there were seven shepherdesses. Between filling buckets, passing them up hill, and keeping the sheep orderly, they had hours of work ahead. Barely would they fill one trough before it was drained. And the girls who were in charge of maintaining discipline guided the willful creatures with bold use of rod and staff.

It was most important that the lambs be satisfied. This was not readily accomplished. The rams pushed their way to the front, and the yearlings, the nursing mothers, and the babies needed to be encouraged forward.

Such a scene was new to the prince. He had seen flocks brought to market, but never had he observed the tender care that went into their daily management.

Each sheep had a name, it seemed. And the girls knew them all. Furthermore, some responded to the voice of one girl, and some another, so that the flock was organized into definite groups.

Not only were they named, but they were treated as individuals, their various personalities calling for varying treatment—the obstreperous demanding a firm hand, the unusually stupid requiring patience, the weak and small calling for gentle assistance.

Moses was amazed that the women lavished an almost maternal love upon the smelly beasts, treating them more like children than like chattel.

As the spectator sat upon the ridge, having forgotten his task of gathering firewood, he noted that one girl seemed to be the leader of the crew. As to her appearanace, he could make out only so much, for she alone wore a veil across her face. But he could see that she was tall and graceful, and her voice rang clearly as she called out directions.

When the shepherdesses had first entered the vale, this girl had led them, skipping and laughing just like the others, but a bit more cautiously. Looking about the wadi, she had made sure it was safe to enter, and even now scanned the hillsides with a protective glance.

Her bearing was reminiscent of Miriam, Moses's sister, strong and confident. But her demeanor was not masculine. Her tall form was more willowy than Miriam's, her arms and legs lithe and long. Though he could not make out her face, Moses could see that her eyes were large and dark, like an intuitive doe's, and her head was held erect, like that of a proud gazelle.

Though Moses enjoyed an uninterruped view of all the ladies, his eyes most often lingered on this one. How he wished that her veil would slip or that she would remove it for a moment!

But a sudden movement on her part diverted his attention to the foot of the wadi. It seemed she had heard something as she turned her head in that direction, and she called out to her sisters.

"Ishmaelites!" she cried. "They are coming again!"

With this, the girls scattered, flanking themselves at intervals along the sides of the flock.

Moses stared down the wadi, wondering what the women heard. Whatever it was, it was apparently more audible to them than to him, as it funneled up the little canyon.

Within moments, he too discerned the sound of many riders and saw the dust of their mounts billowing up the vale.

Though the women must be afraid, they were wondrously brave, emitting not a squeal of fear as a dozen Arabs charged them on camelback, shouting and driving directly for them.

Despite their bravery, however, the girls could not withstand the enemy's advance. At last they fled the ravine, leading their flock as quickly as possible from the water troughs.

Gaining their primary objective, the capture of the troughs, the camelriders hailed their companions, a larger group of shepherds who were followed by an enormous herd of sheep and goats. As the newcomers took over the site, allowing their flock to drain the narrow reservoirs, the riders turned their attention to crueler sport.

Laughing and spewing out crudities, they chased toward the terrified girls, snatching at them from their high saddles.

Seeing this, Moses was spurred to action. Hardly thinking of the danger, he leaped to his feet, standing tall upon the ridge.

Flinging his cloak off his back, he unfurled it to the wind and whipped it back and forth over his head like a battle flag.

Revealed for all to see was not only his presence, but the distinctive Egyptian tunic which he had worn since leaving the palace.

Such a sight he made—bold and regal in his strange attire, shouting and threatening revenge! The Ishmaelites stopped still and surveyed the ridge in fear.

Taking a cue from their astonished faces, Moses turned about as though to address a great, unseen army. "Advance, men!" he cried, pretending that a vast host awaited his command on the downward slope.

The Arabs cried aloud, looking to one another in terror. Not waiting to see their fears confirmed, they took flight, exiting the vale the same way they had entered.

As the sound of their racing mounts and bleating herds faded toward the open desert, Moses glanced up the gorge. Emerging cautiously from the folds of the gully were the shepherdesses, trembling like deer who had been spared the archer's arrows.

Their eyes wide, they crept forward, looking to the ridge where their rescuer stood. They, like the Arabs, expected the advance of some great army behind him. But when nothing more transpired, no sound, no sight of the anticipated troops, they were perplexed.

"It is all right!" he hailed them. "Do not be afraid."

When they shrank back, he decided to introduce himself. Descending from his hiding place, he joined them beside the spring and bowed to them genteelly.

For a long time he held this posture, until they began to giggle. Then he stood up, smiling broadly.

"There now," he said. "That's better. How could one lone male do you any harm?"

Clinging together, the girls watched as their savior set about to perform yet another service. A bucket, discarded in their hasty retreat, lay near his feet, and he bent over, snatching it up.

"Gather your flock," he commanded.

Then he turned to the bubbling well, filling the bucket and carrying it to the troughs. Over and over he did this, until they saw he meant to help them complete their job. At last they began to work beside him, leading the sheep to the troughs and hauling water.

Soon laughter again filled the little gorge. Skipping up and down the slope, the girls lost their timidity and began to flirt with the handsome stranger.

"Who are you?" they asked, their eyes bright and teasing. "You are Egyptian, aren't you?"

Moses gave vague replies, keeping his mind to the work and avoiding their coquettish glances.

But as he returned again to the stream, ready to fill his bucket for the tenth time, he found himself face to face with the veiled woman.

There she stood, studying him with commanding curiosity. Her large, dark eyes thrilled him with their insistence.

"Who are you?" she demanded.

All her sisters had asked the same quesiton. But this time he could not refuse to answer.

His throat went dry as he gazed upon her. Forgetting to protect himself, he croaked, "Moses. My name is Moses."

30

Moses had plenty of reason to move on. Though he had chosen an isolated area for his camp, it was apparently contested territory, and his presence there could only lead to exposure.

Still he decided to stay the rest of the day and leave the next.

The task of watering the flock, while tedious, had taken his mind off his troubles. When the girls left, he had reluctantly said goodbye and had sat in the shade of his tent ever since, strangely lethargic.

Since his flight from the scene of the murder, he had lived in a state of tension. Dreadful as that state had been, it had kept him going. This morning's adventure had been yet another challenge. Now that it was over, now that he was confronted with the utter silence of the hills and with his perfect loneliness, aimless destitution set upon him.

Though he would select another campsite, he had completed an arduous journey. He had broken with the past as far as possible and was now faced with the vacuum of his future.

As he sat listless, the eyes of the veiled woman passed repeatedly through his mind. It was not until nearly evening that the vacuous spell was broken.

Contemplating which direction he should travel on the morrow, he laid his head upon his rolled-up cloak and closed his eyes. Likely he would have fallen into a dreary sleep had the sound of his name not shot through him like a spear.

Sitting up rigidly, he reached for the small dagger secured to his belt and wondered who had found him.

But as the name was repeated, he recognized the voice, and another emotion thrilled through him.

It was the shepherdess, the veiled woman, who called for him. Not imagining why she would come here at this hour, he poked his head through the tent flap and watched her cross his narrow valley.

To his surprise, he saw that her face was no longer hidden. She had removed her veil before coming here, and as he studied her in the dusky sunset, he found her more beautiful than he had dreamed.

"What is it?" he answered, his reply more self-assured than he felt.

The woman, reaching his campsite, gave him a quiet smile. "So you are still here," she observed. "I am glad."

She stood directly before him now, before his tent door. As he stepped outside, gazing upon her, he was impressed again by her stature, tall and elegant as that of an Egyptian princess.

She was, he would later learn, a princess in her own right, the daughter of a Midianite priest. But for now, he knew her only as a shepherd girl, noble and straightforward as the hills she daily roamed.

"Father will be glad, too," she announced.

"He will?" Moses said. "Your father?"

"Of course," she laughed. "We told him all about you, and what you did for us today. He was quite displeased that we had left you behind and sent me back to find you."

"He wishes to meet me?" Moses marveled.

"Meet you?" she laughed again. "He wishes to reward you!"

These words were spoken matter-of-factly, but the girl grinned at him as though he should realize a greater implication.

Moses, naive regarding Midianite customs, only shook his head. "Oh, no," he replied, "that will not be necessary. I want no reward, though I would be happy to meet your father."

To his bewilderment, this response seemed to offend the young woman. For a long moment, she stared at him, a blush rising to her cheeks. How he had insulted her, he could not imagine, but when her mood turned sullen, he was all the more amazed.

"Come, then!" she commanded. "It is a long way, and the hour grows late. You will at least eat supper with us."

Moses would have received the invitation graciously, but she was already heading back across the valley. Grabbing his satchel, he took the donkey by its tether and beat a hasty path behind her.

Having spent his life in the palace, he was no match for the sturdy girl. Her long legs carried her quickly up hills and across deep wadis. Dark was descending, and he could barely keep up.

"Could you slow down?" he called, when she was about to disappear beyond yet another rise. "I ... the donkey needs a rest."

Turning about, the girl stood at the top of the hill, silhouetted against the purple sky. Her hands on her hips, she was obviously impatient.

"How much farther is it?" Moses puffed as he joined her.

"Not far," was the cryptic reply. With this, she pointed toward a distant circle of lights, the outline of a large shepherd camp.

Relieved, Moses sighed gratefully. But in a flash his guide was gone again, descending the slope in heedless hurry.

"It is kind of you to invite me," Moses called after her, wondering if she would even hear.

The haughty shepherdess tossed her dark head, her voice smiting the hillside like a slap to the face. "Hospitality is the way of the Arab!" she answered.

31

Moses's despondency vanished once he arrived in the shepherd camp. Though he had been raised in the most glamorous circles on earth, not even the glory of Pharaoh's court could rival the gaiety and color of the Midianite settlement. Though he had been amused by the activity and sparkle of the Arab caravan at Migdol, the liveliness of this semipermanent station was even more impressive.

Upon entering the brightly lit tent-circle, he was greeted by a host of smiling folks. Shining more brightly than them all was the most outlandish character he had ever seen. He was the father of the seven maidens, and it was apparent at first glance that he was far more than an ordinary shepherd.

Garbed in a flowing robe, he rushed out to meet the Egyptian with arms outspread, his broad sleeves flapping like banners. "Greetings! Greetings!" he proclaimed, bowing over and over. His long beard, black as lava, was streaked with snowy white, and his hair, surrounding his leathery face like a great bush, was striped with silver.

The most remarkable thing about him was his adornment. While Arabs loved jewelry, the ornaments hanging about this fellow's neck and gracing his wrists and turbaned forehead included the most unusual pendants and amulets.

Since they were reminiscent of the charms and "soul boxes" that Jannes donned for special occasions, Moses deduced that his host was a holy man of some sort.

However, while the ornaments of the Egyptian priesthood were symbolic of their gods, taking the form of moons, fertility fruits, calves and snakes, the emblems worn by this man had no pictorial value. Instead, they resembled small plaques, embellished with Semitic inscriptions.

His garb, fringed in blue and red, sported bell-tipped tassels. Fastened to the straps upon his wrists and forehead were small cubes, the contents of which were a mystery. As to the inscriptions upon the amulets, Moses could not read them for they were etched in tiny characters, but he wondered what god they addressed.

The shepherdess who had come seeking Moses seemed now to be quite indifferent to his presence as she quickly introduced him. "Father, this is the man who helped us today," she simply said. "His name is Moses, and he comes from Egypt." Turning to the guest, her lips a tight line, she added, "This is our father, Jethro Reuel."

Then she stepped aside, joining her sisters who shyly leaned together, giggling and whispering about their intriguing rescuer.

"You have been most kind," the host said, bowing again. "You must join us for supper."

Hardly pausing for a reply, the gaudy fellow clapped his hands, sending a bevy of servants into action. Within moments, a feast fit for Pharaoh himself was spread upon a huge ground-tarp. Platters of roast partridge, boiled grains with thick gravies, and cooked eggs wrapped in spiced cabbage leaves contrasted with tureens of yogurt chilled in mountain ice and trays of fresh condiments. Scattered everywhere were skins of wine and the ever-present pots of thick, black coffee.

As the banquet was laid out, several of the sisters came forward, taking the guest by the arms and leading him to a pile of plump cushions at the head of the feast. Here he and the priest would sit together, along with Jethro's firstborn son, a dashing Arab named Hobab.

No sooner had the three men taken their places than their plates were heaped with food, and music filled the common. People in vivid garments emerged from every corner of the settlement, and the tarp was ringed with eager diners.

The seven sisters would not eat just yet. To the rhythm of pipes and lutes they began to dance, swaying, twirling, and clapping tambourines above their heads. Their multicolored gowns caught the light of lanterns suspended from oak branches, refracting it in prismed rays off sequined skirts. Their eyes likewise flashed, flirting openly with the honored guest.

Only the eldest sister avoided his gaze. For whatever reason, she was still angry.

If the priest noticed his daughter's peculiar behavior, he gave it no mind. "Is she not beautiful?" he whispered, leaning close to Moses and grinning like a cat.

Though he could have referred to any of the seven girls, Moses knew he meant the eldest. "She is," he agreed. "What is her name?"

"Zipporah," the shepherd answered. "I am glad you are pleased."

The stress put on this last comment seemed meant to evoke further response. But Moses was oblivious. "'Zipporah,'" he mused. "That means 'Lady Bird.'"

"Yes," the father grinned again. "She is fragile as a little bird, is she not?"

Moses choked on a bite of food and covered his mouth with a napkin. Hawks and eagles were also birds, he thought—the coldest and keenest of killers.

"Of course," he replied. "She is lovely."

"You appear to be a man of means," Jethro said, noting Moses's fine tunic. "I trust you will care for her in the manner to which she is accustomed."

This was said so casually it nearly passed Moses by. Peering gimlet-eyed at the host, he muttered, "What did you say?"

"The girl," Jethro repeated. "You will care for her in the manner..."

"Wait a minute!" Moses interrupted. "You are giving the girl to me?"

He did not realize how loudly he spoke until the music suddenly stopped and all eyes were on him. The stunned sisters ceased their dance and studied him in horror.

Jethro, sitting back, stared at him. "You did not know?" he stammered. "She, alone of all my daughters, is of marriageable age. And she came to you unveiled! You did not know?"

Moses had been surprised to see the young woman approach his camp with her face uncovered. But being untrained in Arab etiquette, he had not understood the implication.

"I meant no offense," he croaked. "If I had known..."

But this only made matters worse, implying that, had he known, he would not have received her invitation to dinner. As it was, he had already offended her, saying that he needed no reward. How was he to know that she herself was it?

Now understanding the girl's behavior, he glanced at her in shame. She had hidden her face and stood surrounded by her sisters, who huddled sympathetically about her.

Moses felt the blood rush to his cheeks. Hobab, the elder brother, and several men in the group laid their hands upon their belted scabbards.

"I...I am sorry," he said, trying to explain himself. "Your ways are not the ways of Egypt."

For a long moment silence hung in the air as Hobab and his friends fondled their knives, glaring at the offender with piercing black eyes. Only the word of Jethro stood between Moses and death.

"So," the priest hissed, sending a thrill through the crowd, "you do not utterly reject my daughter?"

Murmuring, the Arabs continued to stroke their weapons. Moses knew there was no saving answer. Were he to say that he had not rejected her, he would have to receive her here and now—a prospect he found frightening enough. Were he to say he would never have her, he would not live to see tomorrow.

"Jehovah, help me," he secretly prayed. "How did I get into this?"

As the threatening silence grew heavier, his eyes traveled from the bloodthirsty Arabs to the face of Zipporah. She was no longer hiding, but stood in humiliation, gazing toward the sky.

Observing her, Moses felt his pulse rush. Once again, yearning gripped him. "Lord God, she is beautiful!" he thought.

Barely aware of his own voice, he found himself answering Jethro's question.

"I have not utterly rejected her," he said.

32

The ripple of a desert breeze played upon the broad stripes of the wedding tent like gentle hands upon a colored harp. Dawn lit the interior with a tender blush, casting lazy streaks of maroon and azure across the sleeping couple.

A drowsy Moses was the first to awake. He had slept but little all night, and as he opened his bleary eyes, he felt the rush of excitement trip his heart again. He barely knew this lovely creature who snuggled beside him. Yet he might have known her for a lifetime, so easily was she won.

The night had fled quickly, but it fulfilled an adulthood of suppressed longing, granting Moses the experience of love.

Oh, there had been females for the taking in Egypt. As a prince, he had the luxury of satisfying any whim. But, though he had reached 40 years of age, he had never known a woman.

A son of Pharaoh was encouraged to save himself. He had no harem of his own until he reached the throne, for his life-force was considered sacred. And for Moses, especially, physical pleasures had taken a back seat to more pressing interests—to the confusions and pursuits that had obsessed him since his thirteenth birthday. For this prince, the matter of his secret Hebrew lineage had superseded all else.

No longer, however. Zipporah, the mysterious shepherdess, had invaded his soul like a bird of prey, swooping him up with her first keen glance, and calling to his soul a desert song.

She was neither Israelite nor Egyptian. Yet she was now one with him, claiming his heart like a nestling.

In the dusky light, he reached for her, pulling back the sheepskin blanket that covered their wedding bed. At the sight of her body, soft and lithe, reclined in unself-conscious nakedness beside him, his throat grew tight. A groan arose from deep inside him, and he drew her into his bare bosom like a cherished lamb.

Her skin, dark as the red earth, glowed warm against him, and as he buried his face on her supple neck, she awoke, open once again to his embrace.

"Lady Bird," he whispered, breathing into her dark curls, "how can it be that I love you so soon?"

"Or I you?" she replied, her lips parting in a smile. "I do love you, Moses."

Entwining her slender arms about his neck, she mused over his regal face. "Perhaps the Lord has brought you to me," she suggested.

Moses pulled back and studied her with wonder. "The Lord?" he marveled. "You speak of Jehovah?"

No other religion spoke so simply of its deity. Could it be that the God of Jethro was the same worshiped by Amram and his people?

Zipporah glanced away, fearing she had offended her Egyptian husband. "I am sorry," she said. "I am inconsiderate."

"No, no," Moses interjected, stroking her shoulder. Then, remembering his tenuous safety, he covered quickly. "Since we will now live together, I must know what you believe. You worship the desert god?"

Such a designation did not surprise Zipporah. To the Egyptians, Jehovah was nothing more than an obscure tribal deity.

"Yes," she conceded, "'the desert god.' Papa can tell you about him."

Moses sensed her resentment of the term, but could not spare her feelings without revealing his own history. For now he only gazed at her through the soft light of the love shelter and hoped he had not put her off.

"So," she sighed, returning his gaze, "what of you? Your name tells me you were someone's 'child.' But aren't we all?"

It was true that there was no more generic name in all the world than "Moses." Usually a suffix, it was the most common of all Egyptian personal descriptors. Any answer would suffice, but Moses avoided the subject.

"Is my lineage so important?" he said, playfully drawing her close and stretching himself full against her. "Let it be enough that I am no longer a 'child,' but a full-grown man."

Zipporah giggled softly, nuzzling into his caress.

For now, in the first swell of morning, in the quiet of this place, it was enough.

* * *

In the custom of the Midianites, and all people of the desert, a honeymoon couple was permitted a week of privacy. Such "privacy" was, of course, quite tentative. Given the close community of a bedouin camp, and the flimsy secrecy of tent walls, it was a compromised concept, meaning little more than that the couple was free from the routine of early rising and daylong work.

Tentative as it was, Moses enjoyed the luxury of his time with Zipporah to the fullest. But as the week came to a close, he had some grim realities to face, not the least of which was the knowledge that he must, sooner or later, reveal his identity.

Jethro had called him a wealthy man, and Moses let him embrace this misconception. But soon the father-in-law would wish to discuss Zipporah's future, and Moses had no money.

When the day drew near that he must confront his position, fear once again descended upon him. Perhaps he had saved his skin by fleeing Egypt. Perhaps he had gained a few precious days by marrying Zipporah. But he had no idea what risk he might incur when his story came out.

Would the fact that he was now Zipporah's husband mean safety, or would the Arabs, enraged at his deception, be more determined than ever to kill him?

He would know soon enough. On the eighth morning of Moses's wedded bliss, Jethro Reuel came to the marriage tent. Waking the son-in-law the moment the eastern sky gave light, the shepherd-priest called him forth.

No one else in camp was yet awake, not even Jethro's personal servants. But the elder had fed the night's dying campfire, and simmering above it was a pot of Arab brew.

"Sit, sit," the host said, directive as always. "Drink, drink."

With this, he thrust a steaming mug of thick coffee into Moses's hand. Then clasping his knees and leaning back upon his pillows, he read his son-in-law like an open scroll.

"The time has come," he simply said.

Moses stared into the cup, trying to control his shaking hand. With a twitch of a smile, he gulped, "So it has."

"Do you plan to take my daughter to Egypt?" the elder began.

This caught Moses off guard. "You would allow such a thing?" he stammered.

"She is your wife now," Jethro replied. "But, no, I would not allow it. If you take her there, I will have you hunted down like a fox and killed before you reach Arabah!"

This pronouncement would have been laughable, had Moses not utterly believed it. "Well, then," he conceded, "that is not an option."

Jethro had, of course, closed a door through which Moses would not have walked even if he had been given the choice. But the son-in-law tried not to appear relieved.

Jethro, peering sideways, dissected him with his eyes. "From what were you fleeing when you came here?" he inquired.

Moses gripped the splashing cup and wiped hot liquid from his fingers.

"How did you know?" he managed.

Rolling his eyes, the priest chuckled. "How could anyone not have known? Did you not look the part of a fugitive—you in your fine clothes on the backside of the wilderness, your sole companion a donkey? Do you take us for fools?"

Moses bowed his head. "But...what of Zipporah?" he stuttered. "Why would you..."

"Why would I give her to a runaway?"

Moses set his cup on the ground and turned his face toward the desert, tears rising to his eyes.

Still the elder plumbed his sealed heart, drawing forth its contents like a water-witch. "Perhaps, in giving her to you, I *am* a fool," the old man admitted. "But I have walked many years under heaven, and sometimes heaven guides us strangely."

To this he added nothing. But for the fearful listener, the faith expressed was strangely liberating.

Indeed, this Midianite was a priest. Moses did not know just what his priesthood meant, or how he had attained it, but it was a powerful thing, cutting through pretense like the scalpel of a sanctified physician.

Suddenly the runaway could no longer run. Suddenly he stepped over the edge of abandon, not knowing if he would come to freedom or destruction.

"I am Moses, son of Hatshepsut," he confessed, "son of the queen of Egypt. I am a fugitive—and a murderer. Have mercy on me, holy man. Have mercy."

33

Moses leaned against the sandy hillside of his father-in-law's pastureland and filled his lungs with sea air. The tribe of Jethro had recently moved from the wilderness station to the bank of the Gulf of Aqaba about 25 miles southeast, where they had contracted to pasture their flocks for the summer.

It was cooler here than inland, and the humid breezes that played along the shore were reminiscent of the Nile Valley. But how grateful Moses was to be gone from the land of Pharaoh!

The Egyptian prince had now lived with the Midianites for two years, the happiest years of his life. In those years he had learned the ways of the desert and of a simple, earthy people. He had donned the fluid garb of a nomad, and had let his beard grow. He had experienced a time of freedom such as only one reared in the confines and the expectations of Pharaoh's court could fully appreciate.

But, though the shepherds with whom Moses dwelt were simple folk, they were not ignorant. Jethro's tribe was very knowledgeable concerning deep matters, and Moses had gained insights into the Hebrew faith which he might never have received from the oppressed Israelites of Egypt.

While men like Amram, who had endured great suffering, had taught him much about trust and hope, the oral tradition of the Hebrew slaves was not so well preserved as that of the Midianites. The religion of the

Midianites had not been subject to the outside influences that surrounded the Hebrews of the Nile, and therefore their teachings were more developed.

Jethro's theology, like that of the Levites, was closely intertwined with history. It was also more objective. This the prince learned the day he revealed his identity.

In reckless honesty, he had spilled the entire story that distant morning, the crackle of the campfire punctuating each detail of his life, from birth and rescue to crime and flight. Somehow he knew the secret of his guilt was safe with Jethro, that no one else need ever know.

Awkwardly he explained that he had two mothers, that his dark skin was from his Nubian ancestry, and that the princess of Egypt had found him floating in a river-basket.

He had skirted the fact that he was an Israelite. "My parents are slaves," he confessed. "The princess raised me as her own, not knowing that the nursemaid she hired was in fact my mother."

"Hatshepsut is known, even in this land, as a generous lady," Jethro said. "I recall hearing that she adopted a son without benefit of marriage."

Happenings of the Egyptian court were of international importance. It was no surprise that such gossip should reach the backside of the wilderness.

"But, why did your real mother release you to the river?" the elder asked. "Was your family so poor, they could no longer care for you?"

To the Arab mind, nothing was more precious than children. A man's and a woman's soul continued through the children they bore. To willingly give up a son or daughter was unthinkable.

"They were very poor," Moses replied. "But... there were other reasons. Years ago, the king commanded the death of certain slave babies. My parents hoped to hide me from this danger by placing me in the river. Had it not been for the princess..."

His voice trailed off as Jethro studied him dubiously, stroking his beard and sorting back through the years to the time of which Moses spoke.

The prince, suspecting his thoughts, became more uneasy.

"I remember that edict," the priest recalled. "But it did not apply to Nubians."

Moses shook his head. "You are a very informed man," he conceded.

Jethro nodded. "You think because I am a shepherd I live beyond the reach of the world? Learn this, my boy: The way of the shepherd is not isolated. To survive we must be aware of many things. Events hundreds of miles from our pastures make life easy or difficult for us. We are quite astute, indeed. Otherwise we could not survive."

"Very well," Moses conceded. "So, you can deduce the rest. I am not only Nubian, but... Israelite."

Remembering the Midianite traders at Migdol and their violent reaction to the mere mention of the word "Israelite," Moses braced himself. When Jethro only gazed upon him with amazement, and when that amazement turned to joy, the fugitive was astonished.

"God be praised!" the elder suddenly cried. Throwing his hands in the air, he laughed. "God be praised! You are a son of Abraham!"

With this, he pulled Moses into a suffocating embrace. Back and forth he rocked, tears streaming down his face. "Now I understand!" he wept. "Jehovah has played a trick on me, testing the faith of this old man! Letting me think I must give my daughter to an Egyptian, when all along you were a son of Abraham!"

Working free, Moses stared into the priest's ecstatic face. "You are not angry?" he marveled.

"Angry? I have never been so pleased!"

"But," the prince said, "I thought Midianites hated the people of Israel."

Releasing him, the priest exclaimed, "What ever made you think that? Oh, there are those among my brethren who side with the Ishmaelites. But as you have learned already, *we* are no friends of Ishmael!"

Never would Moses forget the camelriders who attacked Zipporah and her six sisters, driving their flock from the watering place.

"I have heard of Ishmael," Moses said, "He was Isaac's brother."

"Half-brother," Jethro corrected, spitting on the ground. "There are some who believe Ishmael was Abraham's rightful heir. But this is a lie!"

Explaining that the Midianites were descendants of Abraham through his concubine Keturah, Jethro pointed out that there were five branches of the Keturahite line, all sent to the desert country by the Patriarch when he divided up the inheritance among his offspring.

"Some of our people profited from trade with the sons of Ishmael, and others from trade with Isaac and his descendants," Jethro went on. "It seemed everyone must take a side. As for my ancestors, they believed Isaac was the true heir of Abraham, and to this day we have been enemies with the Ishmaelites."

Looking across the desert, he laughed a little. "This is not to say the others have always had successful relations with the wild sons of Ishmael. But that only confirms the prophecy."

Moses leaned in close. "What prophecy, sir?"

"The Patriarch predicted that Ishmael would be a 'wild man,'" Jethro recounted. "He said, 'His hand will be against every man and every man's hand against him.'"

"They are a frightening brood," Moses acknowledged. "What god do they serve?"

At this, the priest shrugged. "That, my son, is a mystery. They claim to worship the God of Abraham, just like you and I. But, if so, they have a strange view of brotherhood, don't you think?"

All of this was new to Moses. Entranced, he could only shake his head. "I have much to learn, Father," he confessed.

So it came to be that Jethro took Moses under his wing. For two years the fugitive sat at the feet of the Midianite teacher. When he was not working for the man, when he was not miles from camp in some distant pasture, he was engrossed in conversations with the elder.

But he did not only commit the teachings to memory. He began to record them on parchment, painstakingly writing them down just as Jethro gave account.

Moses was an educated man, used to meticulous note-taking under the instruction of Jannes and his other Egyptian tutors. Unaccustomed to reliance on oral tradition, he would capture the tales in writing, for his own sake and the sake of those he loved.

Just now the breeze ascending from the gulf ruffled a thin sheet of goatskin spread across his lap. Opening a little box containing a cake of oiled carbon, he licked the tip of his split-reed pen and ran it through the inky substance. In rereading the parchment, he had found that Jethro's account of a particular tale did not coincide with that told by the Israelite slaves. Quickly he made a notation in the margin, reminding himself to ask the priest to clarify the matter.

As he did so, the sound of laughter caught his ears, arising from the seashore.

Running toward him was a wee boy, sturdy-legged, round-faced. And behind the lad came Zipporah, calling sharply, "Gershom! Do not disturb your Papa!"

But the boy was heedless. He had played all morning along the shore and wished to sit for a while on his father's lap.

"Come, Gershom," Moses said, waving the child forward. "It is all right."

Eagerly, Gershom tumbled into Moses's arms, sending the ink box flying.

"See there!" Zipporah chided. "You must discipline the boy!"

Laughing, Moses patted the ground beside him. "Sit down, wife," he replied. "You need a rest."

"And what of you?" she sighed, complying gratefully. "You have been working all morning on that scroll."

Zipporah, who now realized her husband's Israelite roots, and who had named her child after Jochebed's Levite father, still did not understand Moses's fascination with the ancient tales.

"I will watch the sheep," he said with a smile, taking her staff in his hand. "It would do me good to walk a while."

Brushing Zipporah's cheek with a kiss, he stood up and took Gershom in tow. "Come, son," he enthused. "Count the lambs for me."

34

It was winter. As dead and cold a winter as could be had in the plains of Midian.

A wind, bitter and frosty, brought a rare pall to the landscape, descending down the eastern side of the Jordan chasm, from the region beyond Gilead, from the realm of Damascus and the towering heights of Mount Hermon.

In the three years since he had joined the tribe, Moses had traveled far and wide with his father-in-law's flocks, being gone weeks and months at a time from the semi-permanent station east of Ezion-geber. He had gone south along both sides of the Gulf of Aqaba and ventured north into the idyllic fields of Bashan. He had seen the lush beauty that made Gilead the most pleasant land on earth. But he had never seen Damascus or the snowy, leaping crags of Hermon.

This winter the Midianites often talked about those distant pinnacles. As Jethro had said, the shepherds of the deserts were not beyond reach of international affairs. Nor were they beyond reach of climatic changes in the northlands.

Tonight Moses sat huddled inside Jethro's tent, fending off the chill that licked about the corners. It was dreadfully bleak outside, and the priest had been joined by several men of the camp in his large goathair shelter.

The tent of Jethro was more than a private home. Because the master of the place was a priest, and because he was the patriarch of the tribe, his house was the conference room in which the elders and leaders of the Jethroites held council.

It was also a place of manly concourse where males of the community laughed and caroused together, free of feminine scruple.

And carouse they did. Especially tonight.

The announced purpose of their gathering was to sharpen tools together. No outside work was possible in the whipping and driving winds. Underlings managed the flocks in low sheepfolds ringing the village. But the leaders of the tribe passed the evening in a more friendly task.

Every man had brought axes and hatchets of metal and rock, and knives of flint. In the glow of the firepit, they smoothed and honed their blades with sharpening stones.

Set conspicuously in the middle of the room was a smoking pipe. At intervals it was passed about, and the men indulged until their vision grew fuzzy and their heads light as cotton.

They spoke daringly of women—never of their wives, but of women of the inns and the streets of distant towns. They admitted to indiscretions and lied to assure their comrades they were guilty of more than they were.

They spoke of politics and of enemies, of bloody battles past and battles only yearned for. And their speech was punctuated by spits and curses that would have stretched the ears of those unfamliar with their customs.

Most of those present had been initiated into this ritual from the day of their entrance into manhood, from the day they took their first swig of strong drink and quoted for the elders a lengthy passage of oral history.

For manhood was predicated not only on reaching a certain age, or on the ability to drink, spit, and curse, but on one's knowledge of and devotion to tribal lore. That lore was highly spiritual, tightly interwoven with the tribal religion. Incongruous as it may have seemed, these wine-swillers and crude talkers adhered to the ancestral faith as to their own firstborn children.

But, for these people, there was no incongruity. Ribald conversation within these hallowed walls was no irony. For these people, it was like dirt beneath the fingernails, a sign of the earth and of the nature of things.

So was religion. And the conversation as easily revolved around things holy as it did around brothels and smoking dens.

"Father Abraham was a wise fellow to leave Damascus," one of the men observed, waving his hands over the open fire. "If it is this cold here, think what it must be like up there!"

The others agreed, and Moses leaned in close. "Abraham was in Damascus?" he asked. "When was that?"

"Surely you recall," Jethro said, "that Abraham came from Mesopotamia. He passed through Damascus on his way into Canaan."

"Oh, yes," Moses replied, remembering the story received at Amram's knee.

"But did you know that the Damascenes desired to make him their king?" the old priest asked.

"No," Moses answered. "That was not part of the Israelite teaching."

"Ah, well," Jethro smirked, "there are many things about Abraham they would not have told you!"

At this the others laughed, shaking their heads. "I suppose that when your people in Egypt speak of the Patriarch, they say nothing about his many children," Jethro guessed. "You had never heard of the Keturahites before you came here."

Moses's face warmed. "They mainly speak of Isaac and Jacob, and the twelve sons of Jacob, called Israel," he admitted. "Perhaps in these 400 years they have forgotten much."

"Ha!" Hobab snarled, slapping his knees. "We are not only Keturahite, but Kenite, descendants of Cain through our mother Keturah! I suppose they said nothing of the sons of Cain."

Moses fidgeted. "They told the story of Cain and how he killed his brother, Abel," he said. "They spoke of the 'mark of Cain.'"

Murmuring, the group rolled their eyes and laughed again. "And I suppose," Hobab spat, "they considered the mark a curse?"

Moses's silence was reply enough.

Quickly the party atmosphere turned sullen. Moses sensed that they held him responsible for his own ignorance, and he did not know what to say.

"Go easy," Jethro interjected, clapping Hobab on the back. "Moses is a willing pupil."

Then, carefully framing his thoughts, the priest explained, "I am sure your people did their best to instruct you in all the truths they knew. Theirs is only the error of omission. In our tradition, we understand that the mark was set on Cain for his protection, lest any man, finding him a fugitive, should try to slay him."

At the mention of Cain's fugitive status, Moses shrank inwardly. Though he had come to a measure of peace in this foreign land, he had never forgotten his own criminal record. Just like Cain, who murdered Abel, Moses had fled retribution for a crime of passion.

Jethro, who alone knew of Moses's guilt, sensed his shame and moved the topic along. "Suffice it to say, lads, that Abraham had many descendants. We do ourselves disservice when we stir up division."

Then, lifting his face to the firelit ceiling, he called for silence. Everyone knew that the priest was about to rehearse some appropriate portion of the oral record. As he did so, they bowed their heads, listening respectfully. For the chant-like passage was the word of the Lord to Abraham himself:

I am the Almighty God;
Walk before me and be blameless.
And I will make my covenant between me
and you,
And I will multiply you exceedingly.
As for me, behold, my covenant is with you,
and you shall be the father of many of nations.
And I will make you exceedingly fruitful,
and I will make nations of you, and kings shall
come out of you.
And I will establish my covenant between me
and you and your children after you throughout the generations for an everlasting covenant. I will be God to you and to your children
after you.
And I will give to you and to your children
after you the land wherein you are a stranger,
all the land of Canaan, for an everlasting possession; and I will be their God.

With this, Jethro opened his eyes, and the men lifted their heads, gazing into the fire. In one accord they began to chant the conclusion of the passage, as was their practice:

Now as for you, you shall keep my covenant,
you and your descendants after you throughout their generations.

The beauty of the words swelled through Moses's soul. Hanging on them, he wished for more. But the men were finished, their voices trailing off with the last syllable as though enough had been said.

Emerging from their trancelike state, they nodded to Jethro, blessing him with the traditional "Jehovah be praised." Within moments they had returned to their partying mood.

Moses sat speechless, staring into the licking flames. How he longed to ask for more, wondering about the covenant of which they spoke.

He had often heard the elders of Israel talk of the Promised Land, saying that it belonged to the heirs of Jacob. This was the first time he had heard that all Abraham's children should share in that longed-for inheritance.

But it was also the first time he had heard of the covenant.

Drawing his coat to his chest, he was lost in contemplation. Thoughts of his pathetic people, bound under Pharaoh's cruel hand, tugged at his heart, filling him with sorrow. Memories of Amram and Jochebed, of Aaron and Miriam, haunted him.

Then, before him, were these strange folk, equally the sons of the Patriarch, yet generations and miles from their intended glory.

What had gone wrong? Where had the sons of Abraham lost their way?

Images of Cain, tormented, wandering, blended into the scene before him, into the memory of the disinherited along the Nile.

And the refrain quoted only moments ago, filled him with questions.

"...as for you...you shall keep my covenant..."

"...keep my covenant..."

Over and over the message seared his soul.

But he did not know what covenant they should have kept. And he feared to ask.

35

It would be weeks before the subject of the mysterious covenant again arose. Though Moses could have inquired of Jethro regarding the matter, he hesitated to do so. He sensed that to know more would require something he preferred not to give, and he clung to ignorance as if it were a shield.

Moses was tired of expectations. He had been raised on them—expectations imposed by the court, expectations imposed by his own knowledge of who he really was. Though he had escaped the demands of the throne, and though his Israelite heritage had never yet required sacrifice beyond what he was able to bear, he carried always within him a sense of destiny, of a calling he was terrified to hear.

Where this sense of destiny came from, he did not know. But it haunted him like the songs he had once heard in his dreams, like the searching gaze of the dark woman beyond his palace window.

The very idea of covenant, so lightly passed over in Midianite recitations, was, for Moses, a fearsome thing that plucked the cords of his subconscious, carrying across the plains of Sinai the desperate pleas of his lost people.

If the idea of covenant had moved Jethro to speak in lofty tones, it seemed of little consequence in the priest's daily life. Beyond the reference in the oral refrain, the man never mentioned the covenant.

Jethro was provoked to easy oratory when recounting legends, and he loved to talk of the heritage that rightfully belonged to the Keturahites. But he never spoke of requirements. Even his monthly sacrifices, with their attendant pomp—the ceremonial slaying of a pigeon or a lamb, the incantations, and the swinging of censers over altar fires as he prayed for the sins of his people— seemed rather hollow.

For he never spoke much of the sins themselves or of how gracious Jehovah must be to overlook them.

Yet for Moses the "covenant" had not ceased to trouble him from the moment he heard of it.

It was the first day of spring, the end of Moses's third year with Jethro. This afternoon, he and his father-in-law traveled on camelback toward Ezion-geber, trailed by servants who drove empty wagons. When they reached the main junction, where the King's Highway branched off from the Way of the Pilgrim, they would await the arrival of Hobab and an immense caravan from the west.

Moses's brother-in-law had been gone for several weeks on a trip to Egypt, where he had marketed baskets, pottery, jewelry, and other wares made in the Midianite camp. Sheep and goats had also accompanied him, for sale or trade in the land across the desert.

Once Hobab met the party from home, he would continue north along the King's route, where he would barter many of the goods purchased in Egypt. But first he would transfer some of his purchases to Jethro, who would return to camp with the wagons piled high.

Moses, of course, had not gone on the trip with Hobab. He was still a fugitive from the land of Pharaoh, and to set foot in that country would surely mean death.

Regardless of the danger, however, Egypt was the land of Moses's birth, the land where many loved ones still resided. Memories of Jochebed and Amram, Hatshepsut and Jannes, Aaron and Miriam, were wrapped tight about his heart, whispering at night across the miles and waking him at daybreak to sad yearnings.

The expanse between the camp and the highway was studded with few landmarks. Only the padding clop of camels' feet and the gentle clatter of wagon wheels measured the miles, while Moses's mind drifted back in time.

As if he were there, he remembered the thousand hours spent in the slave hut, where Amram unfolded tales of Israel before his eager heart. Had that been so long ago? Was it possible he had been a mere boy when he first discovered his heritage? Just now, it might have been yesterday.

But with these sweet memories always came less welcome ones, scenes of oppression and cruelty endured by the enslaved. While Queen Hatshepsut sought to lighten the load of the Israelites, she had been allowed to do only so much, her authority being constricted by her "husband," Thutmose II.

Hunching his shoulders, Moses tried to shrug off the sad images. Never, in all his years under Amram's instruction, had anyone answered the question of causes. Why, he had often asked, must the sons of Abraham, Isaac, and Jacob suffer as they did? Was there some dreadful secret in their history, some sin committed, which had resulted in this torment?

And where were the promises of God, made to Abraham so many years ago, that his descendants would be a blessing to all nations, that great things would come from them, and that they rightfully owned the land of Canaan?

"Father," Moses suddenly addressed Jethro, "what was the covenant made between Jehovah and Abraham?"

The old priest was accustomed to his son-in-law's inquisitive bent. But after so many miles of silence, the introduction of the topic was almost comical.

"I wondered where you have been all this way out," Jethro said with a chuckle. "I might have known you would be pondering unfathomable things."

"Unfathomable?" Moses replied. "The covenant is a mystery, then."

Jethro sensed his disappointment and decided the matter deserved more sincerity.

"Well," he added, "it is a mystery in some ways, and in others it is quite specific."

This was little help, and when Moses waited for more, Jethro squirmed uneasily in his saddle. His riding chair wobbled atop his tall beast, and he pulled the canopy to an angle against the sun.

"How is it specific?" Moses prodded him. "What were Jehovah's requirements?"

Jethro wrinkled his brow. "Well," he said, "there was the ancient rite of circumcision. I believe the Israelites practice it to this day."

"Some of them do," Moses replied. "My mother placed me in the river before I was circumcised. It was this fact, as well as my dark skin, that allowed me to pass as other than Hebrew all those years." Again, however, he was mystified. "But many of my people do not practice the rite. How can this be, if it is God's command?"

Jethro was not comfortable with the question. Shrugging his shoulders, he replied, "I suppose that many of the bloodier rites have capitulated to time and to more civilized ways. The Midianites do not practice it, nor the Ishmaelites. I know of few outside Israelite circles who cling to the grisly ritual. But after all, surely what is important is the intent of the covenant and not the physical application."

Amazed at this casual view, Moses challenged, "Explain. What is the intent?"

Clearing his throat, the priest waxed philosophic. "Circumcision is a mark of distinction, something that sets the worshiper apart from others. It is, of course, the shedding of blood and a putting off of the flesh. All of this, however, is merely symbolic of a consecrated heart. The act itself is nothing."

For some moments, Moses was silent, contemplating Jethro's logic. At last he shook his head. "So the children of Abraham have relegated the command to symbolism? Why, then, bother with sacrifices of any kind? Why slay pigeons and goats upon our altars if everything is merely symbolic?"

Jethro knew Moses had hit on a key point. He knew his own rationale was flimsy. A twitch worked at the edge of the old man's mouth, as Moses went on.

"The Egyptians, for all their faults, are very pragmatic," the son-in-law said. "They are great believers in cause and effect, and to violate the specific edicts of the gods is sure destruction. In all their religion, they give equal heed to the material and the spiritual. They demonstrate their beliefs in tangible form, from pyramid to priestly vestment, from sacrifice to sheafs of legal code. Perhaps for all the freedom the nomad possesses, he has lost something of structure. Perhaps because my people are enslaved, they have had little opportunity to clarify their faith. Perhaps, in the practical application of religion, we can learn something from our enemies."

When Jethro stared at him in horror, Moses added, "Oh, I do not say we should honor the Egyptian gods. I say only that we can take a lesson in obedience from the Egyptian's model. Is Jehovah worth less devotion than the gods of the Nile?"

Jethro smiled vaguely. "You are an able opponent," he conceded.

Moses sat back on his camel and gazed across the desert. The highway wound into view across the sunlit sands, reminding him of his fugitive state, of his crime, his cowardice.

"I do not mean to oppose you, Father," he said. "I am not a righteous man, as you well know. And surely circumcision is only a part of the covenant. What, sir, is the rest of God's demand?"

"The rest," Jethro admitted, "is even more mysterious. 'Walk before me and be blameless,' says the Lord."

Moses remembered those words, the opening of the chant recited in Jethro's tent.

"Blameless?" he marveled. "How is that possible?"

Again, Jethro laughed.

"Son," he sighed, "you *are* a challenge! What can I say except that honor and integrity are what God looks for. A willing and an honest heart are his sacrifices."

Moses lingered over the words, but they only aggravated him. "What does *that* mean?" he wished to cry out. "How can a nation survive with no more direction than that?"

Ahead, the highway rose to meet them, circling toward the hills like a quiet snake. Emerging along the horizon was a great caravan, marked with the flag of Jethro's tribe.

"Hobab!" the old man cried, spurring his camel on. "We will be with him by sundown!"

Speeding across the desert, he left his son-in-law behind.

As Moses watched his hasty departure, he thought how fine it would be to rest so easy in God's hand, to shed weighty matters with such childlike abandon.

As for himself, he could not avoid the thought of the covenant.

Therein lay a secret, he was sure, that could lead his people out of bondage.

36

It was evening when the two caravans met on the plain of the King's Highway. They would camp together for the night, and Hobab would turn north in the morning.

Because Jethro and his son had not seen each other for weeks, the two caravans would spend the time celebrating. As with all cultures, certain occasions always called for revelry: birthdays, weddings, holy days. But for the desert dwellers, who spent weeks on end following dusty trails and counting sheep and goats, other occasions were equally noteworthy. Partings and reunions, for instance, called for song and dance, tears and laughter.

Moses had lived among the Midianites three years. He had married one of their daughters and was son-in-law to one of their priests. Still he was a newcomer, a foreigner. He had never learned to mingle easily when they began to frolic and drink. The parties of Pharaoh's palace were always staid events, invested with so much protocol that the prince had never embraced the art of casual merriment.

Tonight, he would try to enter in.

Surveying the drinkers and revelers whose shadows played in lacy silhouette around the fire, he sought a companion. Jethro was busy talking with Hobab, devoting his full attention to his son's account of bartar and trade. But over against a small bank of palms, where the little pond of the oasis curved into a sandy hollow, one servant sat with a donkey saddle spread across his lap.

The fellow was occupied with oiling down the leather, working a tallowy mass of lanolin into the hide.

Joining him, Moses attempted light conversation.

"It seems your master was successful on his venture," he began. "Was this your first trip to Egypt?"

The servant was young, barely out of puberty. At the question, his eyes lit. Flattered that the priest's son-in-law would single him out for attention, he replied, "Oh, yes sir! It was a trip I shall never forget!"

Moses smiled at his enthusiasm. "You found Egypt to your liking?"

"Oh, indeed, indeed!" the fellow asserted. "Never in my life have I seen anything to compare!"

Moses beamed. "I understand you went to Raamses."

"Yes. And to Thebes and Memphis and ..."

"Did you see Pharaoh's palace?" Moses asked.

"We did!" the youngster exclaimed. "How beautiful it is! How very big and beautiful!"

Moses wondered what it would be like to have grown up in the wilderness, to have never set foot in a city until manhood.

"Yes, it is beautiful," he agreed, his voice so soft the servant leaned close.

"Forgive me, sir," the young man said. "I had forgotten that you come from there. You have seen the palace many times!"

Moses knew that Jethro had never revealed the secret of his royal past. The most this lad could know was that he was indeed from Egypt. He did not know that he had been raised within the walls of the palace itself.

"Many times," he nodded.

For a long while, Moses said no more, gazing sadly across the desert.

At last the youngster broke the silence. "When you lived there, did you ever see the queen? I hear she is lovely and very kind."

Moses's throat tightened. As though he were a child, he could see the queen's smile and feel her tender caress.

"I saw her now and then," he replied.

The servant sighed. "A hard life she has had, losing first her son, and now her husband."

Moses cocked his head in surprise. "What did you say?" he asked.

"You know," the young man shrugged. "Everyone has heard how her son mysteriously disappeared, and how he was charged with murder. There has been a warrant for his arrest for years!"

"Of course..." Moses muttered. "But what else did you say?"

"Her husband. Thutmose II is dead, three years into his reign!"

The prince was numb, his face fixed in an astonished mask. "Thutmose?" he croaked.

"You had not heard!" the young man marveled.

"No," Moses whispered. "When did this happen?"

Suddenly the lad stood up. "But, of course! He died while we were there. The news would not have reached you yet. To think," he boasted, "I am the first to tell you!" Then, begging his leave, the boy said, "I shall go tell the others, if I may."

Relieved to be left alone, Moses waved him off. As the fellow hastened away, he leaned against a palm tree's spiny trunk.

Questions swirled through Moses's head. What of his queenly mother? Would she be dethroned now that her "husband" was gone? Would she maintain her position, but only as a puppet of the state? Or would the constituents force some other man upon her, unwilling to allow a widow the right to govern alone?

Hatshepsut was, as the servant had said, a good and gentle queen. She had tried, despite her husband's restrictions, to bring humane reforms throughout the empire. To some degree, even the slaves had benefited from her kind intentions.

But what now?

Suddenly the face of Moses's rival, the simian face of Pharaoh's bastard son, leaped before him. It had always been the king's desire that his low-browed offspring, Thutmose III, child of a concubine, should reign after him. Would Hatshepsut be forced to concede the throne to him?

Standing, Moses left the partying crowd and drifted into the dark desert. A sliver of moon did little to light his way, and the night crushed in upon his spirit.

"Mother," he whispered, "forgive me. I should never have left you. Forgive me."

PART V
The Burning Bush

37

Hatshepsut paced her darkened chamber, impatiently plotting her future. The month of obligatory mourning was nearly over. As soon as the sun arose this day, she would emerge from her enforced isolation, and she would take her rightful place upon the throne of Egypt.

She wondered what that little squirrel, Thutmose III, was thinking this morning. Surely he did not miss his deceased father! He had loved Pharaoh no more than she, and his "time of weeping" had been just as much a sham.

No, she knew where his thoughts were. She knew he anticipated power. She knew he believed he would take over where his father had left off, in utter command of the empire.

But, though Egypt was no more democratic than any other monarchy, the sentiment of the people was a powerful force. Hatshepsut had no doubt where that sentiment lay.

She was a popular queen. Because of her benevolent spirit, she had outshown the king whom the public had forced upon her. This day, when she and her stepson would ride through the streets, ushering in a new administration, they would supposedly be equal heirs to the throne. But they would be no more equal than she and Thutmose II. While that autocrat had overstepped her at every opportunity, it was her turn now. With the support of the masses, she would be the acknowledged ruler of Egypt.

After all, her stepson was yet a child. Only 21 years old, he was half the age of Moses. Though he would one day prove to be a powerful monarch, as long as Hatshepsut was his rival, he would never rise above her.

The strong-willed queen had held her "husband" at bay throughout their marriage. Never had he been allowed to lay a hand on her. Never had she been his actual wife. And she was still her father's daughter. The reign of Thutose II had been but a brief intrusion on the will of Thutmose I.

Now the daughter would fulfill her father's wishes. She would be no mere feminine figurehead. If her own son, Moses, could not enjoy his rightful place, she would reign in his stead. She would be Pharaoh, a regal *female* Pharaoh!

Throughout her imposed period of mourning she had contemplated such things. Today she would see her dream fulfilled.

Only memories of Moses, still close and fresh, prevented total happiness. Where, in this wide world, was he? Countless times she had asked this question of the silent air, the vacant sky, the mute and unmoving gods.

She knew Moses was a fugitive. She knew he was in hiding. He would never have left her otherwise.

But was he well? Was he alive?

Her mother-heart always broke anew when she allowed herself to ponder the fate of her lost son. She had never known a heart could break again and again, repairing itself only to be shattered once more.

Moses should have been the one anticipating a royal future. Gladly would she have shared her throne with him! Gladly would she have passed it on to him at the moment of her death!

But the best she could do now was see to it that her ape-like stepson enjoyed nothing that rightfully belonged to the departed prince.

The dawn sun was just painting a yellow hem across the horizon when Hatshepsut was struck with an idea. Yes! She knew how she could honor her son this day! It came to her like the light, how Moses could share in the glory of her coronation.

Rushing to her chamber door, she threw it open and confronted her guards.

"Call for Jannes!" she commanded. "Bring him here at once!"

* * *

The sleepy priest shuffled down the gray corridor behind his quickly moving queen. In his hand was a key, and he turned it over skeptically, muttering to himself.

It was the key to Moses's locked room. He had been its keeper since the prince had run away, just as he was keeper to the keys of each dead pharaoh's chamber.

"I do not understand," he groaned. "Why would my lady wish to stir up sad memories on such a grand day?"

Hatshepsut did not even glance behind her at the question. Speeding ahead, she urged him along.

"I have a right," she said, "to enter my son's suite. Just because I have not done so in all this time does not mean I do not care."

"But I thought you wished it this way," the priest grumbled. "I thought it would help you to forget..."

"Forget?" the queen snapped, wheeling about. "Do you really think I shall ever forget? Now," she said, snatching at the key, "let me in!"

With a sigh, the priest clutched the key to his chest. "It seems somehow...improper," he replied.

But as the woman glared at him, he complied, unlocking the latch.

With a creak the door swung open, and Hatshepsut was confronted with an interior as dark as a tomb.

Holding her emotions in check, she advanced, pulling the priest by his coat sleeve.

"Open the curtains!" she commanded, and Jannes crossed the room reluctantly.

As morning light spilled into the musty chamber, the queen's pulse raced. Jannes watched in amazement as she went directly to the prince's wardrobe.

Nothing had been touched since Moses had left. All was as it had been the day he departed.

Fumbling through rows of robes and tunics, racks of headdresses and gilded sandals, all arrayed like soldiers on command performance, Hatshepsut found her hands trembling.

"Where is it?" she sighed. "Where?"

Jannes peered over her shoulder. "What do you seek?" he inquired.

"Hush!" she ordered. "Help me."

Obediently, the priest joined her inside the closet, though he knew not what to look for.

Suddenly Hatshepsut stopped still. She had come across something. Though but it was not the item she sought, she pulled back from an entwining klatch of clothes, stood breathless, and held up a small, striped shawl.

"By all the gods!" she cried, tears arising in her eyes. "I *had* forgotten!"

Jannes immediately recognized the little blanket "You knew, then?" he stammered.

With spasmed fingers, the queen quickly rolled the shawl into a tight bundle. Clutching it close to her breast, she fought back the agony of her child's sweet memory.

In reverie, she walked with her maidens beside the river, and as though no time or sorrow had intervened, she reached for the reed basket, gazing for the first time upon the baby's lovely face. When she had called for a blanket, her maid had taken this very shawl from the little ark. A sure sign of the child's race.

"Of course, I knew," she faltered. With this, she hastily stashed the precious blanket in a drawer and gave the priest a beseeching look. "Apparently you have known as well."

"I have never told a soul," he said, revealing his own unsullied love for the vanquished prince.

For a long while, Hatshepsut studied the wizard's crinkled face. Without words, they acknowledged their mutual bond, the determination that Moses's identity would die with them.

Then, turning again to the rack, the queen continued her search.

At last she cupped her hand over her mouth, stifling a cry of joy. "Jannes!" she declared. "Here it is!"

The priest leaned close, watching in stupefied silence as the queen drew forth a royal garment, the very tunic and shoulder shawl that had been prepared for Moses's coronation, a coronation that had never come to pass.

"He should have worn this," Hatshepsut sighed. "He should stand beside me when I take the throne!"

Jannes could not help but agree. Moses's secret would always have been safe with him.

"What do you mean to do?" the priest asked as Hatshepsut stepped out into the room.

"I mean to wear it myself!" she declared.

"But...but..." Jannes stammered.

"I know," the woman snapped, her voice ringing with sarcasm. "It is a man's garment. It is *improper*."

The priest's face went white. "By the gods!" he objected. "You cannot mean..."

"Ah, but I do!" Hatshepsut proclaimed. "My son cannot be here, but I shall see to it that he is not forgotten. If he cannot reign beside me, he shall reign within the people's hearts. And no one shall call me queen. No one shall call me empress. I shall be called Pharaoh, fully and with honor!"

38

In the wide valley of er-Raha, south on the Sinai Peninsula from the Way of the Pilgrim, two colorful tents broke the monotony of the landscape. Intruding upon the scattered clumps of sage and the uniform beige of the sifting desert, they were like flashing smiles.

Red, maroon, and orange, they would have caught the eye of any wanderer, had there been a wanderer to see them. As it was, the only people near enough to appreciate them were their owners, a small family of shepherds.

For these folks, the two shelters were home away from home for as long as they wayfared in this valley.

One was larger than the other and was the nighttime quarters of two brothers: Gershom, now a grown man, and Eliezer, a child of nine.

The other had long ago been a wedding tent, the love shelter of Moses and Zipporah. Forty years of marriage had not cooled their affection. In fact, time had deepened their loyalty, and they still took the tent with them wherever Moses sojourned with his father-in-law's flocks.

When Zipporah had designed the larger tent for her sons, she had patterned it after the first, selecting the same colors and stripes. For Moses it was a testimony of his wife's enduring love.

Not that Zipporah had always been easy to live with. She was still the spitfire he had met those many years ago, the strong-willed girl whom Jethro had named "Lady Bird." Now and then Moses still teased her about her name, reminding her that birds of prey used sharp talons and screeching threats to great advantage.

Yet while 40 years had not dimmed Moses's love for his wife, neither had it dimmed his yearnings for his people in Egypt. Though he had come to love a new family and the shepherd life, he had never resigned himself to it. He sensed that this time in the wilderness was just that: a time, a season, a transitory interval.

Never had he shared this feeling with anyone. To his own mind it was an enigma. Forty years of anything was surely more than an interval!

Many times, when he had pondered this puzzle, the words of Aaron, as he had left him at the edge of the wilderness, returned to Moses. "Don't you see?" the elder brother had said, "God rescued you from the Nile, and he will rescue you from exile. He will return you to us, in power beyond anything you have ever known."

The first several years of his sojourn here, Moses had only been glad that his past had not found him. Though he could never return in safety to his homeland, a sense of security, the love of his Midianite family, and the ease of the nomadic way had prevented any longing for power.

Yet he could never escape the memory of the oppressed who labored beside the Nile.

As he had grown in knowledge and understanding of the Hebrew God, informal though his theology might be, he had continued to seek after the "covenant." He wished to "be perfect," as God was perfect, according to the chant recited in the Midianite tradition. Though it had strained his relationship with Zipporah, he had seen to it that first he, and then Gershom were circumcised. And he continued to ponder what else God might require.

Eliezer, his younger son, had still not received the mark of distinction. Zipporah was adamant that the child should be unscathed. Bowing to her pressure, Moses had let it go.

Still he was troubled by the injunction and wondered if he could ever be received in God's sight, so long as he did not comply.

Because he longed after the ways of God, he learned to pray. Weeks of desert quiet, as he tended the flocks, allowed for introspection and meditation.

Sometimes he thought he heard God speak to him. When he was at prayer, or when he sat, hour upon hour, poring over his beloved scrolls, trying to sort out the history he took from Jethro's lips, trying to remember the stories heard at Amram's knee, he would sense a stirring, like the rush of wings or a delicate whisper. And he would be spurred to pray longer or to write more precisely.

Still, he did not know the God of Abraham, Isaac, and Jacob as those men must have known Him. He felt his own impotence so keenly he was jealous of the intimacy those patriarchs had shared with the Almighty.

Indeed, he wondered if such intimacy were relegated to times past, if such closeness to the Lord were even possible in his day and age. But who was he to wonder such things—he, the mongrel, the murderer? And just *who* was he, anyway? Was he Israelite? Midianite? Egyptian? Prince? Shepherd? Madman?

Today, as he headed out from his tent and whistled to his flocks, the sight greeting him was impressive as always. Leaping up from the valley floor was the single geographical feature of the landscape, Mount Horeb. Like three gargantuan sentinels, the promontories of the mountain stood guard over the vast plain. Could they have talked, Moses would have inquired what was so important in this vacuous tract that they should pass the years watching over it.

So out of keeping with the flat and tedious terrain were these granite monarchs that they seemed a holdover from some past dynasty, as though, at some distant, anonymous time, they had served to intimidate invaders.

Now there was nothing to be invaded, nothing to protect. Yet the craggy zeniths persisted, pressing out of the floor like the knuckled fist of a collosus, in silent threat above nothing more than grazing land.

Sometimes when he saw the triple-peaked mountain, he was reminded of the fortified palace of Pharaoh, his long-lost home. Today, he thought again of Hatshepsut, and he smiled a little.

Once he had worried over her welfare, having learned that she would be left to rule with the little monkey, Thutmose III. But he need not have troubled himself. From the news that had come his way over the years, he knew the spunky woman had done more than well for herself and for Egypt.

While other kings had invested imperial resources in the military, Hatshepsut preferred to send squadrons of scouts into distant lands for the purpose of treasure-hunting. She had determined, long ago, that her reign would be peaceable, her power not based on military expansion, but on obedience to humanitarian pursuits.

She had spent great sums on bettering the cities, hiring out work to freemen, and paying the more talented slaves for their specialties.

She had completed the temple of Deir el-Bahri and had established herself as a respected pharaoh, easily overruling her rival.

Certainly her avant-garde clothing (for she still persisted in wearing the garb of a man) had been cause for snickers and scoffing, but as time proved her able administration, few continued to belittle her.

Peace was her byword. What, after all, had her husband's expansionism accomplished? Certainly Egypt had a stronger southern front, having brought the Nubians to their knees. But once the king was dead, after his three short years of reign, the southern tribes had become restive again. Hatshepsut's long reign, 37 years, turned the empire's attention to nobler goals.

Moses's goal, at this moment, was a narrow fissure at the base of Horeb. This time of year a spring bubbled there, and his flocks ran for it eagerly.

The cool shade of the steep-walled wadi and the soothing sound of the spring made for a peaceful retreat. Moses's hours of deepest contemplation had been spent in the narrow vale, and here, a time or two, he had felt the presence of the Lord.

The little gorge, with its ascending path and high, confining walls, always led his thoughts upward. Above the gurgle of the spring it sometimes seemed he heard a voice. And above the cool depths of the cavernous rift the slit of sky was transcendentally blue, its sunny brilliance a heavenly contrast to the dark interior.

Today as he entered the wadi, following his sheep, he headed for a certain flat stone where he customarily sat. From this stone he could gaze all the way up the rift and could spy one summit of the mount.

As usual, peace enveloped him, and he leaned his head back with a contented sigh.

"Shalom," he whispered, as if in greeting. "Peace to you."

But today the peace was imbued with urgency, as though Moses needed more than contentment, as though he needed...comfort. Suddenly his heart quickened, and his eyes opened inquisitively.

"What is it, Lord?" he asked.

While Moses felt free to address the Almighty, he never anticipated a direct response. The few times he had sensed the presence or the "voice" of God it had been only a fleeting impression.

But today, the impression was more vivid, like a gentle hand upon his head.

For a moment he reveled in the comforting gesture. But then he became troubled.

"What is it, Lord?" he repeated. "Is there some sorrow?"

Now the voice was quite distinct. For the first time in his life, Moses heard the words of God, directly and clearly.

"Go and return," the voice insisted, "return to Egypt. All those who sought your life are dead."

Shaking himself, Moses leaped to his feet and looked about in fear.

"Lord?" he cried. "Is that you?"

Silence filled the vale, but within the silence was a deeper, shimmering stillness.

"Return," it came again.

"But...how...why..." the man stammered. "My grandfather is dead and my mother's husband is gone. But is my rival gone as well? Does the queen reign alone?"

Again a sense of sorrow filled the peace. And Moses fought the implication.

"Does the queen reign alone?" he argued with the air.

Still the quiet made no reply, and Moses stumbled backward, glaring into vacant space.

It seemed the Almighty waited...waited. And Moses was left to interpret the message on his own.

If Thutmose III was still on the throne, how could he return in safety? Unless...

No! Surely not...surely the Lord was not saying that the reign of the monkey king was now unrivaled. If that were the case, a drive to eliminate Moses would be unnecessary.

As the fugitive hit upon this explanation, the comfort emanating from the hand of God made sense. "Hatshepsut!" he cried. "No, Lord, not my mother!"

Yes—the queen was dead.

As the realization flooded over him, Moses again remembered her tender smile, her saving hands—the hands that had lifted him in mercy from the waters of death.

Weeping disconsolately, he slumped against the rocks.

And the Presence hovered over him.

Always he would remember that the Hand of Mercy had been with him in this place.

And, someday he would seek it here again, beside the cool waters of the Horeb grotto.

39

Moses was afraid. For three months, he had avoided the call of God, the clear command that he must return to Egypt.

He excused the delay on the grounds that he must finish the spring season in Horeb Valley. He had, after all, only just arrived there when the Lord met him in the wadi and pressed the commandment upon him.

But the real reason for his reticence was fear.

Shortly after he knew Hatshepsut was dead, travelers from Egypt confirmed the news. Now and then word as to the state of things in his homeland trickled from the distant highway toward Horeb.

During her reign as Pharaoh, Hatshepsut's personality had held all rivalry in check. Since her death, there had been violent political reaction as the ambitious followers of Thutmose III tried to turn the empire against her memory. All her cartouches, the ornamental inscriptions on monuments and buildings that contained her name and likeness, were defaced. The king saw to it that all references to the woman-pharaoh were removed from the public eye, and even commissioned the desecration of the tombs of her faithful servants.

Presently the royal scribes were obliterating her name from all king lists in existence, replacing it with the names of Thutmose I, II, and III.

So quickly did all of this memory-washing take place, that by the end of spring it could hardly be proved that such a strong lady ever existed. Her favorite project, the mammoth temple at Deir el-Bahri, and her other great edifices were gradually being hidden by grander buildings, commissioned by the king and designed especially to overshadow her works.

Yes, Moses had good cause to be afraid. Although the Lord had clearly said there was no reason for him to remain in exile, he had trouble believing it. If the king was so determined to do away with the memory of Hatshepsut, how could her son set foot in Egypt without risk?

Latest word had it that, even now, Pharaoh marched against Syria, meaning to quell a revolt that had arisen upon the death of the queen.

No, Moses argued, surely the Lord did not mean he should return just yet.

Today Gershom and Eliezer had gone with their flock toward the northwest slope of Horeb, called Ras es-Safsaf. Zipporah tended the ewes and lambs near the tents, and Moses took yet another flock along the foot of the southeast slope.

Spring was in full bloom, as full as could be seen around Horeb. The name of the mount meant "dryness," but during this brief time of year, the mountain provided shelter from the heat and was ringed by a few seasonal ponds, surrounded by flowering cacti and filled with water lilies. Small white flowers splashed the clumps of sage as far as the eye could see, turning here and there to a dusty pink where the earth was reddest. And the sage, though always a muted silver, was tinged with baby green.

Moses loved the smell of the desert in spring. Pleasant breezes wafted the spicy aroma of sun-warmed heather across the sands, and patches of grass, coveted by the hungry flocks, gave off a minty scent. The desert, lacking promise at all other seasons, was at this time of year encouraging.

Still, that phenomenon of nature that always attended heat and vast stretches of horizon manifested itself today. Mirages, steamy and shimmering, caught Moses's eye every time he scanned the wilderness. Summer would soon be here.

Moses whistled to his sheep and goats, leading them to a shallow pool that lay in shadow. Once they were settled, he rested in a sunny place, pulling back his mantle to let the sun stroke his brow.

He tried not to think of Egypt or of Thutmose. But the attempt negated itself. Not to think was to think.

Off to the west, a wavering mirage drew his gaze. During his years in the wilderness, he had seen countless such ghostly distortions. He had learned to distinguish the imposters from the real oases and flowing streams they mimicked. But the one which had captured his attention pretended to no such thing.

Nor did it depict tall palms or traveling camels as some did. Many fantastic things could be seen in a mirage, just as in a bank of passing clouds. But as Moses studied this phantasm, it frightened him.

Within this steamy vision masses of people huddled, hunched under burdens and crying out from the indignities heaped upon them. Sighing and groaning, they beckoned across the miles. And it seemed they called to Moses, wordless pleas for help.

Covering his eyes, the shepherd turned away.

Surely the oppression of the Israelites had increased greatly since the death of Hatshepsut. While Moses feared Thutmose for his aggressive moves against the queen's supporters, he also knew the plight of his truer people must have taken a horrendous turn.

"No!" he cried. "I cannot see this!"

But, as though his eyes were forced open and his head turned back against his will he was obliged to watch the miserable ones who crouched beneath their torment.

Had not the Almighty told him to return, to go back to his suffering people? Moses was now twice the fugitive, in exile for murder and running just as surely from the call of the Lord.

As he observed the tortured souls within the mirage, tears flowed down his face and into his beard. Suddenly the entire desert was alive with the unseen Presence, brooding over him.

Moses did not need to ask the cause of the Almighty's sadness. He feared to utter a word, for he sensed that an unspeakable sacrifice was about to be required of him.

Shuddering, he buried his face in the lap of his robe and wept.

But there was no resisting the persistent Visitor.

The morning sun was growing hotter. As it pelted his back, he tried to think on other things—his flocks, the tribe in Midian, Zipporah. But as he did, a shadow passed between himself and the sun, like a cloud, close to the earth. A chill went through him as the shadow moved by, for it brought with it a wintry blast.

Looking up, Moses saw nothing—no shadow, no cloud. There was only the insistent cold. And it was followed by another round of heat, more intense than sunshine, scorching like the surge of a furnace.

Cringing, Moses shielded his eyes. Across the shallow pond, in a dry hollow, a man-sized clump of sage crackled with fire, its flames reaching out to him.

Amazed, he watched as the bush, which should have been consumed within seconds, burned ever more brightly. And just like the mysterious mirage, it contained an image—an imposing, solitary man, lifting a golden sword in his hand and beckoning to him.

Moses was on his feet, backing away from the flame, away from the intervening pond. Flinching, he ran, a cry of fear pushing from his throat.

But he knew he could not avoid the call of God forever. Stumbling to a standstill, he waited, quaking, fearing to look behind him.

At last, with a sigh, he conceded, "I must go back and see this great sight...why the bush is not burned up."

He knew he was privy to a miracle. But he was not ready to admit this.

Bracing himself, he turned about and went to investigate the phenomenon. He made a wide path around the pond, coming upon the bush cautiously.

"Calm yourself, Moses," he reasoned. "You are overwrought. Surely this is nothing more than a grassfire, started by the sun."

But this did not explain why it burned on and on, as though fed by more than dry tinder.

He was within feet of the little inferno. Again he was obliged to cover his face, for the heat was intense.

As he lifted his long-sleeved arm, he was suddenly smitten backward, pushed as by an invisible hand.

"Moses! Moses!" an unearthly voice shouted.

Crumpling to his knees, the shepherd trembled. The sound was unmistakable; his name was being called from the midst of the burning bush. Afraid to look for fear of seeing the ominous, sword-wielding figure, he replied, "Here am I!"

"Come no closer!" the voice commanded. "Take off your sandals from your feet—for the place on which you stand is holy ground!"

40

How Moses managed to unlatch his sandals and remove them, he would never remember. His mind and his emotions were a chaotic blurr, as the heat of the bush and its rushing blast surrounded him.

No sooner had he complied with the order than he cast himself face first upon the ground, in terror for his life.

From the midst of the bush a pulsating vibration pushed forth, as though the heartbeat of the universe sped urgently. And with it, the voice resumed.

"I am the God of your father, the God of Abraham, the God of Isaac, and the God of Jacob!" it declared, sending a tremor through the listener.

Covering his face, Moses lay prostrate, not daring to look into the fiery plant.

"I have surely seen the affliction of my people who are in Egypt," the voice continued "and I have heard their cry because of their taskmasters. I am aware of their suffering!"

Moses cringed. The statement was almost an accusation. For he also was aware. And yet he had done nothing.

But the voice did not spare him, driving straight for his guilty heart.

"Therefore, I have come down to rescue them from the power of the Egyptians and to bring them up from that land to a large and good land, to a land that flows with milk and honey, to the place of the Canaanite and the Hittite, the Amorite and the Perizzite, the Hivite and the Jebusite."

How familiar was that promise! The promise that accompanied the covenant, chanted time and again about the fire of Jethro and his tribe. Here it was now, from the mouth of the Lord Himself, the promise of the land of Canaan, bequeathed to Abraham's descendants.

Moses barely had time to consider this before the Almighty went on.

"And now, behold!" the haunting voice called. "The cry of the sons of Israel has come to me! And I have seen how oppressed they are in their labors. So come now! I will send you to Pharaoh so that you may bring my people, the children of Israel, out of Egypt!"

Still lying upon the ground, unable to lift his head, Moses felt the earth give way beneath him. Gripping his staff, he braced himself. Yet the ground had not moved. He had not moved.

That which he greatly feared had at last come upon him. In the depths of his soul, he had known for years that this time would come, that the call prophesied by Aaron and planted within his heart when he was but a child would require an accounting.

But who was he that God should single him out? What did he know, severed as he was from his Israelite heritage? What did he know of God, or of things divine?

At last, managing to raise himself from the ground, he struggled to his knees, still avoiding a direct view of the bush. "Who am I," he stammered, his voice barely more than a croak, "that I should go to Pharaoh and bring the children of Israel out of Egypt?"

For a long while, the bush was quiet, sizzling with flame, but unspeaking. Moses wondered if the Lord had even heard him.

But surely God knew he had spoken. Did not God know everything?

When the answer came, it was on wings of mercy. "Surely I will be with you, and the sign that I am with you shall be this: when you have brought the people out of Egypt, you shall worship God at this mountain."

Truly? *This* mountain? Was the Lord saying that the entire nation of Israel, numbering millions of captives, would one day pass through this bleak wilderness? The idea was ludicrous. How should one lone man lead such a company out of bondage, and if he did, why lead them here?

Moses mustered courage to object, but couched his doubts within a seemingly innocent question.

"Very well," he said, keeping his eyes to the ground, "suppose I do go to the sons of Israel, and say to them, 'The God of your fathers has sent me to you.' Suppose they say to me, 'What is his name?' What then shall I say to them?"

In truth, Moses was testing the very nature of the one who spoke to him. He must be certain this was the Lord, the Almighty himself, before he risked all for him.

But at this challenge, the mood in the air and around the bush suddenly changed from patience to anger. Moses thought the ground rumbled, and the mountain loomed in disapproval over him.

As the voice again came from the midst of the flaming sage, Moses covered his head and leaned close to the earth.

"I AM WHO I AM!" the Lord cried. "Tell the children of Israel, 'I AM has sent me to you.'"

Moses's heart pulsed violently. How dare he be so insolent? Yahweh himself, Lord God of the Universe, addressed him. And he had dared to question!

As the cowering shepherd clung to the ground, the voice repeated: "Tell the children of Israel, 'The Lord, the God of your fathers, the God of Abraham, the God of Isaac, and the God of Jacob, has sent me to you.' This is my name forever! And this is the name by which I shall be remembered to all generations!"

In shame the fugitive hunched over, keeping his face to the desert sand. And the presence of the Lord swept back and forth above him, driving home specific instructions.

"Go, gather the leaders of Israel together and say, 'The God of your fathers, the God of Abraham, Isaac, and Jacob, has appeared to me. He says, "I am indeed concerned about you and what you have suffered in Egypt. So I will bring you up out of the affliction of Egypt and lead you to the land of Canaan to a land that flows with milk and honey."'

"And they will pay attention to what you say, and you, along with the leaders of Israel, will go to Pharaoh and say to him, 'The Lord, the God of the Hebrews, has met with us. So now, please let us go a three days' journey into the wilderness, that we may offer sacrifices to the Lord our God.'

"But I know that Pharaoh will not permit you to go unless he is compelled. So I will stretch out my hand and strike Egypt with all my miracles, which I shall do in the midst of it. After that, Pharaoh will let you go!"

As the voice from the bush continued to speak, Moses grew increasingly agitated. Fear overwhelmed him as he imagined challenging the mightiest empire on earth.

He remembered Thutmose III, with his narrow, pea-black eyes, set beneath their overhanging brow. How he had always loathed him! But he also knew that those eyes, set now beneath a crown, could terrify him with a glance.

Lifting his head ever so slightly, Moses cowered before the bush like a dog. "What if they do not believe me?" he cried. "What if they will not listen to my words? For they might say, 'The Lord has not appeared to you.'"

As though the Lord wavered between punitive anger and a patient sigh, the desert was strangely hushed. At last Moses was compelled to study the shepherd's rod which he gripped in his outstretched fist.

"What do you hold in your hand?" the voice asked.

"A staff," Moses replied.

"Throw it down," the voice commanded.

Struggling to his feet, Moses did as he was told. To his horror the staff suddenly began to wriggle. Twisting and turning, it was transformed before his watching eyes into a sleek serpent.

Lifting its head, it faced him squarely, its gaping mouth revealing four great fangs. With a cry of terror, Moses fled away, leaping the edge of the pond and circling back toward his flock.

But before he reached the rock where he had first rested, ready to hide behind it, the voice caught him. "Stretch out your hand," it ordered, "and grasp the serpent by its tail!"

Huddling beside the rock, Moses hesitated. But he knew well enough by now that the Lord would abide no cowardice.

He inched toward the site of the burning bush and warily observed the serpent, which now stood erect on its coiled tail, its head dancing back and forth in deadly, teasing challenge.

How, he wondered, was he supposed to come near that tail, let alone touch it? Surely the snake would strike if he made any move at all.

Never before had his God given him so deadly a challenge.

But this was his first great test. To touch or not to touch; to obey or to disobey.

His very life depended on his choice.

In that moment, there was no time for theology. The core of the man must react. And in that reaction, all his ideas about the Almighty would be manifest.

It was his will that moved his hand. But so automatically did it happen that it seemed the hand moved on its own.

As though he watched someone else's response, he saw the fingers stretch out and the arm reach past the snake's gyrating body to clutch the twisting tail.

Instantly the snake again became a staff, rigid and cooperative in Moses's grasp. Choking with relief, the man held it up, stroking it in speechless amazement.

"So," the Almighty sighed, "they will believe that the God of their fathers, the God of Abraham, of Isaac, and Jacob, has appeared to you."

For a moment, as Moses surveyed the restored rod, he could believe that such a thing was possible; he knew he could indeed return to Egypt and boldly confront his mortal enemy.

But only for a moment. As he remembered the massive imperial walls, the poised bows of its countless archers, he again doubted.

Who, after all, knew better than he just how ruthless the house of Pharaoh was? Had he not been privy to the inner workings of the greatest councils on earth? Had he not been groomed to lead the very nation he must challenge? So what if his staff could turn into a serpent? Pharaoh's magicians performed such feats every day.

Perhaps it was Moses's silence that brought the next response. For the command was not patient.

"Put your hand into your bosom!" the Lord ordered.

The shepherd looked deep into the bush, wondering what evil the Lord intended. But laying his staff upon the ground, he slipped a trembling hand beneath his tunic and held it against his chest.

Within a few seconds he felt a tingling itch upon the back of his hand that spread painfully up his fingers. Wishing to withdraw his hand from his bosom, he nonetheless kept it there until the pain was exchanged for numbness.

Horrified, he wondered if he had lost the hand altogether, if it had vanished like the staff, or, like the serpent, been transformed into an unfeeling stump.

At last he was impressed to pull it out. But having no sensation in the hand, had to lift it up with his good one.

Aghast, he saw the reason for the paralysis. His hand, while still intact, was white as snow—vile with leprous lesions! Crying out, he fell to his knees where he cradled the decaying flesh against his lap.

As he wept bitterly, astonished that his God could be so cruel, the presence of the Lord passed over him once more.

"Put your hand back into your bosom," the Almighty whispered.

Ha! Moses thought. Did the Lord take him for a fool? Was it not enough that he should lose one member to this creeping disease? At least if it were amputated, his life might be saved. But he was not about to contaminate himself further by touching his body with the infested flesh.

Still the Presence was insistent, hovering over him with oppressive love.

Moses watched as his hand obeyed. Into his tunic it went, resting cold and lifeless against his chest.

Suddenly, he could feel the blood surge into the deadened fingers and he sensed life coursing through the withered skin.

Tears flooded his eyes, and doubling over, he held the hand there for a long time, weeping with joy. When he had the courage, he at last withdrew it and saw, as he expected, that it was clean and new.

As he turned it this way and that, the Almighty seemed to embrace him.

"It shall come about that if they will not believe you or take heed to the first sign, they may believe the second sign."

Moses laughed for relief. Never had he heard of the magicians of Egypt performing anything this spectacular. Oh, there were curses, shamanistic voodoo against people whom the priests despised, inflicting all sorts of miseries upon the victims. But he had never heard of leprosy being cured, neither in Egypt, nor anywhere else.

He was beginning to believe. Perhaps he *could* do as the Lord commanded.

As he reveled in growing faith, Yahweh spoke again. "But if they will not believe even these two signs or heed the things you say, then you shall take some water from the Nile and pour it on the dry ground. And the water which you take from the Nile will become blood on the dry ground."

Now why must the Lord have said this? Was not Moses's confidence growing? To refer to the Nile at this moment was to throw a demoralizing spear at his toddling faith.

Only one reared in the ways of Egypt could fully appreciate just how imbued with religious significance was the holy river. Considered to be the very lifeblood of the empire, its waters were sacred, literally flowing from the veins of the gods themselves. And though Moses had been away from Egypt a long time, though he had steeped himself in Israelite theology since he was 13, he was also a product of his upbringing. The Nile for him still represented a fearsome force.

But here was Yahweh, not only defying the sacred river, but threatening to mock its vitality by transforming it into the very substance it portended to be: blood!

Oh, the priests of Egypt would never stand for this! If a representative of an obscure desert deity should tamper with the holy Nile—why he would not live to take his next breath!

Moses looked about, as if seeking someone to rescue him. But he was alone. And should he return to Egypt, taking on the formidable task, he would still be alone, standing before the priests of Pharaoh without defense.

"Please, Lord!" he cried, raising his hands over his head, "I have never been eloquent, neither recently nor in time past. Even now, as you speak with me, I am slow of speech and slow of tongue!"

He knew he strained the patience of Almighty. Moses, of all people, could not claim dull wits or a stammering tongue as an excuse. From the time he had been a child, he had astonished his teachers with his sharp mind and calculating reason. Not even High Priest Jannes surpassed his challenging student.

But the Lord knew Moses's heart. He knew Moses was mortally afraid, and that only tangible support would see him through.

The air quivered as the Lord prepared a response. When it came, it was as gentle as sunlight on the Horeb pond.

"Who has made man's mouth? Who makes him deaf, or dumb, or seeing, or blind? Is it not I, the Lord? Now then, go, and I will be with your mouth and teach you what you are to say."

Moses should have taken strength from this. He should have stood to his feet, taking the staff from the desert floor, and he should have begun his trek to Egypt.

Instead, still huddled over, he whimpered, "Please, Lord, send another messenger in my place."

Suddenly the flames of the bush leaped higher. Forcing Moses back with their intense heat, they threatened to consume him.

"Very well!" the voice cried. "Your brother, Aaron the Levite, speaks fluently. He is coming out to meet you, and when he sees you, he will be glad!"

What? Not Aaron! The pathetic prince shuddered on the ground. Never would he have willingly subjected his brother to this danger! Why must Aaron be involved?

But, of course, Aaron had never been afraid. He had always called the truth as he saw it. Shame filled the cringing shepherd, just as Yahweh knew it would.

"You will speak to him and put the words in his mouth," the Lord commanded, refusing Moses any recourse. "I, even I, will be with your mouth and his, and I will teach you what you shall do. He shall speak for you to the people, and you shall speak for me to him!"

How complicated! Moses thought. *And how unnecessary!* Yet it was because of his own spineless fear that his brother would now be at risk. He could already imagine Aaron's condescension, as once more the older brother must intervene between Moses and the consequences of his frailties.

Barely did Moses have time to absorb the command, however, before the Lord swept over him again, turning his eyes toward the off-cast staff.

"But you yourself shall take your staff in your hand," the voice demanded, "and with it you shall perform the signs as I have said!"

41

The well at Ezion-geber was crowded this night with travelers. A gibberish of tongues filled the night air as companies and caravans settled down to rest, and Moses was reminded of his introduction to the ways of the nomads.

He remembered his fascination and his bewilderment when he had lodged with the Midianites at the oasis of Migdol, when he was on the run from Pharaoh. That had been 40 years ago, and the cacophony of voices, clanking vessels, and bleeting animals still brought a bemused smile to his face.

That Moses could smile at all was evidence of his changed heart. He had every reason to be as fearful as the night he fled Egypt. He was on his way back to the land of the Nile, heading directly into the jaws of the lion. But he was not afraid.

Since the Lord had challenged him from the midst of the burning bush, he had considered and reconsidered his mission. The very day of the encounter, he had packed up his family and headed back to Midian, where he had set his affairs in order, asking Jethro's permission to depart and to take his wife and sons with him. That interval had allowed time for introspection.

Once upon a time, Jethro had warned him never to take Zipporah away. But that had been years ago, and since then, the elder had come to believe Moses was especially touched by the hand of God.

Graciously he consented, and so Moses and his little family had set off across the desert.

Moses no longer doubted God's calling, or the fact that he would have what he needed to fulfill it.

As for Zipporah, however, her outlook was different. She was not smiling tonight.

To the feisty woman, Moses had always been an enigma. She loved him passionately, but everything about him, from his abrupt entrance into her life to his elusive past and his fascination with her father's teachings, mystified her.

From the beginning, she had attributed his idiosyncracies to his foreign heritage. But this had never fully satisfied her. Surely not every Egyptian was bookish, so often lost in thought or piqued by melancholy as her husband was.

Her way of handling the mystery was to sublimate it to more practical interests. Moses was a good shepherd, a tender and caring father. He had learned to mingle with her people. And he adored her. However strange his private bent, this was enough for her.

Sometimes, however, he infuriated her. What he had in mind, taking her and her sons into a foreign land, she could not imagine. Never had he hinted at such a plan. Never had he mentioned a longing to do so. Midian had always seemed precious to him, like a haven, though even this she had never understood.

Surely this sudden move had it roots in that ever-obscure part of him—that part which defined his mystique. But Zipporah had no patience with his decision and fought it every step of the way.

Her anger over this turn of events was as pointed and dramatic as her feelings the day Moses announced he would undergo circumcision. How she had fought that! None of the men of her tribe were so disfigured.

How silly and worthless the bloody ritual had seemed to the highstrung woman! Yet she might have accepted even this had he not insisted on inflicting the same brutality on little Gershom.

Never would the tribe forget her desperate pleas as her husband had taken the lad by the hand and had disappeared with him into the striped tent. Moments later Moses had emerged, cradling his teary-eyed son in his arms.

Gershom had been incredibly brave that day. But Zipporah had never forgiven Moses the unalterable abuse, calling it up to him many times over the years when she was angry.

This present journey earned the same volatile reaction. Though the Midianites were nomads, their lives followed a predictable routine. To remove them from the wilds to the confines of civilization was just as unnerving as to uproot a pampered city-dweller and cast him to the hyenas.

Still Zipporah had had little say over her husband's choices. Just now, as she and Gershom erected the family's small traveling tent, she cast a piercing glance over her shoulder, hoping to catch Moses's eye and drill him once more with her helpless frustration.

Nine-year-old Eliezer performed his usual duty of unloading the water bottles from the backs of the donkeys and filling them at the wayside well.

As he carried them into the tent, Zipporah nodded to him proudly. At least over this child's welfare, she had been influential. Somehow she had raised enough protest to dissuade Moses from circumcising Eliezer. The younger son had never been subjected to the ordeal. And never would he be, she had determined.

As he passed by her once again, heading to the well, she reached out and stroked his dark curls, running a hand over his smooth cheek. But with this she took a sharp breath. The boy's face was flushed, his skin hot to the touch.

"Son," she said, bending anxiously over him, "do you feel well?"

The boy looked up at her with drowsy eyes, and she saw that they were tinged with feverish red. "I'm tired, Mama," he answered. "I want to go to bed."

Quickly she took him into the shelter and began to undress him. No one must see that he was sick. If word spread through the camp that he carried a fever, the family would be required to leave.

Her heart fluttering, Zipporah bedded him down. "Hush, now, Eliezer," she tried to comfort him. "Don't cry. I'll fetch Papa."

Hugging him close, she caressed his hot face again and went to get Moses.

Gershom was just pounding the last tent stake into the sandy ground when Moses hastened into the shelter with his wife. Kneeling over the boy, the father held his small, sweaty hand to his lips and prayed in silence.

"Surely it will pass," he whispered, trying to calm the fretting Zipporah. "It will probably be gone by morning. He is simply overtired, and probably frightened."

"Of course!" the woman snapped. "Why shouldn't he be? Taken from home and loved ones for no reason!"

Gershom joined them and listened anxiously. "Mother," he warned, "someone will hear."

Choking on her anger, Zipporah bit her tongue.

"Get a rag," Moses commanded. "Wet it and cool his brow."

As Zipporah obeyed, Moses threw back the tent flap and trudged into the desert a way, pondering this strange turn. Here he was, at last, fearlessly following the call of God. He was no longer resisting, but had forsaken safety and certainty to return to Egypt. What evil could come upon him or his own so long as he did the will of Yahweh?

Yes, surely the fever would quickly pass. Surely this was only one more test of faith, and the boy's strength would revive by morning.

But something deeper troubled Moses. He felt somehow out of harmony with the Lord.

The feel of Eliezer's flushed cheek was still hot upon his hand.

Fearful it was, like the heat of the burning bush.

42

Night descended quickly over the oasis at Ezion-geber. Almost eerie was the darkness, and coming on too fast.

Moses did not go so far out into the desert that he lost sight of the camp lights. But he trudged aimlessly for a long while, gripping his staff in a stranglehold, prayer constricting his breath, and a nameless dread throbbing through his heart.

Something was wrong. Terribly wrong. He knew that Eliezer's fever involved a spiritual battle, and he must know the cause.

Weak-kneed, he at last stopped his pointless pacing, and resting his staff across his lap, sat down beside a mound of sage. This time no divine fire raged through the brittle bush. But Moses could sense the exacting presence of the Lord.

"What is it, Master?" he pleaded. "You know I will do whatever you wish. Have I not proved myself?"

No answer came, only deafening silence. "Please spare my son!" Moses begged. "He has no quarrel with you!"

Again silence. A soft breeze tickled the sage.

When at last the Lord replied, the man listened carefully.

"When you return to Egypt," the voice whispered, "see that you do all the wonders which I have put in your power before Pharaoh."

Moses clutched his sacred staff, the one which had displayed the acts of God's power. But tears clouded his eyes. Did Yahweh care nothing for his present misery?

Must he only repeat his previous instructions and not respond to the crisis of the hour?

Still the voice went on, seeming not to heed his frustration.

"But I will harden Pharaoh's heart, so that he will not let the people go."

Yes, yes. Moses had heard this before. It angered him to hear it again.

Yet now an urgent wind passed through the sage. And Moses sensed that God was just as angry as he.

"Then you shall say to Pharaoh, 'Thus says the Lord, "Israel is my son, my firstborn. So I said to you, 'Let my son go, that he may serve me.' But you will not let him go. Therefore, I will kill your son, your firstborn!"'"

Moses was stunned. This was a new thing, an instruction which the Lord had not spoken before. Never had he indicated that any child of Thutmose would be in jeopardy because of the king's refusal to obey.

But as the man of God pondered this, he suddenly caught a glimpse of himself.

Had he, indeed, always been faithful? Had he not held back for himself a corner of disobedience?

Thinking of his own dear son, Eliezer, lying in feverish torment, he trembled. Yes, Moses was guilty of the same sin as Pharaoh! He had not let his own son go, that he might serve God. He had given in to the demands of Zipporah and had never consecrated Eliezer through the clearly demanded ritual of circumcision.

As the reality of his guilt swept over him, shame contorted his face.

Looking back toward camp, he knew what he must do. He had taken the Lord's patience for granted; he had toyed with the holy demands of God.

Rising on wobbly legs, he hurried home. If he were to face the king of Egypt in righteous boldness, he must himself be righteous. If he were to save his own son, he must surrender him to the will of God.

The fearful, demanding will of God. He was learning just how inescapable it was, how insistent and unyielding.

* * *

"Zipporah!" Moses called, as he flung back the tent flap and entered the dark shelter. "God has met with me!"

The woman, who had fallen into a restless sleep beside her sick child, jolted awake and peered through the blackness. "Husband?" she replied. "Where have you been?"

Her tone was still accusatory, but Moses was in no mood to endure it.

"The Lord has told me what we must do. And this time, you will not fight me!" he declared.

In a corner of the tent, Gershom awoke and lit the lantern overhead. "What is it, father?" he asked, searching Moses's determined face.

Fists clenched, the man reasserted, "We must not resist the will of God. I know now that I have been wrong."

Zipporah looked on, wide-eyed as Moses searched the supply sacks stored on the floor.

"What are you looking for?" she asked, careful lest she anger him further.

Eliezer, whose fever had escalated, lay beside his mother in a sweaty stupor, oblivious to his father's actions.

"Where is the flint knife?" Moses demanded, impatiently sifting through the bags.

"The flint knife?" Zipporah gasped. "Why would you want that?"

Flint knives were used for surgical purposes. They were part of the gear of every household, but were employed only for delicate operations: the removal of thorns, the letting of blood...

Suddenly Zipporah was on her feet. "Surely you do not mean to bleed him!" she cried, bending over her husband. "That is superstition!"

Indeed, the practice was predominately Egyptian. People of the desert rarely resorted to it, decrying it as barbarous, though the Egyptians were highly advanced in medicine.

"No," Moses replied, not even looking at her. "You know what must be done."

By now he had located the tool and held it forth in shaking fingers, gazing steadfastly into his wife's astonished face.

As his intentions became clear, Zipporah reached for the blade. "Not that!" she pleaded. "You would not betray me again!"

"Betray *you*?" he sighed. "It is the Lord whom I have betrayed! Now he demands an accounting."

"You would butcher the lad as you butchered yourself and Gershom?" she cried.

The elder son stepped close, drawing his mother to his bosom.

"It is the only way," Moses insisted. "Would you rather Eliezer died at the hand of the Almighty?"

Incredulous, Zipporah cried, "So God is responsible for Eliezer's illness? What kind of monster do you take our Lord to be? This is not the God of my father, Jethro!"

For a moment, Moses wavered. Zipporah's argument was strong. Indeed, he did not wish to think God capable of vengeance upon an innocent child.

Still he knew he must obey. He knew, despite all reasoning, that Eliezer's survival depended on his utter abandonment to Jehovah's will.

"Remember Abraham," he countered. "He was obliged to give up Isaac, to offer him on the altar. Only when he obeyed was his son restored to him."

Zipporah was dumbfounded. For a long, desperate moment, silence hung between them.

Then, as though angry lightning moved her hand, the woman suddenly lunged for the knife. Moses thought she would do him harm. But to his amazement, she turned for the lad's bed.

"Very well!" she snarled. "But if it must be done, *I* shall do it. You will not lay a hand upon my son!"

Before Moses could think, she had exposed the boy's genitals. Her hand moving more by spite than by obedience, she circumscribed the lad's flesh.

For Eliezer, the swoon of fever was a blessed anesthetic. Within seconds, his mother held the severed foreskin to the lamplight.

"Here!" she cried, casting the crimson tissue at Moses's feet. "You are a husband of blood to me! A husband of blood!"

With this, she pushed past him, heading toward the door. Though he reached for her, she avoided his touch and ran sobbing into the night.

43

The next morning Moses sent Zipporah and her sons back to Midian.

As he had predicted, Eliezer's fever broke once the circumcision had been performed. Though the lad would be sore for a time, he was no longer ill and had, in fact, been able to sit up and take nourishment almost the instant the Lord's command had been met.

Zipporah was no longer angry with Moses. She was not blind to the truth so plainly proven. Once it was clear that her son would recover, she flew into her husband's arms, her face tear-streaked and her heart yearning for forgiveness. Even now as he helped her mount her donkey and hugged her good-bye, she clung to him, weeping on his shoulder.

But Moses felt it best that she go back. "I never should have forced you to come," he said, smiling weakly as he lifted her into the saddle. "God called me to this journey, but he did not call you. Return to your father. I will send for you when the time is right."

"I love you," the woman whispered, her voice plaintive.

"And I you," Moses replied. Then turning to Gershom, he instructed, "Take care of my family for me."

That had been four days ago. Moses had resumed the journey toward Egypt on his own and was now half-way across Sinai.

Since leaving Ezion-geber, his soul had been a jumble of emotion. He missed Zipporah. He missed Gershom and Eliezer. Midian had become home, and he was homesick. But with each step west, he was filled with mounting anticipation. Although he could see only vaguely into the future, he knew he had prepared for this journey all his life.

He had begun in Egypt, and he must return there. His years in the wilderness had served him well, hardening his body, teaching him self-reliance, and educating him in divine matters both at the feet of Jethro and through experiences that would not have been his elsewhere.

If he pondered the future too closely, he always met with fear. But this was overcome when he remembered his mission—and God's promise to be with him.

The dust of the Sinai highway sifted through his sandals. The sound of his sacred staff, as it struck the ground beside him, emphasized the silence of the desert. Occasionally he came upon a group of travelers, and always he greeted them heartily, clinging to the sight of them as they passed by. For of all his feelings, loneliness was the keenest.

He was headed toward the Bitter Lakes. Ahead stretched 75 miles of desolate wasteland. Steeling himself against the inevitable vacuum of solitude, he looked for anything on which to focus—a rock, a tall plant—so he would not lose touch with time and space.

He was relieved when he saw yet another traveler heading toward him. The figure was wavery, clouded by distance and desert steam. But the closer it came, the more distinct was its form, and he knew it was a man.

Savoring the sight of life, Moses kept his gaze riveted to the fellow. All too quickly they would pass, and he would again be alone.

But as he watched the oncoming traveler, he thought

he had seen him before. In his stride and his bearing there was something familiar.

Suddenly Moses's heart leaped. Flashing to the burning bush, he remembered that God had promised to send...

"Aaron!" he cried. "Aaron! Is that you?"

Energized by joy, the two men erased the distance between them. Running like schoolboys, they met with arms outspread, and embraced hilariously.

"Moses!" the elder greeted, clutching him in a bear-hug. "I have found you! Just as the Lord said!"

Pulling away, they surveyed one another up and down, turning each other about and laughing like children.

Aaron was still tall and strong, handsome as dark cedar. But his younger brother matched him now, his years in the wilderness having strengthened his lithe body and given character to his face.

"I would know you anywhere!" Moses declared. "But what is this?" Teasing, he pulled at the silver in Aaron's beard.

"The wealth of old age!" the elder returned. "But what is this?"

He, too, tugged at Moses's beard. But he saw there more than silver. He saw the loss of the cleanshaven, Egyptian look, and in its place the face of a sun-kissed shepherd.

"The wealth of old age... and of a freer life!" Moses laughed.

As he said this, however, he felt of twinge of regret. "How is it that you have met me here? You are not a free man."

Aaron understood Moses's embarrassment. When last they had been together, Moses was a fugitive and Aaron a truant bondman.

"The family was emancipated some years ago, when the queen was on the throne. She allowed indentured servants like us to earn our freedom."

Moses choked back tears. How much he did not know! How much he had missed!

"But what of you?" Aaron sighed. "What of the two of us? I hear God has great plans!"

PART VI

Man of God

44

As though time had folded back on itself, the walls of Raamses loomed before Moses in the blush of an Egyptian sunset.

How many times in his life he had witnessed such a view! And how long ago! Coming upon them from the wilderness side, rather than glimpsing them from the window of a palace chamber, made the walls all the more awe-inspiring.

The last time he had seen them had been from the seat of Aaron's wagon, as the two brothers had fled to the wilderness. Now Moses would reenter, having taken on a holy calling.

During the journey from Sinai, Moses had described for Aaron his encounter with the burning bush and had rehearsed all the instructions the Almighty had given. The brothers knew that their first duty was to call together the leading Israelites and to announce to them God's love and his promise to rescue them from bondage.

Just how this would be performed, they could not predict. But they would set about tomorrow morning to fulfill the Lord's commands.

Tonight they headed directly for the house of Amram. The anticipation of seeing his family was as exciting as any work of God Moses could imagine.

Aaron had assured him that Amram and Jochebed were alive and well, and Miriam was as fine a woman as Israel could claim. The sister had never married, but had devoted her life to serving her parents and to easing the burdens of her people. She was, Aaron said, still a fighter. Had she only been born a man, she would likely have led a revolution by now.

As the two men entered the city, the business day was winding down. Soon the guarded gates would be shut for the night, barring all going and coming.

To all appearances, the brothers were both commoners, arousing no suspicion in their simple robes and dusty sandals. Each of them carried a walking stick, and no one would have suspected that Moses's staff was the tool of mighty miracles, or that he had once been heir to the throne.

Traversing the main viaduct, the men came to the turnoff that led to the slave compound. Years ago, Moses had followed that road to the low wall-within-the-walls that had hid slave town from the view of passersby. Behind that humble wall were the huts and dirt paths of the Hebrew ghetto, where he had first learned of Jehovah. And it was there that his heart had returned again and again during his years in exile.

Lightheaded with anticipation, he followed Aaron closely, but was surprised when he skirted the turnoff. Instead the elder brother led him to a middle-class section of town. "Where are we going?" Moses asked, surveying the neat, whitewashed buildings and the clean pavement.

"We live here now," Aaron replied. "Amram and I have done well working for the stonecutter, and mother and Miriam receive good wages tending the children of wealthy families. We get by."

It seemed they did more than "get by," Moses thought, as Aaron led him to the polished wooden gate of a modest cottage. From the entryway glowed the soft light of a brass lantern, and the sound of music floated out from the courtyard.

"Apparently we have guests," Aaron said. "Most likely mother and father have gathered some of the elders to celebrate your return."

As Moses followed him into the house, he found himself taking the role of the younger brother, hoping Aaron would speak for him. Regardless of the fact that he had been raised in the courts of Egypt, had been a brilliant student, and had been groomed for the throne, he had always bowed to Aaron's shadow.

"Mother, Father," Aaron called, greeting the little company gathered about the brick oven, "see who is here!"

Moses hardly recognized the elderly couple who turned about at the call. Had Jochebed's face not lit with joy, and had Amram not rushed to greet him, the returning son might not have singled them out from among the other aged members of the group.

But when the slight woman, with her hair of silver wool and her dark, crinkled face, stepped forth, her eyes brimming with tears and her feeble arms outstretched, he knew her. And when the elderly gentleman, with his patriarchal beard and his silent prayer of thanks, stood beside her, Moses knew him.

Never had there been such rejoicing in Egypt as took place that hour. Laughing and crying, the parents clung to their long-lost child, alternately clutching him close and holding him at arm's length, looking him up and down, marveling at his equally changed appearance, and leading him from stranger to stranger in the room.

"We knew you would come! We knew!" Jochebed cried, burying her tear-streaked face on his shoulder.

"How could you know?" Moses wondered.

"God knew," Amram said matter-of-factly. "And he told Aaron."

Could Moses have doubted such a thing—he who had heard the voice of God from within a burning bush?

"Of course," he smiled.

Looking about the court, he saw that the family had put action to their faith, decorating the room as for a great party. Colored lanterns hung from the open rafters, and the low dinner table was spread with holiday fare.

Already, before the brothers had arrived, merriment had begun with men playing pipes and lutes, and women singing.

But it was a secret gathering, its purpose known only to those people whom Amram and Jochebed considered trustworthy. Because the prince might still be considered a fugitive, no one outside this company had been informed of his homecoming.

Most of the folks in the courtyard were advanced in years. Some of them Moses remembered as respected leaders in the Israelite community. The men in the group had reached the status of "elders," and the women were matriarchs of the Hebrew slaves. There were younger people, however, and Moses could see that they were strong personalities who could be trained for leadership.

A young man by the name of Hoshea had come with his father, Nun, and his grandfather, Elishama. He had been a mere child when Moses left Egypt. Now he was tall and handsome, his dark-bearded face and snapping black eyes evincing intelligence and courage. Moses would be watching him over the next days.

Along with Hoshea was another young fellow, named Caleb. Following in his father Jephunneh's footsteps, he was already a leader of the tribe of Judah. Moses would ask Aaron about him.

In all, there were about 20 men and women in the courtyard: wise old people who had suffered much under Pharaoh and had grown stronger through their sufferings, and bright young activists ready for a change.

All of them had heard of Moses; many had known him from his earliest years. And all believed that he had been spared the wrath of Pharaoh, twice in his life, for some great purpose.

To this point only Aaron had been told Moses's specific calling. Before the night was over, everyone here would have heard the story of his years in Midian, of Jethro, the man of God, and of the burning bush. They would gaze with awe upon the sacred staff, which had been turned to a serpent, and upon his hand, which had once been leprous. They would marvel to the account of his son's illness and recovery, and they would begin to believe that all things were possible.

"Jehovah has promised to bring us out of bondage," Aaron said as he sat with his brother beside the fire. "Moses has much to tell you, and he has asked me to help him choose those who will work beside him. I am sure that you can help him stir up the hearts of Israel."

Eager agreement showed on every face. The elders leaned together in excited whispers and the young men appeared ready to take orders, then and there.

But before Moses spoke, there were a few more people to meet. The sound of the courtyard gate, opening on its hinges, announced the arrival of newcomers. When Moses turned to see who entered, he had no doubt as to the identity of the central figure.

The latecomers were three women, two very elderly and one a few years older than Moses. On the instant, he recognized Miriam. She was still a striking lady, her Nubian features softened by her Hebrew heritage. That nearly masculine ambiance was still in her bearing, yet she was beautiful.

Nor did she hesitate to identify Moses. "Brother!" she cried, rushing to his arms. "I had hoped to be here when you came."

"It is enough that you are here at all," Moses returned. "How I have missed you, my sister!"

Wiping tears from her eyes, Miriam introduced him to her two friends. "You remember Shiphrah and Puah, the midwives who did us such kindness years ago?"

"I do," Moses assured her, as pieces of his past reclaimed him. Surveying the two ladies, plump Puah and the always-willowy Shiphrah, he marveled. As though he were a boy again, he remembered the night of his thirteenth birthday party, when the two women had sought him out on the veranda. That night they had presented him with the first proof of his Hebrew heritage.

His face stretched into a smile as he took their frail hands in his. "Dear ladies," he laughed, "do you never tire of surprising me? Had it not been for you, I should be sitting this day upon the throne!"

Befuddled, Puah blushed and Shiphrah chuckled softly. "We never tire of it, my lord," the tall one sighed. "In fact, we have a gift, again, for you."

"Yes," Puah giggled. "When Miriam came to fetch us at the royal house, we were still wrapping it."

From behind her back, Puah drew out a package, and Moses took it in trembling hands.

He knew what it was, and he could barely bring himself to open it for the shaking in his heart.

"It was in the queen's chamber for years," Shiphrah said. "Before she died, she sent it to us. She must have known we helped you escape the wrath of Pharaoh. It was her way of saying 'thank you.'"

Jochebed and Miriam drew close, leaning against Moses as tears clouded his eyes.

Gently he drew back the wrapper and there, just as he had suspected, was the little blanket in which he had been wrapped within the bulrush ark—the blanket which had become his Hebrew mantle, and beneath which he had said his forbidden prayers as a secret Israelite.

Jochebed reached out and touched it, her own heart too full for words. Her hands were now wizened and arthritic, but once upon a time she had woven tenderness and prayers for safety into the blanket's every warp and woof.

Lifting it from the wrapper, the old mother held it up. And as Moses bowed his head, she placed it over him— the certain mark of his salvation, and of his mighty calling.

45

The next morning, the small congregation that had gathered at Amram's house followed Moses and Aaron into the public marketplace. It was not a day to report for service to their Egyptian masters. It was a day to announce liberty to the captive Israelites!

Their entrance into the square was not questioned, as people of all social levels mingled there. But those who observed their tight-knit company wondered why they kept so close together and what the excited gleam in their eyes was all about.

Hoshea and Caleb followed directly behind the two brothers, ready to assist in any way. For Moses, who felt as though he had stepped out from a high precipice, their support was a comfort.

Many times in his memory, Moses had passed through this market. But those memories were of a far different time, when he rode in the finest carriages in the realm, and when onlookers bowed before him as he went by. Now he was unrecognized, one face among thousands in the jostling, noisy bazaar. Though he kept his chin high and held his sacred staff close to his side, he felt anything but regal.

When he and Aaron came to the center of the square, they waited a while, wondering how to proceed. Their followers were silent, placing more confidence in them than they did in themselves.

All about the busy market were the trappings of commerce and competition. Merchants stood at their booths, crying out to be heard above the throng, peddling whatever handmade goods, imports, or homegrown foods they wished to sell. And slaves were everywhere, running errands and assisting their masters and mistresses in countless ways.

Most of the slaves were, of course, Hebrew, and most were Israelites. Here and there an especially capable one had full charge of his owner's booth and property, and worked unsupervised, his master having entrusted his business to the slave. Aaron referred to such people when he leaned close to Moses and whispered, "Many of these are also leaders in Israel. They are some of the brightest and the best, and have risen to positions of responsibility since you were here. Pay attention to them."

"Very well," Moses said. Then, heaving a sigh, "It is time now."

Aaron nodded, and looking about, saw a pile of crates near the bazaar's center aisle. "Come," he replied.

Fully aware that they risked their lives, they climbed up on the pile and Aaron began to cry out in a loud voice, "Men of Israel, draw close that we may speak to you!"

At first the voice was only one of hundreds vying for attention in the market. Aaron might as well have been selling a special variety of grape, as proclaiming salvation from bondage. For the marketplace was not only the site of bartar and trade, but the wholesale clearinghouse of fresh ideas and the place to air any philosophy new to the empire. Here politics were debated with relative freedom, and so were religious ideologies. So long as no insurrection was advocated, even Thutmose tolerated free thinking.

Nevertheless, as Aaron continued to shout across the heads of the milling crowd, his words began to pique the interest of the crowd. He addressed his message to slaves, an unheard of thing, and very dangerous. How dare he distract them from their work or imply that they merited a moment in the public eye?

As the elders and the young leaders who had followed Moses out from Amram's house looked on, their fellow slaves hearkened to the call.

And Aaron repeated himself over and over: "Come, gather about us, all you sons of Israel! If there be elders among you, fetch them and bring them here!"

Moses tried not to stand in Aaron's shadow. He was, after all, the chosen one, and Aaron was his spokesman by default. Moses knew God would not allow him to resist his position of primary responsibility.

Yet looming above and about them were the parapets of Egypt, the fortified walls and gates of the capital city. And all along those walls were royal guards, the keen-eyed police of the kingdom. Moses knew that any moment the soldiers' spears and arrows could be leveled at them.

Had he a mind to shrink into the crowd; however, he could not have done so. For Aaron was drawing attention directly to him.

"I am Aaron, son of Amram," he hailed the people. "And this is my brother. You have all heard of him, though you do not recognize him now!"

The crowd's attention settled on the peculiar fellows atop the crates. Gradually a few brave souls left their stations, Israelite slaves who had no right to do so. Attracted by Aaron's boldness, they gathered about him until their number was considerable.

Trying not to show fear, Moses glanced toward the walls. Yes, the police were on alert, and they watched the response of the slaves with grim displeasure.

They had not raised their weapons yet. Nor had any warning been shouted. But Moses swallowed hard as Aaron forged ahead.

"The one who stands beside me is none other than Moses, son of Queen Hatshepsut!" he cried. "You have all heard how he fled for his life, charged with the defense of a Hebrew slave 40 years ago!"

Incredulous, the audience studied Moses, and a huzza filled the air. Though many of those present had not even been born when Moses dwelt here, the story of the fugitive prince was anything but musty history. In fact, unknown to himself, Moses had become a legend in his own time, and among his people the crime that had sent him fleeing for his life had come to be regarded as an act of heroism.

Even among the Egyptians, the story of Moses was a popular tale, as popular as that of the queen mother herself. The runaway did not realize that the story had grown to messianic proportions, even among Israel's oppressors. But the Egyptians who loved Hatshepsut had always hoped her son might one day return to vindicate her name.

Therefore, at this introduction, not only did Hebrews come forward, but Egyptians also crowded about, wondering if the quiet, bearded shepherd could actually be their lost prince.

"But this fellow is a sand flea!" some mocked, referring to his desert robe and bushy beard. "The son of Hatshepsut is of royal blood!"

"Get down from there!" others laughed. "You profane the queen's name!"

Aaron gave ready defense. "Don't you remember the story of how the queen received her son?" he countered. "Was he not borne on the waves of your sacred Nile, carried directly into her hands? He was not of royal blood, but the son of slaves, spared by Jehovah to save his people!"

Now the crowd murmured, divided over Aaron's account. Even the slaves mocked him. "The one beside you is no Israelite!" they cried. "He is ruddy as the riverbanks!"

"And I am not?" Aaron returned. "See my face? Is it not also dark? And yet you all know me as the son of Amram and Jochebed! This is my brother, prince of

Egypt and savior of Israel! You would do well to bow, and not to mock!"

Moses wished Aaron would not go so far. He was uneasy enough already. Looking again toward the walls, he cleared his throat and tapped his brother on the shoulder.

Aaron, caught up in his own rhetoric, jolted at his touch. But he moved aside as Moses stepped forward.

"Men of Israel!" Moses called, his voice not so dramatic, "The God of your fathers, the God of Abraham, Isaac, and Jacob, has appeared to me, saying, 'I am indeed concerned about you and what you have suffered in Egypt!'"

Surprised at his own boldness, he tried not to think of the consequences. As the crowd stood riveted to his words, he gained courage.

"'Therefore,' says the Lord, 'I will bring you out of the affliction of Egypt and lead you to the land of the Canaanite and the Hittite and the Amorite and the Perizzite and the Hivite and the Jebusite, to a land that flows with milk and honey!'"

Yes, those had been the words of the Lord. He remembered them exactly. And though he did not know it, his face was radiant with zeal as he spoke them, his voice ringing with authority.

As he paused, quaking at his own courage, he found that a hush of awe had overcome the crowd. Even Aaron looked at him in amazement.

No man made a move against him; even the guards upon the walls were astonished at his speech. But gradually, as the crowd whispered among themselves, dissension again manifested itself.

"Ha!" someone challenged. "So you say the Lord has sent you? Just who is this Lord of whom you speak? If you are a son of Israel, tell us his name!"

Now this was a fair test. Most folks knew that the Israelites worshiped Jehovah. No one was afraid to say the name. But only those reared in the most orthodox circles of the race had been privileged to hear the true form of the word.

"Jehovah" was a substitute for "Yahweh," which only the most respected Israelites, family priests or patriarchs, were allowed to pronounce. Any slave present would have been impressed if Moses had used the holy name.

But God had told Moses just how to answer, the day he had spoken to him from the burning bush. And his answer would be even more profound than the Israelites could have wished.

Drawing strength from a source beyond himself, Moses threw back his shoulders and closed his eyes, repeating the words that the Lord had given him.

"The Lord, the God of your fathers, the God of Abraham, the God of Isaac and the God of Jacob, has sent me to you! I AM WHO I AM is his name! I AM has sent me to you!"

Suddenly, as though a mighty wind passed through the crowd, the people gasped. Like the voice of the sea was the sound of their amazement, as the elders looked at Moses through tear-filled eyes, and the young people pondered the mystical words.

It had been perhaps generations since the name of God had been so clearly interpreted. Even the use of Yahweh was not so profound. On a tide of wonder, the words were passed from mouth to mouth, and Aaron stepped to the front of the rickety platform.

"Hear this, Israel!" he cried. "Today the very words of God are spoken!"

As Aaron repeated the message that Moses had given, again acting as his spokesman, Moses knew what the Lord would require next. There was one thing God had not allowed him to shirk, and which Aaron could not do for him.

He must take his staff in his hand and perform the signs which the Almighty had commanded in the wilderness.

Even as Aaron went on, Moses again took the lead from him and raising his eyes toward heaven, breathed a silent prayer. Then, waving the staff like a banner over his head, he cast it down upon the crates where, to the horror of all the people, it wriggled into the form of a snake, rising upon its tail and hissing.

Falling back, the audience crushed in upon itself. "See, Israel, the power of your God!" Aaron cried, stepping away from the gyrating creature.

Without a pause, Moses bent down and grasped the serpent by its tail. Just as before, it returned instantly to its original form, a compliant staff within the shepherd's hand.

"Thus says the Lord," Aaron declared, throwing back his arms, "'I have surely seen the affliction of my people, and have given heed to their cry because of their taskmasters. For I am aware of their sufferings! So I have come down to rescue them from the power of the Egyptians, and to bring them up from that land to a large and good land, to a land that flows with milk and honey!'"

Moans and weeping flooded through the crowd as slaves moved forward like a wave, pressing in about the flimsy stage.

Heedless of the Egyptians all about them, they bowed down in worship or stood boldly, hands raised to the sky.

Those who had known beatings and days of endless oppression, lifetimes of toil and hopelessness, suddenly cried for joy. And spontaneous songs, sung for years in dreary tradition, muttered for centuries among the chained and shackled, swelled through the throng, taking on volume and new meaning.

"Milk and honey!" they chanted, repeating the ancient phrases. "We shall have milk and honey!"

As their tears flowed and their songs rose, so their dreams reawakened, dreams long stifled and hardly ever believed, of a promised land whose very breezes were the breath of God.

46

Had ever an Egyptian lived so long as Jannes? He had not been a young man when Moses's grandfather, King Thutmose I, had been alive. And he had now seen the rise of that king's grandson to the throne.

Sometimes he lost count of the administrations he had advised. The various pharaohs to whom he had ministered blended embarrassingly in his memory. It was hard for him to recall just who had built this or that monument, who had warred in this or that province, who had quelled which riot, who had passed what law. Of all the monarchs whose lives he had overseen and whose souls he had guided, Hatshepsut alone stood out.

This was not only because she was a woman. It was because she cared as much for justice and peace as for fame and glory.

Moses would have been like her, Jannes knew. But Moses had been cut off in his prime. Jannes had grieved for him, as surely as if he had died. And he had prayed for him to the many gods of Egypt.

Once, in desperation, when Moses had been gone for several months, and when Hatshepsut swore her heart would not recover, Jannes had even prayed to Jehovah. He had not known just what to say to the desert god. But he had tried to reach his ears, just in case...in case he might have some power in the matter.

That one prayer had left him miserable. Never had the old priest been miserable when he prayed. He knew the gods of Egypt, and with them he had influence. Sometimes he even felt superior to them and wondered why they seemed always to need his advice.

But Jannes would never forget the single time he had invoked the blessing of Jehovah. He had felt very awkward doing so, and the prayer had been followed by strange dread, as though Jannes treaded on ground too holy.

Quickly he had passed over the impression, not allowing it to burrow through his soul. But he had never forgotten it. And he had never prayed to that god again.

Still the memory of Moses was as fresh as yesterday. Whenever the present king called for Jannes in the stateroom, the old man felt a lump in his throat. He loathed Thutmose III. Though he had served his administration nearly four decades, Jannes still thought of him as Moses's rival.

No, no one had ever lived so long in Egypt as the ancient priest. Yet for Jannes, life had stopped the day Hatshepsut died, the day the hope of Moses's kingship died with her. On that day Thutmose III had taken over, and there was no reason to hope.

The old priest, his bald head bowed beneath the wall torches, passed down the king's corridor, answering a stateroom summons. He knew he was old beyond accounting because he lived more in the past every day. The ghosts of yesteryear were, in fact, more real to him than the living, breathing people with whom he must interact. The corners of the palace were full of whispers, conversations that lived in his memory word for word. And the rooms were full of apparitions, each room he looked into.

Just now as he shuffled toward the meeting place, he glanced into his old classroom, the one where he had taught countless young princes the ways of the court and the dogmas of Egyptian theology. His teaching duties had long ago passed to men younger and more energetic. But the challenging students whom he had instructed over the years still called out to him as he passed by, waving and smiling as they had always done, though now they were only a dream.

"Oh, Moses...Moses..." he whispered, shaking his head as he walked and tapping his cane abjectly against the tiled floor. The stateroom guards saw him muttering to himself as he approached, and they looked at one another from the corners of their eyes. Jannes knew what they thought. He often muttered to himself, and people thought he was senile.

But he was not senile. He was only lonely. If it had been Moses who summoned him to this meeting, he would be stepping lively. He would not have withered in his advancing age. As it was, his heart had died a long time ago, and he did not care what anyone thought of his muttering.

"Jannes," Thutmose hailed him as he entered, "there is a commotion in the streets!"

The announcement jolted the priest from his sad reflections.

"Commotion?" he repeated, a little absently.

"You know nothing of it?" the king barked.

"I did not know there was one. How should I know anything of it?" Jannes countered.

It was Jannes's way with Thutmose to always be taciturn. He did not cooperate because he did not care.

"Old man," the king breathed, trying to keep his temper, "what use are your charts and your star-maps if you cannot prepare me for such things?"

Although Thutmose's reign had begun as anything but peaceable, and despite his Cretin looks, he had established himself by a remarkably efficient administration. Surprising his critics, the past several years of his reign had gone smoothly. He had followed in his grandfather's footsteps, pushing the empire's boundaries to their farthest limits. And he would eventually go down in history as the greatest of the Pharaohs.

Nonetheless, from the moment he ascended the throne, factions who loved Hatshepsut had resented him. His attempts to eradicate her memory had estranged him further from many of his people.

Jannes especially had little respect for the man. Walking to the great arch which commanded a view of the main street and the marketplace, he saw that a restive crowd was indeed gathering outside the compound. "It could not be much," he said, shrugging.

In his heart, however, he hoped it was much. Whatever had stirred up the people, he secretly delighted in Thutmose's discomfort.

"There is strange news circulating," the king whined, gesturing to a small group of police who stood at attention before the throne. "Laughable... but strange."

Jannes had always hated the king's querulous voice. He could have sworn it had not changed with puberty, but still bore that grating pitch that had made him such an obnoxious, though bright, student.

Yet his words were intriguing.

Commotions in the streets of this city were not unusual. Crime was a problem, as were the inevitable uprisings when people went hungry or when workers were too much oppressed. Raamses had been remarkably peaceful under the queen. But those days were over and still it was more than a commotion that troubled Thutmose.

"What is this news?" Jannes asked the soldiers. "Speak."

The lead officer cleared his throat, uncomfortable with the assignment. "We were on the wall today, Your Holiness, when a group of slaves upset the marketplace. Two of them, claiming to be brothers, stirred up the people with most peculiar talk."

"Yes, yes," Jannes muttered impatiently. "So what did they say?"

The big guard looked at his companions and shrugged. "One of them introduced the other as... Prince Moses, son of Hatshepsut."

Jannes's hand flew to his chest, as if to shield his aging heart. "Say again," he whispered, shooting a keen glance at the speaker.

"Moses, sir," the embarrassed man reported. "But... surely it cannot be true."

At the mention of the name, however, the breeze of hope blew across the ember of a dream, and Jannes's spirit, so long dormant, was aroused.

Saying nothing, he bored through the guard with an insistent stare. Yes, there was more to the story, and it soon came forth.

"The two brothers claim that the god of Israel has sent them—has sent Moses in particular—to set the people free."

No one in the room—neither Thutmose, nor the guards, nor the half-dozen counselors who stood by— could have known what such words evoked within the old man. As if it had not been 70 years ago, he remembered young Moses debating the injustices of the Egyptian system in his very own classroom. He remembered coming upon him in his chamber and finding the forbidden Hebrew mantle in his hands. He remembered the countless nights when he had watched the young man creep out of the palace, thinking himself unobserved as he headed for the fellowship of the slave village. And he remembered the lad's fascination with all things Israelite. Most especially with the Hebrew God.

A tremor started deep within the elder's heart and worked its way outward until he feared he might sink to his knees. But no one in the room saw this. He gripped his cane more tightly and steadied himself against the wake.

"These men," he managed, "where are they now?"

"They have been arrested, Holiness," the guard replied. "Shall we bring them to you?"

47

Perhaps it was because he had known Moses since infancy, perhaps because the prince had spent more time in his presence than with anyone else, that the priest recognized him immediately. Jannes had witnessed the growth of Moses's mind and spirit as no one else on earth had been privileged to do. If anyone had ever been a son to the old man, Moses had.

Jannes had never spoken his heart to the prince. He knew, in fact, that Moses had feared him, thinking he might betray the secret of his heritage to the court.

But this was only because the priest had never confided to the lad the abiding love he had for him.

Not even Aaron, Amram, or Jochebed had recognized Moses as easily as Jannes did. It did not matter that his arrival was announced beforehand, or that he stood in the palace stateroom where the priest had seen him a hundred times. The old man would have known him in the darkest alley of a foreign city as easily as here. Despite the dusty robes and the beard, so un-Egyptian and unregal, despite the 40 years' absence and the character they had imprinted on the fugitive's bearded face, Jannes would have known him anywhere.

The old man knew likewise that Moses remembered him. The moment the insurgent stepped into the room, his eyes flitted only briefly toward the king and then settled with great feeling upon the shriveled priest. Like a vapor the years dissipated, leaving the two to confront the chasm of disparate beliefs that had always separated them.

At one time their differences had been merely philosophical, affording scholarly challenge and schoolroom debate. But as the prince had come into his own, he had begun to act on his views. And now, a lifetime later, his faith would challenge the empire.

Jannes and Moses did not greet one another as Aaron and the Israelite leaders filed into the room. There was no time for pleasantries as the king mounted his throne, ready to address the troublemakers.

Outside, the growing masses, both slave and free, pressed in against the palace gates. A mighty swell of sound rose from the streets, and here and there the Israelites continued the song they had sung in the marketplace. Chanting and bold demands thrilled through the crowd, and the names of Moses and Aaron rose on the warm air, threats of war.

As the king poised himself on the edge of his throne, his simian eyes betrayed that he, like Jannes, recognized Moses. He had no more affinity for his rival now than 40 years ago, and his strident tone said as much.

"So, it *is* you!" he snarled, leaning forward and studying his old enemy. "Beneath the hair and the sand I see the face of Moses!"

Aaron would have made retort, but Moses nudged him to be silent.

"What is your playact this time?" Thutmose laughed. "You were always a great impostor, pretending to the throne when you had no right. Do you pose now as a shepherd chief?"

Aaron tensed, and Moses moved forward. Bowing his head in deference to the king's position, he spoke forthrightly.

"I am no longer the son of Hatshepsut," Moses began. "I come to you now as a son of Abraham, Isaac, and

Jacob. I bring you word from the God of Israel, saying
'Let my people go!' "

Thus was all protocol set aside, leaving the king
stunned at the sand flea's boldness.

Looking about the court, Thutmose sought an explanation. But his advisers, muttering among themselves,
were no help.

"The god of Israel?" the king spat. "You threaten me
with the god of slaves?"

Moses, unmoved, only repeated, "Thus says the Lord,
the God of Israel, 'Let my people go into the wilderness,
that they may hold a feast to me there.' "

"Ha!" cried the king. "Do you forget that you are a fugitive from justice? A criminal, untried and unpunished?
How dare you make demands?"

Hoshea and Caleb, who had come with the others
from Amram's house, stood behind their hero with worried faces. Indeed, his life was at risk, and they could be
counted among his accomplices.

But Moses remembered the words of the Lord, that all
those who had sought his life had passed away. Understanding, now, that he was a legend among the people
whose cries filled the streets, he knew that Thutmose
would risk great public displeasure, should he move
against him.

"Do as you will unto me, O King," Moses answered.
"Only, let my people go!"

The rush of sound outside was increasing, shaking the
very walls of the royal mansion. Thutmose rubbed his
hands along the arms of his chair and glanced at Jannes.
But the old priest had buried his nose in a scroll and
busied himself with note-taking.

Nevertheless, Pharaoh seemed to address his next
question as much to the old theologian as to Moses. "Who
is this 'Lord' that I should obey his voice?" he hissed. "I
do not know the Lord, and I shall never let Israel go!"

If the king had been sensitive to the priest's response, he might have been more cautious. A twitch worked down the old man's jaw at Thutmose's flippant talk, and his quill quivered in his hand. The wizard knew that Jehovah was a force to be reckoned with. And he wondered, now, if he shouldn't have warned the king.

Swallowing hard, Jannes looked up from his idle work.

Aaron had taken the floor and pressed the monarch with political savvy. "Should the king risk the well-being of his many slaves?" he challenged. "The God of the Hebrews has met with us. Please, let us go a three days' journey into the wilderness, that we may sacrifice to the Lord our God, or he may fall upon us with pestilence or with sword!"

Ah, thought Jannes, *this Aaron is a clever fellow!* The entire economy of Egypt depended on slave labor. How could Thutmose know but what this obscure god might indeed take such action?

But this king was just as headstrong as his grandfather, Thutmose I. He was no more prone to listen to reason or to be cautious than his forebear.

Jannes braced himself as the emperor rose up from his throne and pointed an angry finger at the brazen Hebrews. "Moses and Aaron," he shouted, "cease your foolishness! Why do you entice the people from their work? Get back to your labors!"

As though the masses outside the palace knew what proceeded within, their chanting became louder, their demands more insistent.

Darting an anxious eye toward the archway, the king tried to keep his composure. He knew that there were thousands beyond the gate, perhaps tens of thousands.

Still he was unrelenting.

"Look!" he cried, gesturing toward the arch, "the people of the land are now many, and you would have them rest from their labors?"

Furious, he stepped down from his throne and went to the opening. Jannes knew the look upon his face. It was the same look which had often colored the face of his grandfather, revealing an obstinate pride that only grew more unreasonable when challenged.

But, it was more than this. It was the look... Oh, when had Jannes first seen it?

Suddenly, like a tourniquet, the memory tightened itself about the priest's heart. Arising from the deep recesses of his spirit, it pushed forward like a fist, gripping his soul in a stranglehold.

It had been long ago. So long... ages and ages...

Eighty years ago!

Yet how could he have forgotten? Had it been suppressed by more than decades of time? Had it been suppressed by Jannes's own pride and resistant fear?

Now the memory was clear, coming back to haunt him like a prophecy fulfilled: the dream of a boy-child, which he had told to a long dead pharaoh.

As if it were yesterday, the priest remembered standing at the bedside of the lazy, headstrong king, the king whose equally proud descendant now paced the stateroom floor. "I have had a dream," the priest had announced. "I see a child... a Hebrew child. And then, he is no child, but a prince, garbed in Egyptian gold... and from his dark brow go forth the rays of divine ordination."

For the moment, Jannes did not know what time it was, what year, what century. He was not sure if the one who wore the crown this day was Thutmose I or II or III. His frail body quivered at the sound of the slaves outside, and he felt his breath hiss from his lungs.

"...Through his hair trickles the oil of anointing... and his tongue is like a sword... like a sword..."

Had those been his words? Yes. How could he have forgotten?

Suddenly the priest was speaking aloud, and the king stopped his pacing, glancing at him in bewilderment.

"In my dream, the prince is adored by thousands," Jannes said, reciting the very warning he had given long ago. "His believers slough off the chains of bondage, following their leader to freedom beyond Egypt's gates!"

Staring at the priest, Thutmose shook his head. "What is this babble, old man?" he quipped. "So you have found your voice, after all?"

Jannes could barely hear himself as he talked. It seemed he slipped between realities, uncertain just which pharaoh he addressed.

"There is more, O King," he added. "But you cannot bear it now."

Thutmose I had been full of fear when he heard this. But the man who now stood before Jannes was not as easily shaken. Not comprehending what transpired within the priest's fragmented mind, he only laughed.

"Do not kill the babies..." Jannes groaned, reaching out a withered hand and clutching the king's sleeve. "Not again!"

"Madness!" Thutmose suddenly raved. "I am surrounded by madmen!"

Heading for his throne again, he fell into it and desperately surveyed his challengers. "Shall you toy with my patience forever?" he growled. "See what good comes from your threats! If your people have time for a trip to the wilderness, they must not have enough work to do!"

Motioning to the priest, he ordered him to record an edict.

"Tell the taskmasters, they are no longer to give the people straw to make bricks. Let them go and gather straw for themselves! But their quota of bricks shall remain the same. It shall not be reduced! They are lazy, with too much time on their hands. Therefore they cry out, 'Let us go and sacrifice to our god!'"

The king's face was livid, his tone enraged. "Let their labor be heavier, so they have no time for such folly!"

At this, Thutmose rose and hastened from the stateroom, his counselors cringing and his attendants white of face.

Aaron and Moses stood silent as the king passed by. Only Jannes said a word.

Muttering to himself, he passed the quill in incomprehensible scrawls across his vacant scroll.

"There is more, O King," he whispered, shaking his bald head, "but you cannot bear it now."

48

The parasol atop the king's royal cab swayed gently in the afternoon sun as Thutmose rode past his many work projects. Leaning out from under the concealing shadow, he pointed to a tall tower and spoke brightly to a small boy cradled on his lap.

"See, son, there it is," he said. "They are building it just for you."

The boy's dark eyes followed his father's finger, up, up the monolith. His cherubic lips parted in wonder.

"For me?" he repeated. "But what will I do with it?"

To his childish mind, such a gift had little practical use. He was accustomed to receiving fine presents, toys and games to occupy his pampered life. But what good was a stone tower?

Thutmose laughed. "Someday you will understand," he said. "When you are king, the tower will have your name upon it, so that all who pass by will think of you and pray to the gods for your well being. Is it not beautiful?"

The boy shrugged and pressed himself back against his father's chest. "I suppose," he sighed. "I want to go home now."

"In a moment," the king nodded. "I have one more stop to make."

At this, he directed the driver down the street in the direction of a great pit, where a thousand slaves were treading yellow mud with their bare feet.

"Here," the king ordered. "Stop the cab."

Taking his son by the hand, he stepped down from the seat and walked to the edge of the enormous mudhole. His bodyguards nervously paced beside him, wishing he would not be so public.

Scanning the muddy hollow, he was unmoved by the hopeless labor of the beleagured ones below. For two days the workers in the pit had tackled the futile task of pounding out clay fit for the making of bricks without straw to give the mud the right consistency.

Yet the king's decree could not be mistaken. The Hebrews were required to meet their daily quota, straw or no straw. And their foremen, people of their own race, were required to beat them when they failed.

Hunched with pain, most of the slaves had felt the sting of the whip, and they had no reason to expect they would escape more punishment. Despite the fact that an occasional wagonload of stubble was brought from the fields outside the city where other desperate slaves scrounged day and night, there was never enough to make a difference. The mud remained loose and wet, and the paltry deposits of dried grass were swallowed uselessly into the ooze.

As Pharaoh watched from the rim, a pallet was being hauled up the side of the pit, covered with a layer of mud loaves, lopsided and uneven. The little piles, which would not hold a rectangular shape, were supposed to be bricks, ready for drying in the sun. But anyone could see they were worthless.

A sneer passed over the king's face. Snapping his fingers, he called to the Israelite foremen who oversaw the quarry.

"You, there!" he shouted. "Let me see your records."

The foremen, realizing that the monarch had come out to check on them, bowed rigidly and walked up the slope toward him.

One of them bore a long, heavy whip in his hand, and its jagged lash was caked with blood. The man looked quite weary, and his face bore the stress of his job—a job which he had come to loathe, though it once represented power.

The other carried beneath his arm a clay tablet upon which were tallied the bricks produced this day. He knew the record would not please the king and hesitated to show it.

Saying nothing, the two men fell to their knees before Thutmose.

"The tablet," Pharaoh muttered.

Holding it forth in shaky hands, the second foreman cringed as the monarch took it. Both men watched in silence as anger darkened the king's face.

When at last Thutmose addressed them, staring at them from beneath his protruding brow, his voice was snakelike.

"Why have you not completed your required amount?" he asked, turning the tablet over and over. "Neither yesterday nor today have you made bricks as previously."

The men looked at each other, having no answer. Nor were they given time to formulate ones, before the king summoned the Egyptian taskmasters from the sidelines.

"Beat them," Thutmose snarled. And standing aside, he drew his son close, whispering, "See what becomes of the enemies of Pharaoh."

The taskmasters, too, bore whips in their hands. These were used to keep the foremen in line, and were not so worn or bloody as those of the Hebrew overseers. But they were equally effective when called into action.

The young prince clung to his father's skirt as the beating commenced, and he put his hands to his ears as the foremen cried out.

But Pharaoh would not let him cover his eyes. He must become used to such sights if he were to rule with power.

When 30 stripes had been administered, 15 for each

foreman, the king called a halt. "Enough!" he commanded. "Perhaps they will do better now."

As the Egyptian taskmasters bowed and backed away, the foremen struggled to their knees, the flesh of their backs quivering with bloody welts.

The recordkeeper, however, did not cower before the king. Daring to speak, he demanded, "Why do you deal this way with your servants? There is no straw, yet they keep saying to us, 'Make bricks!' Here we are being beaten, but it is the fault of your own people!"

Incredulous, Thutmose glared at the presumptuous Hebrew. "You are lazy!" he cried. "Very lazy! This is why you say, 'Let us go and sacrifice to the Lord.'"

Turning for his cab, he led his son away. "Go now. Get back to work!" he spat over his shoulder. "You shall be given no straw. But you must deliver your quota of bricks!"

As the king settled into his cab, he pulled the parasol close to his face and, without so much as a glance back, ordered the driver to take him home.

As the foremen watched him leave, they rose to their feet and turned for the pit again, helping each other to walk.

But the recordkeeper stopped short, caught by the sight of two Israelites standing nearby.

"Look," he whispered to his partner. "See who takes pleasure in our suffering."

It was Aaron and Moses who stood upon the rim, only just arrived. Staring up at them, the first foreman spat, "So, have you come to save us? Some good all your promises have done!"

"We were told there was trouble here," Moses called. Drawing near, he looked through tear-dimmed eyes upon the beaten men. "I will summon the physicians," he said. "Sit here in the shade."

With this, he tried to lead the men to a palm-sheltered corner of the quarry. But they would have none of it.

Pulling away, the recordkeeper grumbled, "May the Lord look upon you and judge you! For you have made us loathsome in the sight of Pharaoh and his servants. You have put a sword in their hands—a sword to kill us!"

49

It was twilight along the Nile. Moses walked the bank in desolate silence.

He had left Aaron at the mud pit, telling him he would join the family at Amram's house later in the evening. And he had chosen the solitude of the riverbank, wishing to be alone.

It seemed he was the desperate prince again, as though 40 years had not intervened between himself and the night he had last paced this bank in the dark. It had been at this very place that the river had called to him, tempting him to jump, to end his miserable existence and solve the dilemma of his double life.

It had been the following morning that he had witnessed the beating of the Hebrew slave in the sandlot. And it had been at that moment that he had acted out his frustration, violently taking the life of the fat Egyptian slaveowner.

How the incidents of his past had a way of repeating themselves! As he stumbled through the riverside's graying light, the incident at the mud pit and the scene in the sandlot blended together. It must have been the hand of the Lord that spared him the witness of the foremen's flogging. He knew he would have tried to intervene, that he could no more have stood by uninvolved today than 40 years ago.

Why, he wondered, had God returned him to Egypt? Was it only to show him that nothing had changed, that his people were just as oppressed as ever, and that he was helpless to save them? Sometimes Jehovah seemed no more than a cruel jokester, whose chief delight lay in revealing to men their hopelessness.

It would not have mattered if Moses had lifted a hand to help. Years before when he had done so, his Israelite brothers had scorned him as a murderer. Today when he had arrived late upon the scene, he was accused of instigating the cruelty, of making life even harder for his people, and of putting a sword in Pharaoh's hand.

Dark was descending quickly. As Moses paced the Nile's persistent current, he steadied his feet upon the slippery bank. For an instant it seemed he might fulfill the river's seductive command. How easy it would be to free himself from the riddle of his life!

But as he slid to the ground, he dug his heels into the wet earth and cried out, "O Lord, where are you? Have you forgotten me? Have you forgotten all of us?"

He had not noticed the humming song of crickets along the shore. But as he cried out, the low droning ceased, and he felt its absence keenly. The silence surrounding him was abysmal. Save for the mocking rush of the water, he was alone.

Still he cried again in desperation, "Why do you hurt my people? Why did you ever bring me back? Ever since I came to Pharaoh to speak in your name, he has done harm to my people. And you have not delivered us at all!"

Anger at the carelessness of God, at his seeming disregard for the atrocities and injustices of the world, welled up from Moses's heart. Burying his face in the dirt, he wept, deep, throaty spasms shaking his body. Whether he wept for himself or for others was unimportant. For he suffered with all the oppressed of earth.

But as he cried, the rushing current seemed to bear the whisper of a voice, and this time the voice was not mocking.

This one did not woo him to destruction, but seemed the voice of the very one who had made the river and all the world about.

"I am the Lord," it said. "Now you shall see what I will do to Pharaoh."

Quivering, Moses lifted his tear-stained face, scanning the gray waters.

Again it came. "I am the Lord. I appeared to Abraham, Isaac, and Jacob...and I established my covenant with them...I have heard the groaning of the children of Israel...and I have remembered my covenant...I will redeem you with an outstretched arm and with great judgments...I am the Lord."

50

Over the next two weeks, only the promise of the Lord received upon the bank of the Nile kept Moses from losing heart.

As he tried to reassure his people of God's plan, he met with nothing but angry scoffing.

A second meeting with Pharaoh produced equally frustrating results. For the king put Moses and Aaron to a test, insisting that they prove themselves and their god by a display of miraculous signs.

Twice, the sons of Amram showed that the power of Yahweh was with them, as they fulfilled the Lord's instructions given to Moses in the wilderness. The sacred staff became a wriggling serpent, astonishing Pharaoh and his court. And the morning following, in confrontation with the forces of darkness, Moses and Aaron turned the waters of the Nile and all the reservoirs of Egypt, large and small, a fetid blood-red.

While the country often contended with a seasonal change in its rivers, streams, and reservoirs because of the infusion of decomposing organic matter and the proliferation of invisible plants, the blight Aaron produced when he passed his rod over the earth caused an actual alteration in the water's composition. Never before had the streams been putrified and undrinkable, and never before had the fishes and animal life within the sacred river died off.

To the brothers' dismay, however, the king called for his magicians, commanding that even old Jannes appear; and he ordered them to show their own secret arts.

When the magicians proved that their craft could also change the waters of the Nile to "blood," they convinced the king that Yahweh was nothing to fear. And when Aaron threw down the staff before the throne of Pharaoh, the wizards and magicians who had accompanied Jannes into the stateroom matched the miracle with mighty works of their own. They, too, had brought sticks in their hands—the long, silver wands with which they worked their magic. No sooner did the shepherd staff become a serpent, twisting upon the ceramic floor, than a dozen others joined it, the priestly batons hissing and slithering all about.

The fact that Aaron's staff raised itself full length from the floor, and one by one, picked off the others, swallowing them head to tail, did not persuade Pharaoh to relent.

Today, the last day of the second week, Moses marched with Aaron down the Boulevard of the Gods, heading once again for the royal house. He tried not to think about the old priest, whose shriveled face haunted him day and night. He tried not to think in terms of doing battle with the kindly fellow. But he knew they were indeed locked in spiritual warfare, Jannes representing the forces of Egypt, and Moses the will of the Lord.

Had it not always been this way? From the time Moses had been a young student in Jannes's classroom, he had been compelled to debate with the priest. Over time the debates had become more than a game of rhetorical exchange. They had taken on philosophical importance, indicating a mysterious difference between the two thinkers, a difference which was now clearly defined.

Still Moses hated to be at odds with Jannes. Throughout their recent deadlocked interchanges, the Israelite often found Jannes's eyes upon him. Sad eyes they were.

Not vengeful. Not full of spite. It seemed, in fact, that the old man loved him, and always had. It seemed the warfare in which they engaged was nothing Jannes would have chosen.

The last seven days had brought great misery throughout the land. The waters were only now returning to normal, and for the past week the people of Egypt had been forced to dig new wells, lest they thirst to death.

It was time for the Lord to move in stronger force. Pharaoh's heart had only been hardened by the volley of miraculous acts performed by the Hebrew leaders and his own wizards.

As Moses and Aaron approached the palace, leading their disciples, they were taunted and jabbed by their own people. Rumors of their encounters with the priests had won them no support, and the Israelites hated them for the hollow hope they offered.

It was some comfort to know that the young men, Hoshea and Caleb, were close behind. Over the past days, Moses had come to appreciate their supportive presence. Even now as the company neared the guards stationed at the palace entrance, Hoshea leaned close and whispered, "The Lord is with you."

Moses glanced back at him, taking courage from the smile in his kind, dark eyes.

The palace guards, knowing that Moses needed no introduction, admitted the company to the front lobby. "Pharaoh is in the porch of the baths," the head guard said. "You will have to wait."

"I think not," Moses replied. "We will see him there."

When the shepherd and his followers pushed past the astonished sentries, they did not lift a weapon to stay them, for they had heard of the powers displayed by the sons of Amram.

The hallways and chambers of the palace were etched upon Moses's memory. With unerring directness, he led his people to the king's suite, and once there, pushed past another set of guards who stood watch outside the spa.

The broad porch, which commanded a view of the Nile and was rimmed by large pools, had always been the most pleasant and luxurious part of the royal house. Though Moses had been a prince, he had been privileged to enter it only a few times in his life. It had been upon those rare occasions that he had felt closest to his grandfather, Thutmose I, for it was then that the king actually touched him, drawing him onto his lap and speaking to him as to a son.

Resisting those memories, Moses braced his heart. He was here for no sentimental reason, but to call down judgment on Israel's oppressors.

His unexpected arrival created no small stir in the porch. Thutmose III lay upon a narrow cushion, face down, when Moses and Aaron barged toward him. Several bare-breasted concubines hovered over the king, massaging his back and his forehead, giggling in his ears, as a band of court musicians played erotic rhythms for a klatch of dancing girls. This was Pharaoh's private place, his most intimate domain. At the entrance of the slaves and shepherds, the careless spell of pleasure was broken.

Lurching upright, the masseuses quickly pulled light shawls across their torsos, and the dancers stopped in midbeat. The music ceased, and Pharaoh, bleary-eyed, turned in bewilderment toward the visitors.

Sitting up on his pallet, the king sputtered, "How dare you? I'll have your necks!" Grabbing a towel, he wiped his forehead and called for the guards.

But Moses spoke forthrightly. "Have you learned nothing, O King? Why do you still resist the will of the Lord?"

Gesturing toward the pools, he sniffed in disgust. "Are these the royal baths, Your Majesty? Why is no one bathing today?"

Of course, he referred to the scarlet sheen of the waters, the blood-like residue which had not yet been eradicated. Day after day, fresh water from distant wells had been hauled to the palace for deposit in these pools. But the crimson curse was still in evidence.

"Guards!" the king repeated.

"It will do you no good to resist," Aaron said. "You seek your own destruction when you avoid Jehovah's command."

When the sentries hastened into the room, responding to their master's call, they brought another surprise visitor, the high priest.

Jannes needed no invitation to enter the king's suite. He had access to him at all times, a privilege he did not hesitate to exercise and which was no end of consternation to the monarch.

"Call off the guards!" the old man demanded. "We need not resort to force."

How was it that the king always felt like a child when Jannes was near? Squirming upon his pallet, Thutmose objected. "But...the intruders have no right..."

"Let us hear what Moses has to say," the priest insisted. Deferring to the Hebrew, he waited.

"I have a word from the Lord," Moses began. "You have heard it before. 'Let my people go, that they may serve me!'"

Yes, they had heard it before. And there was no softening on Thutmose's part. His expression was as hard as ever.

"Ha!" he laughed. "Do you not tire of this, Moses? Your god is no greater than the least of Egypt's gods. Haven't my magicians proved this? Why should I let my servants go?" Pulling his towel over his head, he sighed lazily.

But it was Aaron who spoke next, his forceful manner demanding attention. "Take heed, Thutmose," he warned, lifting his rod in his hand, "and take heed, priest of Egypt. Is not the Nile your sacred river? Yet the Lord has shown power over the Nile. And do you not have a thousand other gods, great and small? The alligator and the cat and the baboon, and even the frog? Jehovah will show himself greater than all your gods! For this is the word of the Lord: 'If you refuse to let my people go, behold, I will smite your whole empire with frogs. The Nile will overflow with frogs. They will come up and go into your house and into your bedroom and onto your bed! They will enter the houses of your servants. They shall crawl upon your people, and shall burrow into your ovens and into your kneading bowls! Yes,'" he cried, passing his rod over the room, his eyes wide and wild, "'the frogs will come upon you and your household and all your servants!' Thus says the Lord!"

As Aaron's warning echoed through the glossy hallways, fading into rafters far away, Thutmose sat like a horrified statue.

Jannes's ears burned as he contemplated the blasphemous curse. Surely the frog was not the greatest of Egypt's gods. It was one of the least. But it *was* a god, and it was spawned by the fertile waters of the Nile, making it a kindred spirit to the holy river.

Scanning the red waters that flowed past the broad porch, he shuddered. How was it that Jehovah could turn the gods of Egypt against their own worshipers? Such a thing made no sense in his theology. But his fretful musing was interrupted.

"So, priest," the king sneered, "have you nothing to say? Shall you let these sand fleas profane our deities?"

Jannes heard the frantic plea within the question. But he had no answer.

The sun was setting across the Nile. The evening sound of croaking frogs, low and distant, was the only reply.

Always before, that sound had been a comfort, soothing away the tension of each day. But tonight it was an omen, fearsome and foreboding.

51

Moonlight, red as the Nile waters, filtered through the summer dust above the streets of Raamses. Entering the high arch of a palace bedchamber, it touched the cheek of a small boy, causing him to turn his face to the wall, but not waking him.

Upon this very bed, within this very room, another boy used to sleep—his dreams full of the grandeur of the court and of the fulfillment of his royal training.

This had once been Prince Moses's room. Now it was occupied by the son of Thutmose III.

The boy was a handsome child, taking after previous strains of the family rather than his father. Anyone seeing him here might even have thought him to be young Moses, except for his fair, olive complexion.

Tonight his dreams took him to the foot of the obelisk that the king had shown him a few days before. In childish fantasy he scaled it, reaching the pinnacle and standing atop it like a god.

But suddenly the dream became a nightmare as a flying lizard, wet and cold, slipped down from heaven and placed its clammy claw upon his shoulder.

Lurching awake, the boy drew a fearful breath and rubbed his eyes. He found he was not atop a tower, but was only in his room. He should have felt safe, but something was wrong.

The clammy feel of the visionary lizard still clung to his bare shoulder. Wiping the spot with one hand, he recoiled. The skin was damp—cold and damp—as though some amphibious creature had actually rested there.

Stifling a cry, he peered through the darkness toward the hazy, red moon. Its strange scarlet glow illumined his floor, and he thought he saw movement along the tiles.

The prince drew up his knees and tried, with admirable maturity, to reason with himself. He had not had many nightmares in his life. The few times he had called out for his governess, she had assured him, by fetching a lamp and surveying each cranny of the chamber, that there was nothing to fear. He was too big, he thought, to call her this time.

Yet now the movement seemed to carry a sound, a slopping, padding sound, as though someone or something walked through a puddle on his floor.

Crawling to the edge of his bed, the boy got courage for a closer look. What met his wide, round eyes was more horrifying than the dream.

For through the crimson darkness, other eyes stared into his—small, beady, moonlit—the eyes of a hundred little demons.

Gasping, he drew back only to find that his bed was now occupied, dozens of the slimy creatures sitting on his linens and lining the pillow pile.

His bravery vanished, and from his chest arose a piercing cry. "Dofda!" he squealed. "Dofda!"

Over and over he shouted the word, the Egyptian name for the sacred river frog.

He did not cry out for his nanny. As hysteria overtook him, he instead called for his father, tears running down his face.

"Papa! Papa!" he shrieked. "Help me!"

Instantly his cries were echoed by his wet, green companions. Their mouths agape, as though they mocked him, they set about croaking until the room was bedlam.

From down the hall came the boy's governess, half-a-dozen guards, and the old priest, Jannes.

By the time they reached him, he had worked himself into a frenzy. Frogs were loping over his bed and crawling up his arms and legs, the sticky suckers of their long toes clinging to his flesh like leeches.

Jannes brought a candle to the bedside and gazed in horror upon the ghastly spectacle. Never had he seen such a thing. He believed that the souls who passed through the netherworld endured such torments as part of their testing. But what he witnessed was taking place this side of Hades.

Quickly he began snatching the wriggling creatures from the boy's body, and the governess and guards followed suit.

But the faster they removed them, the faster they replaced themselves, swarming up from the archway, in from the hall—jumping, croaking, clinging.

"Summon the king!" Jannes commanded, shooing one guard from the room. "Tell him the curse is upon us!"

52

Pharaoh paced the top of the high wall surrounding his palace. The fortification was wide enough for a chariot to travel upon and provided a sweeping view of his capital city. Many a quiet evening he had spent walking here, proudly surveying his kingdom and commending himself for his many accomplishments.

Today, however, a dreadful stench rose on the warm air from the streets below. Though he had come here by choice, to oversee the grisly work being done on every corner and in every alley, he could barely contain his churning stomach.

Covering his nose with his sleeve, he called for his servant to hand over a vial of perfume brought along for the purpose of masking the odor. With liberal splashes he soaked his sleeve and breathed deep of the more pleasant aroma.

"When will they be done?" he growled. "Is there no end to the monsters?"

He referred to the project being carried out by slave crews, the piling up of dead, decaying frogs into heaps as they were removed from houses, silos, courtyards, and fields. Only after seven days of the atrocious plague and the invasion of the slimy creatures into every nook, every kneading trough, every bedchamber of the land, had Pharaoh again summoned Moses and Aaron to his stateroom.

Amazingly humble, he had wrung his hands, pleading, "Entreat the Lord, that he might remove the frogs from me and from my people! If you do, I will let the Israelites go, as you have asked."

Without hestitation, Moses had bowed. "As you ask," he replied. "Then you will know that there is no one like Jehovah."

Huge bonfires now raged throughout the land as the stinking heaps of rotting frogs were torched. A sickening pall of black smoke filled the sky.

"We think the job will be done by tomorrow," the servant answered. "It is a blessing the Israelites have stayed on to see it through."

The man meant no offense by what he said. But the king bristled at the remark.

Sensing his displeasure, the servant said no more, but he studied Thutmose's haughty face in wonder. Just days ago, the monarch had been desperate, forced to plead with his enemy like a helpless pawn. Tonight, as he watched the removal of the blight, he seemed to have regained his obstinate pride.

At last, unable to refrain himself, the servant dared to question. "You *do* mean to let the people go, don't you, Majesty?"

53

With unrelenting purpose, the Hand of God moved across the face of the land.

The people beneath the great Hand could not see it, bound as they were by their finite vision. But as the vengeance of the Lord took its unimpedable course, all who lived in Egypt, slave or free, rich or poor, powerful or weak, began to know the fear of Yahweh.

Day in and day out, two men especially represented the polarities of good and evil. Stationed at opposite ends of the capital city, separated by class, by race, and by heart, were Moses and Thutmose. Daily the antagonism between them grew.

All focus in the land was centered on these two, all thought, all conversation. Though the people went about their affairs as best they could, their minds were never off the battle raging between the shepherd and the emperor.

Week after week Moses trekked to the palace, calling down yet another act of God upon the unyielding king. Time after time the king repented, promising that if only Moses would remove a given curse, he would grant the Israelites their freedom. And plague after plague the monarch reversed himself, refusing to make good his word and keeping the slaves in bondage.

As the news went out each day regarding the most recent move on Moses's part and the king's vacillating temper, the two men became more than men in the people's eyes. They were archetypes of a universal battle—a battle that had always raged, but that was usually carried on in secret.

It was natural that the men to whom the nation looked should take on the very qualities they represented. Moses, once the reticent, self-effacing prophet, became less reticent with each encounter. Though he no longer wore the garb of royalty, and though he lived and ate with slaves, he carried himself with more confidence, walked taller, and spoke more boldly each time he confronted Pharaoh.

Thutmose, on the other hand, was shrinking within himself. Decked in the finest of clothes, surrounded by the luxuries of earth's highest station, he nonetheless seemed every day more monkey-like, less the king and more the hunched and fretting quarry of a cosmic cage.

Likewise, the two nations, Israelite and Egyptian, increasingly represented the two sides of the battle. For Yahweh had put a distinction between them that protected the Israelites from the worst consequences of the plagues.

Miraculous as the plagues were, the fact that they did not touch the children of Israel was even more mysterious. When the dust of the earth produced swarms of biting gnats, which hovered over and invaded every Egyptian house, the homes of the Israelites were spared. Not a welt or a sting marred the flesh of a child of Jacob, so that even the priests of Pharaoh were obliged to acknowledge, "This is the finger of God!"

Then came insects in greater numbers, larger and more vicious. Still the mighty king would not yield, thinking to bargain with the Lord and sneering in the face of his prophet.

When the livestock of Egypt were attacked by an invisible pestilence, left to writhe in torturous death upon the streets and fields, Pharaoh's heart was full of fear. But seeing that not one horse, donkey, camel, flock, or herd of the Israelites had been affected, he simply took them for himself and spat at the feet of Moses and Aaron.

There were, of course, other slaves in Egypt besides the Israelites. The way in which the catastrophes affected them was yet further evidence of God's power. For those ethnic groups who were closest and most sympathetic to the children of Israel were least troubled by the round of torments.

The Lord's favoritism displayed itself most clearly on the day the hail and lightning came.

That day opened with the sunshine and soft breezes typical of the Nile Valley. Of course, evidence of the most recent devastations was to be seen on every hand. The streets were filled with rotting carcasses and the stench of decimated cattle yet to be removed. Flies buzzed in and out of every window, driving householders to near madness. But at least the plagues of bugs and disease had been lifted, and the country was in the process of cleaning up. The crops in the fields had been ravaged by insects. But there was hope that the stubble of life yet visible might produce enough food for the coming year.

The most dreadful reminder of the Lord's vengeance was in the bodies of the people themselves. As they went about their tasks in city and field, the majority worked against the pain of crippling boils—putrid, running sores inflicted upon every man and beast of the enemies of God.

Throughout the months of plague and pestilence, people became accustomed to starting their days in conference. Before going to the fields or to their various jobs in the city, they would gather together in the market or along the roads to hear the latest word from the prophets. The plague of boils was still in process when news came that Moses and Aaron predicted devastating climactic changes.

"'Behold,'" Moses quoted the Lord, "'I will send a very heavy hail, such as has not been seen in Egypt since the day it was founded!'"

Giving ample warning, he told the people to prepare by bringing their livestock and possessions in from the fields. Every man and beast remaining in the open when the hail came would surely die.

Despite all evidence, however, many persisted in unbelief. Stubbornly logical, they reasoned away the former plagues, attributing them to quirks of nature or to temporary disruption of the elements. Forgetting the frogs, the lice, and the bloody waters, and even disregarding the present plague of running sores, they refused to accept that a minor deity could upset the temperate climate of their sacred land.

Therefore, the day of the hail and lightning found many men, women, children, and beasts of labor working unsheltered in the fields, roaming the streets and totally unprepared for the prophecy's fulfillment. While many of the slaves who were forced to work outdoors may have believed in Moses and Aaron, they were not granted safety if their masters and mistresses ignored the prediction.

When ugly clouds began to collect along the horizon, the hard-hearted foremen of the slave gangs paid them no mind. And when, by midafternoon, a strange, pelting rain moved between crackling streaks of lightning across the grainfields, it was a rare Egyptian slaveholder who called his people in.

As the rain descended to the rhythm of pealing thunder, the drops began to freeze, hardening and collecting upon themselves until they grew to the size of pomegranates. Like volleys spewed from mythic canons, the barrage smote the earth, crushing anything in its way—crops, wagons, animals, human beings. Barn roofs and house roofs buckled beneath the weight of the frozen artillery. Within half an hour, the valley floor was strewn with battered bodies.

Again however, a distinction had been made between the children of Jacob and all others. Though the Israelites and their sympathizers stumbled and cried as they fled, they managed, one and all, to escape the cataclysm.

Huddling together along the city walls or under any available roof, they gazed in horror across the ice-scattered wasteland.

Protruding from beneath heaps of hail were the arms and legs of countless Egyptians and their hapless cattle. Shaken and weeping, those who had been spared clung to one another, surveying the evidence of their God's discerning power and knowing now, more than ever, the intention of Yahweh to save them.

54

For months the curses of God had ravaged the land of Egypt. There was not much of Egypt left, stripped as it was of life, and of the potential for life.

What little greenery had not been spoiled by insects had nearly been obliterated by the hail. Then all other fragments of vegetation had been wiped out by locusts, the most recent devastation.

The only hope against starvation among those who had survived lay in the stockpiles of food stored in silos throughout the realm. But even this was meager comfort. There was no governor in Egypt like the famed Hebrew seer, Joseph, who centuries before followed God's guidance and told the king to amass seven years' worth of provisions. There was presently enough in the silos to see the people through only a few months.

Yet not even the most horrible plagues had humbled Thutmose III. His unprecedented stubbornness would not allow repentance. Since he believed himself to be the incarnation of the highest god, he continued to hold his fist to heaven, spitting in the face of Jehovah and his prophets. In time, he reasoned, the measly deity of slaves would run out of tricks, and Egypt would rise again. When it did, he told himself, it would be on an overwhelming tide of vengeance stored up by Osiris, Isis, Ra, and all the protective spirits of the Nile. Israel and her sympathizers would be squashed.

It was under the delusion of such logic that Thutmose made his way, this evening, down the bleak halls of his palace.

Had anyone observed him as he passed by the many chambers of his counselors and servants, he would have appeared less than mighty. Hunched in his simian posture, he hobbled against the pain of lesions and boils not yet healed. And he braced himself against the walls as he moved, his breathing hard and raspy.

But no one saw his dark passage through the corridors. There was a peculiar blackness to this night, a shadow almost palpable, that spilled through the streets and entered the palace like a stalking spirit. No one would have seen the king, had he come upon him face to face. For the darkness was so heavy it defied sight.

Yet the king denied even this phenomenon. The night was black because it was moonless, he reasoned, and its depressive quality was merely a reflection of his own withdrawn spirit.

Such was the thinking of one who considered himself divine. If he was sad or troubled, the world must necessarily be so. If the night was black and heavy, it was because the incarnate deity was depressed.

Just now he sought the only comfort he could be sure of. He would find his little son, draw him to his bosom, and listen to his gentle voice. In his son, his own life abode. As long as he had a son, he knew he was immortal.

He ignored the fact that the wall torches along the hallway were strangely smothered, giving off just enough hazy glow to show the door to his little boy's room. Feeling for the latch, he rapped lightly and entered on quiet feet.

"Son," he whispered.

"Papa!" the youngster replied. "Is it you? It is so dark, Papa!"

By the sound of the lad's voice, the king knew he had been crying. Feeling his way through the blackness, he reached his bed and sat down.

"Papa," the boy said again, "I have been afraid. I can feel the night against my skin."

Thutmose drew the lad to his heart and cradled his small head against his shoulder. From the dark outside the palace, the sound of soft weeping could be heard, arising from the houses of Raamses.

"Why do the mothers and children cry?" the prince asked. "Are they all afraid like me?"

Thutmose did not know how to answer. Earlier he had convinced himself that the eerie sound was just the wind. Now he knew it was the voice of fear pushing through the streets.

"These are hard times for our nation," he finally replied. "The people are very weary. But we must not despair. The mighty gods of Egypt will subdue our enemies."

The boy knew the "enemies" were the Israelites. But he wondered at the designation.

"Papa," he said innocently, "how is it that slaves have gained such power? Are they not less than the dogs of the earth?"

Pulling back, the king strained to see his son's face through the pall of black between them. Such a bright boy he was! But his pointed question was an embarrassment.

With a sigh, the king answered, "The Israelites worship an evil spirit. That spirit is stronger than we had thought. But the gods of Egypt have let him have his day. Any moment, they will take action, and then everyone will see that Ra and Osiris and Isis are supreme."

For a long while, the boy pondered this. Then, rising, he found his way to the tall window of his room. Looking out through the thick night, he called his papa to his side.

"But why," he said, "if the gods of Egypt are so great, is there no light in any house below? Only on the far side of town, in the houses of the Israelites, is there any light at all."

Amazed, the king scanned the morbid streets. Just as the prince pointed out, there was only blackness in every window and doorway of the Egyptian houses. But from the distant huddles of the slave compounds, scattered about the edges of the city, a warm glow emanated. Yes, from every hovel within the Israelite quarters, light penetrated the darkness in swordlike shafts!

At the witness of this phenomenon, the king's heart suddenly sank. None of the plagues and pestilences had affected him so much as this simple observation. There was light in the houses of the Israelites, and only darkness in all others!

While the boy could not clearly see his father, he could feel the man's body tremble.

"Oh, Papa!" the prince cried. "I did not mean to frighten you!"

Taking a deep breath, the king tried to turn things about. Had he not come here to reassure himself, to assure his own son of their glorious destiny?

"It is only the night breeze that makes me shiver," Thutmose lied. "It is chilly at this window."

Leading the lad to the bed again, he tucked him in and kissed his forehead. "Sleep now," he whispered. "I will see you in the morning."

He could feel his son's questioning gaze through the darkness, but he could not bear to speak further. Stumbling for the hallway, he shut the door behind him and slumped against the wall outside. His heart drummed so that he thought it would push through his chest. Unearthly fear consumed him, and with threatening clarity he remembered when Moses had first come before him, demanding that he let the Israelites go.

Such a strange day that had been! Though he had never admitted it, he had sensed great power in the prophet.

Yet he had resisted. Not even the warnings of his high priest, Jannes, had turned him aside.

With great effort, he moved himself down the corridor, determined to find his chamber and sleep away his mounting terror.

With haughty obstinacy, he reasoned against despair. He had a son, a bright, handsome son. The gods would not have given him so marvelous a child if they did mean to safely seat the boy on the throne!

Yes, in time all this misery would pass. Thutmose would die in a good old age, assured of the ongoing strength of his realm.

But just as he turned the last corner to his suite, the memory of that first meeting with Moses reasserted itself. Yes—Jannes had been present that day, hunched in a corner and babbling to himself. With a shiver, the king remembered how the wizard had clutched at his slave, gazing into his eyes in warning.

What was it the old man had said? Something about the future...

On a hissing swell, the words framed themselves fresh in the monarch's mind. "There is more, O King," the feeble priest had said. "There is more...but you cannot bear it now."

55

Not only was there light in the houses of the Israelites, but there was merriment.

Since the pall of blackness continued for a full week to dominate the land, fear filled the hearts of all Egyptians, just as it did the heart of their king. Although every slaveholder in the country had witnessed the devastations wrought at the hands of Moses and Aaron, nothing worked such terror as this unending night.

As a result, the slavemasters lightened their demands upon their Hebrew servants. Spiritual dread forestalled harsh treatment of the Israelites as their oppressors acknowledged their connection with the Almighty. And the slaves found themselves free to celebrate.

Therefore, there was revelry within the slave camps and within all houses of the children of Jacob.

The home of Jochebed and Amram was no exception. For days, the modest courtyard had been the scene of much coming and going, as renowned elders and young Israelite leaders visited with Moses and Aaron, speaking of the hope inspired by recent events and boldly planning for the future.

For Moses himself, it was a time of confirmation and assurance. Increasingly his mind turned to the desert and to his imminent return "home." Just as his journey back to Egypt from Midian had been a homecoming, so also would his return to the land of the shepherds.

However, when he pondered the fulfillment of God's plan for Israel, knowing that he would be responsible for somehow leading millions out of bondage, his mind boggled. He could never think on that certain destiny with any confidence. That one lone man should set out from the gates of Egypt with millions of human beings trusting him for guidance—why, to dwell on such a concept was like pondering infinity. It left him numb.

Far more comforting was the realization that he would soon see his beloved Zipporah, that he would be reunited with his sons, and that he would be with Jethro once again. In fact, this evening as he sat beside the fire in Jochebed's kitchen, he savored just such anticipations.

For the past few moments there had been no visitors in the house. Not even Aaron or Miriam were nearby. Amram napped in a soft parlor chair, and Jochebed busied herself in clearing the evening dishes.

As Moses allowed his thoughts to drift eastward, visions of his lovely wife dominated his thoughts. Although Zipporah was always in his heart, only such rare moments as this permitted him to give his full attention to comforting thoughts of his wife.

When last he had seen her, she had been leaning from her saddle, pleading with him not to leave, pleading that he return with her to Midian. Still beautiful despite her advanced age, her smooth, dark face had radiated love for her husband, and the feel of her slender arms clinging to his neck had filled him with yearning.

Remembering their countless nights together, their lifetime of love within the "wedding" tent, he could still feel the caress of her curls against his neck, and he longed for the pleasure of her kiss. Her hair was now laced with silver, it was true, and her body was not so round and supple as in youth. But she was still his Lady Bird, the only woman who had ever moved him.

His throat tightened, and for a long while he let his mind wander among the flames of the oven fire, passing through the familiar stretches of Midian and the wilderness between that sweet land and this.

At last his reveries took him to Sinai, and he remembered, vividly, the burning bush. Brought up short by the recollection, he was confronted once again with his greater calling. He remembered that the Lord had told him he must lead the people to that sacred mountain, and that there they would meet Jehovah, just as he had done.

How jealous was the Lord! Moses thought. It seemed he would allow his chosen man only fleeting fantasies of personal comfort. Once more he was left to wonder just how a solitary human should manage the exodus of three million slaves. And once they had left Egypt, how should one man oversee the welfare of such a throng?

With the magnitude of the challenge, the weight of the universe descended upon Moses's head, bowing him down in the stillness where he sat and leaving him smaller than an ant in the path of a hurtling planet.

"I cannot do it," he whispered. "I cannot do it alone."

The quiet of the house could not last forever. It was inevitable that company would come calling. As Jochebed hastened to answer a knock at the door, throwing it open to the thick black outside, a smiling face greeted her.

It was the young man, Hoshea, who had repeatedly lent support to Moses and Aaron over recent days.

"Is the prophet in?" he asked, leaning eagerly into the entryway.

"He is," Jochebed replied, thrilled to admit yet another guest.

So heavy was the darkness beyond the door that it seemed to push through the opening. But as it did, it was absorbed into the light, and Hoshea shook it from him as he soaked in the warmth of the happy room.

It was with the slightest hint of envy that Moses watched the young man cross the court toward him. Such energy and expectation he evinced, such youthful zeal!

Moses remembered when he had enjoyed the strength of 40 years, before he had been tested by 40 more.

"Good evening, sir," Hoshea greeted him. "When will you go again before the king?"

"It will not be long, I am sure," Moses sighed, smiling despite his weariness.

"Ah, then!" Hoshea exclaimed. "The time draws close for our deliverance!"

Moses nodded, impressed as always by the confidence his young friend exuded.

"You must let me go with you when you stand before the king!" Hoshea insisted. "Promise me!"

Moses's eyes glistened. Jehovah was ever the God of surprises. Sometimes he took years to answer prayer, and sometimes only moments.

"You may go with me," Moses assured him. "You may help me anytime you wish, for I cannot manage on my own."

Astonished, Hoshea took a deep breath. "Surely you are the chosen one, and Aaron is your spokesman," he deferred. "But if I can be of help, I will gladly do so. I will be your right-hand man if you but say the word!"

Surveying the fellow's handsome face, his strong chin and bright eyes, Moses took courage.

"'Hoshea,'" he said. "That means 'salvation,' does it not?"

"Yes," the young man nodded.

"From now on you shall be 'Joshua,'" the prophet announced, "for '*Jehovah* is salvation,' and you are his special servant."

56

The two gigantic doors to Pharaoh's stateroom swung open on squeaking hinges. The tangible darkness that had filled the palace for days had brought with it a dank humidity, producing a thick, green coating on the ornamental brass that defied polish.

The guards who opened the doors were no less affected by the gloomy curse. Trying to maintain their dignity, they appeared limp and disheveled in the dim yellow light of the wall torches.

"The king will receive you," one of them announced as Moses and his companions came upon them.

Normally such an announcement would be delivered in a warning tone, as no one went before Pharaoh casually. But today the guard's words were tinged with defeat.

As Moses entered the stateroom, he was flanked by his brother, Aaron, and followed closely by Joshua. Their bearing, in contrast to the Egyptians', was confident and strong. They knew this was the hour of destiny, the last time the leaders of Israel would ever stand before their oppressor.

If Thutmose had not been seated on his throne when they approached, Moses would not have recognized him. Slumped and smaller than he remembered him, the king appeared mummy-like in the morbid pall, his royal poise whittled at last to nothing.

Without formality he addressed the prophet from across the room, calling out to him as he was still at the door. "I would ask you to remove this curse, as you have removed the others!" he cried, his voice wheezing and dry. "But I know you would only bring another! Go!" he shouted, pointing his finger toward the east. "Take your people hence, and serve the Lord! Only leave your flocks and your herds behind, or we shall surely starve!"

Drawing near, Moses studied his enemy's shriveled face. "Do you still bargain with Jehovah?" he marveled. "You must let us have our animals, that we may sacrifice to the Lord our God, for thus he has commanded. Our livestock will go with us. Not a hoof will be left behind, for we shall take some of them to serve the Lord our God. And until we arrive there, we ourselves do not know how many he shall require."

Although the king had been beaten to the ground, rage still smoldered within his proud heart. Seeing that Moses once again resisted his will, he began to quiver. The anger of a headstrong child surged through his emaciated frame, and he clenched his fist in spite.

"Get away from me!" he suddenly screamed. "Take heed! Do not see my face again! For in the day you see my face, you shall die!"

As his screech pierced the ceiling and splintered down the halls, Joshua moved close to Moses's back.

But the man of God needed no assistance.

In righteous indignation, Moses moved close to the throne, lifting a finger to Pharaoh's nose. "You are right," he replied, staring at him eye to eye. "I shall never see your face again. But one more plague will the Lord bring on you and on your people."

Then stepping back, he lifted his voice to the rafters, and his words shook the building. "Thus says the Lord," he proclaimed, "'At about midnight I will go into the midst of Egypt. And all the firstborn in the land of Egypt shall die, from the firstborn of Pharaoh who sits on his throne, even to the firstborn of the slave girl who is behind the millstones! All the firstborn of the herds as well! And there shall be great wailing in all the land, such as there has never been before and shall never be again!'"

Leaning forward in horror, the king gripped the arms of his chair. Moses, taking a deep breath, continued: "'But against any of the Israelites a dog shall not even bark, neither against man nor beast, that you may see how the Lord makes a distinction between Egypt and Israel!'"

Looking again at Thutmose, Moses lifted a fist. "When this happens, your servants will come bowing before me, saying, 'Go out, you and all the people who follow you!' And after that, I will go out!"

Turning on his heel, Moses swung his robes about him and headed for the door. Joshua and Aaron followed.

Too late did the king raise a beseeching hand, as if to call them back. Never would he see the prophet again. And never would the Lord grant another chance for salvation.

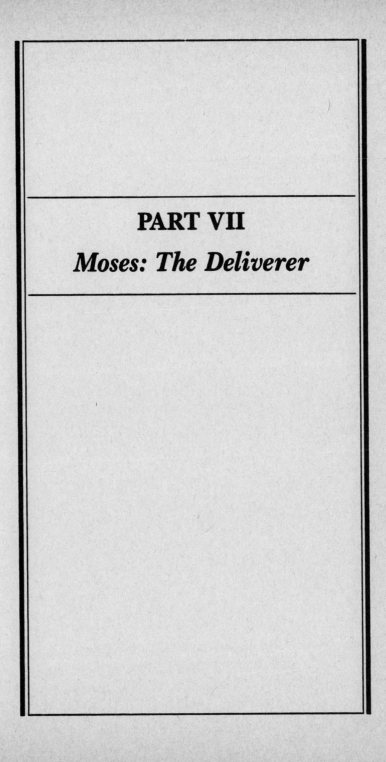

PART VII

Moses: The Deliverer

57

It would be yet two more weeks before the Lord brought his final plague against Egypt. But it was an indispensible time of preparation among the Israelites.

During these two weeks, Moses began to establish a system of regulations for his people that would be the foundation of their newly born nation. Since he had been a child at Jannes's knee, he had understood that what made Egypt great was her elaborate social and legal system. The more evolved the nation, Jannes had taught him, the more specific was its system of order. Slaves were kept in slavery by virtue of the fact that their nationhood had been stripped from them. For the slave, the only law was his master's word. Beyond this he had no conscience, no will, and therefore no identity.

It was during this brief 14 days, that Moses made good on the conviction that had burdened him for 40 years, the conviction born of hearing the words of God chanted beside Jethro's fire in Midian:

> Now as for you, you shall keep my covenant,
> you and your descendants after you through-
> out their generations.

When Moses had pressed his father-in-law regarding this covenant, the elder had acknowledged that the mark of circumcision was one of the specific requirements which Yahweh had placed upon Father Abraham and his descendants. Although Jethro had spiritualized the concept,

Moses was not convinced it should be so easily passed over.

Of course, the Lord had affirmed this to him when his own son, Eliezer, had taken ill. Only when the lad was circumcised was he spared. That example of God's clear command was still fresh in Moses's mind, having been demonstrated only a few months earlier.

Therefore the Lord's prophet moved quickly to establish this ordinance among the still-captive Israelites. Sending forth the first edict of his administration, he decreed that each male, young and old, must be circumcised.

The command met with objection, but by now no Israelite doubted Moses's sacred calling. Though it was a bloody ordeal, it was carried out.

Meanwhile the prophet gave other orders. During the lull before their deliverance, the families of Israel were to ask for provisions from their Egyptian neighbors. Given the recent displays of Yahweh's power, what Egyptian would deny an Israelite anything he or she asked?

Thus the slaves despoiled their masters, requiring of them articles of gold, silver, and clothing—anything that met their fancy. In baskets and crates, the haul was stored up, ready to accompany the Israelites on their emigration from the land of bondage.

Ten days into the two weeks, Moses gave his final command for preparation. Each Israelite household was to select a lamb or a kid for themselves, an unblemished year-old male. Four days hence, it would be slain for a feast and for a sacrifice.

The feast would establish the beginning of the Israelite calendar and become the first of the national festivals.

But there was a purpose more profound in this last command. The feast about to be celebrated would introduce God's greatest show of power and the day of his mighty deliverance.

* * *

It was the evening of the fourteenth day. Blackness no longer veiled the land. Morning, noon, and night again graced the Nile Valley, but the fear of the Lord still rested on the oppressors of Israel.

Into the soft gray of twilight ascended the smoke of a million household ovens, bearing across the country the aroma of roasted meat. In this there was nothing unusual. It was, after all, dinnertime. But outside the door of each Israelite home a peculiar rite was enacted.

The men of the households held in their hands small bowls of red liquid, blood from the slain lambs that were being cooked. Into the bowls they dipped small swatches of hyssop mint. Following Moses's orders, they reverently sprinkled the blood upon the doorposts and lintels of their homes, keeping their heads covered with the sacred mantles of their tribes and invoking the blessing of their God.

Having performed this, the men ducked inside their homes where they and their families would eat the meat, the unleavened bread and bitter herbs that their wives had prepared. Nor would they set foot outside their houses until morning, as they awaited the moving of God.

In haste the families fulfilled the feast, garbed as for a journey and even holding their staffs in their hands in anticipation of the great exodus.

* * *

At about midnight, the old priest, Jannes, suddenly lurched awake, sitting up rigidly on his bed. With a shiver he peered through the dark of his chamber and drew a shawl about his feeble shoulders.

When he had gone to bed there had been a full moon over the city. As he gazed through his window he saw that it still shone bright overhead. Had he only dreamed that a shadow passed over it?

Getting to his feet, he shuffled across the floor and stared over the rooftops. He had seen the Israelites' peculiar ritual, the sprinkling of the blood, performed earlier in the evening. He had not known what it meant, and it had troubled him, but not enough to keep him from sleep.

When he saw that lights still shone in the houses of the slaves, he was perplexed again. Apparently the strange people were still awake, anticipating something.

As for himself, he knew that something ominous had roused him from slumber. Jannes had spent a lifetime investigating the realm of spirit. He was sensitive to its vibrations, and he perceived a dreadful moving.

Glancing again at the moon, he shook his head. Surely, as he had slept, a cloud had passed over it. A shadow, yes, a shadow...

Suddenly the priest's perceptive gaze shot along the rooftops until it rested upon the wing of the royal house where the young prince, Pharaoh's beloved son, resided. With instant intuition, terror passed through the old man.

Out into the hall he ran. As quickly as his arthritic feet could carry him, he headed for the prince's suite.

But he was too late. He did not reach the boy's room before a piercing cry shattered the silence of the palace.

"By all the gods!" someone shouted. "The prince is dead! The prince is dead!"

Gripping his heart, the old wizard slumped against the wall. It was beginning—the final and the worst of the curses.

With vivid clarity his own words returned to haunt him. As he stumbled again along the hall, he whispered to himself: "There is more, O King. And the time has come for you to bear it."

58

It could not be seen, but it could be felt. And its mark was irrevocable. Beginning at the royal palace and proceeding on a relentless passage from the estates of the nobility to those of the aristocracy, from the houses of the middle class to the abodes of the merchants and the workers, the avenging spirit stalked the land. Everywhere it touched down, it was greeted with shrieks and wails of terror, by a cry ascending to the heavens such as never had been heard in Egypt and never would be again.

As the death angel prowled the dark streets, stopping before every gate and every door, the people within could sense its scrutiny. Quickly it became obvious that the destroyer was passing over houses where blood marked the lintels and doorposts, and the only cries arising from those places were of relief and joy.

As for the others, the grim reaper acted without mercy, threshing the breath from the lungs of every firstborn male, Egyptian or foreigner, human or beast. Within every barn and stable, bulls, camels, donkeys, and mules were felled. In every bedchamber or parlor, not one firstborn man or boy was left alive, and not one Egyptian house was spared the horror of death.

As the destroyer moved through the streets, those who abided in the house of Amram and Jochebed girded themselves with prayer. That evening, Amram, like all who followed Moses, had sprinkled the blood of the festal lamb upon his doorway. Jochebed had prepared the household feast in accordance with her son's instructions and now waited with the others for the imminent unfolding of God's plan.

Surely the Lord's mercy to Israel was manifest this night. For Jochebed, however, the sounds of weeping and horror beyond her door stirred up terrible memories.

Her husband, knowing she relived the holocaust wrought by Thutsmose I, went to her side and sat with her, holding her hand.

"It seems like yesterday," she whispered, "only yesterday..."

Amram, seeing the tears in her eyes, tried to comfort her. "But this night is different," he said. "This time it is the Egyptians who weep, and not the mothers of Israel."

Pulling away, Jochebed stared angrily at her husband. "Do you think I delight in any mother's suffering?" she rebuked him. "That any child should die is a tragedy!"

"Of course... I did not mean..." Amram bowed his head.

The sounds of despair were moving closer through the streets. Neighbors on every side succumbed to loud mourning.

As Aaron and Miriam huddled about their mother, the old woman stretched out a hand to Moses. "Do something, son," she pleaded. "Can't you do something?"

But the prophet knew the Lord would have his way. Drawing her hand to his lips, he kissed it lightly.

Just then, a knock was heard at the entry. Fearful to answer it, Jochebed was relieved when Moses bade her remain where she was.

"Have faith, Mother," he said, "It will not be long." Crossing the room, he opened the door.

What greeted him in the light of torches was a group of soldiers and high servants from the king's house. Foremost was the familiar face of Jannes, his skin drawn and ribbed with deep wrinkles over jagged cheeks and brow. Bowing his bald head, the elder spoke in breathless wheezes, rubbing his hands together like two bones.

"I bring word from Pharaoh," he rasped.

"I knew you would," Moses replied.

" 'Rise up,' says the king, 'get out from among my people, both you and all the Israelites. Go, worship the Lord, as you desire. Take your flocks and your herds, and go!' "

Not once, as he said this, did Jannes look Moses in the eye. But the remainder of the message was most important, and he at last glanced up. "The king also asks..."

"Yes?" Moses spurred him.

"He asks that you bless him."

Not gracing that request with so much as a nod, Moses only stared with pity into his friend's face. "And what of you, old man?" he asked. "Will you turn at last from your gods, and come with me?"

Taken by surprise, Jannes quivered, and for a moment, Moses thought he might have won him.

But at last, like a prisoner accustomed to his cell, the priest stooped his shoulders. "We took our separate paths a lifetime ago," he confessed. "As for me, there is no turning back."

59

Up from the fields and the cities of Egypt, from the fields stripped bare by the plagues and the cities humbled by disease and death, a great swell of sound, jubilant and festive, arose. It was the sound of captives set free, captives who had bowed to the whip of Pharaoh and the oppression of the slavemasters for 430 years.

Yes, it had been 430 years to the day since the sons of Jacob first entered the land of the Nile. In the beginning, their sojourn here had been pleasant, greeted as they were by the outstretched arms of their brother Joseph, who had risen to the seat beside the throne, and who had power to settle them in luxury. For a time the children of Israel had dwelt in Goshen, tending their flocks and raising their sons and daughters in plenty. But when Joseph died, they were left to the mercy of a king who would enslave them. And for over four centuries they had suffered untold misery.

Tonight all that was changing. They were no longer a small company. During their service in Egypt, their ranks had swelled to nearly three million. And tonight that formidable throng was leaving. From every corner of Egypt they set out, from Raamses, Thebes, Memphis, Heliopolis, Bubastis, and all points in between.

They were an encompassing group, containing within their ranks sympathizers of many races. For there had always been those who sided with the Israelites in their troubles, and those numbers had grown during the period of the plagues, as the power of Yahweh became known. Having submitted to the rite of circumcision, Nubians, Libyans, Ethiopians, and the dispossessed of countless tribes were interspersed among the liberated slaves.

Indeed, there were even a few Egyptians who, despite great personal risk, had befriended their Israelite neighbors.

When the sons of Jacob had entered Egypt four centuries before, they had been on the verge of starvation, driven to beg for help from the richest land on earth. Overnight they had now become fabulously wealthy, hauling with them wagonloads of booty demanded of their oppressors. On their backs were satchels full of fine clothes, and on their arms and necks were layers of gold and silver jewelry. Like children in a sweets shop, they had let their appetites run wild and were taking with them everything they could lay hold of. Having owned little, they were now giddy with wealth, gaudy with opulence.

Of course they took their flocks, herds, livestock. Since the plagues had destroyed all cattle belonging to the Egyptians, the land would be devoid of most its animals.

But even so, the Egyptians did not detain the Israelites Instead, they encouraged them, begging them to make haste before Yahweh took further vengeance. "Go!" they shouted from city walls and housetops, as the former slaves passed through the streets and down the highways. "Get out of here! Or we shall all surely die!"

But, though no one challenged their exodus, the Israelites went forth in martial array, carrying swords and spears and flanked by shieldbearers. Perhaps they felt this was all too easy, that at some point, further on, they would be required to defend themselves.

For now they were eager to follow their leader, Moses, to meet him in the wilderness beyond Egypt's border. It would take many days before all three million, from every corner of the land, congregated upon the delta plain. But as they went forth, they did so with dancing and singing, lifting their voices in the song of promise:

> Milk and honey,
> We shall have milk and honey.
> In the land of Father Jacob,
> In the valley of Jehovah,
> We shall rest ourselves.

EPILOGUE

Lord, my heart is not haughty,
nor mine eyes lofty:
neither do I exercise myself in great matters,
or in things too high for me.
Surely I have...quieted myself,
as a child....
Let Israel hope in the Lord
from henceforth and for ever.
Psalm 131

Across the vast wilderness south of Goshen, a shimmering red glow lit the earth. For many miles in every direction, from the borders of Raamses to the rim of Great Bitter Lake, the scarlet light could be seen. And high above the sands, filling the sky with its flashing aurora, was a fiery pillar.

Taller than the world's highest mountain, stretching between the earth and the distant stars, the phenomenon hung in eerie splendor. The first night of the exodus, the pillar had formed itself above the host of Israel and had gone before them, leading the way toward Succoth. With morning it had cooled to a white, cloudy column, and had again passed southeast, leading the numberless throng.

During the day it was a wonder to behold, with its billowy folds and undulating rhythm. But at night it was more spectacular, sending reassuring warmth across the desert.

Where it stopped, the three million stopped, camping beneath it. And all night long it was stationary, save for a slow, spiraling dance that gave it the aspect of a watch-carer in his tower, who turns this way and that as he overlooks his charges far below.

For the Israelites who had witnessed Yahweh's power in plagues and devastations, it was encouraging to sense his fatherly side. Theirs was a fledgling faith, timid and uncertain. Like small children, they required tender parenting as well as the fear of the Lord.

As for Moses, he was familiar with the fiery aspect of his God. He had seen him first in the burning bush, and he knew that fire could hurt or heal, it could warm or sear. But Moses, too, was a child. Despite 80 years of learning, he had much more to understand.

Tonight he sat beneath the shadow of his tent at the head of the vast human flock that rested on the plain. The crimson glow of the gigantic pillar cast his shadow across the ground, depicting him in silhouette much larger than he was. He did not feel large. He felt very small.

The enormity of the task before him had not diminished. Although the Lord continually showed Moses that he went before him, to smooth the way and provide all means necessary to perform his calling, Moses still had times of doubt.

What lay ahead, he could not imagine. He knew that he was to lead the people to Sinai, across 200 miles of rock and sand. How the Lord would provide for so great a company along the way, he dared not guess. And what would happen from that point, he knew not.

There could be enemies in waiting, or Pharaoh could reverse himself and come after them. They were not trained in battle and had no means of survival beyond the supplies with which they had escaped.

Among them were many elderly, like Amram and Jochebed, Shiphrah and Puah, and many little children. Moses tried not to think how helpless they would be should any disaster overtake them.

He thought instead of Joshua and his friend, Caleb. They were among thousands of strong young men in Israel. On them he must rely.

And he thought of his longed-for reunion with Zipporah, Jethro, and his two fine sons.

When he dwelt on such things, he was more confident. Looking above to the flashing pillar, he smiled. A corner of his mantle, drawn over his head, impeded his view, and he brushed it aside. But as he did, a comforting warmth filled his heart.

Removing the striped shawl, he draped it across his lap and recalled the day the midwives had presented it to him. He remembered hiding it from Jannes and wearing it when he said his first, hesitant prayers to the God of Israel. He remembered when Hatshepsut had found it, and how she feared she might have lost his love.

Tracing his finger across its beloved pattern, he recalled the dark woman who had stood outside his palace window, longing for a glimpse of his face. To this day Jochebed wore the headband of the Levites, the stripes which denoted her husband's tribe.

With a lump in his throat, Moses realized how intimately his life was bound up in every fiber of the little blanket.

In reverie, he could almost remember how it had felt to be set adrift upon the Nile, to see the sunlight through the slats of a basket lid. Helpless and weak, he had floated at the mercy of the river, cradled only upon this small swatch of cloth.

Even as an infant, he had not been alone. The Lord had been with him, directing him, pushing him, teaching him the way he should go.

Now as much as then, he must rely on the strength of Yahweh. This he knew, as he lifted the mantle to his cheek and held it there.

"Keep me, Lord," he whispered. "Keep us all. For we are your children. And our life is in your hands."

ELLEN GUNDERSON
TRAYLOR

JOSHUA

GOD'S WARRIOR

HARVEST HOUSE PUBLISHERS
Eugene, Oregon 97402

JOSHUA, GOD'S WARRIOR

Copyright © 1991 by Harvest House Publishers
Eugene, Oregon 97402

Library of Congress Cataloging-in-Publication Data

Traylor, Ellen Gunderson.
    Joshua, God's warrior / Ellen Gunderson Traylor.
    ISBN 0-89081-853-3
    1. Joshua (Biblical figure)—Fiction.   2. Bible. O.T.—History of Biblical events—
Fiction.   I. Title.
PS3570.R357J65   1991
813'.54—dc20   90-24542
                                                             CIP

Printed in the United States of America.

To all
who wage peace
by
staff or sword

Other Books by
Ellen Gunderson Traylor

Song of Abraham

John—Son of Thunder

Mary Magdalene

Noah

Ruth—A Love Story

Jonah

Mark—Eyewitness

*Esther—The Story of
a Woman Who Saved a Nation*

Joseph—Dreamer of Dreams

Moses—The Deliverer

Contents

A NOTE TO THE READER

It was hard to walk in Moses's shadow, to miss the calling of prophet and be appointed instead to fulfill a role that seemed less spiritual.

But Joshua needed to learn that all God's callings are holy, and that there are many ways to serve.

As promised in the preface to *Moses: The Deliverer*, *Joshua: God's Warrior* follows the children of Israel from their escape from Egypt to their entrance into the Promised Land. While these chapters continue the saga of Moses, Joshua looms larger with each episode, and earns his place in history not only as right-hand man to the prophet, but as a mighty leader in his own right.

This is the story not only of God's working through prophecy, but of his special ordination of a military general. It reveals the demanding character of Yahweh, as well as his fatherhood, as he prepares Israel for its inheritance. And it lays the sword parallel with the shepherd's staff, as Joshua fulfills his purpose.

But *Joshua: God's Warrior* is also a story of one man's personal journey. The one who knew the lonely path of leadership would be surprised by love, both human and divine. In finding the Promised Land, tradition says, he also found a home for his heart and embraced a Gentile woman as part of his rightful inheritance.

May this book bless you as you pursue your own Promised Land.

Ellen Traylor

The Lord your God is
He who fights for you.

—Joshua 23:10 NASB

PROLOGUE

Joshua knew where Moses was camped. He had followed close beside him all day, this third day of the great exodus from Pharaoh's Egypt. But as the Israelites had settled down for the night, beneath the orange glow of the miraculous fiery pillar, the young man left the prophet to himself.

This was a fearful night, and he knew the man of God wished to be alone. It was the first night on the very edge of the wilderness, and he had sensed a heaviness in Moses as they approached it.

He had rarely been beyond view of the great leader since they had departed Raamses. Only a few days before, Moses had promised him that he could be his servant, that second to Aaron he was his right-hand man. With eager devotion he had seized the role, happily answering to the name Moses had given him.

Father Nun and Grandfather Elishama were having trouble becoming accustomed to the new name. They still called him Hoshea, if they were not careful. But they were old men. Joshua did not correct them.

His friend, Caleb, had taken easily to the name change. Joshua's closest companion since childhood, the young Judahite had stuck with him and with Moses through the dramatic days when they had gone before Pharaoh. He had witnessed the king's resistance, and encouraged the man of God to hold firm.

It was Caleb whom Joshua sought this night, as he wandered through the great camp of the Israelites. Many dark thoughts were his, and he wished to fill someone's ears with them. He knew Caleb would listen.

As he made his way between the staggered rows of tents, he was glad he had no immediate family. Though he often

11

longed for the comfort of wife and children, the sounds of whimpering babies and the sight of young women cradling them against the peculiar cold that always descended upon the nighttime desert troubled him deeply.

The Israelites had borne with four centuries of misery as slaves to Egypt, laboring beneath whip and rod. The ordeal had toughened their bodies and their spirits. Each new generation was hardier than the last, as those who could not survive died off, and those who could gave birth to strong children. Yet these people were accustomed to the mild climate of the Nile Valley and the region of Goshen, most pleasant land on earth. They had never walked through scorching daytime sands, nor had they shivered with the chill of Sinai nights.

How would they survive the journey ahead?

Indeed, the journey itself was a mystery. Never in human history had three million people set out across unknown terrain, in pursuit of an uncertain destiny, and following a leader enigmatic as his demands. Upon their backs were only the clothes they had taken from their former masters. True, they bore layers of heavy golden bracelets and neckchains upon their arms and torsos. In their wagons were clanking silver vessels and boxes full of coins. But what good were such treasures in the lifeless sands about them?

They had enough food in their colossal company to last only a few days, though they had taken as much as they could carry from the anxious Egyptians. "Go! Get out of here!" their terrified masters had urged. "Take what you want, but go, lest your god send another plague upon us!" While the Israelites lived on the memory of Yahweh's saving hand, on the witness of devastations wrought upon Egypt by the rod of Moses, Joshua wondered how long their faith would last when hunger gnawed at their ribs.

Yes, he was glad, just now, that he had no wife or child. But he did have an aging father and an elderly grandfather. In his extended family, there were many young ones, feeble widows, and nursing mothers. Concern for them, and for all the helpless folk of this exodus weighed heavy upon him.

Joshua was a young man, only forty-five years old. He had not attained the status of an elder among his people. But he was already highly respected for his keen mind and obvious leadership abilities. Hundreds greeted him as he walked through the vast crowd this evening.

When he saw Caleb seated beside an evening fire, he eagerly called to him, "Friend, walk with me."

Glad to be singled out, Caleb rose to meet the handsome Joshua, and joined him on his rounds. Each evening the servant of Moses ventured forth among the people, doing what he could to oversee their welfare, and Caleb was happy to assist.

The two of them made a striking pair, both tall and broad-shouldered, with dark hair and bright, black eyes. Many times, as youngsters, people had taken them to be brothers, and though Joshua was seven years Caleb's senior, they had always been best of friends.

Of course, the fact that they had both served the same Egyptian master gave them much in common. When they were children, they had been wrested from service on the chain gangs, and taken to the home of a wealthy man. Trained as valets to his stable of fine Arabian horses, they had risen in the household to the status of indentured servants, capable of eventually earning their freedom. Accustomed to order and refinement in their master's home, they bore themselves with dignity unusual in slaves.

Tonight, as they walked through camp, Joshua's face was pensive. Caleb, who knew Joshua better than anyone, anticipated his need to talk.

"Look," Joshua sighed, passing his hand over the vast company, "there is no order, no arrangement to this huge population!"

Caleb surveyed the rows of tents, which stretched so far they blended with the dark horizon. As closely as possible, families had tried to stay together. But in the mayhem of the flight from Egypt, this had been difficult. And in many cases, family members would not even have known each other, having been separated by the slave system all their lives.

"Leaders are emerging among the people," Joshua acknowledged, "and groups are forming. But there is no clear organization. Already there is squabbling and division. If Moses hopes to manage such a horde, a chain of command and an appointed government will need to be established."

Caleb scanned the sea of faces all around him. Shaking his head, he shrugged his shoulders. "Have you spoken to Moses about it?" he asked. "Surely he is aware of the need."

"Of course he is," Joshua replied. "But he is overwhelmed, and to this point there has been no time for anything but flight. See," he sighed, "again this night we will be allowed only a few hours sleep, and then we will be on the march once more."

Caleb need not be reminded that all three million were fugitives, that the possibility existed that Pharaoh could change his mind and come after them.

Furtively he glanced toward the north, half expecting to see the torches of the king's army lighting the line between earth and sky.

Because Moses had ordered the people to go forth from Egypt in battle array, Joshua and Caleb had come out tonight bearing swords on their thighs. They tried not to be awkward with them, but though they had sometimes polished their Egyptian owner's ceremonial armor, they were not soldiers. As boys they had received sound thrashings if they were caught playing with the master's weapons, and neither of them had been closer to the things of war than any spectator at one of Pharaoh's flashy military parades.

Nor were any of the men who populated this company men of war. They had never been trained in battle, save for a select few who had served in the king's guard. Israelites had never been allowed to bear arms, and they did not know how to use them.

Yet, everywhere in this vast host were weapons to be seen, lying beside campfires, leaning against tent poles, perched inside tent doors. In the feverish despoiling of the Egyptians, the Israelites had taken spears and hatchets, chariots and bucklers. At Moses's command, they had laden themselves with military paraphernalia. But no amount of martial array would make up for ignorance in battle, and few men kept their weapons in their hands.

Not that they had never yearned to rise up against their oppressors. Every boy of the slave villages had dreamed of revolution. Joshua and Caleb were no exception. When they had lived in the ghetto, and when they were allowed an hour of recreation, they had inevitably turned to games of war, taking on their enemies in a more fortunate, imaginary world.

But they were now men, and having been conditioned by a lifetime of subservience, they were unused to bearing arms. Though their latent longings to subdue the Egyptians had risen with the courage of recent days, they did not know how to fight.

Joshua had no intention of visiting Moses this evening, but a circuitous path had brought him and Caleb near the front of the great company. When the prophet's tent appeared before them, Joshua held back.

"Why don't we speak with him?" Caleb suggested.

"Not now," Joshua said. "There will be time enough for questions later on."

Turning aside, he led his friend toward his father's camp. But as he did so, they were obliged to pass by the company's only hallowed station, the guarded coffin of the great patriarch, Joseph.

Overwatched day and night by a dozen armed men, the laquered sarcophagus gleamed in the towering light of the fiery pillar. At Moses's word, the shining box had been wrested from the mammoth Pyramid of Zaphenath-paneah in Avaris, final resting place of the mighty Hebrew prime minister, and named by his Egyptian name. From the moment it had been brought forth, the coffin had been treated with the respect due the revered ancestor. Borne through the desert upon golden poles, it would not be allowed to touch ground until it reached Palestine. Once there, its sacred contents, the bones of Joseph, would be buried in the holy soil. This had been the patriarch's dying request, passed down through the generations, and Moses would not forget it.

Awestruck, Joshua walked around the hallowed coffin. "Isn't it magnificent?" he whispered to Caleb. "I wish I had been chosen for this duty! To guard the bones of Joseph, I would gladly bear a hundred swords and spears!"

Caleb smiled, and placed a hand on Joshua's shoulder. He knew that Joseph was not only the honored patriarch of the Hebrew slaves, but that he was Joshua's direct ancestor. Joshua was an Ephraimite, descendant of Joseph's second son, and Caleb understood the pride his friend took in the fact.

How many generations had passed since the death of that mighty savior, the one who had spared his traitorous brothers from famine and brought Israel safe into the land of plenty? Had it not been for Joseph, no Israelite would have lived to see this day.

"Just think!" Joshua enthused. "Three hundred years have intervened between us and the rule of Joseph. Yet we would gladly give our lives to preserve his powdery bones!"

Caleb pulled his mantle close to his chest and doubtfully stroked the hilt of his sword. "Well," he sighed, "let us hope there will be no need for that. We are not warriors, Joshua."

PART I
The Slave Set Free

1

King Thutmose's physicians hovered over his bed, speaking in anxious whispers, peering at him from beneath their red fish costumes. The fish, Egyptian representative of health and well-being, was a fitting symbol for their profession, and the doctors always donned the glittering, scaly garb, their faces framed by the open mouth, whenever they tended royalty.

But, today, no matter how fervently they chanted to the river god, no matter how much fish oil they spread upon the king's throbbing temples, they could not rouse him from his stupor.

In vain did they massage his wrists, hoping to spur the blood through his body. In vain did they bathe his limbs with Nile water, petitioning heaven for his escape from the land of Lethe.

Thutmose had succumbed to this morbid fever the night the Israelites had fled. He had been a mere shadow of himself for weeks before, but on that night he slipped into this palsied state, and had not rallied.

Dauntless, he had withstood the blows his enemy dealt him. He may have bowed briefly to the Hebrew's onslaughts, giving in to his demands when plague after plague ripped through the land. But always he had revived, refusing, ultimately, to let the slaves go free.

Only the death of his dearly beloved son had at last devastated him. When frogs and insects and dying cattle, boils and hail and locusts had failed to undo him, he had inspired his people, and Egypt had held strong. But with the death of his son, and the death of all the firstborn of Egypt, something in the king had also died.

19

Perhaps it was merciful that he had been unaware of the slaves' mass exodus. Lying upon his bed, his bony frame curled into a fetal position, he had slept through the great escape. He had not seen the millions walk boldly through the streets and highways, heading straight for the borders of the land. He had not heard the frantic cries of his own citizens as they had rushed the slaves out the doors, filling their arms and their wagons with the wealth of the country, and begging that they never return.

Perhaps it had been a mercy that the king had been spared the witness. But his people needed him now. Egypt needed him.

The old priest, Jannes, had been called night after night to add his prayers to the physicians' efforts. Each time his petitions had been fruitless. And tonight he expected another failure.

Deep in his heart, he knew his prayers lacked fervor. Scarcely had he maintained his own faith in the face of Moses's powers. It was all he could do to appear devout, when he doubted the truth of his own teachings.

Nevertheless, he had gone through the motions, saying the right words, mixing the right potions, and trying not to think of Yahweh. Tonight, as he stood over the king's bed, he managed to say a believable prayer, and was stunned when the patient opened his eyes.

Bleary eyes they were, red and filmy, for they had not seen the light for four days. When the lids fluttered, Jannes took a sharp breath.

The priest had no love for Thutmose. His heart had always been devoted to the vanquished prince, Moses. But he did love Egypt, and since he still believed that the fate of Pharaoh was the fate of the land, he was grateful for this sign of life.

Taking Thutmose's hand in his own feeble fingers, he lifted it to his withered lips. "Return to us, Son of Light," he groaned. "Bring the daylight to your people."

When the king spoke his first words in days, all the doctors gathered close about his bed.

"Darkness..." he hissed. "Nothing but darkness..."

Though his eyes were open, he seemed not to see the yellow glow of the lampstands in the room.

"He dreams of the dark plague," one of the physicians guessed, recalling the three days when no light shone in all the land, when a black pall so thick it was tangible had overwhelmed the sun and every candle, every ember, for seventy-two hours.

"Find your way through the night," Jannes pleaded, pressing close to the king's ear. "Return to your children!"

Motioning toward the windows, the priest sent a servant to throw back the blinds, and afternoon sun flooded the chamber.

"See," he urged the king, "it is the Sun, your Majesty. Add your light to the light of Ra!"

Suddenly the king awoke, raising a hand to wipe the film from his hazy vision.

"Return, O King!" Jannes cried, lifting him to a sitting position. Propping him up with pillows, he ordered the physicians aside, that the sun's rays might spill across the bed.

As the light touched the king's face, he seemed to draw energy from it.

"My son," he rasped. "Where is my son?"

When Jannes did not readily answer, the king stared wildly into his averted eyes. Grasping the priest by the collar, he pulled at him with amazing strength. But, just as it seemed he would choke the old man, reality sparked into memory, and his face twitched.

Releasing Jannes, he fell back again into his pillows, a sigh like a death rattle gurgling from his throat.

"The king is well," Jannes whispered, when the doctors reached for him. "Let him be."

In a moment, the ailing monarch again sat up, this time fully aware of himself and his surroundings. His last recollection was of sending word to Moses and Aaron, telling them to leave, and to take the Israelites with them.

Oh, let it not be! Thutmose thought. Turning fevered eyes to the priest, he clutched at his arm. "Where is Moses?" he cried.

Again, the priest hesitated to answer, and the king became enraged. "Send for Moses, now!" he shouted. "This very instant!"

"Of course, you could not know," Jannes stammered, leaving his arm in the king's grasp. "You have not been with us, so you could not know..."

"Know what?" Pharaoh screamed, his voice taking on the shrill tone Jannes had always loathed. "What does he say?" he demanded, turning to the doctors.

"Do not agitate yourself, Your Majesty," one of them advised. But as he ran a cold cloth over the patient's head, Thutmose jerked away.

Taking a deep breath, Pharaoh tried to calm himself. "What is it I do not know?" he asked through gritted teeth.

Trembling, not for fear of Thutmose, but for fear of Yahweh, Jannes at last replied, "Moses is not here, Your Highness. He has not been here for four days."

A sneer crossed the king's face. He had no patience for half-answers.

"Must I strangle the truth from you, Jannes?" he cried. "Where is Moses? Where is Aaron?"

Swallowing hard, the priest answered, "In obedience to Your Majesty, they have left the country... they and all their people."

2

Joshua awoke with a start. A voice, soft but urgent, called to him, and when he sat up he was greeted by the moonstruck silhouette of a man outside his tent wall.

"Come," the voice insisted. "Moses needs you at once!"

"Aaron?" Joshua replied. "Is that you?"

"Hurry. Meet me at my brother's tent."

With this the shadow departed, and Joshua pulled on his tunic. Fumbling for the door, he stepped outside just in time to see Aaron hastening up a staggered row of tents toward the front of the great company.

Joshua glanced above as he tied his sandals. By the moon's position, he judged it must be the middle of the night. What the prophet and his spokesman could want with him at this hour, he could not imagine.

Between the countless lean-tos and goatshair shelters strewn upon the sand, Joshua found his way, once more, to the tent of Moses. Aaron had already entered when he arrived, and when he hesitated outside, the elder poked his head through the tent flap.

"Come!" Aaron spurred him.

Out of respect for Moses, Joshua did not take a seat until Aaron pointed to a cushion on the floor, and for a while none of them said a word.

Moses, who had apparently not slept all night, sat beside a small, smoking lamp, his dark face pensive, and his hands folded quietly in his lap.

When at last the prophet spoke, his two servants were unprepared for his instructions.

"We must tell the people to turn back," he said.

Astonished, the listeners gaped at Moses, then at one another.

"Turn back?" Aaron stammered. "You can't mean it!"

"Retreat?" Joshua marveled. "Into the jaws of the lion?"

Apparently expecting such a response, Moses only nodded. And Aaron objected loudly, "Have you lost your mind, brother? We have come this far, and against such odds, only to turn back?"

"If it is food we need," Joshua challenged, "we should trust Yahweh to supply!"

"Of course!" Aaron echoed. "He has not saved us with many miracles only to see us perish now. We need not turn back for lack of food!"

With a sigh, Moses looked into the faces of his two best friends. "It is not for food that we turn north," he explained. "And it is not to Egypt that we go, but only as far as Yam Suph."

Aaron shook his head. "The Reed Sea?" he laughed, interpreting the name. "But we have already passed by there. It has nothing to offer but bulrushes. What would we find at Yam Suph?"

"A foil for Pharaoh," was Moses's gentle reply.

Bewildered, the two servants pondered the words. Was the prophet saying that the king of Egypt had had a change of heart? Would he come after the fleeing Israelites?

Aaron and Joshua would have asked the question directly, but Moses was speaking again, his face uplifted to the ceiling and his tone reminiscent of the many times he had spoken for the Lord.

"'Tell the children of Israel to go back and camp before Pihahiroth, between Migdol and the sea. You shall camp in front of Baal-zephon, opposite it, by the sea. For Pharaoh will say of the children of Israel, "They are wandering aimlessly in the land; the wilderness has shut them in." So I will harden the heart of Pharaoh, and he will chase after them. And I will be honored through

Pharaoh and all his army, and the Egyptians will know that I am the Lord.'"

So, it was true. Pharaoh would indeed come after them! Fearfully, Aaron and Joshua turned the phrases over in their minds.

Joshua had not known Moses long. It had been only a few weeks since the holy man had appeared in Egypt, preaching liberty. It was clear, however, that he was a man of God, not only because of the miracles wrought at his word, but because of the spirit of authority with which he spoke.

Still, tonight's instruction did not sit well with Joshua. He had not been trained in war, but he did have common sense. And he had not been called to this little council to hold his peace.

Swallowing hard, he dared to question.

"Sir," he croaked, "though we far outnumber Pharaoh's armies, we are children when it comes to fighting. Can Yahweh truly mean for us to go to war?"

Moses gazed fondly on his young friend. But his reply was unsatisfying. "I wish I knew," he sighed. "In this matter, I have no leading."

Joshua's face reddened. "Very well," he managed. "But, if we *are* to face Pharaoh's men would we not do better with our backs to the open wilderness? To be hemmed in by a marshy sea is suicidal!"

Out of the corner of his eye, Joshua saw Aaron nod in agreement, and he privately commended himself for his courage.

But when Moses also agreed, he was deflated.

"So it would seem," the prophet replied.

Would he say nothing more than this? Joshua bit his tongue, choking on frustration.

"We have the word of the Lord. And sometimes his word is a mystery," Moses concluded.

Silence hung in the council tent as the two servants digested the truth.

Taking a deep breath, Joshua assented weakly. "We turn back tomorrow?"

"Tomorrow," Moses replied.

3

Barely stronger than a rag doll, Pharaoh Thutmose gripped the side of his two-wheeled chariot and peered across the open desert. His driver, armed from head to toe, avoided the ruts and stones of the ancient highway that stretched out from Raamses east toward the wilderness. Thutmose, sensing his protective hesitancy, growled at him.

"Am I a babe-in-arms that you drive like an old woman? Whip your horses, fool!"

Chagrined, the charioteer complied, and the gilded chariot leapt forward. Following the king's lead, all the vast host of the Egyptian army picked up speed, the ten thousand other chariots whose columns stretched for two miles behind him, the twenty thousand horsemen who followed them, and the nine hundred thousand foot soldiers who marched on their heels.

Nearly a million strong was the army of Pharaoh. And this was only the best of his fighting forces. Others occupied his many tributaries or waged war in rebellious provinces. The best he had brought with him to retrieve his fleeing slaves.

Scarcely now could he believe that he had been so foolish as to let the people go. True, the awful plagues brought upon the land had tested him. The puny god of Israel had somehow cowed the "greatest of the Pharaohs." But was not Thutmose also the greatest of the gods, incarnaton of Ra himself? What could he have been thinking, to let the mainstay of the Egyptian economy and the foundation of its social order flee the country?

Well, he reasoned, he had *not* been thinking. Some infernal voodoo had twisted his head.

Not for long, though. Thutmose had regained himself. With the help of Ra, invoked by the holy priests, he had emerged from his living grave, and like the Morning Sun, he shone forth now upon the valley of the sacred Nile.

Through Goshen tramped the mighty million. The shepherd country, ancestral home of the fleeing Israelites, was vacant now. No slave towns filled the green hollows. Not one sheep or goat was left upon the hills, as the slaves had taken every creature of worth from Egypt's delta country. Ahead stretched the lifeless desert, and soon Pharaoh would be returning this way, the slaves and all their booty in tow. Within days, the Goshen hills would be full again of tended flocks, and the slaves would have forgotten their rebellion.

As the king surveyed the bleak wilderness beyond, he wondered how far three million Hebrews could have gotten. Only four days had passed since he had fallen into his swoon, since Moses had wrested his possessions from him and the defiant rabble had looted the land. Surely, with women and children, flocks and herds, old people and laden wagons, they could not have gotten far.

Straining his vision across the hot sands, he gripped the rim of the chariot tighter and remembered his younger days. He had been a mighty warrior, once upon a time. He had led many valiant armies, conquered countless foes. Under the command of this Pharaoh, Egypt had risen to her greatest military glory.

He doubted, however, that there would be need for fighting this time. In reality, the tramping horde behind him was for show, more than for war. It would take no more than a *show* of force to bring the Hebrews to their knees. Why, the very sight of the dust cloud raised by the Egyptians' marching feet should be enough to bow them to the ground!

It was reported that the Hebrews had gone forth in battle array. Stealing weapons and chariots from their masters, they had left Egypt "prepared" to fight. Pharaoh smirked to himself, as he imagined how silly they must have looked, like little children dressed in daddy's armor, swaggering and bumbling.

Glancing behind him again, he commended himself on the proud demeanor of his six hundred most select charioteers, the captains of his host. Looking neither to the right nor the left, chins held high, they peered straight ahead from beneath the brims of their brass helmets, standing upright and arrow-sure in the spurs of their magnificent vehicles. Upon the hubs of their wheels revolved sharp-honed blades, capable of cutting the legs off man or beast that came too near, or of chewing the wheels off enemy chariots. The very appearance of the six hundred commanders and their steeds would cause Moses and his foolish followers to pray for mercy!

But who would hear their prayers? Yahweh had led them to slaughter when he seduced them from Egypt's protective embrace.

Emulating his captains, Thutmose struck a noble pose in the spur of his own vehicle and cast his gaze again toward the wilderness. The three million could not have traveled more than a few miles out. Within a day or two, he would see them upon the horizon.

And when he came upon them, they would be face down in the sand, making obeisance and pleading for forgiveness.

4

What Pharaoh did not know was that the Hebrews had been traveling by night as well as day. Moses allowed them a few hours respite each evening, but beyond this, they did not sleep, following the fiery pillar in the dark hours, and its counterpart, the colossal pillar of cloud, by day.

When a full three days had passed, and Pharaoh still had not found them, his soul began to shiver. The same spiritual dread which had descended upon him with each devastating plague hovered over him once more.

He might have turned back, he and all his men, thinking that the wizardry of Moses had lifted the entire nation of Israel from the face of the earth, had he not reached Yam Suph, or Lake Timsah, called the Reed Sea, by the third night. And had it not been nearing dusk when he came upon the three million camped there, he might have thought a mirage tricked his eyes.

But at twilight there were no mirages.

Leaning over the rim of his chariot, he nudged the driver in the ribs.

"Yes, Your Majesty. I see them," the charioteer confirmed. "The great company has come to rest on the shore of Yam Suph."

A catlike grin stretched the king's face. Throwing back his shoulders, he raised a fist to the air, signaling his captains that the time had come.

Like a tidal wave, the fearsome million poured down the desert slope toward Lake Timsah.

*   *   *

Long before Pharaoh laid eyes on the Israelites, those on the northernmost edge of the encampment saw the dust cloud raised by the sprawling army. Moses was notified of their approach, and stood on a sandy cliff beside the lake, trying to calm his frightened people.

Joshua, who stood alongside him, tried to calm his own fears. Had not Yahweh spoken through Moses until now? Surely the man of God had not led them astray.

Yet the young Hebrew sympathized with the frantic millions who heard the threatening drums of Pharaoh's hosts, and the awesome tramping of their feet.

"What have you done?" the Israelites cried out to their leader. "Is it because we had no graves in Egypt that you have taken us away to die in the wilderness?"

"What is this?" they shouted. "Why did you bring us out of Egypt?"

Desperately did the women weep and the little children scream. Men slumped to their knees, quaking uselessly behind their shields.

"Did we not tell you to leave us alone?" they accused him. "You should have left us to serve the Egyptians! We were better off serving them, than dying in the wilderness!"

Only Aaron and Joshua stood between the prophet and his manic followers. Trying to be heard above the din, the two servants demanded quiet.

But it was no use. Some of the people already lifted stones in their hands, ready to pummel the man of God. Women spit at his feet and clawed at the limestone cliff, ready to pull him down.

Throwing his arms wide, Moses called above the throng. Over and over his authoritative voice pierced the sky, until those nearest grew silent.

"Do not fear!" he commanded. "Stand still and see the salvation of the Lord!"

When he had repeated these words again and again, they somehow pricked the hearts of the people. Little by little, quiet spread through the crowd.

"Do not fear!" he insisted. "See what the Lord will accomplish for you today! The Egyptians whom you see today, you will never see again, *forever!*"

"But Moses," the men objected, "we cannot fight so great a host! We have not been trained in war!"

Joshua clenched his teeth. That had been his very objection to this venture! Why, oh why, had Moses not led them further south? If they had not turned back, Pharaoh might never have found them.

But as he watched his mentor, who stood boldly before the unbelieving masses, he was reminded of the first day he had seen him in the marketplace. He remembered how Moses and Aaron had mounted the storage crates in the middle of Raamses Square, and he remembered how dauntless Moses had been in the face of his mockers and beneath the leveled weapons of Pharaoh's guards.

Once again, the prophet was proving himself worthy of his calling. It did not matter who opposed him. He declared the words of Yahweh, come what may.

"The Lord knows your weakness!" Moses cried out. "He will fight *for* you, while you keep silent!"

Against this, what could anyone say? A shudder of compliance swept through the crowd, as the Israelites recalled the many times God had saved them by a miracle.

Indeed, the fact that three million could keep silent for any length of time was a miracle in itself. But so they did, until the Egyptians drew so near that their hearts nearly broke for fear.

"God save us!" they pleaded. Pushing down the shore, they began to retreat the way they had come.

But Moses would have none of it. "This way!" he commanded, pointing toward the sea.

Was he lunatic? Would he direct them to march into the miry waters of the Reed Sea?

Yes, it appeared this was his intention, as he stretched his rod out over Lake Timsah and cried, "Go forward!"

At that one instant in eternity, the descending troops of Pharaoh so close upon them they could feel their breath, and the marshy waves of Yam Suph licking at their toes, three million souls made a decision. Knowing they could drown, knowing they should never survive, they moved forward at Moses's command.

But the moment they made their first childlike steps toward the water, the earth began to shake. It was not the tramping of Pharaoh's army that shook it, nor the quaking of the fearful Israelites. It was the sigh of Yahweh, sweeping over the desert floor, sloshing the waters of Timsah back and forth like wine in a goblet.

Suddenly, the waters moved back from themselves, parting like hair is parted as a comb runs through it. Where the waters left a void, the lake bottom saw the sky. Earth water-soaked for thousands of years was suddenly drained dry, as though sucked clean by subterranean lips.

The Hebrews, who teetered upon the shore, rushed forward, pushed by fear, pulled by the pathway stretched before them.

Surging past the cliff where Moses and his servants stood watch, the three million fled across the seabed, between walls of standing water. Barely a soul looked back, as the stampeding horde raced for the eastern shore.

Only Moses, Joshua, and Aaron witnessed the next miracle with a clear view. As the escaping slaves made their desperate course, the cloudy pillar that had led them thus far suddenly lifted higher, and whisked back toward the oncoming army.

Spiraling downward, it spread out between the sea and

Pharaoh's million, obscuring their path and blocking their vision.

Like circus clowns, the troops collided into one another, and the chariots careened to a halt.

Foggy darkness descended upon the confounded army, causing the soldiers to grope for direction.

It was the Egyptians' turn to cry for help. And their fear was greater than any Israel had known.

5

The next morning, there was a great party on the eastern bank of Yam Suph. So great a celebration there had never been in all of human history!

Not only did it involve the largest number of people ever to celebrate together, but there had never been a more worthy cause to celebrate.

Pharaoh and his army, to the last man and beast, were dead.

It had taken the whole night for all three million Israelites to safely pass through the sea's narrow corridor. During that time, the pillar of cloud had kept the Egyptians from pursuing them.

When morning came, the pillar had risen again into the sky, and Pharaoh's men once more took up the chase.

Any fear this inspired in the Israelites, as they watched from the far shore, was quickly quelled. As though rattled by the hand of a giant child, the king's toylike chariots stuttered across the seabed, their wheels swerving and their horses stumbling over invisible obstacles. While the walls of water still stood firm to either side, the army began to cry out in confusion, many of the men turning back and fleeing the unseen challenger.

"Go back!" they cried to their companions. "Flee from Israel! Their god is fighting for them!"

While the amazed Israelites looked on, Moses again stretched his rod over the sea, and the waters closed in upon themselves. Panicking, the Egyptians fled directly into the tumbling walls, their chariots capsizing, and their horses being thrown head-down beneath the overwhelming tide.

Within an hour, there was no sign of the vanquished host. Swallowed alive, they had disappeared beneath the bubbling waves.

By midmorning, the only evidence that such a company had chased after Israel was a few corpses, washed up on the shore.

So now it was time to celebrate! Singing and dancing broke out among the Israelites. Up and down the beach they ran, laughing and pulling more booty from the soldiers' bloated bodies.

Gathering around Moses, Aaron, and Joshua were a thousand maidens, tossing their dark locks and swaying to tambourines and flutes.

Taking Moses by the hands they swung him about, and passed him from girl to girl. Joyous, the prophet laughed with them, while Aaron and Joshua, likewise, were spun around.

Then, emerging from the crowd, came Miriam, Moses's beloved sister. As though she were not a very old woman, she also danced, clapping a tambourine high above her hoary head, and directing all the women of Israel to follow her.

Within moments, a serpentine line of swaying, singing women was winding through the midst of the congregation, thousands upon thousands of them, pounding on hand drums, rattling cymbals and fingerbells, shimmying timbrels against their thighs.

During 400 years of slavery, the Hebrews had developed a knack for spontaneous chorus. Their slave songs had helped them work more easily together, and while often cast in sad, haunting harmony, they had helped to keep the Israelites' spirits from withering.

Today, however, the song was joyous. It mattered not who composed the words. It became a merry chant, voice answering voice, men calling to women, and women to men, African and Egyptian rhythms contributing to a gay symphony of sound:

I will sing unto the Lord, for he is highly
  exalted;
 the horse and its rider he has thrown
  into the sea!
The Lord is my strength and song,
 and he has become my salvation.
He is my God, and I will praise him;
 my father's God, and I will exalt him!
The Lord is a warrior;
 the Lord is His name!

On and on the song went, and Joshua danced and sang along with the others, laughing with his friend, Caleb, who cavorted beside him.

His heart had never been so free. He had seen the miracles of Moses in the plagues and in the exodus. He had been released from chains of slavery, and had followed the fiery pillar, the cloudy pillar, leaving the land of bondage.

But it was not only this that gave his soul wings, and set his feet to dancing.

He had been afraid of war, and the Lord had fought for him. He had feared taking up the shield and sword. But Yahweh had spared him.

Just as the song said, the Lord was the warrior. Israel had not needed to fight.

PART II
The Reluctant Warrior

6

South along the Gulf of Suez, along the western edge of the Sinai Peninsula, the people traveled, until they had gone out from Raamses a hundred and fifty miles. It was slow going. What would have taken a family two weeks to cover had taken the three million three times that long.

It was the fifteenth day of the second month after their departure from Egypt when they entered the wilderness called Sin. It was a bleak wasteland they traversed. With each passing day, the people became more restive.

They were running dangerously low on food. Moses had miraculously provided them with drinking water some days before, when they found the wells of one oasis bitter to the taste. And they had next arrived at Elim, a pleasant respite from their journey, full of a dozen sweet springs and a luscious date grove. Now, however, they were on the brink of Sinai's most lifeless tract. And they saw no prospect for sustenance should they venture further.

This evening, Joshua sat with his father, Nun, and grandfather, Elishama, beside the family stewpot. An uncomfortable hush had descended upon the Israelite camp. None of the three men commented on it, but as Joshua studied the firelit faces of the two elders, he knew they were thinking his thoughts.

The people were hungry. Likely, every family in the mammoth camp had sat down tonight to a paltry supper. The ominous quiet denoted growing desperation.

As Joshua dipped the ladle into his father's pot, it thudded against the bottom, and he scraped the last of a red porridge from the kettle. He would have offered it to

Elishama, but just as he called for his bowl, the old man shook his head.

Beside the family tent stood a small boy, son of a widowed relative. His dark eyes round and large, he watched the three men eat, and wistfully gazed upon the ladle in Joshua's hand.

In his own hands was an empty soup bowl.

"Give it to him, Hoshea," Elishama directed, bowing his head so that his long beard swept across his lap.

"But...Grandfather..." Joshua hesitated.

"Do as he says," Nun whispered.

Elishama was not well. He was frail, and might not make the journey across the desert. Still, the child's beseeching eyes tugged at Joshua's heart as well, and with a sigh, he called him close.

Pouring the last of the stew into the boy's bowl, he patted him on the head and sent him away.

Joshua, like everyone else, was becoming familiar with hunger. Holding his arm firm against his growling stomach, he asked to be excused, and left his father's campfire.

In recent days, as his energy had ebbed, the glory of past miracles was hard to recall. Despite the miseries of slavery, in Egypt he had never gone hungry, and it was difficult not to be bitter as his strength dwindled.

As he passed through camp, heading for Moses's tent, the quiet oppressed him. He could feel the people's eyes following him, steely eyes, accusing eyes. Tomorrow, or the next day, the camp might not be so still. When the people sat down to empty bowls and another hungry night, they would begin to make demands.

In fact, it might not take that long before they rebelled.

"We should have died in Egypt!" someone spat as he walked by.

"Yes!" another grumbled. "There we had plenty of meat, and we ate our fill of bread!"

"Do you go to see Moses?" a young mother cried. "Ask him why he brought us into this place? Does he hope to kill us all with hunger?"

As Joshua grew accustomed to his role as Moses's servant, he was also becoming more bold. Tonight, as he approached the holy man's tent, he did not announce himself, but walked right in.

"Master, the people have no food," he said.

In the lamplight, Moses sat reading a scroll full of Egyptian hieroglyphs. Joshua recognized it as one on which his mentor had been laboring for many days. The handwriting was Moses's own, and Joshua had often been curious as to the scroll's mysterious contents.

The prophet did not look up. "Do you remember when we came to Marah?" he asked.

"Of course," Joshua replied. Marah, meaning "bitter," was the name the Israelites had given to the oasis where the water was undrinkable.

"Why do you think the water was so useless?" the prophet inquired.

Joshua thought a moment. "It was standing water, not a spring," he answered. "Standing water can become rank."

"Yes," Moses nodded, "but that oasis has been used for years, by countless travelers. When I worked the shepherd route for my father-in-law, I went there many times."

Joshua shrugged. "Then I cannot say," he admitted. "It does seem strange that it was rancid."

"Not so strange," Moses replied, leaning back and looking at Joshua. "It was the people's ignorance that caused the problem. Don't you know that they fouled the waters themselves?"

Joshua pondered this. He remembered that the people had eagerly used the waters as a bathing pool. When millions of sweaty bodies had entered and left, the waters had indeed been murky.

"Not only did they swim there, but they relieved themselves there," Moses explained. "God, in his patience, showed me the way to purge the waters, but our people must learn new laws of cleanliness. The ways of the slave camps will not do here."

Joshua vividly recalled Moses's strange command that several shittah trees be chopped down, and thrown into the huge pool. Within a few hours, the waters had cleared and become drinkable.

On that day, Moses had strictly forbidden the people to enter the water. From his scroll he had read to them an edict, instructing them, furthermore, to relieve themselves outside the camp.

"'If you will give earnest heed to the voice of the Lord your God, and do what is right in his sight, and give ear to his commandments, and keep all his statutes, I will put none of the diseases on you which I have put on the Egyptians,'" the prophet had pronounced, "'for I, the Lord, am your healer!'"

At the time, Joshua had seen no connection between the ordinance Moses gave, and the problem of the waters. The Egyptians paid little heed to such matters, and the moving waters of the Nile suffered little for it. Still, from time to time strange ailments did sweep through the land of Egypt, especially through the hovel-lined alleys of the slave camps. Life in this enormous company was even more precarious, and the people must learn a new set of standards to survive.

"So," Joshua wondered, passing his eyes over the open scroll, "has the Lord given you more rules for us to follow?"

Moses reverently lifted the parchment to the lamplight, and scanned it quickly. Then, rolling it up, he placed it in a leather wrapper, and tucked it beneath his pillow.

"Every day God speaks to me, Joshua," Moses answered. "His words are wonderful. I do not understand them all.

But they always pierce my heart like shafts of light. In time I will share them with you."

Joshua bowed respectfully before the prophet. "I shall be honored," he said. But then, clearing his throat, he pressed him. "Sir, what about the present problem? The people are becoming disillusioned. They cry out for food, and soon there will be none at all!"

Nodding, Moses drew out the leather folder once again, stroking it gently. "On that matter," he said, "the Lord has revealed himself this night. Bring the people before me in the morning, and I will calm their fears."

7

The next night, the great congregation slept soundly, having no enemy to fear, and their stomachs full.

Just as Moses had promised, the Lord had taken care of them.

Early that day, the prophet had called the people to him, speaking words of comfort, and rebuke.

"Come near before the Lord," he had cried out, "for he has heard your grumblings!"

In that moment, as the people looked toward the wilderness, the cloudy pillar began to glow and throb, streaks of lightning flashing through it.

Falling back, the crowd gasped, and Moses shouted, "Your grumblings are not against me, but against the Lord! Thus says the Lord, 'I have heard the grumblings of the children of Israel. At twilight you shall eat meat, and in the morning you shall be filled with bread. Behold, I will rain bread from heaven for you, and you shall know that I am the Lord your God!'"

Suddenly, from the midst of the pillar, a smaller, darker cloud emerged, heading straight for the camp.

Covering their heads, the people ducked as the strange configuration swept over them.

Not knowing what to expect, they could barely believe their ears when the cloud swooped toward the ground, shuddering and squawking.

For this cloud had wings, and countless, feathered bodies! It was a gigantic flock of quail that descended from the flashing pillar, and the quail now skittered across the ground, pecking at the lifeless sand and surprising the feet of the bewildered Israelites.

With a shout of hilarity, the people scooped them up in their hands. That night there was meat in the stewpots of Israel, more meat than they could eat.

Next morning, Joshua, having had the best night of sleep since leaving Egypt, awoke to a peculiar sound.

In fact, it was not sound, but the lack of sound that roused him, and as he opened his eyes, the light entering his tent seemed unusually bright.

Sitting up, he cocked his head and listened to the shining stillness. He had never seen snow, but he had heard travelers tell of the bright dawns in mountain countries, and of the peculiar quiet that always came with a snowfall. If it had only been cold this morning, he would have expected to see a frozen landscape when he opened his tent door.

What met his eyes, when he did step forth, was far stranger.

It seemed a fine frost mantled the earth, but when Joshua reached down to touch it, it did not melt.

When he stepped forth, it crumbled into large flakes beneath his feet, but was not cold against his skin.

It was very early, but the sunlight glancing off the white ground was waking the whole camp. As news spread of the strange phenomenon, people cautiously studied the flaky substance, lifting hunks to their noses and smelling its subtle aroma. Like sweet honey, it melted in their mouths, and soon they were gathering it up in handfuls, eating it eagerly and laughing together.

"What is it?" Caleb asked, running to Joshua with a handful.

"It must be the bread the Lord promised," Joshua replied. And sampling it for himself, he shrugged. "Whatever it is, it is very good!"

8

For each of the children of Israel, through all their years of bondage in Egypt, there had been a dualism to life that was unique to their race. While the cultures of other enslaved tribes and nations had been absorbed into the Egytian system, losing their identity over time, the Hebrews had maintained their integrity. No matter how oppressed, the Israelite was first a son or daughter of Jacob, and second a slave.

Though their racial imprint might have been oblite-rated by intermarriage and by the cares of the world, it somehow survived, passed on by word of mouth, by sto-ries of the patriarchs told around evening fires, by cradle songs, and by stubborn tradition. Their identity, more than anyone else's, was preserved by an ancient and persistent faith. Challenged though it had been, that childlike ideology had endured the ravages of persecu-tion, and the encroachment of other teachings.

A few select names from their national genealogy served to give them a sense of solidarity. For four hun-dred years the names of Abraham, Isaac, and Jacob had helped the Israelites see themselves in one another.

For Joshua, his ancestral link to Joseph had been a proud distinction.

Blessed with a godly father and grandfather, he had been raised on the legends of Joseph and his brothers. Early on, the longing for freedom and the longing for his people to achieve their true potential had been planted deep within his heart.

Thus it was that while many of his fellow Israelites had scorned Moses when he first returned to Egypt, Joshua had not. Trained up on the truth, he had recognized it when it was spoken. And he had quickly identified Moses as a man of God.

As for the character of God himself, Joshua and all the people were only beginning to know him. They realized he was their protector and their savior, for they had witnessed his miracles on their behalf. But in many ways his dealings with them were mystifying, and the requirements he made of them were difficult to comprehend.

The days following the first provision of the quail and the manna were illustrative of the Lord's strict commands. According to the words of Moses, the men were to gather enough manna each day for the number of people in each household; no more, no less. They were not to have leftovers, for if they left it overnight, the manna bred worms and became foul. If they did not comply with the command to gather the manna before noon, they went hungry, for the strange substance melted in the sun.

The miraculous nature of the peculiar foodstuff was borne out in the fact that it never appeared upon the ground on the seventh day of the week. The Israelites were told that they must gather enough for two days upon the sixth day, and that the amount set aside for the seventh day would not spoil.

"The seventh day is a sabbath observance," Moses explained to them, "a holy sabbath to the Lord. On that day you will not find manna in the field. The Lord has given you the sabbath. Remain in your places on that day, and rest. No one should go forth on the seventh day."

Little by little, Moses was imposing such regulations on the people. And while they were strange laws, they did serve to bind the people together, bringing some sense of order to their lives.

Not that the concept of sabbath was entirely foreign to them. The idea of a "day of rest" was common to many cultures, and the word "sabbath" itself was Babylonian.

Always the Hebrews had maintained that the last day of the week was special, because the Lord God had rested from his work of creation on that day.

But the restrictions on work were new to them, as they had been forced to serve their Egyptian masters regardless of the day.

With the provision of food and the institution of the sabbath, the journey became more relaxed. There was no more Pharaoh to dread, no looking back in fear of his pursuit, and there was one day a week of sheer rest.

In safety and in peace did the people at last come in view of Mount Horeb, or Mount Sinai, the holy mountain where their leader, Moses, had first encountered the Lord.

Four days of travel across the sands had brought them from the Wilderness of Sin to the grazing land of Rephidim, just ten miles west of the sacred site. It was nearing noon when the vast company caught its first glimpse of the mountain's three craggy pinnacles.

Joshua was walking beside Moses, at the head of the congregation, when Horeb appeared on the horizon. As the prophet gazed upon it, a look of awe and reverence lit his face, and Joshua knew he was remembering the hallowed day when the angel had spoken to him from the burning bush.

Truly, the mountain would have inspired awe in anyone coming upon it. For centuries it had been a legendary landmark, lifting the thoughts of passersby toward the heavens. For it was the solitary feature of a barren landscape. In an otherwise drab, flat terrain, it seemed to have no reason for being, other than to take the mind to higher things.

Guardian of the wilderness, it had also guarded the souls of shepherds who walked in its shadow, and merchants who skirted its caverns. To many tribes and tongues it was known as a holy place.

But for Moses and for the children of Israel, it represented more. It was the birthplace of their liberty. Moses's experience there had fathered their freedom.

As the three million made camp at Rephidim, every man, woman, and child scanned Horeb's distant, hazy slopes, hoping for a glimpse of Yahweh himself.

What would the Lord teach them there? they wondered. He had taught them much already. But this was his home, and they were entering holy ground.

As Moses and Joshua made camp at Rephidim, the master was increasingly private.

At last, his servant dared to speak.

"Was it high on the mountain that the Lord appeared to you?" he asked.

Moses smiled and shook his head.

"No, my son," he replied. "Shepherds do not climb Horeb. They tend their flocks in the lowlands."

"So the Lord appeared to you at the foot of the mount?" Joshua deduced.

"Yes," Moses answered. "He did not wait for me to find him, but met me where I was."

9

Joshua rode through the oasis of Rephidim, where the Israelites were resting. Tomorrow they would set foot in the shadow of the sacred mount, and spirits were high in the camp.

People greeted the young Hebrew with smiles and cheers, for though he was only Moses's servant, they respected the regard their leader had for him.

Though Joshua returned their greetings, he shook his head at their inconsistency. Just yesterday, when they had first entered this place, rebellion had once again nearly broken out.

It would have been so easy to slip the last miles toward Sinai on feet of faith. All had been going smoothly since the children of Israel had left the Wilderness of Sin, where they had first received the manna. But it seemed Yahweh would not allow them to enter the holy mountain before they were again tested.

In years past, and during the time of Moses's stay in this region, the wells of Rephidim had always provided respite from heat and thirst. And a great hill which sheltered the wayside gave good shade against the sun. The Rock of Horeb, it was called, being in view of the sacred mount.

What the Israelites found here, however, was dismaying. It had been only a few months since Moses had watered his father-in-law's flocks at this very site, but the wells had now gone dry. Although the people had brought water from Marah, their jugs and flasks were nearly empty. And though it was only a matter of miles before they reached the pasturing land of Sinai, they might not survive the journey in between.

Yahweh had once again proven that he was with Moses by delivering the people through a miracle. From the midst of the Rock of Horeb could still be heard the sound of gushing water. When Moses had, at God's instruction, struck the giant monolith with his staff, it had split asunder, sending a pristine river across the sand.

But this had not happened before insurrection threatened to undo the progress the people had made toward unity.

Reigning his horse along the border of the camp, Joshua dropped in on various families, checking as to their welfare this last night before entering Sinai. Would they forever prove themselves to be fickle under pressure? he wondered. If only they could believe once and for all that God was with them!

Venturing into the night desert, he marveled that anyone could doubt. They had been spared from Pharaoh, from the waters of the Reed Sea, and from hunger. When the reassuring billows of the cloudy pillar dissipated each night, the glow of the fiery pillar was always with them.

Even now, as Joshua headed out from camp, the spiraling watchtower lit the ground.

It was wonderful to be so free, to have the liberty to race across the sands and to return at will! Never in Egypt had he known such freedom. He was still not used to it.

When he heard someone call to him from behind, he sighed. He was not ready to go back. He wanted time to savor the desert quiet.

Turning about, he saw that the one who hailed him came not from camp, but from the direction of Sinai. Dressed in heavy, dark robes, he appeared to be a bedo, a nomadic tribesman, and he rode a galloping camel.

At every wayside along the wilderness route, the Israelites had encountered bedouin clans and caravans of many nationalities. Thus far their exchanges had been friendly, for what could small companies do against so great a horde of people?

But this bedo hailed Joshua with great urgency, and as he drew near, his face was full of fear.

Though Joshua was unfamiliar with the man's native tongue, the fellow broke in and out of Hebrew, interpreting himself as he frantically addressed Joshua.

"We want no violence here!" he cried. "Joshua, son of Nun, take your people hence! We will have no war in our desert!"

Dumbfounded, Joshua watched as the stranger bounded across the sands toward him. He was certain that he heard him clearly, now. But his words made no sense.

"Do not fear," Joshua called, as the man reigned his camel close beside him. "We come in peace, I and all my people."

Breathless, the bedo leaned down from his high saddle, and flailed his arms. "Peace?" he cried. "We have heard of your exploits against Pharaoh! We are not fools. And neither are our neighbors!"

Joshua would have laughed, so desperate did the man appear. But he respectfully restrained himself.

"Good man," he replied, "it was not we who overcame Pharaoh, but our God. No Israelite has ever gone to war!"

For a moment, the bedo was silent, seeming to ponder this statement. But at last his lips parted in a sneer, showing a gleam of large white teeth against his black beard.

Bowing low, he nodded. "Very well," he said, "so it was your God who fought for you. Pharaoh had a god or two himself. We all do. But there shall be no violence in this desert! When the sons of Amalek come against you, turn around and go home!"

"The sons of Amalek?" Joshua marveled. "What have they to do with us?"

The bedo sat up and studied Joshua in disbelief.

"You are a commander of your people, and you do not know?" he laughed. "The Amalekites claim the very land you enter! And they are prepared to fight!"

Of course Joshua had heard of the Amalekites, one of the oldest nations on earth, and he knew that they claimed this desert as their own.

"This is a land of many peoples," Joshua argued. "It is a wilderness, and open to all."

"Ha!" the bedo scoffed. "Wouldn't I like to think so! I am chieftain of a tribe myself. But I know when I am outdone. I bow to the Amalekites, and so should you! Take your people and go back to Egypt, before the blood of Israel floods the sands!"

At this, the bedo reigned his camel about and fled back across the desert.

Swallowed by the night, he left Joshua with nothing but the drumming of his heart.

10

All night long a council fire burned in the compound where Joseph's sarcophagus rested. The tent of Moses was not large enough to accomodate all the leaders of the people whom the prophet had summoned.

In the sky above the great circle of men gathered there, the fiery pillar kept vigil, and far into the wee hours the elders talked of war.

When Joshua had returned to camp, he had gone straight to Moses with news of the bedo and his words. He had not told another soul of the stranger's fearsome warning, knowing it could spark panic among the change-able Israelites.

Sending for Aaron and Caleb, Moses sent them forth with Joshua to call a select council, and once gathered, the leaders considered what to do.

Peppering their conversation, the word "Amalekites" never failed to inspire fear. For the huge nation, which claimed for itself several kings and numerous territories from Palestine to Sinai, was the most warlike of all Semi-tic peoples.

Although, as Joshua had said, the wilderness into which the Israelites traveled was open territory, most tribes of the area bowed to the sons of Amalek, and across the Sinaitic Peninsula was evidence of the Amalekites' conquest in thick stone buildings set up as check stations for their occupying troops.

Sitting near Moses tonight was not only Aaron, but Amram, their father. And with Caleb and Joshua sat their own fathers and grandfathers: Nun, Elishama, Jephunneh, and Hezron. But the number of leaders was in the hundreds, men who had shown themselves over the past weeks and during their time in Egypt to be wise, reputable, and courageous. While there was, as yet, no census among the Israelites, and no clear registry of tribes, the men present this night represented a good cross section of families and clans.

As they discussed the matter at hand, it was obvious that none of them underestimated the strength of the enemy.

"They have likely sent ambassadors to all the nations hereabouts," said Hur, a leading Judahite. "We can be sure that if they come against us, we will have no allies, for they will have stirred up the whole region to hate us!"

At this, the council murmured, shaking their heads and huddling in anxious agreement. Though Hur's observation was not made to incite panic, it was a reasonable deduction. Who, after all, would side with three million renegades, whose entrance into the area was so mysterious, and about whom such fearsome reports were circulating? If Israel had "overcome" Pharaoh, as the bedo believed, they must mean to establish a land for themselves, and undoubtedly dreamed of conquest.

"As for the number of nations who might join them," Nadab added, "we would do well to think largely! Are there not many different tribes in Sinai?"

The question was directed at Moses, who had lived in the area for forty years. Thus far the prophet had said little, allowing the men to grapple with the issues. When he did not readily reply, Abihu spoke for him.

"Of course there are!" the Levite said. "Surely, Moses, when you worked here with your father-in-law, you had dealings with dozens of tribes."

Moses looked about him, surveying the worried faces in the company. "Yes," he answered at last, "there are many various people in this land. And most likely they will side with Amalek. And," he said, rising to his feet, "if we look at our options in human terms alone, we have reason to sink from fear. But we must remember that we do not fight in our own strength. If Yahweh is with us, any who come against us are *his* enemies, not ours alone!"

As Joshua listened, he remembered the night when he and Aaron had been summoned to the master's tent. When Moses had told them they must turn back toward Egypt, that Pharaoh was going to come against them, he had wondered how the untrained Israelites could ever successfully take up arms.

Breathing deeply, Joshua smiled up at his mentor. So once again the prospect of war loomed before them. Surely, once again, they would be rescued by a miracle!

Unbidden, he too stood up, taking a place beside the prophet. And presuming he had permission, he began to exhort the crowd.

"Listen to Moses," he said. "When will we ever learn? Has not Yahweh always fought our battles for us? Remember the Reed Sea? 'Stand still and see what the Lord will do,'" he quoted the prophet. "Will Yahweh forsake us this time? Surely we are not men of war!"

Rapt, the great circle of men considered Joshua's words with a hush. Never had the young man used his position as Moses's servant to speak so boldly.

Surely he was right, they thought. When they began to applaud him, Joshua bowed his head.

But soon, his moment in the sun was cut short. When Moses drew near and placed a hand on his shoulder, it was with a look of disapproval.

"May Yahweh reward you for your faith, my friend," the prophet addressed him. "But the Lord has never said we must not take up arms."

Stunned, Joshua listened, his face burning as Moses corrected him before the elders.

"Tomorrow you will go forth among the people, and choose an army," the prophet directed.

An army? The words hung in the air like battle banners.

"*I*, sir?" Joshua stammered.

"Yes," Moses replied. "You are no longer my servant, only. You are now commanding general of all my forces."

11

If ever there had been a reluctant warrior, it was Joshua.

It had been one thing to stand with Moses before Pharaoh, lending support to the man of God as he called down the power of the Almighty against Egypt. It had been one thing to, by faith, sprinkle blood upon his doorpost and await the coming of the death angel through the streets of Raamses. It had been one thing to set out across miles of barren desert, in quest of an unknown destiny. It had been one thing to stand on the banks of Lake Timsah, trusting the words of Moses that God would save them from the oncoming Egyptian troops.

It was quite another to know that within hours he must take a cold spear in his hand, hoist a heavy shield to his breast, and charge into a bloody fray.

Joshua was not a coward. A coward would never have sided with Moses in the first place. But Joshua was a reasonable man. He knew that tomorrow he must raise up an untrained force to battle against the most cunning of enemies. He knew the odds were overwhelmingly against him.

Though the Amalekites were barbarians in comparison to the fine-tuned war machine of the Egyptian forces, they were ruthlessly bold on the battlefield. Caring more for combat than for their own lives, they had made a name for themselves by recklessly rushing into conflict. By sheer bullheadedness alone, they had won countless wars, savagery making up for lack of formal discipline.

Despite all this, however, Joshua would have been less apprehensive if it had not seemed Yahweh had changed his dealings with Israel. Never before had the Lord left them to their own devices, yet this seemed to be the word Moses had given.

With dawn only a few hours away, Joshua sat in the prophet's tent, undergoing an accelerated course in military strategy. Moses had been trained in warfare in the finest military academy on earth, the school for Egyptian princes in the court of Pharaoh. Though he had never been obliged to fight in the king's army, or to lead a force in battle, he well remembered the theories learned as a young man.

"Begin by sending the council elders back to their camps," Moses directed him. "Since, as yet, there is little stratification among the people, and no demarcation according to tribe or household, instruct the elders to call forth the most capable men they can find, register them on tablets, and send them to the front, to stand before you."

Grateful for this guidance, Joshua agreed. "Yes, sir. What next?"

"These men, once gathered at the head of the company, must likewise be given orders to seek out other able men. When you have done this, come back to me, and we will talk further."

Hastening away, Joshua did as Moses suggested. And as the troops were being gathered, he took further counsel.

"Soon you must address your men," the prophet said. "Encouragement is the word of the hour. Let everything you say inspire confidence and daring."

Joshua nodded, but ran a nervous hand through his dark hair, wondering how this was to be done. He longed to tell his men that Yahweh was with them, that he would fight their battle for them as he had done in times past. But he was apparently not free to do this.

"Charge the young men to obey their elders, and the elders to obey you," Moses went on. "Appoint a small party of men to remain near the water of Horeb, to bear it out to the troops, and another to take care of the women and children. Let them know that their role is of equal value to the role of the warriors, but choose the less able-bodied for this duty. Instruct your men to shine their weapons, and to carry them with poise and valor. You have no time to drill them, but you must demand orderliness."

"Yes, sir," Joshua assented. His brow was furrowed and inwardly he trembled at the task before him. But keeping his feelings to himself, he rose to go. "Your advice is most appreciated," he said. "I shall do my best."

Though he did not look Moses in the eye, the prophet easily read his apprehension.

"Joshua," he called, as the general turned to leave, "is there something you wish to say?"

"No, sir," the young Hebrew lied. But Moses knew him well. Stammering, Joshua turned about and faced the man of God.

"Yes, sir, there is," he confessed. "I do not understand the ways of our Lord. We need him now as much as ever. Yet he has withdrawn himself."

Amazed, Moses looked at his servant wide-eyed. "How can you think this?" he marveled.

"You said so yourself," Joshua replied, his face reddening. "Just last night, before the elders."

Thinking back, Moses sorted through the events of the evening.

Suddenly realizing the source of Joshua's concern, he shook his head. "My dear friend," he sighed, "do you think that because Yahweh requires us, this time, to bear arms, he will not be with us, in our very midst?"

When Joshua only gave a perplexed shrug, Moses stood up and placed his hands upon Joshua's shoulders.

"It is true that you and all your army must take up sword and shield," Moses said, "but tomorrow, when the enemy comes against us, I will be stationed atop the hill of Horeb Rock. In my hand will be another weapon, the staff of God. So long as it is raised to heaven, no army on earth can conquer Israel!"

12

By the time dawn had arrived, seven hundred and fifty thousand strong young men awaited orders at the foot of Horeb Rock. Riding his horse halfway up the hill, Joshua overlooked the huge company. Enormous though it was, it was composed of the most disheveled, awkward-looking "soldiers" any commander had ever claimed.

There was no order to the ranks. In fact, there were no ranks. Each man was an entity to himself; no man dressed like any other, and every man, though fearful, stood at ease. They had not been trained to salute. They held what weapons they had in clumsy hands, shields dragging on the ground, spears pointing every direction.

They had come from Egypt as children at heart, raised in a slave system, stripped of a sense of power. They had not studied war, and if they were to succeed in this battle, it must be by force of will.

As Joshua surveyed his "army," he tried not to appear dismayed. But he could not help but wonder just how much force of will they had. In four hundred years they had not risen up against their oppressors. Any sense of duty or obedience they had learned was that of subservience. They did not see themselves as a force to be reckoned with.

And now, their commander must address them.

Glancing over his shoulder, he saw that Moses had taken a station on the top of the hill, and that beside him stood supportive comrades, Hur the Judahite, and Aaron. Taking a deep breath, Joshua wondered how his next words could ever command the same attention as an address from the prophet of God.

Sitting straight and tall in his saddle, he assumed the air of an experienced general, though he felt quite foolish.

"Men of Israel!" he cried. "It is by the grace and assistance of Almighty God that you have been brought out of Egypt, and have attained freedom. Be of good courage and strong heart. Rely today on that same Guiding Hand that has given us victory time and again!"

At the sound of their commander's voice, the troops grew quiet, and Joshua listened to the echo of his own words pass over the plain.

"We go out today," he cried, "against a force that would strip us of all God has given us. We must not think them capable of undoing the work of the Lord!"

Murmuring enthusiastically, the men took heed and seemed now to stand a little straighter.

"You must not imagine that the Amalekites are any more numerous than we, nor that their weapons are any finer," Joshua went on, "because we have on our side the hosts of heaven and the sword of Yahweh!"

At this, a cheer arose from the field, and the men raised their spears and swords to the sky.

"In the eyes of God, the army of Amalek is weak and small!" Joshua shouted. "They have no weapons to frighten the Almighty!"

Another cheer arose, and praises all about.

"What is war?" Joshua cried. And scarcely believing his own wisdom, he answered, "It is a fight against men, only. But you have endured trials far greater—hunger and thirst and oppression of every kind. With God's help you have conquered deserts and the great sea!"

"Yes, yes!" the men shouted.

At Joshua's command, they filed themselves behind select leaders, and began to look the part of an army. With the hems of their garments and the winding cloths of their turbans they began to shine their weapons. And within an hour they had transformed themselves into a reasonably sharp company, spears held erect and chins held high.

As they stood at attention, Joshua descended the hill a little way and passed back and forth before them. He had reason now to be proud. And though his soul still shook at the thought of the conflict ahead, he did not show it.

Turning about, he faced the men on the hilltop. "Master Moses," he cried out, "I present the army of the Israelites!"

A deafening shout ascended from the troops, and Moses smiled.

But as the eager cry filled the sky above Horeb Rock, it was met by another sound, equally deafening and terrifying.

It was the cry of the sons of Amalek, as they raced toward them across the Sinai sands.

13

More fearsome than the sound of Pharaoh's legions was the awesome thunder of one hundred thousand galloping camels. More terrifying than the well-groomed threat of Egypt's marching troops was the helter-skelter onslaught of nearly a million barbaric bedouins.

Dark of face and spewing hate, they careened across the desert toward the uninitiated Israelites. Their long headscarves trailing in the sandy wind, the riders lunged forth upon their gangly steeds, waving razor-sharp swords and broad-bladed machetes in the air. Calling on their god, Allah, foot soldiers raced behind them, swords and clubs held in sweaty hands, and scabbards empty in their wide, cloth belts.

This fighting force bore few shields, so eager were they for hand-to-hand combat. It seemed they had no fear, as they recklessly ran toward the "invaders."

Stunned by the sight of this human stampede, Joshua and his flegling fighters were momentarily paralyzed. But Moses still stood atop Horeb Rock, and when Joshua looked toward him he saw that the prophet had raised his staff above his head.

"Charge!" the commander cried. And with a mighty shout, the childlike troops dashed straight for the oncoming horde.

Slashing and yelling, the newcomers raced directly into the front lines of the Amalekites. They had few camels of their own, and had not ridden them into battle. But they daringly took on the riders, who swooped at them from their high mounts with spears and blades.

So thick was the red dust raised by the troops and

animals that it was a wonder anyone could see to move. Within moments, the Sinai sands were redder, speckled and splattered with the blood of men and camels.

Joshua, buried in the middle of the fray, saw hundreds fall to every side. But he had no notion as to who had taken the worst until a sudden rift grew between the two companies.

To his amazement, the Amalekites were retreating, chasing back across the desert.

As the dust settled, the Israelties looked at one another in bewilderment. But as they realized they had actually driven back the foe, they began to laugh and cry with astonishment.

Embracing one another, they danced up and down, clapping one another on the back and slapping hands together.

Joshua, as astounded as any of them, circled out from the troops and rode quickly toward the foot of Horeb Rock. As before, Moses stood there, Aaron and Hur beside him, his staff raised over his head. Perhaps he was just as bewildered as Joshua, for as the general stood below him, he shrugged and lowered his staff.

Counting casualties, the host of Israel found that relatively few of their men had fallen, as compared to the great many dead who littered the path of the Amalekites.

But they were not so foolish as to congratulate themselves on an early end to the war.

From the direction of Mount Sinai could again be heard the sound of a rushing army. The Amalekites had not accepted defeat but had only regrouped, this time coming forth with reinforcements, having been joined by allies of many nations round about.

To this point, the numbers of each side had not really mattered, for the first battle had seen fighting mainly along the front. Now the war would be more bloody. The chagrined Amalekites were more determined, and the fight would move deeper into the ranks.

This time, also, the Israelites would face multiple enemies spread out to north and south, as well as east.

When Joshua shouted the command to again go forth, Moses once more raised his sacred staff above his head. But the staff was no longer just a bare stick. The prophet had removed his striped mantle from his head—the one in which his mother had wrapped him when she placed him in the bulrush ark, the one beneath which he had said his first contraband Hebrew prayers in the house of Pharaoh—and he had attached it to the top of the rod.

It was a Levite shawl, and it was now the banner of Israel. Over the fray it would wave, until the war be finished.

* * *

It hardly seemed possible, but so long as that banner graced the hilltop, held aloft in Moses's hands, the army of Israel was invincible.

Whenever Moses allowed his arms a rest, the tide of battle turned, and Israelite losses soared.

It was high noon when Joshua first realized this. The battle had gone back and forth between the contenders several times, and each time the Israelites were routed, he noted that Moses had let down his hands.

This fact would have been more obvious to the prophet had he been down on the war stage beside his commander. As it was, with the dust and the inscrutable scuffle of the valley floor, the truth of the matter was not so evident to the three spectators on the hill.

There were now nearly twice as many Amalekites and their allies as there were Israelites. Things had not gone well for Israel for the last hour, although Moses kept his staff aloft most of that time.

Grabbing Caleb, who rode beside him, Joshua commanded him to go to Horeb Rock. "Tell the man of God he must not let his banner slip...not even slightly!" he cried.

Hastening to comply, Caleb raced away, and soon the banner was seen flying higher upon the hill, the prophet standing tall beneath it.

Throughout the afternoon, from this point on, the army of Israel made valiant strides. Though they were far outnumbered, and though the daring men of Amalek were far more capable, the Israelites forced them back toward Sinai.

Joshua's heart surged as he saw the enemy retreating. On the hill behind, Moses now sat upon a large stone, apparently placed there by his two friends. Joshua knew that his arms must be drained of blood, his muscles unable to maintain the banner on their own. To either side of him sat Aaron and Hur, supporting his numb arms, and keeping his hands aloft.

Not once, since Caleb had taken Joshua's message to him, had Moses lowered the staff. Whenever the troops wearied, the sight of the Levite banner, waving over them, gave inspiration.

At sunset, as the last of the overwhelmed Amalekites scurried toward the eastern horizon, the red sun glinting off their lowered spears, such a cry of jubilation went up from Israel, the whole world must have heard it.

PART III
The Right-Hand Man

14

At the foot of Mount Sinai, on the very ground where the enemy had retreated, Israel set up camp. There were no Amalekites left in the plain, and none had been seen since they had been routed.

This night, in the shadow of the holy mount, a great celebration was about to begin. This site had been Moses's first goal since leaving Egypt, and it had been reached over seemingly impossible odds.

Joshua's father and grandfather fussed over him as he made ready to go forth from the family tent. Moses had summoned him to stand before the people, that he might honor him tonight. The two elders helped him look his best, holding up a hand mirror and smoothing his finest tunic in the yellow lamplight.

"You have done us proud, Hoshea!" Elishama boasted, as he coaxed into place a stray lock of Joshua's wavy hair.

"Never was a father more proud than I!" Nun enthused, as he walked around his son, surveying him up and down. "To think! I raised a mighty warrior, and did not know it!"

Joshua smiled, and headed for the door. "Never did an Israelite have finer fathers," he answered, and securing his sword to his belt, he quickly hastened away.

Throughout camp, a million torches competed with a coral sunset, and with the deepening glow of the sky-pillar. Up ahead, at the base of Sinai, Moses waited for him, standing at the very site of the miraculous burning bush. Tonight there was no mysterious flaming bush, but the whole desert was flooded with orange firelight.

Apparently the entire nation of Israel awaited Joshua's appearance. As word spread that he was going forth,

73

music and applause broke loose on every side, and barely could he make it through the pressing throng.

When he at last stood before his mentor, Moses took him by the arm and led him a little way up on the mount, so that he might be seen by the masses.

On the Sinai slope, the prophet had constructed a stone altar, and perched atop it was the sacred staff, adorned with the Levite shawl.

As the great crowd grew quiet, Moses took from inside his sleeve a small scroll. Opening it, he turned to the congregation, and announced, "The Lord has told me to write a memorial, and to recite it to Joshua."

So powerful was his voice, no one would have believed he once objected to the Lord that he needed a spokes-man, that Aaron must speak for him because he was "slow of speech" and "slow of tongue."

"Thus says the Lord," he declared, "'I will utterly blot out the memory of Amalek from under heaven!'"

At this a jubilant cry went up from the people, and Moses raised his hands to quiet them.

"By his own hand, the Lord has sworn!" he shouted. "The Lord will have war against Amalek from generation to generation!"

Joshua's skin prickled as Moses looked him in the eye, and when the prophet placed hands on his head, he knelt to the ground, removing the sword from his belt and laying it at his master's feet.

"Joshua," the man of God announced, "you have proven yourself worthy of honor among your people. Always remember that the Lord is your banner."

With this, the prophet took a small vial of oil from his belt and anointed the warrior in the witness of all.

Then drawing Joshua up, he led him to the altar, where a slain goat had been placed.

Taking a torch, he held it before the commanding general.

"Do this for the people," Moses directed him.

Scarcely believing the holy man could pass this duty to him, Joshua hesitated.

"But, Master," he stammered, "I am not their minister. How can I light the fire of sacrifice?"

Moses studied him compassionately. Taking the staff from the altar, he laid it beside Joshua's sword. "With your weapon you have served the Lord, just as I serve him with my staff. You are worthy, Joshua."

Trembling, the warrior, the one who had feared to fight and who had reluctantly gone to battle, touched the torch to the altar kindling.

Instantly, a fire raged, consuming the sacrificial goat.

Overcome with holy awe, Joshua turned to the people. And raising his hands, he cried, "The Lord is my banner! The Lord, mighty in battle!"

Like a war cry it spilled over the plain, capturing the heart of Israel. And soon, the entire congregation echoed the slogan.

"The Lord is my banner!" they cried. "The Lord, mighty in battle!"

15

All that night, there was a celebration in the camp of Israel.

The mood in the vast company had been festive ever since the defeat of Amalek. But the official celebration had begun on this, their first evening at Sinai.

Indeed, it was not only a celebration of victory in war, but of their arrival at the holy mount.

The ex-slaves had learned how to be festive in Egypt. Under the oppression of bondage, any small happiness was enough to inspire revelry. It was a matter of soul-survival that the slaves learned to forget, however briefly, their hard life, and turn their minds to frivolity. Given their new liberation and the recent evidences of God's blessings, they practiced the art of merriment with greater zest than ever.

Joshua sat with Moses tonight, in the company of Israel's most respected elders. The vicinity of the prophet's tent was always headquarters of the traveling nation, and here the leaders congregated about their own fire, with their own musicians. In the shadow of Joseph's casket, beneath the spiraling light of the fiery pillar, lovely virgins danced, their long skirts and wild hair flying as they twirled and swayed.

As wine was passed, the men laughed and talked together, of freedom and victory and the days ahead.

Mostly, however, their attention was focused on an old man, bushy-bearded and dark of face, who spun an intriguing tale.

Never in his life had Joshua seen a fellow like this one. Except for the bedouin sheik who had challenged him on the desert the night before the war, he had never been close to an Arab patriarch. The Amalekites were wild desert dwellers, but not one of them had been so colorful.

Dressed in heavy, striped robes, he was bedecked with countless charms and baubles. Upon his wide sleeves there dangled little prayer boxes, and his mantle hood sported a dozen more. White teeth gleamed between a black moustache and grizzled beard, complemented by the whites of smiling eyes in an otherwise ruddy face.

When he laughed it was at Moses's expense. For the tales he told were of the young, runaway prince who had become his son-in-law.

Yes, this was Jethro Reuel, priest of the tribe of Midian, and father of Moses's Midianite wife, Zipporah. Moses did not seem to mind his good-natured jabs. The delight they had in one another's presence had been evident from the moment Jethro appeared on the eastern horizon.

Word of his approach had followed on the heels of the ceremony at the site of the burning bush. One of Jethro's servants had been sent ahead, and had come to Moses at the mount, telling him, "Jethro Reuel, priest of Midian, your father-in-law, has heard of all that God has done for you and for Israel, how the Lord has brought Israel out of Egypt. He says to tell you 'I, your father-in-law Jethro, am coming to you with your wife and her two sons.'"

Leaving the holy mount, Moses had wasted no time in rushing out to meet the long-lost family. It had been months since he had left his wife and sons in the desert, returning them to the tribal camp in Midian, and going off to Egypt. Taking Joshua with him, he had ridden quickly into the eastern night, and when he had seen the little company advancing, he had leapt from his camel, bowing and running, bowing and running, until he embraced them all.

Feeling a little out of place as he witnessed this intimate reunion, Joshua had nonetheless observed it with pleasure. He had heard of Zipporah, and he knew Moses had a family on this side of the world, but seeing them together brought the prophet's humanity into sharper focus.

As did the stories Jethro told tonight around the campfire.

"He barely knew a donkey from a mule, when he came to us," the old fellow chuckled, clapping Moses on the back. "Oh, it is good to be with you again, my son!"

For the tenth time since Jethro's surprise arrival at sunset, the two men embraced and tears filled their eyes.

"And you have joined us on our most happy night since leaving Egypt, my father!" Moses enthused. "My life has surely never been fuller!"

As he said this, his gaze traveled past the fire to the radiant face of a woman, the only woman allowed inside this otherwise male gathering.

"Sit with me, wife," he called, extending his arms and beckoning her forth.

Who dared to question this gesture? Was not Moses governor of Israel? If he wished for Zipporah to sit with him, she had every right to do so.

Joshua watched with a lump in his throat as Moses rose to receive her. The look of unfaded yearning upon the master's face tugged at the young Hebrew's heart.

What must it have been like, he wondered, for the mighty prince of Egypt to fall in love with an Arabian shepherdess? Such a romance they must have had—the ruddy, wild girl, and the refined and regal runaway!

In all the fables of every nation, there were such stories. Unlikely lovers—princesses and tinkers, noblemen and beggarwomen—always made for romantic fare.

But the two whose fingers entertwined this night were not the domain of fairytales. They were real and breathing, and as an aging Zipporah cuddled close to a graying Moses, the lingering glances they exchanged pricked Joshua's lonely soul.

Wistfully, he listened as Jethro told of the couple's first encounter. While Moses and Zipporah were real enough, the tale of their meeting was more beautiful than any fanciful lovestory Joshua had ever heard.

"My daughter and her six sisters were tending their flock beside a well in Midian," Jethro recounted, "when they were set upon by Ishmaelites, who meant to run their animals away from the water, and do who-knows-what evil to the girls."

Zipporah nodded, remembering the incident clearly.

"Suddenly, atop a nearby cliff, a strange-looking fellow popped up, hailing the Ishmaelites, and calling over his shoulder, as if to summon a mighty army against them!"

Jethro looked at Moses, who shrugged and laughed a little.

"How were the wildmen to know there was not a soul with the phantom Egyptian!" Jethro laughed. "And how was Moses to know that from that day forth he would be responsible for the eldest girl he rescued!"

Zipporah leaned into the crook of Moses's shoulder, a broad smile stretching her lips.

"Ah, but you have not told the entire truth," Moses jibed, recalling the slippery manner in which Jethro had "bestowed" his bride upon him. "You have not told that it was trickery, pure and simple, that saddled me with this woman!"

Zipporah pulled away, pretending to be offended. But though the audience was not privy to the details of that long-ago transaction, the twinkle in the woman's eye let them know there had never been a happier marriage.

"If you have been saddled," Jethro countered, "it has been willingly. Never did I see a man take the bit in his mouth so eagerly!"

Delighted by this exchange, the listeners applauded.

On and on the stories went, as Jethro and Moses reminisced, and as Moses's sons, Gershom and Eliezer, and

Jethro's son, Hobab, added their own memories to the chronicle.

But as a gigantic moon rose on the horizon, casting the gathering in silvery halo, the mood around the campfire mellowed.

It was hard to be frivolous beneath such a moon. Instinctively, their spirits were stirred, drawn toward higher things.

As the rest of the Israelites celebrated through the night, the elders and leaders of the camp recounted for Jethro the many miracles with which Yahweh had proven himself their protector.

Chapter by chapter, Moses told the glorious story of what God had done to Pharaoh, of the hardships that had befallen Israel on their journey, and how the Lord had delivered them time and again.

The men described for Jethro the parting of the Reed Sea, the gift of the quail and manna, and the miracle of the water at Horeb. As they reported the details of their most recent victory, the defeat of Amalek, Jethro bowed his head and closed his eyes.

"It is too much!" he groaned. "My heart can barely contain such joy!"

Suddenly, the old man stood up, raising his hands and drawing the crowd to its feet.

"Blessed be the Lord who delivered you from the hand of the Egyptians and from the hand of Pharaoh!" he cried. "Now I know that Yahweh is greater than all the gods!"

At this, he turned to Aaron, who sat beside Moses.

"I understand that you have ministered to your brother since he left my camp. I am a priest," he said, drawing Aaron close, "but you are more worthy than I, for you have *seen* the hand of Yahweh, and I have only believed in him. You *know* him, and I am only learning. Come with me."

To the amazement of all, Jethro led Aaron toward the site of the altar, where only hours earlier Moses and Joshua had sacrificed to the Lord.

Summoning all the elders before him, he requested that another sacrifice be made, this time by the hand of Aaron, invoking the guidance of Yahweh on them all.

As flames parted the dark above the altar, Jethro embraced Moses his son-in-law again.

"I was once your teacher," he said, remembering the naive fugitive who had first entered Midian. "Now you shall teach me. Though you are hated by Ishmaelites and Amalekites, though you will endure the reproach of many nations, my people and yours shall be one together, sons and daughters of Abraham!"

16

Joshua crept forth from his tent, rubbing his eyes in the morning light. The celebration of the night before had lasted until near-dawn, so that by the time he had slipped to bed, only a few hours of sleep were his.

Beneath one arm he carried a bundle of scrolls, a record of disputes between the people, which had been brought to Moses since the journey from Egypt had begun.

At various intervals along the trip, Moses had set aside time to hear such matters. In a company as huge as Israel, there were many contentions. Tempers were short among the weary travelers, and with few distinct boundaries and fewer clear rules, arguments and rivalries escalated from hour to hour. The days of the hearings were always arduous, as Moses sat in his camp and the contending parties came before him, hundreds of them at a time.

Joshua was not looking forward to the ordeal. He was Moses's attendant, and it was up to him to keep order as the people waited in the hot sun for their turn at court.

Though the master sat as judge from morning until night, he had never once cleared the docket of disputes. Some of the scrolls that Joshua carried with him today went back to their stay at Timsah.

What would make matters worse this day was the fact that many of the people who would come before Moses would be suffering the effects of the previous night's revelry. As Joshua arrived at Moses's tent, nearly two hundred disheveled, bleary-eyed folk awaited trial.

The master himself was not in the best of spirits. As Joshua called to him, entering his striped shelter, he found the man of God just pulling on his sandals, his brow furrowed.

"What is the first subject I must deal with?" he asked, hardly glancing up at his servant.

"One we have discussed before, master. The matter of the young girl who cried 'rape.'"

Moses shook his head. "Did we not settle that?" he groaned. "That was weeks ago."

"It was, sir," Joshua sighed, "but her father is not satisfied. He wants to see the man marry her."

Moses shrugged. "Poor girl. Caught in the middle. I am sure her attacker is the last man on earth she wishes to spend her life with. But who will have her, now?"

At this, he stood and threw back the tent flap, squinting against the desert sun.

He did not stop to see how many stood outside, awaiting his emergence. Walking straight for the chair of judgment, a highbacked throne brought from the palace of Egypt and placed atop a mound of crates, he sat down and took the first scroll from Joshua's hands.

"What else?" he muttered softly, so that the crowd would not hear.

"I am sure the girl's father will have more witnesses. You will be involved with her trial until noon."

"And then?" Moses snapped, already weary.

"Well, sir, there is an accusation of thievery against a Kohathite, by his younger brother. The man claims that the elder took more than his share of the birthright when his father died during this journey. The elder claims the possessions were never his father's in the first place, as he himself took them for spoil from his own Egyptian master."

"Witnesses?" Moses asked.

"On both sides," Joshua replied.

The prophet now looked up, quickly surveying the host of petitioners and defendants who anxiously waited for a moment of his time.

"I am ready," he said.

Joshua felt the weight of his master's responsibility as he faced the crowd and called forth the first party. It was good that Israel had finally come to rest for a time at Sinai. The roster of hearings could well take several weeks.

*   *   *

It was nearing sunset. Moses had heard four trials this day, and had reached decisions on them all, a feat which amazed his servant, Joshua. Yet still, there were one hundred and fifty Israelites, representing over thirty unheard cases.

As he sent these people back to their camps, he could feel Moses's exhaustion as if it were his own.

He had just rolled up the last scroll and was about to accompany his master to the headquarters tent, when a voice from the twilight hailed them.

"Son, may I have a word with you?"

It was Jethro, and Moses greeted him with a vague smile.

"Joshua will prepare us a cup of wine, Father," Moses replied. "Do come."

As the three of them sat in the smoky lamplight of the prophet's tent, Jethro intently studied his son-in-law's face. In his always-direct manner, he came to the point of his visit.

"What is this thing that you are doing for the people?" he asked. "Why do you alone sit as judge, and all the people stand around you from morning until night?"

Taken aback, Moses sputtered, "Well, because, Father, the people come to me to inquire of God!"

Jethro looked at the floor, and Joshua wondered what he was thinking.

"When they have a dispute," Moses went on, "they come to me, and I judge between one man and another, and make known to them the statutes of God and his laws."

"These laws," Jethro paused, "they are made known to you of the Lord?"

"They are," Moses replied. "At least, I trust that they are."

Jethro leaned back, and gazed at the goatshair ceiling. "I remember when you used to come to me, asking how we may know the right from the wrong. You wanted to know how a nation and a people may be righteous."

Moses, too, remembered those long-ago conversations.

"I wanted to know about the 'covenant' of which your people so often spoke," he acknowledged. "'Be perfect, as I am perfect,' was God's demand, so you told me."

"You were not very satisfied with that, were you?" Jethro recalled.

"I did not see how such a command was specific enough," Moses admitted.

"So...now the Lord tells you, and you alone, every day, just what is right in every case?"

Moses squirmed, obviously uncomfortable with the intimation.

"It seems so," he answered. Then he defensively pulled forth the thick scroll he had once shown Joshua, on which were scrawled dozens of edicts. "As the Lord gives me his judgments, I write them down. These are the laws of Israel."

Looking at the collection, written in bits and pieces along the journey, Jethro seemed doubtful. "Very well," he said. "But the thing you are doing is not good."

Joshua felt for his master. What did Jethro know of the pressures he endured day after day? But the young Hebrew did not interfere.

Sighing, the Midianite summoned his most diplomatic skills. "I am only concerned that you require too much of yourself," he explained. "I, also, am master of a nation," Jethro reminded his son-in-law. "Were I to try to administer justice as one man, I would go mad!"

This seemed to take Moses up short. "Yes," he acknowledged. "I know you handle things differently."

"Well, then, take my advice," Jethro said. "You will surely wear out, both you and the people who are with you, for the load is too heavy for you. You cannot do it alone."

Leaning close to the lamp, so that his aged features were illumined clearly, Jethro insisted, "Now listen to me. I shall give you counsel, and God be with you. You will still be the people's representative before God, and you will bring the disputes to God. But teach them the statutes and the laws, as the Lord gives them to you. And make known to them the way in which they are to walk, and the work they are to do, once and for all. Furthermore, select out of all the people able men who fear God, men of truth, those who hate dishonest gain, and place these over them, as leaders of thousands, of hundreds, of fifties and of tens. Let them judge the people at all times. And let them bring every major dispute to you, but every minor dispute they themselves will judge. So it will be easier for you, and they will bear the burden with you. If you do this thing, and God so commands you, then you will be able to endure, and all your people will complete their journey in peace."

Astounded, the two Israelites took in the wisdom of the Midianite. As though a huge weight had been lifted, they looked at one another with brighter eyes.

"Last night you said I was to be your teacher," Moses sighed, laying a hand on Jethro's knee. "But once again, you prove yourself the wiser man."

"By experience, only," Jethro said with a smile. "God speaks to all people in all places."

Hugging Moses to him, he added, "But surely the Lord

has great truths to show you, greater than anything I have ever taught. When he reveals to you the full meaning of the covenant, share it with the world."

17

After Jethro left the tent, Moses asked that Joshua stay for a while. As it turned out, the young servant never went back to his own camp that night, but sat up talking with the prophet till dawn.

Though he had come to know Moses well during the journey, that night's conversation exposed to him parts of the master's soul which had before been hidden. As never before, he came to understand what a toll leadership could take, and as never before he came to appreciate the heart of God's chosen one.

For some time, they discussed who might best fulfill Jethro's description of the judges to be set over Israel. Moses best knew the elders of the nation; Joshua the younger, rising leaders. The names of Hur, Amminadab, Zuar, Helon, Shedeur, and others came easily to mind, for these were the most reputable and respected patriarchs of various tribes. And then Caleb, Nahshon, Nethanel, and Eliab, to name a few, seemed likely candidates to put beneath them, training to take their places when necessary. It seemed reasonable that the first should be placed over the "thousands and hundreds," as Jethro suggested, and the younger over the "fifties and tens."

Of course, Moses would confer with Aaron on these matters, but for now, he seemed content to consult Joshua alone.

Though the choice of governors was crucial, Moses often sidetracked to a discussion of "covenant," that mysterious concept which had apparently been a theme of frequent debate between himself and Jethro in years past.

It was when he spoke of covenant that Moses revealed his most personal agony.

His face pensive, he seemed to hope the ex-slave whom he called his right-hand man would be able to illumine the subject.

"I used to torment my poor father-in-law," he confessed, "with my need to know more of God's demands. But, as you have seen, Jethro, for all his savvy, is a rather simple man. For him, the way of God is the way of the desert. He does not dwell deeply on the ways of 'righteousness,' for right and wrong are a matter of expedience and survival. To be perfect, in Jethro's unwritten code, is to be both strong and kind. When problems of justice or issues of cleanliness are brought before him, he follows an elementary code: Do unto others as you would have them do unto you."

As Moses spoke, the young Hebrew sensed that he was still debating with the old priest, at least in his mind.

Joshua shrugged, and prodded the tent fire with the sword he was now accustomed to keeping with him.

"In Jethro's defense, sir," he offered, "his nation is very old, and its ways well established. He is not faced with the complexities of our new society, with the variety of people, and with the confusion that comes with their new freedom. If he were, he would understand the necessity of a fully defined code."

Standing, Moses paced the small chamber, his fists clenched. "I, of all people, should have such a code at my fingertips!" he complained. "What laws are more intricate and sophisticated than those of the Egyptians? I would have been Pharaoh! Yet I cannot compose a set of regulations for this most childlike of people!"

Joshua, not knowing what to say, gazed into the fire.

"What good will it do to assign ten thousand governors, if they have no laws to govern by?" the prophet went on. "I have searched my memory for help from Hammurabi, the Babylonian lawgiver. I have pondered the laws of my Egyptian mother. All of these help. But this is not Egypt or Babylon. These people have known only the law of whip and chain, and cannot govern themselves. Every morning I am faced with unique problems, demanding a wisdom which is beyond me."

By now, Moses had gone to the tent door, and stood looking out at the moonlit sky. Over all there was the every-night glow of the spiraling pillar. But the master's face was dark with gloom.

Turning about, he inquired of Joshua, "What am I to do? Oh, Joshua, how I would love to say, 'Go to, Israel! Judge yourselves by this or that code!' But God demands perfection, and there is no perfect code."

18

Joshua's heart was heavy. He had known fear on this journey, and joy. But he had not known heaviness since he laid aside his slavery and joined the exodus.

The master had been gone for days, and he missed him. Moses had excused himself from his duties, leaving Israel in Joshua's charge, and he had disappeared into the folds of the mountain.

He wanted to be alone, he said. If he was to establish the laws of Israel, he must have guidance. God had spoken to him on Sinai before, and he would not leave the mountain until he spoke with him again.

That had been three days ago, and no one had seen or heard from the prophet. Though Joshua was kept very busy as commander of three million people, desperate thoughts sometimes raced across his mind, fears for the master's safety, and fears that he might be Israel's overseer indefinitely.

The young administrator had called a gathering for this afternoon of all the elders and leaders whom Moses had approved, the chosen judges of the new order. For the first time they were meeting together, and they all expected that Joshua had some important word for them.

Indeed, Joshua had expected to have more to offer. When he had announced the meeting yesterday, he had hoped that Moses himself would be here, to take charge and pass to his men the Lord's commandments.

Instead, he was left alone to face the most prominent Israelites in the nation.

As he looked over the crowd, congregated in the shadow of Joseph's coffin, he felt a lump rise to his throat. There must have been hundreds looking to him who were far more worthy to carry such responsibility, and who would have done the role greater justice.

Would he ever have the confidence of a Moses or an Aaron? Once again, he found himself wondering how he, of all people, had attained such a position.

Raising his hands, he called for quiet in the milling audience. Though many of the leaders were older than he, they respected him as a military hero, and as Moses's servant. Quieting, they sat down upon the ground, their mood eager.

"Three days ago, our governor, Moses, went into the mountain," he announced. "We have all been waiting for his return. As yet, he has not chosen to come down."

Obviously disappointed, the men turned to one another, murmuring among themselves.

Quickly, Joshua covered. "This is not necessarily a bad sign, gentlemen. Surely, the Lord has met with our master, and the time is well spent. The longer he is away, the more he will have to tell us!"

Perhaps Joshua's tone was not convincing, for the men only shook their heads and muttered more loudly.

"Didn't he say when he would return?" someone challenged. "Did he leave you with no instructions?"

Joshua thought he heard laughter at the back of the crowd. But he lifted his chin.

"It is enough for you to know that I *am* in charge!" he retorted. "Until we hear otherwise, we shall conduct ourselves as Moses would wish."

This silenced the challenger, but the men grew more restless.

"We understand that we have been chosen to help Moses govern Israel," another called out. "We need to learn just how to do that!"

Joshua nodded. "And so you shall," he replied. "You have been chosen for your wisdom and endurance. Let patience accompany these qualities."

The crowd sensed that the general was buying time.

"Would you have us go back to our camps with no instructions?" someone else inquired. "How can we be effective? We will be laughed to scorn!"

"Hear! Hear!" others agreed.

"We know you are a mighty warrior, Joshua," one of the younger men shouted, "but how do we know that Moses left you to rule over us?"

"Yes," another cried, "perhaps Moses is not returning, and you have taken the lead presumptuously!"

Joshua's heart stuttered. How could they make such accusations? Daily he was gaining a greater appreciation for the endurance Moses displayed in the face of the headstrong and hot-blooded Israelites.

Again, he raised his hands, demanding silence. But many of the men were standing, turning to leave.

"Call us when Moses returns," they hooted.

Humiliated, Joshua watched them disperse. And with stooped shoulders, he turned toward the master's empty tent.

But suddenly, the crowd was called to a halt by a voice, loud and commanding, ringing from the mount.

"'You have seen what I did to the Egyptians,'" it cried, "'how I bore you on eagles' wings, and brought you to Myself!'"

There was no mistaking the voice of Moses, and everyone knew he spoke for the Lord. Hurrying back toward the foot of Sinai, the men huddled together and watched their prophet descend the mountainside.

"'Now then, if you will obey my voice and keep my covenant, you will be my own possession among all nations, for all the earth is mine!'"

Trembling, Joshua listened with the others, to the awesome pronouncement.

"'And you shall be to me a kingdom of priests and a holy nation,'" Moses concluded. "These are the words of the Lord!"

Joshua was forgotten in the tide of wonder that over-swept the audience. Joshua himself forgot his shame as he watched his beloved mentor striding down the jagged slope.

"All that the Lord has spoken we will do!" the men cried out. "Tell us, Moses, the words of God!"

Passing his hands over the crowd, Moses stilled them, and one by one, then as a body, they fell to their knees.

"Consecrate yourselves!" he commanded. "Wash your garments, and make ready. For in three days, the Lord himself will come to you. In three days, the Lord himself will speak to you. At the sound of a trumpet blast, he will descend!"

19

With blistered hands, Joshua gripped the tongue of a wagon and pulled it into line behind a hundred others, helping Caleb and a dozen young men construct a barrier along the foot of Sinai Mount. All night they had worked, fulfilling Moses's command that a barricade of carts and bales must be made between the people and the site where Yahweh had promised to appear.

Word spread quickly of Moses's encounter with the Lord, and of the revelation soon to come. Like a tide, the mass of Israelites spilled toward the mountain, pressing in about the barricade, so that Joshua was afraid it would not hold.

"Back!" he cried, gesturing to the people. "The prophet has told us that we must not go up on the mountain or touch the border of it! Whoever touches the mountain shall surely be put to death!"

Crushing in upon the makeshift boundary, the Israelites waited for dawn, sensing that sunrise would herald the Lord's approach. When Moses emerged from the headquarters tent, just as the sun broke over the horizon, a hush of awe spread through the crowd.

Stepping back, Joshua let the prophet pass, and quickly closed the boundary again. He was almost afraid to say a word, but so insistent were a thousand would-be trespassers that he cried aloud, "You must not break through! He who looks upon God Almighty shall surely die!"

His heart drumming, he then turned about, watching his master ascend the dewy slope.

Suddenly, as the prophet trekked high enough that all the people could clearly see him, the earth quaked. It was dawn, the sun was shining, but in an instant a thick blackness arose from the mountaintop, cloaking the sky above the highest pinnacle, and blotting out the light just breaking across the easterly summit.

From the midst of that black cloud there came a rumbling, as of thunder—a thunder sympathetic with the rumbling of the earth. And out of the shroud's interior there flashed lightning, jagged bolts of searing white.

Clutching a wagon rail, Joshua tried to stay erect on his wobbly legs. But when another sound, the blast of an unearthly trumpet, shook the mountain, he could no longer stand. Slumping behind a hay bale, he closed his eyes and tried to control his chattering teeth.

It seemed the trumpet took on the semblance of a voice, dreadful, indecipherable. Finding courage to peer through the slits of his eyes, Joshua saw that the cloud was descending the mountainside, and as the trumpet voice grew louder and louder, he stopped his ears, fearing he would go mad.

Again, a quake shook the earth, this time rattling through the mount itself. Smoke and fire, as if from a colossal furnace, belched into the air above Sinai, so that Joshua thought the mount would be consumed. In horror he watched as Moses ventured into the heart of the holocaust, and was swallowed by the living cloud.

It seemed the prophet was gone an eternity. Actually, he descended once or twice, warning the people to stand back, for the Lord would surely break through upon them if they disobeyed. But all this was like a dream to Joshua, who waited in the darkness, alone and fearful, waited for the quaking and the nightmarish voice to end.

As horror and wonder stretched into hours, Joshua felt as though his soul was not his own. It seemed to scale the mountain heights, wandering through the loud phantasm like a ghost. And it seemed an unclean ghost, sorely in need of redemption.

Joshua had dwelt often in his life on God and on things holy. He had done his best, according to the light he had, to lead a holy life. But today he felt unclean. In the presence, or beneath the presence, of an almighty God, he sensed the raw weakness of all his efforts.

Sinking further down behind the hay bale, he forgot his whereabouts, lost as he was in the supernal horror of heavenly blackness.

Sometime that day Moses came again to the people. On every side, and stretching back as far as the eye could see, men and women lay prostrate upon the ground, all fearing, like Joshua, to look upon the mount, upon the lightning and the dreadful cloud. Everywhere men and women shut their ears, terrified of the howling trumpet, the sealike voice.

"Fear not!" the prophet cried. "God is testing you, so that the fear of him may remain with you, and you may not sin!"

Sin! Such a confounding word. Joshua had never felt sinful in his life, not until today. Today he hid his face in shame, despising the feel of his own unclean hands upon his face.

But somehow, he managed to stand again. Not because he was haughty, but because he longed to be whole.

"Moses!" he replied, shouting toward the mount. "We would be holy, just as God is holy. But we do not know how! We cannot understand his ways!"

Through the smoke and dusty ash, Moses's eyes met the eyes of his beloved servant. The prophet knew he spoke for the entire nation, and listened respectfully.

"Tell us the ways of God!" Joshua pleaded. "Speak to us yourself, and we will listen!" Tears poured down Joshua's face and into his dark beard. Like a child he wept, his arms thrown open wide. "Please!" he cried. "Tell the Lord to keep silent, lest we die!"

20

Two weeks later, Joshua sat in a niche of the mountainside, high, high above the camp of Israel.

The warning of Moses, declared over and over, during the great revelation, still haunted him: "Beware that you do not go up on the mountain or touch the border of it. Whoever touches the mountain shall surely be put to death!"

Yet, here he sat, having been led by his master into the very sanctuary of Yahweh.

So much had happened since the great day when the mountain had shaken that Joshua would never recall it perfectly. He knew that Moses had descended to the people, recounting for them all the laws that God had given them, a multitude of ordinances, some general, and many more specific, regarding the behavior expected of them as a holy nation. But the commandments had been so foreign, and so numerous, Joshua wondered if they could be kept.

Only the first ten had pierced his heart, and had riveted the attention of all the listeners, for they cut through all confusion. On these Joshua had dwelt these two weeks, hoping to inscribe them on his memory:

You shall have no other gods besides Me...

You shall not make for yourself any graven image...

You shall not take the name of the Lord your God in vain...

Remember the sabbath day, to keep it holy...

Honor your father and your mother...

You shall not murder...

You shall not commit adultery...

You shall not steal...

You shall not bear false witness...

You shall not covet...

Again and again he had pondered these words, finding them more than enough to live up to.

More potent, however, than thoughts of God's law, was the memory of the sight of him.

Yes, Joshua had seen God!

He, along with Aaron and seventy elders, had been summoned by Moses to the mountainside the day after the laws were given. That morning, at the site of the burning bush, Moses had constructed yet another altar, this one surrounded by twelve pillars, one for each of the twelve tribes of Israel. Young men had been chosen to offer burnt offerings upon those pillars, and Moses took half of the blood and put it in basins, and the other half of the blood he sprinkled on the altar. When he had once more read all the laws to the people, they cried out, "All that the Lord has spoken we will do, and we will be obedient!"

Sprinkling the blood of the basins over the audience, Moses had announced, "Behold, the blood of the covenant, which the Lord has made with you in accordance with all these words!"

Then, taking Aaron and Joshua by the hands, and followed by the seventy elders, Moses had led them higher up on the slopes of Sinai.

This very moment, Joshua could remember the feel of the master's hand in his. Terrified of letting go of it, he had held on tight.

Leading them into the very midst of the smoky darkness, Moses told them to shield their eyes. And when they were completely enveloped, he bade them sit down upon the ground.

Suddenly, the air about them shimmered with stillness, and through their closed eyes they sensed that light surrounded them.

One by one, they took courage to look up, and to their astonishment they found that a brightness divided the dark in a halo.

Though no one on the plain below could have known it, in the center of the swirling roar of smoke and cloud that blanketed the Sinai summit there existed a chamber of perfect calm, flooded with an aura indefinable in human terms.

As their eyes adjusted to this brightness, a figure, tall and glimmering, became distinct before them. At his feet was what looked like a pavement of sapphire, clear as the sky itself, and from his face radiated beams, as pure as sunlight.

Falling down, Joshua lay prostrate, just as did Aaron and all the elders. From deep within him Joshua felt a quaking, a tremor moving from his innermost soul to the tips of his fingers and soles of his feet.

Surely he would not survive. Surely he would never stand again or breathe again.

Today, as he sat in a lonely niche of that same mountain, not far from the very site where he had seen the Lord, he could scarcely remember more. He knew that somehow he and the elders had been encouraged to rise up, that food and drink had mysteriously appeared before them, and that they had partaken of a celebration meal in Yahweh's presence.

But this he could only vaguely recall.

The laws of the Lord and the Lord himself were his sole concerns. On these laws he had dwelt day and night since that hour.

But he was now alone, and loneliness also consumed him.

When the meal had ended, the Lord had vanished, taking the light with him, and night had covered the mountain.

Sending the elders and nobles back toward camp, Moses had singled out Joshua, and told him to accompany him further up the mount.

"We will return," Moses told the others. "Wait for us and take charge of Israel. If any disputes are brought before you, on which you need advice, bring your questions to Aaron and Hur."

He did not explain to Joshua why he must stay with him. But together they had hiked nearly to the peak of the highest pinnacle of Sinai.

Slipping and sliding on the red sandstone, they arrived at a flat spot near the top, their hands and shins scraped and bleeding.

"I will leave you here," said Moses. "You may not enter the holy of holies. Make camp here, and wait for me."

Camp? Joshua had no provisions for a camp, no tent, no firewood. But without further word, Moses disappeared up the highest slope, into a misty veil.

Night was coming on. It was much colder here than in the desert, and a shrill wind stung Joshua's eyes with red grit.

Through a glimmer of biting tears, he spied a fissure-like cave notched into the mountainside. Quickly he scrambled toward it. At the mouth, a clump of brittle sage, the only vegetation on the lifeless slope, offered fuel, and rummaging in his pouch, he drew forth the flint with which he had sparked a hundred campfires during the journey from Egypt.

If he built a fire at the cave's entrance, he might be safe from prowling beasts. Deftly he did so, and soon he was bundled in his mantle, deep within the rift, drowsily watching, through the thick cloud, the leaping flames and the swirling fiery pillar that lit the valley below.

Thoughts of food would wait until morning, when his growling stomach would awake him.

* * *

Where was Moses, he wondered, as sunlight penetrated the cave. How had he fared through the lonely night? Or *was* he alone? Perhaps he was, once again, in the company of Yahweh, and only Joshua must spend the bleak hours in solitude.

Solitude. Moses had often spoken highly of the condition, saying that his greatest spiritual lessons had been learned during his forty years in the wilderness.

Joshua shivered at the thought. Were he to spend a week here, he believed, he would go mad.

That had been two weeks ago. In that time, he had learned to track down his food, to stab lizards (or anything that moved) with his sword, to roast them over his daily-gathered brush fire, and to swallow the most noxious fare with a less-than-queasy stomach.

In these two weeks, he had seen Moses three times. Each time the prophet had come from the summit famished and exhausted. Though his face was radiant, having confronted the face of God, he did not speak of his hours in his presence, and was drained of strength.

Eagerly, Joshua would prepare for him a meal, stoke the campfire that he might be warm, and remove his sandals. But all too soon, the master would rise again to go. And each time he vanished up the mountain, Joshua was more miserable.

Today it seemed even the ten laws which had thrilled his soul were difficult to recite. He wondered if he would be able to obey them if they were lost to mind all together.

But then, if Moses never came to him again, if he had

disappeared forever into the mountain heights, what purpose did the laws serve?

What purpose did Israel serve?

Gathering his robes close to his legs, Joshua drew his feet under him and tried not to fear. Like a loyal dog, he listened for the sound of his master's footstep on the slope outside.

To Joshua, Moses was Israel, Moses was the law. Without him, there seemed no purpose to anything.

21

Forty days and nights had passed. Joshua lay at the mouth of his cave, his hollow eyes closed and ready for death.

He was healthy enough. He was worn, but strong. It was not physical depletion which had beaten him down, but loneliness and doubt. It was not the elements or the cruel mountain that had defeated him, but emotional exhaustion.

Joshua had been a mighty warrior before the Lord, but he was not well trained in prayer. Forty years in the wilderness may have lifted Moses to spiritual greatness, but forty days had brought Joshua to despair.

With only sporadic visits from Moses, and with his sole duty that of survival, Joshua sorely wished he had remained a slave in Egypt.

This morning a light frost covered the ground where he lay. Fitting, he thought, with what strength he had for thinking. Frost and death were good companions, and if he never had a grave, snow would be a fitting shroud.

Half-consciously he moved his fingers through the frost, and lifting its moisture to his lips, he left a residue of dirt upon his mouth. To his dreaming mind, the frost was manna, and the red earth was meat.

Across the years his drowsy thoughts meandered, to times in his Egyptian master's stable. Reliving those years in his confused state, he thought he groomed one of the glorious horses, and that, as chief valet, he rode him through the streets of Raamses.

On all sides, people cheered him, for was he not a military hero? When the streets of the king's capital

became the desert highway, and he rode in the ranks of
Pharaoh's army, tall and proud, he suddenly awoke.

His heart was pounding to the sound of Egyptian
drums ringing through his dream, and as he realized
how perverse was this fantasy, his face grew hot with
shame.

Struggling to a sitting position, he ran a hand across
his brow. It seemed a fever raged within him.

"Forgive me, God!" he cried out. "I am an Israelite! A
son of Abraham! And I love you!"

A brilliant winter sun seared the cold sky. There was
surely no winter like winter in the desert, at once chilling
to the bone, yet demanding a lively heart.

Joshua stood up, still reeling from the shame of his
dream and hoping Yahweh could forgive such trespass,
when he was hailed by the voice of Moses.

Wheeling about, he saw the master descending the
mountain, this time not with an exhausted stride, but
with determined purpose. In his arms he carried something. Joshua could not make out what it was, but joyously
ran to greet him.

Yes, Joshua ran! The man who had lain half-dead
moments before was suddenly infused with zeal.

"Master!" he cried, leaping up the slope, dodging
crags and shale like a mountain goat. "Is it over? Are we
going home?"

Moses would have embraced his beloved servant, but
would not release the burden he bore in his arms.

"What are these?" Joshua marveled, seeing that the
objects were two smooth stone tablets, etched with perfect characters. Sensing that they were very holy, he
feared to touch them, and as he gazed upon them, his
soul trembled.

"My friend," Moses replied, "they are the words of the
Lord, engraved by his very own hand. Without them, we
are prone to evil. But with them, we may learn to keep the
covenant by which we are true sons of Abraham."

PART IV
The Faithful Friend

22

It was with a light heart and a nimble foot that Joshua descended the mount with his master, Moses. Night was settling across the wintry desert, but he was not any longer afraid.

As he trekked down the Sinai slope, he often glanced at the miraculous stone tablets cradled in the prophet's arms. Such strength they gave him, just to gaze upon them!

For engraved there were the most awesome words ever recorded, the ten commandments that would forever constitute the covenant between the Lord Almighty and his people, Israel.

How long Master Moses had sought after the simple thoughts contained there! During his forty years with Jethro he had yearned to know God's requirements, and now that they were established, how compact they were!

Nor were they written on parchment only, or transferred by word of mouth. They were registered in rock, a permanent record for the nation to embrace.

So long as Israel had these two tablets, it had the mind of God.

So it was that Joshua was lighthearted, able-footed as he headed with the prophet back toward camp, eager to witness the celebration certain to commence when the tablets were displayed before the people.

They were only halfway down the mountain, however, when a frightening noise ascended from the valley floor. Loud shouts and the rhythm of drums hammered up the slope, filling Joshua with apprehension.

Automatically, his hand went to the hilt of his sword, secured in his belt.

"Master," he gasped, "there is a sound of war in the camp!"

Moses had already stopped, and stood still in the path, his head cocked as he listened to the reverberations.

Suddenly, his face was clouded, and Joshua wondered if that was anger flashing in his eyes.

But before he could inquire, the prophet was heading downhill again. "That is not the sound of war!" he shouted over his shoulder. "It is not the cry of triumph or defeat, but the sound of singing I hear!"

Singing? Joshua followed after him, racing behind the elder who moved at a surprising pace. What kind of singing was it? he wondered. As he drew closer, its gyrating beat pulsed through him like the throb of unclean thoughts.

And to his dismay, the scene he came upon, when they reached the foot of the mountain, was far worse than the music suggested.

Reminiscent of the free-for-all festival of Bast, which annually raged through the streets of Egypt, the licentiousness of the people was beyond recounting. Apparently having given up hope that the prophet would return, they had also given up all decency, abandoning themselves to revelry of orgiastic proportions.

In the leaping light of bonfires, aflame throughout the camp, could be seen the silhouettes of lewd dancers, and at the head of camp, in the very place where the sacred bush had burned, a golden image reflected the glowing fires.

Pausing behind his master, Joshua stood with him, gazing in horror at the excesses of his people.

Glaring at the image of a golden calf, which profaned the holy site, Moses clutched the tablets to his breast.

"The Lord told me the people had corrupted themselves!" he groaned. "Oh, I did not want to believe it!"

Then he was off again, striding downhill with great

fury. Joshua ran to keep up with him, feeling the slap of master's robes against his own shins.

From Moses's dark brow sweat streamed, and if a face of retribution could kill, the entire nation would have been leveled.

Casting his arms wide, Moses straddled the mount above the camp, and holding aloft one tablet in each strong hand, he shouted over the din, "How quickly you have turned to sin!"

Over and over he repeated the words, until the music and the dancing ceased, and the cry of the camp was silenced. All eyes traveled to the mountain, and the besotted gaze of the people met the angry countenance of God's man.

Gesturing to the golden calf, Moses cried, "Is this your god, O Israel, who brought you up from the land of bondage?"

Chagrined, the revelers covered their nakedness and slumped to the ground, shielding their shameful faces.

Unable to contain his fury, Moses raised the sacred tablets, the stones carved by the hand of God himself, and threw them to the ground. Into a thousand pieces they shattered, and though the people did not know what they were, they gasped with terror.

His hands now free, Moses approached the profaning idol, and toppling it from its pedestal, sent it likewise crashing to the desert floor.

"You deserve no greater god than a golden calf!" he howled. "May the Lord reject you!"

Whipping his robes about him, he turned, trudging into the black of the Sinai heights.

Stunned, Joshua fell to his knees. Before him, in the sand, the remains of the tablets lay scattered about the fallen baal.

Through a haze of tears, he rummaged through the dirt, trying to retrieve the covenant.

But it was no use. The site of the burning bush and the words of the Lord had been profaned. Israel was still enslaved and should have stayed in Egypt.

23

The next day there was another cry in the camp. This time it was not the cry of riotous celebration, but of mourning.

Joshua sat outside his master's tent, far out on the desert. Incensed by the sin of the people, Moses had removed his headquarters a great distance from the population, and the young servant stood vigil as the prophet prayed inside.

There was much to pray about, much to grieve. After destroying the tablets and the golden calf, Moses had summoned the sons of the tribe of Levi, the only group which had largely abstained from the follies of the apostate crowd. Commanding them to strap their swords to their thighs, he had sent them throughout the congregation with orders to kill those most responsible for the sinful excesses. In that night, over three thousand men had fallen. Regardless of their status, even if they were friends, brothers, or sons of the avengers, they were cut down. And by morning the sands of the Sinai valley were crimson with blood.

"Take off your ornaments, take off your party clothes!" Moses had cried to the horrified onlookers. "Let the widows, the orphans, and all the bereaved weep for their own sin, in sackcloth and ashes! Weep for yourselves, and not for the fallen ones only. For the Lord says whoever has sinned against him, he will blot out of his book!"

As the dawn sun touched the blood-soaked earth, a putrid steam arose from the ground, and the people sat in the doors of their tents weeping and wailing.

"Listen to the words of the Lord!" Moses challenged. "From this day forth he leaves us to ourselves! Though he will send his angel before us, he himself will stand afar off. For you are an obstinate people, and should he stay in your midst for one moment, he would destroy you!"

At this, Moses had turned from the great company, and had trekked out into the desert, to the site where Joshua had moved his tent. The pillar of cloud, the symbol of the Lord's presence, had followed him, standing a good way off from camp, hovering over the prophet's sanctuary. All day long, Moses had been inside, weeping and wailing himself, for the iniquities of Israel.

And all day long, Joshua had sat outside the tent, guarding it. He had not gone inside, for he could hear more than one voice through the tent flap. Yahweh was visiting with Moses, and Joshua dare not look in.

Sometimes the conversation emanating from the interior sounded like an argument, not violent or loud, but a bargaining session, full of pleas and objections, requests and concessions. Now and then, Joshua caught a phrase or two, though he tried not to eavesdrop.

"Forgive them," he once heard. And to his horror, he had clearly picked up the Lord's response. "Whoever has sinned against me, I will blot out of my book!"

Yes, Moses had told the people this was true. But to hear it direct from the Almighty caused a tremor to pass through Joshua's soul.

"If you do not go with us, do not lead us any further!" Moses had wept.

On through the day the dialogue had continued, until Joshua wondered that the master did not faint dead away.

And the cloud remained at the entrance to the tent, hovering over the desert floor, until the sun began to set and the pillar took on its reddish glow.

Perhaps Joshua fell asleep. He only knew that when Moses at last emerged from the tent, he was unprepared for him, and jolted by the sound of his voice.

"Stand up!" Moses commanded. "Come with me!"

Rubbing his eyes, Joshua obeyed, trudging out with his master across the desert.

Glancing over his shoulder, he saw that the fiery pillar no longer stood over the tent's entrance, but had risen again to the sky and taken its customary place above the camp.

Did this mean that the pleas of Moses had prevailed? Would the Lord once more dwell in the midst of the people?

Anticipating his question, the prophet pointed across the sands. "Ahead is the Rock of Horeb," he said. "We must cut out two new stone tablets. The Lord is going to restore the covenant."

24

Joshua sat at the top of a great dune, overlooking the westerly desert. In the distance, three days' journey from the setting sun, could be seen the craggy summits of Mount Sinai, where the law and the covenant had been given and restored.

So much had happened on the journey from Egypt and during a full year at the sacred mountain that the children of Israel might always have considered Sinai their home, had the great pillar of cloud not lifted and begun to lead them to the east. They were not intended to live forever in the sifting sands of the Arabian Peninsula. A land had been promised to them centuries ago, to their fathers Abraham and Jacob. A destiny greater than Sinai beckoned to them.

This evening, Joshua, Moses, and Aaron waited on the crest of the great sand hill, looking back across the wilderness as the three million whom they had led out from the holy mount spilled toward them in waves.

The sight of this huge company, when viewed from any distance, had always been awesome. But never more than now.

When the fugitive slaves had left Egypt, they had been a disorderly mob, with no sense of rank or file. At Sinai, a degree of division and hierarchy had been established, with the assignment of judges over thousands, hundreds, fifties, and tens. And by then, the people had largely arranged themselves according to what they knew of their ancestries, into tribal companies.

Before setting out from Sinai, however, Moses had assigned more specific order, and along with teaching

116

them the laws and ordinances of Yahweh, he had instructed them to build a tabernacle for the Lord, a traveling sanctuary to be the fulcrum point from which all justice would be dispensed, and to which all reverence and homage would be made.

No longer would the humble tent of Moses be the only council chamber of Israel. A glorious meeting place would go before the people, the house of God himself, upon which the presence of the Lord would continually dwell.

Little by little, the nation of Israel was becoming a formal entity. Though it was on the move, with no fixed resting place, it had its seat of government and its own intricate legal system. It had its governors, its priests, its rituals, and its army. It was becoming a formidable force, and the lands across which it traveled quaked at its coming.

This evening, as Joshua watched the Israelite tide spill across the desert, he marveled that this was the same throng that had only months before fled for their lives from the Nile Valley.

They tramped across the sands in cadence with the rhythm of drums and flutes and singing. Had one been blind, upon whom they had come, the sound alone of their marching and their music would have inspired great fear. But the appearance of the vast congregation was enough to make the heart stop.

Divided into seven neat companies, they were headed by the camp of Judah, with the tribal armies of Issachar and Zebulun. Behind these came the Levite tribes of Gershon and Merari, bearing the dismantled tabernacle, and followed by the camp of Reuben, with the tribal armies of Simeon and Gad.

The Levite tribe of Kohath was next, bearing the most holy elements of the sanctuary, the very house of God himself, and behind them came the orderly ranks of Ephraim, with Manasseh and Benjamin; then the camp of Dan, with Asher and Naphtali.

Bringing up the rear of the mammoth march was a mixed multitude, the multicolored, multilingual horde of people who had sympathized with the Israelites during their struggles in Egypt, many of them Egyptian themselves, or members of countless Semitic and African nations who had likewise endured oppression under Pharaoh's cruel hand.

At the head of each great camp was a banner, the green standard of Judah leading them all, and graced by the design of a noble, golden lion. The banner of Reuben was scarlet, its motif a human head. And last to come into view was the eagle-crested flag of Dan, its red and white emblem flashing in the sunset.

Before the banner of Dan, however, was one other, and upon this regal standard Joshua's eyes lingered longest. For it was the golden flag of Ephraim, and though Joshua was privileged, as Moses's servant, to travel at the head of the company, his heart was with his family and with the host that carried Joseph's coffin.

Strange, he thought, as he sat upon the dune, absorbed in the wonder of the oncoming throng. Strange that he was equally proud to be an Ephraimite as an Israelite.

"Sir," he sighed, leaning close to Moses, "did you ever think so many different people could march together in harmony?"

Moses scanned the ranks who pressed toward them. At the very head of the march, coming even before the camp of Judah, was a small cluster of men, bearing poles upon their shoulders. Atop the poles was a gleaming gold box, overwatched by the likeness of two golden angels, their wings stretched across it. It was the ark of the covenant, containing the tablets of the ten commandments, and it always led the way before the nation.

Pointing toward the hallowed box, Moses replied, "So long as the covenant is our guide, we will work together, and our enemies will be scattered before us."

25

It was true that as they marched in their orderly files, each family and tribe in its place, each banner held proudly aloft, the nation of Israel appeared to be harmonious. But their unity was a tenuous thing, easily weakened by the least adversity.

On the seventh day out from Sinai, Moses stood with Joshua at the head of the camp, preparing to say the evening prayer for safety over his people. As his servant lifted the sacred mantle over the prophet's head, Moses raised his hands toward the pillar of light. "Return, O Lord, to the many thousands of Israel!" he cried. And the pillar, which had come to rest over the congregation, descended, marking the end of the day's journey.

But though the pillar rested, the people were anything but serene. Throughout this past week of travel, as had so often happened in the past, they were complaining.

As Moses and Joshua walked back through camp, women were fretting over their cooking. They had grown very weary of manna. They were tired of gathering it, grinding it, beating it into batter, boiling it in pots, and pounding it into cakes. Men sat in their doorways griping that they had no meat and recounting fondly the variety of fish and fowl they ate in Egypt; the succulent cucumbers and melons; the zesty leeks, onions, and garlic.

"Who will give us meat?" they cried out as Moses and his servant passed by. "What became of the quail the Lord provided before Sinai? Will he never do so again?"

Joshua walked close to his master, shaking his head as Moses sighed, "Do you believe it? After all the Lord has done for them, they still complain!"

Moving faster, Moses angled out from camp, toward his own tent. Joshua could see that he was anxious to be free of the protesters.

"Well, sir," he tried to console him, "they *do* grow weary of the same fare day after day. I suppose even a miracle can become bland when it is revisited too often."

When Moses turned on him with a storm in his eyes, Joshua looked at the ground. "I...I only meant..."

But the man of God was right to be angry. And Joshua was chagrined as Moses lifted a tormented face to heaven and began to remonstrate.

"O Lord!" he groaned. "Why are you so hard on me? What did I ever do to deserve these people? Did I conceive them? Did I give them birth, so that I must carry them like babies?"

They had come to the tent now. All the way out from camp, Moses had ranted. "Where am I to get meat for so many? 'Give us meat! Give us meat!'" he mimicked them.

Dejected and frustrated, the prophet did not even bid Joshua good night as he threw back the flap of his tent and disappeared inside. Joshua's ears burned as he rolled out his own pallet and made ready for bed outside the door.

He knew the burden of his master was great. But he feared Moses took too seriously the cries of the disgruntled masses. And his own heart sped fearfully as he heard the despair in the prophet's voice, still raving within the shelter.

"I cannot bear it!" the master cried. "These people are too much for me! If you are going to deal thus with me, please kill me at once! If you love me, kill me! Do not let me suffer any longer!"

* * *

All night the prophet struggled with the Lord. Joshua slept fitfully, awaking often to the sounds of anxious and angry conversation issuing from the shelter, and trying not to eavesdrop.

At dawn, the man of God emerged, a look of retribution etched upon his face.

Joshua hung back, following at a distance as Moses strode across the sands toward camp.

Every other morning since leaving Sinai, the prophet had gone to the head of the nation and had called upon Yahweh to lead them forth. "Rise up, O Lord!" he would cry, lifting his arms to the pillar of cloud. "Let your enemies be scattered, and let those who hate You flee before You!"

At this, the cloud would lift and move northeast across the desert, guiding the people toward the promised land.

But today, no such prayer would be said, no such guidance would occur. Instead, the prophet trudged to the top of a high dune and shouted to the people, "Consecrate yourselves! For tomorrow you shall eat meat! You have wept in the ears of the Lord, saying, 'Oh that someone would give us meat to eat! We were well-off in Egypt!' Therefore the Lord will give you meat and you shall eat!"

The millions who heard this proclamation might have cheered heartily had it not been for the vengeance in their leader's voice and his angry gestures. Bewildered, they listened breathlessly as he declared the Lord's intent.

"You shall eat, not one day, nor two days, nor five days; neither ten days, nor twenty days! But a whole *month*, until it comes out of your nostrils and becomes loathsome to you! For you have rejected the Lord who is among you and have cried before Him, saying, 'Why did we ever come out of Egypt?'"

Aghast, the people heard their fate, and not daring to dispute, they bowed to the ground, weeping this time for shame.

Joshua's throat was tight at the witness of the repentant horde. How many times had he seen them driven to their knees? Would they never grow beyond their faltering faith?

Observing his master, who stood upon the windswept hill with his eyes closed and his head back, Joshua was grateful for his example. He, the prophet's servant, was also weak of faith, and he knew he would have been among the dissenters had he not been afforded months of intimate companionship with the man of God.

At that moment, as the three million crouched upon the ground, pleading for forgiveness, and as Moses stood strong and tall before them, Joshua loved him more than he ever had. At that moment, also, he realized what a dreadful void would be left in his heart and in his soul should the master ever leave him.

Though the prophet was a pillar of strength this morning, his words of the night before still haunted his servant: "O Lord, please kill me at once! If you love me, kill me! Do not let me suffer any longer!"

Joshua knew very well his master's humanity. Moses had experienced the hand of God and had received many evidences of Yahweh's saving grace. But over and over he had also been tested by his temperamental and fickle followers, his always-demanding and rarely grateful children. Joshua had been privy to his moments of despair, his hours of heartbreak.

Surely Yahweh did not intend for Moses to bear such burdens, but if the Lord did not act soon to relieve him, he might not survive the journey to Palestine.

Longing to reach out to him, Joshua crept up the hillside and drew alongside the man of God. Stretching forth his arms, he was about to embrace him when Moses turned away. Unaware of his servant's presence, he blinked back tears and descended the dune, plodding in dejected solitude across the sandy waste.

26

Once again alone, Joshua waited that morning beside the tent of meeting, wondering when his master would return. The camp of Israel was busy making preparation for the ominous visitation which Moses had promised, washing and consecrating themselves as he had commanded. Joshua had completed his own oblations and tried to devote himself to prayer.

Pondering the events of the night before and the sad words that Moses had spoken, Joshua did manage to pray for his master's welfare.

But though he longed to see the prophet's burdens lightened, he was unprepared for the way in which that longing would be answered.

At high noon, a movement along the edge of camp caught his attention. A large company of men was gathering there, and another figure was leading them toward the meeting tent.

Standing, Joshua shaded his eyes against the sun and watched them approach. It was Moses at the lead, and as the group came closer the servant recognized them as members of the seventy whom Moses had taken up Mount Sinai to see the Lord.

In fact, as they gathered outside the shelter, Joshua realized that all but two of that select group were present.

"Circle the tent," Moses instructed them. Quickly they did so, and the man of God motioned to Joshua to stand back, well away from the house of meeting.

When Moses raised his hands, the pillar of cloud descended above the tent's entrance. As had happened on Sinai, a voice like thunder, but this time gentle, issued from the cloud, and something like a mantle of fire was lifted from the prophet's shoulders. Moving quickly over the elders, who waited with their heads bowed, the fiery cloak settled on one after another, until the entire meeting house was set aglow round about, and every face was upturned to the sky, radiating divine light.

As the spirit settled on them, each man in turn began to speak out with authority. Some repeated the commandments that God had given Israel, some raised their voices in songs of praise, and others entoned the warnings against ungodliness which Moses had so often given.

Amazed, Joshua huddled behind a clump of sage and watched the supernatural ordination of 68 new prophets.

But, while he could have been delighted at this intervention on behalf of his master, he was not. When governors had been raised up to help Moses bear the burden of judging and overseeing the people, Joshua had been grateful. But to think that his master's gift of prophecy should now be shared among these men sparked a protective jealousy he did not know he possessed.

This was obviously the work of the Lord. What right did he have to question it? Certainly he would not do so in the presence of the men themselves.

Still, he bowed his head and stared at the ground, tracing his toe aimlessly back and forth through the sand. And as the prophets continued to preach and sing, his brow furrowed.

Barely did he understand his own emotions. He surely did not admit to himself that he was envious. But when opportunity presented itself, he was surprised by his own response.

His fretful ruminations were interrupted when a voice hailed the master. Running out from camp was a young fellow, one of the nobles who served with Aaron in the service of the altar. Although he was respectful of the events transpiring about the tent, he bowed furtively and spoke in urgent tones.

"Sir," he called, catching his breath, "strange things are happening in the congregation!"

Gradually the elders ceased their expounding and their singing, listening as the young man exclaimed, "I thought you should know, sir, that there are two men prophesying in the camp! They say they are among the seventy you called, but they did not come out with you to the tent, and they are wandering through the camp, preaching!"

Now this was all Joshua needed to give courage to his jealousy.

"Preaching? In the camp?" he snarled, as though it mattered greatly where such activities were carried on. "Who are they?"

The young noble, surprised at Joshua's interruption, replied, "Eldad and Medad, sir. Are they among the seventy?"

Indeed they were. But Joshua, already incensed, did not care whether they were or not.

Turning to the man of God, he heaved an exasperated sigh. "Moses, my lord," he pleaded, "restrain them!"

Taken aback, Moses surveyed his servant's distraught face. Quickly interpreting Joshua's reaction, he shook his head.

Placing an arm about his shoulders, Moses looked deep into Joshua's eyes.

"My friend," he replied, "are you jealous for my sake?"

When Joshua only looked away, his face coloring, the man of God declared, "Would that all the Lord's people were prophets, and that the Lord would put his spirit upon them!"

27

The visitation of the Lord, against which Moses had forewarned the people, was meant to be a punishment. But by their reaction to it, it seemed instead a blessing.

Initially, as it appeared on the eastern horizon, heralded by a strong wind and a dark, ominous cloud, it sparked fear. But when that cloud swooped over Israel in a flurry of wings and squawks, a shuddering cheer arose from the great congregation.

Moses had told them they would have meat. The Lord was giving them quail, just as he had done before Sinai. And as the birds toppled to the sands, tottering among them, the people went wild with greed.

Joshua stood with his father and grandfather, and with his friend Caleb, in the midst of the ravenous mob. Astonished, they watched as the manic, meat-hungry crowd gathered up the birds, wringing their necks and stuffing them into bags and baskets.

"Don't they hear the prophets?" Caleb marveled, noting that the seventy wandered everywhere through the throng, preaching destruction and warning of retribution.

On every side the people grappled over the live food, cursing and tearing it from one another's clutches. Nun and Elishama huddled together, fearing that riot would soon break out.

"They did not listen to Moses," Joshua answered. "Why should they listen to anyone else?"

Shaking his head, he led his three companions outside the camp. The sky was so darkened by the living cloud, which continued to come in from the east, that it might have been nighttime.

"Hurry!" Joshua cried. "We will be safer at the tent of meeting."

Though it was midday, people were building fires in the camp, not only for light, but for cooking. By the time Joshua and his little company reached the tent, the aroma of roasted fowl already filled the air.

He and his family had longed for the taste of meat, just like every Israelite. They too had had their fill of manna and its bland variations. But as the smell of quail, fried, broiled, and boiled, wafted toward them, they covered their noses.

Joshua held his stomach as the sounds of fighting and frantic feasting filled the desert.

He would not have eaten of the windfall were it set on a golden plate before him. And he doubted that Yahweh would long abide Israel's gluttony.

* * *

All that day, all night, and all the next day the people gathered and ate fallen quail. But on the third day a nauseating stench replaced the aroma of cookfires and banquets.

Joshua and his party feared to go forth to see the source of the foul odor, for they knew it was the reek of death.

They might have thought it was only the stench of rotting birds. Certainly this was part of it, for the windfall of quail was so vast it spread as far as the eye could see, a day's journey in every direction, so that the quail lay writhing in their death throes to a depth of three feet upon the ground.

Of course, the tent of meeting was within the radius of their fall. All night long and all day, Joshua and his companions had huddled inside the shelter, listening to the small, feathered bodies hit the goatshair walls and tumble to the earth about.

A nightmare it was, and the odor was disgusting. But they also knew it was not only rotting birdflesh that drew flies and choked the air with rancid steam.

People were also dying, hundreds, thousands of them.

Yes, the Lord's patience did have an end, and by the second day greedy feasters throughout the camp had taken sick. A plague tore through the huge company, and the sound of merriment gave way to weeping and mourning.

On the third night, Joshua and his three comrades emerged from their shelter. No plague had reached them there, and they hoped it was safe to venture forth.

But just as they took a few wary steps into the darkness, they decided to retreat. The moonlit scene before them, mounds of dead flesh both poultry and human, was too grotesque, and the womb of their tent was a comforting haven.

They would wait for Moses. And when the nation moved on again, they would name this place Kibroth-hattaavah, "the graves of greediness."

For here they would bury yet another rabble element. And again Israel would be purged.

28

The oasis of Hazeroth was a welcome respite from the tragedy of Kibroth-hattaavah. This pleasant dot of green in the monotonous Sinai landscape had been a stopping place for countless generations of caravanners and bedouin tribes. Many had left permanent marks here, erecting small sandstone huts and low corrals, so that the place-name meant "villages."

That a company so vast as Israel could be impressed by a tiny parcel of vegetation testified to the bleakness of their desert sojourn. They were weary. They missed not only the food of Egypt, but its temperate climate and lush riverbanks.

They had learned, for now, not to grumble over their condition. But Moses would at least allow them a time of refreshing, permitting them to stay here for several days.

Not only was Hazeroth a beautiful oasis, but it received breezes from the Gulf of Aqaba, almost twenty miles east. Indulging himself, as well as his people, Moses set up the tent of meeting, which was his dwelling place, on the east side of camp, where he could best enjoy the cool air that spilled across the dunes at sunset.

Not only did he move his shelter there, but for the first time since leaving Sinai, he brought his family out from the camp to reside with him.

Joshua might have felt awkward with this arrangement, especially considering that the family Moses invited was an extended one, including not only his wife and sons, but his sister Miriam, brother Aaron, mother Jochebed, father Amram, and his wife's brother, Hobab, who had stayed with them when Jethro departed. Rather than feeling awkward, however, Joshua was glad for the company. Though he would never have told Moses, his role as solitary servant to so private a man was often very lonely.

What neither he nor Moses anticipated was the incendiary atmosphere that would be created by bringing so diverse a group together.

Moses's kin had never lived with Zipporah and her relations. The fact that Moses had married a Midianite and had managed to coexist with her family for forty years was no guarantee that his Hebrew family would mesh well with them.

Indeed, it had only been Moses's quiet and humble personality that helped him endure the high-spirited Arabs. A more volatile temperament would have clashed endlessly with the feisty Zipporah and her hot-blooded brother.

As it was, the mixed group experienced difficulties from the beginning.

Joshua sat this afternoon in the shade of the tent, chatting with Moses's sons, Gershom and Eliezer. He tried not to glance too often toward the abode of Zipporah, the striped wedding tent that had for all her married life been her conjugal home. She had pitched it close to the tent of meeting, too close, according to Miriam, and just now the two women were outside it, engaged in a boisterous exchange regarding its location.

Joshua had heard the women argue before, always differing over one trifle or another. He had managed to steer clear of involvement, and was determined to do so again. Pretending not to notice their conversation, he focused on the two young men at his side.

But with each passing minute, the argument grew louder, until Miriam, in a huff, wheeled about and stormed toward her own tent.

"Selfish!" she was shouting, her wrinkled face livid. "I never met a more selfish woman than you, Zipporah!

How my gentle brother could have chosen you, I will never know!"

Zipporah, not to be outdone, waved her small fist in the air. "Perhaps he learned patience from dealing with you!" she cried. And with this she flung back her tent door and slapped it shut behind her.

Gershom and Eliezer looked at the ground, their faces red. Doubtless such embarrassment was not new to them, and they had learned not to interfere.

Not so with Aaron, Jochebed, and Amram. Naturally siding with Miriam, they huddled close about her, listening to her grievance. "It just isn't proper!" the spunky woman complained. "To erect a love-house in the shadow of the tabernacle is indecent. I tell you, it is not right!"

Aaron nodded and Jochebed flashed angry eyes at the colorful shelter. But though Amram agreed in principle with Miriam, he tried to calm her.

"Now, daughter," he said, "we must not be hard on her. She is new to our society, you know."

But when Zipporah stuck her head out her door and made another catty remark, even Amram clenched his fists.

"How can it be improper for the shadow of God's house to grace my marriage house?" she spat. "But then you have never been married, Miriam. You wouldn't know about such things!"

When Miriam lunged forward, ready to engage her sister-in-law, Aaron and Amram restrained her. Flailing her arms, the outraged woman yelled, "Will you teach us the ways of the Lord?"

And Aaron, unable to hold his tongue, added, "You would do well to listen to us. We know a few things about God! Has the Lord spoken only through Moses? Has he not spoken through us as well?"

To this point, Moses had been oblivious to the dispute. He had been in camp all morning, and had only just returned home. When he walked in on the contest, he was befuddled.

Running to him, Joshua beseeched him. "They are fighting again, Master. Is there nothing you can do?"

Moses had heard enough to be deeply troubled. But it was not the issue of the tent and its location that aggravated him.

"It seems my own family doubts my calling," he observed. And going directly to his brother, he demanded, "You and Miriam come with me!"

Surprised by his sudden appearance, the two drew back. But taking them firmly by the arms, Moses led them to the very door of the meeting tent.

Suddenly, from the midst of the tent, a quaking could be felt. And the cloudy pillar, which hovered over it, descended and stood before the door.

"Aaron! Miriam!" came a trumpeting voice. "Hear now my words!"

Trembling, the two squabblers shielded their gaze.

"If there is a prophet among you, I the Lord will make myself known to him in a vision," the voice pronounced. "I will speak to him in a dream!"

Aaron and Miriam took in the words fearfully and looked sheepishly at one another. Neither of them had ever had such a dream or vision, and they stood corrected before the Lord.

"It is not that way with my servant Moses," the voice went on. "He is faithful in all my household. With him I speak mouth to mouth, openly, and not in dark sayings. And he beholds my very form!"

At this, Moses also bowed his head, humbled by such distinction.

And now the pillar moved from side to side, as if surveying the prophet's shamefaced siblings.

"Why were you not afraid to speak against my servant Moses?" the voice demanded.

Still emanating anger, the cloud ascended, departing from them. But when Aaron turned to Miriam, ready to lead her away, he suddenly gasped. Creeping forward, the rest of the family looked upon her, and fell back horrified. For she was white as death, her skin suddenly leprous.

Falling to his knees, Aaron clutched Moses about the legs and wept, "Oh, my lord, I beg you, do not charge this sin to us! We have acted foolishly. Do not let her be like one who is dead, whose flesh is half eaten away!"

Leaning his head back, Moses too wept, stretching his hands heavenward and praying, "O God, heal her!"

For a long, tense moment, the family waited for a reply. And when Moses opened his eyes, he heaved a sigh.

Turning to Joshua, he instructed, "Take her. Lead her by the hand into the desert. There she must stay for seven days, until this curse be lifted. These are the words of the Lord!"

Swallowing hard, Joshua stepped toward the snow-white Miriam, toward the one whose skin had been ruddy and dark from birth, just like his master's. Fearing to touch her, he nonetheless obeyed.

And as he led her forth, Joshua saw Moses draw Zipporah to his bosom. Like a bird she nestled into his embrace. Though he sadly watched his sister depart, and though the family would no longer reside so close to the holy tent, he clearly drew great comfort from his wife's caress.

PART V
The Leading Spy

29

Joshua sat on a rim overlooking the Gulf of Aqaba, the northeastern arm of the great Red Sea. Framed by white sands, its pure, azure waters stretched to the southern horizon as far as the eye could see.

It seemed forever since the people of Israel had been near a great body of water. The last time had been when they crossed the Reed Sea, or Lake Timsah, under the miraculous intervention of the Lord. So long had they been hemmed in by desert and endless miles of sand that the proximity of water was refreshment indeed.

So was the proximity of civilization.

At this northern tip of the gulf lay the small town of Ezion-Geber. Beginning as an Egyptian outpost, it had become a full-fledged settlement, having permanent residents. While the Israelites might have been uneasy with the fact that it represented Egypt's farthest imperial reach, they were not. What could Egypt do against millions of them, so far from the Nile Valley? Instead, the sight of buildings and commerce, however modest, was consolation that they had at last come through the Sinai.

Of course, if they were to reach Canaan, they must go through more wilderness. But none would be so bleak as the desert which had been the scene of their journey thus far.

As Joshua sat on the rim of the gulf, he was stirred with anticipation. But that anticipation was mingled with another emotion, his all-too-familiar soul mate, loneliness.

Glancing north, he knew that Canaan lay more than one hundred miles ahead. He also knew that great things would be required of him as the immigrant nation of Israel attempted to take their place within its borders.

Not that Israel was truly immigrant. By the promise given to their forefather, Abraham, the land was rightfully theirs. Though they had been away for 400 years, they still believed in the covenant. And though to the current inhabitants they would be invaders, they considered themselves returning heirs, ready to lay claim to their inheritance.

Joshua drew his cloak tight to his chest. He knew that the birthright would not easily be won. He would have been a fool to think war was not inevitable.

And he was the commanding general of Israel.

Closing his eyes, he clenched his teeth. He still had trouble thinking of himself as a warrior. What he would have given for a comforting word, for a touch of human reassurance!

Despite the agitation that Moses's family often caused, Joshua envied him the tender joys of wife and sons. And not for the first time in his life, he regretted that he had never married.

But, he told himself, lifting his chin and striking a dauntless pose, it was probably for the best. A man in his position, a man who would soon risk his life, was better off without attachments.

"Good day, Joshua!" a voice hailed him.

Jolting from his ruminations, the young Hebrew glanced down the incline leading to camp. Walking toward him was Moses, his step eager.

"Such a noble look you have today," the master greeted him, "as though you could take on the world!"

Joshua's face colored. "I . . . I was just thinking . . ."

But he did not wish to divulge his thoughts.

"You were thinking of Canaan, and the days ahead?" Moses guessed.

Joshua gazed north again. "Partly, sir."

"That is good!" Moses said, clapping him on the back. Sitting with him, he drew forth a parchment and unrolled it on the sand.

Upon it were not the usual hieroglyphs and words of law that Joshua was accustomed to seeing. Instead, it was a map, carefully drawn.

"Here!" Moses enthused, pointing to the topmost section. "Here, my boy, is Canaan!"

"Yes, sir," Joshua replied.

"And here," Moses went on, moving his finger southward, "is Ezion-Geber."

Joshua studied the pinpoint on the map, and then the real-life village on the desert floor.

"There are many miles between us and the promised land," he noted. "How many days will it take to get there?"

Moses shrugged. "I do not think that is the question to concern ouselves with. Not yet, anyway."

Keeping the chart before him, he explained, "Hobab drew this map for us. He has traveled much for my father-in-law, and knows every inch of the terrain between here and Canaan, as well as Canaan itself. He will be an excellent aide as we approach the land. But we must not be hasty."

Joshua listened attentively as Moses laid out the plan for the next few weeks.

"We will not invade immediately," Moses began. "The people have come to me, suggesting that first we spy out the land, to see what our challenge is. After all, we have fought only once, and that was against desert dwellers. Canaanites are city dwellers, and their region is very different from the Sinai."

Joshua nodded. "Very wise, sir. Besides, the Canaanites have likely heard of our intentions by now. Surely the whole world has heard! They will be ready for us."

Even as he said this, an unwelcome twinge worked

across his shoulders. He hoped Moses did not read his fear.

"I am glad you agree," the prophet went on. "So our next task is to choose men to send forth as spies. We must choose one for each of the twelve tribes, each man a leader."

Again, Joshua nodded. But as his quick mind composed a list of likely candidates, he was unprepared for Moses's next words.

"Of course, you will represent the tribe of Ephraim."

Taken aback, the young general looked at his master in amazement.

"I, sir?" he marveled.

"Who would be better?" Moses insisted. "For their commander to accompany them would give the young men courage. Besides," he admitted, "I will rest easier if you are in charge."

Flattered, Joshua tried not to smile too broadly. And he attended closely to his master's instructions.

"Head directly north and then west," he said, tracing the route. "Avoid the King's Highway, which runs northeast. There are too many settlements there, and relations with the Edomites are uncertain. Start in the Negev," he directed, pointing on the map to the southern edge of Canaan. "Then go up into the hill country and see what the land is like, whether the people are strong or weak, whether they are few or many. And how is the land in which they live, rough or smooth? What are the cities like? Are they open camps or fortifications? And is the land rich or poor? Are there trees and orchards, vineyards and farms? It is now early spring. Try to bring back some of the produce."

Joshua took all of this in, committing the map and its place-names to memory.

"I shall do my best," he promised.

Pleased, Moses rolled up the map and handed it to his servant. "I know you will," he said.

Then with a sigh, the prophet looked over the little village below. "How well I remember this place!" he said. "When I was running from Egypt, I stopped here. This time, it is a starting point, but back then, it was like the end of the world. The end of Egypt and her reach, for sure."

His mind drifting back, Moses reminisced. "I was very frightened then, just as you are now. I knew not what lay ahead. And I was very lonely."

At this, he stopped and gazed deep into his friend's eyes. Joshua had hoped he had not detected his fear, his loneliness. But as he proceeded, the young man was grateful for his insight.

"I had no idea what I would find in Midian," he continued. "I did not know that I would dwell there so long, or that my life would be so happy. May your life be full when we reach Canaan," he smiled. "May you find life and love, as I did."

30

A cooling breeze blew across the shepherd hills of southern Canaan, caressing the faces and bare torsos of twelve young men. Sprawled beneath the open blue sky, they laughed and talked together, enjoying one of the rare hours of rest they had permitted themselves since leaving the Israelite camp in the wilderness of Paran.

They had headed out on their investigative expedition three days ago, making short work of the forty miles between the Negev and the Hebrew encampment at Kadesh-barnea.

Just this morning they had entered the shepherd district, and had donned the disguise they would wear throughout their sojourn, the long headscarf and cloak typical of Canaanite herdsmen. They hoped to avoid scrutiny by passing themselves off as just another group of transient shepherds. If they could avoid speaking much with the locals, they would do well, for their Egyptian tongue and Hebrew dialect, the only languages they knew, would surely give them away.

But though they rested, they were on the alert. A group of real herdsmen might come upon them at any time, for the hills were full of them. And finding them without a flock, they would surely be suspicious.

A few miles away, according to Hobab's map, a highway would lead them to the town of Hebron. Once on that road, they would be able to move more freely, for passersby would assume their flock was in the hands of comrades in the hills.

Keeping their eyes and ears atuned to danger, they were nonetheless grateful for the hour's reprieve.

Not since leaving the Nile Valley had their eyes been blessed with green hills, or their ears with the music of songbirds. The rounded terraces of southern Canaan were full of color and melody, trees blooming with spring flowers and narrow wadis alive with the sound of running water.

Joshua lay upon his back, his cloak open to the breeze. For a brief moment he closed his eyes, soothed by the rush of wind in tall grass.

He had just come from the brook that ran alongside the hill. Having washed his face and neck, he had splashed the cooling water all over his head, and now enjoyed the feel of sunlit air upon his wet hair and beard.

Sad, lonely thoughts had kept their distance since he had set out on this adventure. Eagerly he contemplated the next weeks, wondering what lay in store.

When a shadow moved across his face, he opened his eyes and found that Caleb had joined him. Stretching himself full-length beside Joshua, Caleb shook his own wet locks in the warm air.

"The brook feels wonderful!" Caleb exclaimed. "Much better than those stagnant oases in the Sinai."

"Are you just now done with your swim?" Joshua laughed. Gesturing toward the others, he said, "They have all dried off long ago."

"I could stay at the brook all day!" Caleb replied. "But I suppose we should make Hebron by nightfall."

"Yes," Joshua said, sitting up. "We will move out soon."

Gazing over the green folds leading toward the highway, Caleb marveled. "Perhaps I never really thought we would see Canaan. I can scarcely believe we are here!"

Joshua ran his hand through the lush grass at his side, disturbing a fat bee, who bumbled drowsily away. From someplace in the hills the sound of bleeting sheep reached his ears, and the clanking of heavy bells about the necks of milkgoats echoed up the ravines.

Reminded of a refrain from a slave song often heard among the Hebrew chaingangs in Egypt, he whispered, "Milk and honey..."

Caleb looked at him in surprise, a smile lighting his face.

"A land flowing with milk and honey!" he cried. "Oh, Joshua, I remember the song well!"

Suddenly, they were singing, rocking back and forth upon the hill, their arms wrapped about one another:

> Milk and honey,
> We shall have milk and honey.
> In the land of Father Jacob,
> In the Valley of Jehovah,
> We shall rest ourselves!

Barely were they aware that the others had now joined them, until ten more husky voices rang out across the hills, and each heart was lifted in song.

Yes, they had come at last to Canaan! Somehow, the trek through the arid Negev had not impressed them with this fact. But today, as they reveled in the joy of pleasant surroundings, in the tune of birds and bees, it occurred to them that they were the first Israelites in four hundred years to set foot upon the holy soil promised to their ancestors.

The more their souls swelled with song, the more the reality of their privileged position settled in on them, until tears filled their eyes and spilled down their ruddy cheeks.

Weeping for joy, they embraced one another, dancing up and down the hill like children.

But suddenly Shammua, representative of the Reubenite tribe, stopped short, his glistening eyes caught by a movement along a distant ridge.

"Brothers!" he gasped. "Look, over there!"

Quieting, the men followed his pointed finger to the top of the ridge, where a handful of people could be seen traversing it.

There were half-a-dozen of them, men dressed not like shepherds, but like cave-dwellers, in short skin skirts and highlaced sandals. Upon their torsos they wore nothing at all, but two of them bore upon their shoulders a long pole from which was suspended the carcass of some large animal.

Because there was so great a distance between the hill and the ridge, the Hebrews might not have realized just how gigantic these fellows were. It was the animal they carried, and the size of the men in comparison, that told Joshua and his followers that the hunters were huge.

Even if the quarry was a stag of unusual proportions, the men bearing him were over seven feet tall. And if the deer was of normal size, they were even taller!

Clustering behind some bushes, Joshua and his followers lay low, watching the hunting party descend the far slope, apparently headed for a camp in the wadi below.

"So...it is true!" whispered Shaphat, the Simeonite.

"What is true?" asked the Benjamite, Palti.

"The legend that Canaan is full of giants!" answered Ammiel, the Danite.

Joshua was familiar with that rumor, but quickly challenged it.

"Now, men," he warned, "we have seen many Canaanites along the way. None of them were giants!"

"We must not stir ourselves up with silly stories," added Caleb.

Looking at him wide-eyed, Geuel, the Gadite, argued, "Silly? Do you call what we have just seen 'silly'?"

"Right!" exclaimed the others.

Soon they were trading tales, of ogres and colossal bogeymen, of cannabalistic Canaanites who would as soon eat them as talk to them.

All but Joshua and Caleb. To no avail, they tried to reason with the rumormongers, until Joshua, in anger, commanded, "Put on your coats and your cloaks! We go to Hebron today! If there are giants there, we will tell Moses."

31

While the Canaanites were a rugged, handsome race, strengthened by generations of pleasant climate and good food, Joshua and his companions encountered no one of unusual stature as they set out the next day, traversing the highway that ran up the Jordan Valley.

Climbing the steep road toward Hebron, they passed people of many nationalities, for this was one of the three main trade routes from the east. Yet none of the folks they saw were giants.

Nor were the Hebrew travelers suspect along this international highway. Though Canaan, like every land, had heard of Israel's exploits, of its marvelous exodus from Egypt, and of its amazing defeat of Amalek, a little company like Joshua's sparked no suspicion as it passed through the region.

Hebron, the first city of any consequence the Israelites had seen since leaving the Nile, was a refreshing stop-off. Though they had to be cautious as they entered this Canaanite town, they reveled in the experience. For this place was more to them than a center of commerce or entertainment. It was the longtime home of their ancestor Abraham. And their entrance here brought Israel full circle.

Privately they delighted in the knowledge that they represented the return of the lost child, Joseph...the return of Jacob and his disenfranchised descendants. Though Israel had not yet conquered the region, they believed such conquest was inevitable.

As they headed north from the hilltop city, highest town in Palestine, they viewed the outlying fields with quiet pride. Just as in Abraham's day, the fields were dotted with sheepfolds and clumps of low-lying oaks. Somewhere out there Abraham had tended his own flocks, and one of those leafy arbors might be the Oaks of Mamre, where he had been a yearly tenant.

Then, too, one of the caves on the surrounding hills surely housed the bones of Sarah, Abraham's beloved wife. For legend had it that the patriarch had purchased such a sanctuary as her burial place.

Yes, this area was rich in history precious to the twelve Israelites. No Canaanite could have cared less for such stories, but as the young spies made their way through the territory, they thought of little else.

They would not stay long in one place. Moses had given them forty days to survey the land, and the more quickly they passed through it, the better. They were not here as tourists, and any lingering was risky.

But as the grade of the highway descended toward the northeast, they entered a most fertile little plain, and amazed by the lustrous vegetation growing along the easterly streams, they chose to camp there for the night.

On the green hillsides were many of the oaks they had seen from the highway. Quickly Joshua and the others gathered kindling from beneath the bows and proceeded to build an evening fire. In moments they had caught enough fish from the nearest brook to feed the entire company, and soon the delicious aroma of roasted trout spiraled up from the coals.

Leaning back with a sigh, Igal, of the tribe of Issachar, licked his lips, savoring the last of his dinner, and gave a contented belch. "I almost feel guilty," he laughed.

"I, too," replied Gaddiel, the Zebulunite. "When I think of our poor people, stuck back there in that desert, I wonder how we got so lucky!"

Caleb chuckled, rolling out his bed beside the fire. "Just suppose," he exclaimed, "that we are camping in the very place where old Abraham camped. Wouldn't that be something!"

Joshua nodded. "It's very possible!" he said.

No sooner had the words left his lips, than Nahbi, representative of the tribe of Naphtali, rushed up from the brook into the firelight.

"Men!" he cried. "See what I've found!"

Thrusting his fist toward the fire, he opened his palm for all to see. Lining it were four of the fattest grapes the Hebrews had ever laid eyes on, purple and luscious in the golden light.

"Where did you get those?" Joshua marveled.

"In the wadi, sir," Nahbi replied. "There is a whole vineyard only yards from here!"

Darting a glance at Caleb, Joshua rose to his feet, suddenly on alert.

"A vineyard?" he repeated. "We are on private land!"

But Nahbi shook his head. "I don't think so, sir," he replied. "It is not a tended vineyard."

Dubious, Joshua took one of the enormous grapes in his fingers, turning it over and over. "Impossible," he objected. "Such fruit could not possibly grow wild."

"But there are no fences, sir," Nahbi argued, "no trellises, no poles. The vines grow every which direction, even into the water itself!"

Passing the grape to Caleb, Joshua enthused, "This is indeed a holy land! Where but on holy soil would such riches grow free for the taking!"

32

Though the twelve Hebrews must be moving on, they marked firmly in their memories the exact location of the vineyard camp. One of Moses's requests, when he had sent them forth, was that they bring back a sample of the fruit of the land. What better example would be found than those magnificent grapes?

And so they determined that they would find the place again on their return trip, to take a cluster to Moses.

From here, their immediate destination was the city of Jericho, two days' journey to the northeast. The most important city in the entire Jordan Valley, it was a strategic fortress, commanding the eastern entrance to Canaan and the three trade routes that branched north, south, and west from the Jordan River. No investigation of the land would be worthwhile without a report on Jericho. For if Israel intended to invade the territory, they would inevitably go against that place.

Though the highway led directly from Hebron to the great walled fortress, the traveling was not easy. Hebron sat well over half-a-mile *above* sea level, and Jericho was positioned in a parched valley eight hundred feet *below* sea level. The descent toward the Jordan through the shepherd hills made for treacherous going.

When, by evening of the second day, the spies glimpsed the city, their hearts froze. If ever legends of Canaanites had stirred their souls to fear, the sight of Jericho and its formidable walls did more so.

Jericho's name had several interpretations, and it was thus called "the city of palm trees," "the place of fragrance," and "city of the moon." Though it was nearly night when the spies came upon Jericho, its silvery light illumined gleaming turrets and enhanced the foilage of towering trees. Exposed as it was in this wide, dry vale, Jericho was indeed moon-kissed, its palm-lined streets a thrill of green. And even to this distance the aroma of gardens and flowers was borne through the desert air.

But it was none of these attributes that caused the Israelites to tremble. Huddling together upon the sloping highway, they spoke in hushed tones, marveling over Jericho's impassable walls.

More like a castle than a town, the city covered only six acres, its tiny streets so jammed with houses that sunlight rarely touched them. The gardens and bowers that lent their green to its glory grew atop the flat roofs, and while the palace of the king sat perched at the crest of the mound which was the result of three thousand years of habitation, other residences were literally hung along the space that separated the city's inner and outer walls.

Creeping down the sunset highway, Joshua leaned close to Caleb. "Those walls must be as tall as six men standing on each others' shoulders!" he whispered.

"And the thickness of them!" Caleb added. "Why five men stretched full length across would not reach from side to side!"

Pausing for breath, Joshua sat down beside the road and gathered his men about him.

Surveying the crowded city, he shook his head. "To think, we were afraid of giants!" he sighed. "What we see before us is far more awesome! Like a town built by a giant's hand!"

His eleven companions sat with him in silence, paralyzed by the prospect of taking on so substantial an obstacle.

Surrounding the mound was a glacis of cracked and broken stones, a sheer drop-off which would slice an invading army's feet to shreds. And that hazardous slope led directly to a wide moat, which encompassed the entire circumference of the city.

"Sir," said Sethur, the Asherite, "even if we could scale that wall, how would we ever make it across the water? Who knows what creatures lie beneath the surface, just waiting for the taste of human flesh!"

Nodding in agreement, the others murmured fearfully, and Joshua knew their imaginations were again running wild.

"Let us deal with what we know!" he squelched them. "Not with what we do not know!"

"Very well," replied Gaddi, of the tribe of Manasseh, "but what we know is bad enough! I think we should turn back and tell Moses what we have found. What is the point of going further, when Israel will never get past Jericho?"

Astonished, Joshua confronted his kinsman. "Gaddi!" he cried. "You are, like me, a son of Joseph! I expected greater courage from you!"

Shamefaced, Gaddi looked at the ground, but his comrades rallied to his defense.

"Moses told us to bring back a report," they argued. "We know enough now without going further. We know enough to tell him that invasion is suicide!"

Flushed with anger, Joshua glared at them. "Do you all feel this way?" he snarled.

"Not I!" Caleb answered. "Brothers, where is your faith?"

Silenced by this question, the objectors squirmed, and Joshua stood up, heading down the road.

"Come!" he shouted over his shoulder. "We will camp with the caravans outside the wall, and tomorrow we will spy out the city!"

* * *

Joshua could not sleep that night. It was not the noise of the encampment that kept him awake, as caravans and bedos from the three major trade routes settled beneath

the shadow of the great wall. It was the attitude manifested by his fellow spies that would not let him rest.

As his companions slumbered, he lay staring up into
the star-studded sky, fretfully recalling the many times
Israel had resisted the will of God.

Were it not for Caleb, even Joshua might have given up
this venture by now, so weary was he of struggling with
his followers' unbelief. Why was it that these young
leaders, the choicest men his nation had to offer, were so
easily intimidated? How fitting had been Caleb's question! Where *was* their faith, anyway?

Giving up his attempt to sleep, Joshua threw back his
covers and stepped into the moonlight. All about him
were travelers of many nations, waiting for morning
when they would enter Jericho to do business, or, having
completed their work there, to move on. This was the
first time since leaving Egypt that Joshua had been in
close quarters with so many Gentiles. He felt quite alone.

Most likely everyone in this campground had heard
of Israel's miraculous flight from its four-hundred-year
bondage. Doubtless they had all received news of its
exploits in the desert, and wondered when the Hebrews
would make their next move.

If the identity of Joshua's men were ever suspected,
their lives would be in jeopardy. Therefore, as he paced
through camp, he spoke to no one and hid his Hebrew
face behind his mantle.

Ironic, he thought. If the Canaanites knew how spineless his spies really were, they would laugh at them rather
than fear them.

I keep company with cowards! he sneered. *These ten
"leaders" might as well be the enemy, for all the good they will
do me!*

The enemy. Joshua paused over the phrase. He was
commanding general of Israel. He had better concern
himself with the nature of his adversary, as well as the
nature of his own men.

Walking out from camp, he stood upon the bridge that spanned the moat, and he surveyed the walls up and down.

What sort of people lived behind them? he wondered. Proud people, they must be. Strong and ruthless. What other sort could build such a fortress? And merciless. They were surely a cold, heartless people, to have taken command of Canaan and to have held it against countless invaders for so long a time.

One thing he knew for certain: They were pagans, idolators. They worshiped a pantheon of false gods and goddesses, and had long ago abandoned themselves to the most sensual and depraved practices.

Cringing, he tried not dwell on the horrors that attended their religion, on the fornication and bloodlust that went with their rituals and sacrifices.

Clenching his fists, he dwelt instead on the righteous calling that was his, the destiny that would lead him to overthrow this wicked place.

Tomorrow he would take his men inside the walls. He would show them the reason for their venture, and inspire them with such zeal for their cause that they would put aside their childish qualms.

Feeling better, he knew he would sleep now. Or if not sleep, cogitate on strategies and plans. Returning across the bridge, he headed back for camp.

But just as he came again beneath the shadow of the moonlit wall, his eyes were drawn to a movement in a window, high atop the fortress.

One of the houses built along the wall was still alight, its owners apparently yet awake. And silhouetted against the window's yellow glow was a young woman, leaning on the sill.

Apparently seeking a bit of fresh air, she sat with her face upturned, the moon touching it sweetly. She ran a comb through her hair, which tumbled in long, red waves about her shoulders.

She was very far away in that high window. She did not look toward the camp, and was unaware of the solitary Hebrew and his admiring gaze.

But Joshua could see her clearly, and following her gaze toward the moon, he wondered what thoughts possessed her.

Only for a moment, however, did his eyes leave her face. For she was far more beautiful than the moon.

Unnoticed, he was free to linger over the graceful curve of her bare arm, where it peeked from beneath a scarlet gown. One dainty hand rested like a white bird upon the window sill, and as she lifted it to brush back her hair, he likewise lingered on the line of her neck and gentle fullness of her bosom.

"My lady..." he groaned, as feelings he had long denied himself rushed forth.

No one heard him. No one knew what surged through his masculine heart as he stood entranced upon the Jericho bridge.

Even he was unaware of himself, until a group of rowdy young Canaanites passed him, heading for the city just before curfew. In a moment the drawbridge that spanned the moat would be taken up, and the clatter of streets, taverns, and brothels would dwindle to a hum.

Suddenly aware again of his surroundings, and of the fact that he was in alien territory, Joshua felt the blood rush to his face.

Tearing his eyes from the woman in the window, he determined not to look that way again.

No matter how sweet her aspect, no matter how lovable her moonstruck face, she was, after all, a heathen. And no Israelite had a right to look upon her.

33

With daylight, the full color of the city was evident. While at night, the moon had played up the verdant vegetation and the clean white walls, sunshine showed another side of the pallet.

The moment Joshua awoke, the raging red of fire-trees, a plant peculiar to the area, stung his eyes. Bearing the brightest, poppy-colored flowers he had ever seen, these trees grew all about the roadways leading to Jericho. And as Joshua and his men entered the city, they found bright clusters of the scarlet blossoms in every niche of the marketplace.

The broad plaza where business was transacted was the only part of the congested city open to the sun. And in the light of day, what bold business was carried on!

Since Jericho controlled all access routes to the interior of Canaan, merchants from every land brought wares here to be sold. Goods from as far away as India, Egypt, Assyria, and Anatolia were on display. Joshua's men found that the language barrier was of little concern, as folks conducted trade by facial expression and wild gestures more than by the word of mouth.

But it was not only the produce and handcrafts of all nations that were traded here. Reminiscent of Egypt were the platforms of the slave merchants, who bought and sold human beings as though they were cattle.

Pierced to the heart, Joshua and his men watched as captives of foreign wars and young people born to slavery were auctioned off like sheep and goats. Their faces full of fear, or evincing no feeling at all, they stepped one by one upon the block, and listened as their prices were determined. Bound and shackled, they stepped down again, to be hauled away by new owners. If their eyes met the eyes of the Hebrews, they found there a sympathy new to them. But there was no chance for explanations, and no way to offer help.

As the slaves were led away, they met with the bite of cruel whips, and from their backs streamed another form of scarlet.

Yes, the streets of Jericho raged red in the daylight. From the far side of the square came the sound of drums and tambourines, as people brought sacrificial animals to be offered on the altars of Baal and his consort, Astarte. There would be no human life offered up today, for such sacrifices were made just once a year. But the gifts given daily to the priests were so numerous that the drain ditches leading off the main thoroughfare were choked with blood by noon.

All of this Joshua observed with growing disgust. It had been just such sights he had determined to show his men. But he had been unprepared for his own reaction.

While he had always been a hesitant warrior, he experienced today a rush of desire to wipe these people out. Egypt, for all its cruelty, had at least covered its shame with sophistication. Jericho's bloodlust bore not even a veneer of decency.

And it was not only the sacrificial system that carried the scarlet theme to the gutters. Hand in hand with bloody Baal walked his licentious lady, Astarte. On every corner, in broad daylight, her prostitutes flaunted their wares.

"Men," Joshua whispered, drawing his comrades about him, "can there be any doubt that Yahweh will destroy this place? Why would he promise this land to our fathers, yet allow this pollution to remain?"

Thoughtful, the men nodded, peering into the dark corners where all manner of lewdness abounded.

Walking toward the center of the square, Joshua led his men to the town fountain, a terraced pool fed by underground springs and graced with three tall geysers. Sitting on its ledge, the men cooled themselves from the heat of the hammering sun.

"I agree, sir," said Nahbi. "But those walls are insurmountable! How would our army ever gain a foothold?"

"How have we done any of the things we have done since the day Moses came to us?" Joshua argued. "Yahweh is the God of miracles!"

Looking at one another, the men recalled the many ways in which the Lord had intervened, from the plagues on Egypt to the quail and manna.

But as they considered Joshua's words, their contemplation was interrupted. A group of harlots, all dressed in red, had seen them sitting near the fountain, and had decided to approach them.

They did not know what tongue the Hebrews spoke, but sidling up, they bent over seductively and offered their services with universally understood body language.

Pulling back, Joshua denounced them, and muttered to his men, "Remember Sodom and Gomorrah? God told Abraham he would save those cities if only ten righteous persons could be found in them. But there were none!" Passing his hand over the market scene, he sighed, "I doubt even *one* could be found here!"

When he stood and turned for the city gate, about to lead his men away, the departing harlots jeered at him, hooting and laughing and calling unwanted attention to his little group.

To his relief, they were distracted by a party of would-be customers just as the crowd began to close in. But as the women left, one remained behind, studying the newcomers with uncommon kindness.

Instantly, Joshua recognized her. When she had been with the bawdy klatch of streetwalkers, he had not singled her out. But as she stood now alone, gazing upon him, his heart tripped.

She was the woman whom he had seen the night before, the beautiful young lady whose moonlit face had held him captive upon the bridge.

Just like the others, she was dressed in scarlet. While her scarlot garb had not impressed him last night, today it carried significance.

She was a harlot! His lovely lady was a prostitute of Astarte!

Dumbfounded, he backed away, his throat choked with shame that he could ever have given her a second glance.

But as he withdrew, her face colored, and she turned her sad, aqua eyes to the fountain.

"Will you have a drink of water?" she said softly.

Incredulous, Joshua glanced at his men, who observed her with wonder.

"She speaks Hebrew!" Caleb whispered, drawing near his elbow.

"Indeed!" Joshua stammered.

"How can that be?" his friend marveled.

But the others were frightened by the fact. "We have been found out!" they speculated. "She will report us!"

Anxiously they spurred their leader to depart.

But not before the young woman had drawn closer, offering them a skin of water, which she had just filled at the splashing pool.

"Come again," she bade them. "My house is your house."

With this she gently thrust the water bottle into Joshua's hot hands, and bowed quickly before him.

Then she hastened away, vanishing into the dense crowd like a ruby arrow.

"Let's go!" the men exclaimed, pulling on Joshua's cloak.

Complying, he followed them to the gate.

But now he knew less about Jericho than he had when he entered. The soft, kind face of the scarlet woman had made a muddle of his heart, setting up an obstacle far more confounding than the walls of her profligate city.

34

Before Joshua had entered Jericho, he had been un-afraid. Though his men had been squeamish since their sighting of the Anakim, or giants, at Hebron, it took Jericho to fill Joshua's heart with apprehension.

Nor was that apprehension based on the size of the walls or on the ferocity of the Canaanites living there. It was precipitated by a quandary of the heart, a bewilder-ment of the spirit.

His two encounters with the woman in red caused him to question the nature of his enemy. He wondered not only where such a lady had learned to speak Hebrew, but he wondered how someone so lovely, so apparently kind of spirit, could be evil.

Yes, she was a harlot. Harlots were wicked, were they not? Doubtless, she worshiped a heathen goddess—not only worshiped her, but prostituted herself in her name.

Still, he sensed in her a seeking soul. He wondered how he could go against her city when it would mean her destruction, and the destruction of others who might be like her.

When Joshua had fought the Amalekites at Rephidim, he had encountered the most vicious of warriors, men bent on bloodshed and filled with hate. It had been easy to oppose them with strength of purpose.

But Jericho was inhabited by families, by women and children, as well as men of war. How to hate them, he knew not.

Such thoughts filled his head during the remainder of the venture through Canaan.

Following the Jordan, the spies and their commander hugged the folds and creases of the mountain highway leading toward the northern limits of the land. They had been given forty days to complete their round-trip, and when they left Jericho they tried to travel at least ten miles a day, stopping only briefly to investigate various locales along the way to Rehob, the last city on the itinerary.

While Amalekites and other warlike groups were concentrated south of Jericho, the northern half of the land was dominated by Canaanites, likewise students of war, but more deeply rooted in towns than their transient neighbors. Joshua and his men found that most of the cities were walled, and though none of them was so strongly fortified as Jericho, each would be a difficult obstacle to overcome.

To their relief, they saw no more gigantic Anakim on their trip north, and might have avoided giants altogether had they not ventured toward the seacoast on their return.

Making a side jaunt to spy out the cities of the Philistine plain, they came across the tall, pre-Hellenic sea-peoples who inhabited that region. Intermingled with them were remnants of the giant race, the Zamzummin. Together the bloodlines had created an exceptionally powerful populace.

It was with skittish glances over their shoulders that the Hebrews set out at last for Kadesh and the camp of Israel. If Joshua had had trouble maintaining morale during the early days of the venture, he had even more once his followers had been through Philistia. He hoped that their long-planned return to the wild vineyard outside Hebron might renew their spirits, for they must soon give an account of the land to Moses, and in their present mood, that report would be anything but encouraging.

It was a bright, sunny day once again when the men found the vineyard just north of Abraham's city. Laughing and running, the weary travelers headed for the brook where the thick vines trailed into the current, and stripping themselves they plunged in, playfully splashing one another.

Joshua seated himself on the bank and dangled his feet in the stream.

"We have seen much on this trip," Caleb noted, joining his friend by the water's edge, "but this place is the most impressive."

"More impressive than the giants?" Joshua tested him.

The Judahite shrugged. "Canaan is indeed a land of mighty people," he acknowledged. "But if we are meant to take it, we will overcome them."

"Well spoken, " Joshua praised him. "It seems I can always rely on you."

Caleb took the compliment graciously, and breathed deep of the warm air, a smile of contentment on his face. "We should give this place a name!" he suggested. "When we tell Moses about it, we should call it by name."

Pondering this a moment, he traced the vines where they grew down the shore. Lush with purple fruit, they beckoned to the hungry Hebrew.

Leaping to his feet, Caleb exclaimed, "Eshcol, Valley of Eshcol!"

The Hebrew name meant Valley of the Cluster, and repeating it joyously, Caleb ran down the bank to where a huge clump of swollen grapes hung shining in the sun.

Emerging from the brook, his companions gathered around him, and one drew a sharp knife from his belt, offering it to him.

"These will do, to show Moses just how lush this land is!" Caleb proclaimed. Taking the knife, he eagerly sawed through the thick vine, until the grapes fell with a thump to the earth. Then breaking off a length of the vine, he ran it between the stems of the cluster and lifted one end to his shoulder.

Nahbi hoisted the other end, and as though they bore between them a slain buck, they carried the grapes to Joshua.

The commander laughed as they approached, and stood to greet them. "Moses told us to bring a sample of the fruit of the land, but you bring the entire vineyard!"

Though they pulled off handfuls of the succulent grapes, ravenously cramming the sweet morsels into their mouths, the men barely made a dint in the cluster. Between the sounds of lips smacking and juice trickling, they sang together as though they drank fine wine.

But just as they had nearly forgotten all care, a sound less palatable interrupted their little party. Low and gutteral, it issued from the slope behind, and thinking it must be the growl of a wild animal, the revelers leaped to their feet, drawing their swords in a flash.

From a clump of bushes, a creature emerged, his shadow falling across their gathering like a thundercloud.

Mouths agape, the Hebrews surveyed their visitor. This was no animal. This was a human being. But he was enormous, taller by a cubit than the tallest of them!

And he was built like the Jericho walls, his trunk thick and muscular, his arms and legs rippling like iron. The scantiest of clothing served to enhance rather than conceal his powerful physique. A small leather breastshield was his torso's only covering, and beneath a short, rawhide skirt, swelled well-defined thighs. Crisscrossed up his limbs, from toes and fingers to knees and elbows, were studded straps of leather, and in one rocky fist he bore a spear taller than himself.

This he shook violently, throwing his huge head backward and roaring like a lion, shaking also his black mane of hair and beard.

Falling back in terror, Joshua's men clattered their swords together, endangering one another in hasty retreat.

"Anak!" they cried, knowing that they confronted one of the legendary giants.

"Stand still!" Joshua commanded. "We are the Lord's!"

But his companions ignored him, all but Caleb, who managed to take courage.

The colossus was now within feet of Joshua and his friend, still roaring and flashing his weapon like a lightning bolt. Looming over the Hebrew leader, he sneered at him like an ox above an ant, until Joshua felt his hot breath upon his face.

Then, to his surprise, the giant lowered his spear, not to drive it through him, but to point at the abandoned cluster of grapes.

Anger flamed in his huge eyes, and shaking his enormous head again, he bellowed like a wild boar.

"This is your land?" Joshua interpreted. "Your vineyard?"

Of course, the giant could not understand a word he spoke, but Joshua knew he got the message.

Snorting, he nudged at the cluster and waved his spear under the Hebrew's nose.

Swallowing hard, Joshua and Caleb listened as the towering challenger replied in his own tongue, flinging his hands toward the vineyard, and stamping his feet.

"Yes," Joshua said, his heart surging. "We will go. We will take no more grapes."

Joshua's tone convinced the titan he would comply. And while the Hebrews tiptoed backward, expecting him to wait until they vanished down the road, it was instead the giant who turned to go.

Watching him depart, Joshua and Caleb could scarcely believe they were still in possession of their lives. For a long while they stood silent on the shore, thinking the fellow would come back, and likely with an army.

But the sun was setting and night was coming on. As the first stars appeared in the black sky, the two Hebrews were joined by their companions, who one by one crept forth from places of hiding.

"We will not camp tonight," Joshua whispered to his men. "We will travel by cover of darkness."

Relieved to be going, the men headed with him toward the highway.

But Caleb was not so hasty.

"What about the grapes?" he called after them.

Joshua turned around, and seeing the pile of discarded fruit lying in the moonlight, he sent Nahbi back to help carry it.

"What if the giant returns?" the others objected.

"We have our orders," Joshua reminded them. "Moses wants to see the fruit of the land, and we will take it to him!"

35

Miles before Joshua and his men laid eyes on the camp of the Israelites, the sound of music and celebration reached them across the wilderness. Messengers who had been on the lookout for them heralded their return, and the people made ready to greet them, eager to hear their report and to plan the next steps toward their long-lost homeland.

It had been over four centuries since the children of Jacob had dwelt in the promised land. Anxious to regain their inheritance, the people who had been tested in Egypt and tested in the Sinai believed nothing more could stand in their way.

Yes, they had often failed the Lord. They had not always been strong of faith. But surely they had learned their lessons now. They had survived, had they not? Once they entered the land of milk and honey, they would never look back.

Joshua should have been glad to return to camp. This should have been a momentous occasion. But, despite the evident enthusiasm of Israel for his homecoming, it was with a leaden heart that he descended the last sandy hill and witnessed the enormous population spread out before him.

Ever since the encounter with the giant at Eshcol, his men had spoken only of defeat. Joshua knew that the report they would present to Moses and the people would be full of discouragement, and though he would try to inspire the opposite, their voices would outnumber his.

Therefore, when Moses sent a committee to meet him, asking him to address the congregation, the lift of his

167

chin and the resolute expression on his face served only to cover a despondent spirit.

"Greetings, Master," he hailed the prophet, joining him upon a slope overlooking the crowd. "Greetings, Aaron," he said to the prophet's brother, bowing low. "Your servants are safely returned."

At this, applause rang up from the desert floor, as Israel showed appreciation for their twelve heroes.

Moses, relieved to see his closest friend, embraced him fervently, and with tears welling in his eyes, he presented him to the people.

"We are all anxious to know what you discovered in the land of our fathers!" he announced. "We want to know what lies before us as we reclaim our heritage!"

Again, applause and cheers filled the air, and Joshua tried to appear zealous.

Turning to the congregation, he held up his hands, calling for silence. "We went into the land where you sent us," he began, "and it certainly does flow with milk and honey!" Then calling forth Caleb and Nahbi, who bore between them the grape-laden vine, he proclaimed, "This is the fruit of the land!"

Amazed at the sight of the monstrous grapes, the people gave a great shout, and instantly broke into song:

> Milk and honey,
> We shall have milk and honey.
> In the land of Father Jacob,
> In the Valley of Jehovah,
> We shall rest ourselves!

To the sound of timbrels and horns, they clapped and danced, seeing the first tangible evidence of their racial dream. When at last, Moses commanded silence, he addressed the men who stood with Joshua.

"You have done well," he praised them. "Tell us, then, about the people of the land, and their cities."

Caleb would have spoken, but before he could get a word out, his fellow spies took over.

Shamelessly they circumvented their commander's positive approach, coloring Canaan in the bleakest of terms.

"It is indeed a land of milk and honey," Shaphat said, "but the people who live there are strong, and the cities are fortified and very large!"

"Moreover," interrupted Igal, "we saw the descendants of Anak there!"

At the very mention of the name, fear pushed through the crowd, and the people murmured in horror.

"Amalek is also living in the Negev," added Palti, "and the Hittites and the Jebusites and the Amorites live in the hill country just north of us!"

No race of warriors was more greatly to be feared than those already mentioned, but as the crowd grew restless with dread, Gaddiel inserted the obvious.

"And the Canaanites live by the sea and by Jordan!"

By now, the people despaired indeed. Old men clutched their chests in horror, and women wept aloud. Little children clung to their mother's robes and able-bodied men trembled.

Seeing that Joshua had lost ground, Caleb managed to gain the front, and cried out for the crowd's attention. "Brothers and sisters!" he shouted. "Do not be disheartened by this evil report. Canaan is the land of Jacob, the land vouchsafed to us and to our children! Regardless of the challenge, we should by all means go up and take possession of it. For we shall surely overcome it!"

This seemed to prick the spirits of the people, but only for an instant. No sooner had Caleb spoken than Gaddi forced him aside. "Do not be foolish!" he growled. "We are *not* able to go up against the enemy. They are too strong for us!"

"Yes!" cried Ammiel, his eyes wide and his hands gesturing wildly. "The land through which we have gone is a land that devours its inhabitants! All the people we saw are men of great size!"

Flabbergasted by this gross exaggeration, Joshua tried to take control, stepping to the fore and calling for peace.

But it was too late. The ancient legends of the Canaanites and their neighbors were too deeply ingrained in the memories of the Hebrews. Passed down through generations, they required only such lies to make them flower into wild imaginings.

Vainly did Joshua attempt to regain the people's confidence. When Sethur added his account, the crowd was lost forever.

"There also we saw the *Nephilim*!" he cried. "And we became like grasshoppers in our own sight, as well as theirs!"

The *Nephilim*? The Anak were bad enough. But the Nephilim, a legend reserved for campfire tales and nightmares, were the most notorious monsters of Hebrew folklore.

Believed to be the descendants of the titanic race that dwelt on earth before Noah's flood, they were half-human and half-demon. Of unearthly stature, their descendants were of preternatural dimensions.

Utterly terrified, the people greeted this account with loud distress. Standing aside, Joshua looked on helplessly as the Israelites stirred themselves into a frenzy of weeping and wailing.

Directing their fear and their resentment at their great leader, they began to shout at Moses: "Why didn't we die in Egypt, or in the wilderness? Why is the Lord bringing us into this land, to fall by the sword? Our wives and children will become plunder! Wouldn't it be better for us to return to Egypt?"

Soon even the most respected men of the camp, the very ones whom Moses had selected as his governors, were taking up the cry. Conferring amongst themselves,

they rushed up the slope, ready to overthrow Moses and
replace him with one of the rebellious spies.

"Let us appoint a leader," they called to the people,
"and return to Egypt!"

Cheers rose from venomous hearts, and as a body the
people moved forward, ready to tear Moses and Aaron to
shreds.

Surrounded, the two brothers were thrown to the
ground, and there they lay, facedown in the dirt.

Always Joshua had been amazed at the ease with which
the Israelites could be turned from the right to embrace
the wrong. But somehow he had always held out hope for
them, believing that in their hearts they must have a core
of good. After all, were they not "the chosen people," the
sons and daughters of Jacob, Isaac, and Abraham?

But this moment, as he observed their callous cruelty,
their changeable spirit, he gave up that hope. In terror
for his master's safety, he ran to him, throwing himself
across his prostrate body, and shielding him from the
blows of fists and feet.

"Back! Back!" he cried. "Do not do this evil, my
brothers!"

Somehow, his voice penetrated the soulless mob. Somehow, they heard him, and dismayed at their own actions,
they pulled away.

Raising himself from the ground, Joshua stood again
to his feet, finding, to his amazement, that Caleb had
likewise protected Aaron. Together, the two Hebrews
managed to make a dent in the crowd, and sent the
governors back to the desert floor.

Their faces tearstreaked, Caleb and Joshua paced back
and forth before the people, pushing aside their fellow
spies and commanding the attention of the crazed congregation.

Tearing the necklines of their own tunics, they threw
dust over their heads until their tears trickled through a
coating of dirt.

"The land which we passed through is exceedingly good!" Joshua proclaimed. "If the Lord is pleased with us, He will bring us into this land and give it to us—a land flowing with milk and honey!"

"Listen to Joshua!" Caleb joined in, his arms spread beseechingly. "Do not rebel against the Lord! And do not fear the inhabitants of the land! For they shall be our prey! Their defense has been removed from them, and the Lord is with us! Do not fear them!"

Again, it seemed the people might give heed. But it took only a hint of rebellion on the part of their leaders to kill their faith.

Where it began, no one would be able to recount. But from somewhere in the crowd a pebble was thrown, and then a rock, and another, and another. "Stone them!" someone cried. And soon the cry became a chant.

Driven like lepers from the edge of camp, Joshua, Caleb, Moses, and Aaron took flight. Bleeding and battered they took sanctuary in the rocky hills where the sons of Amalek dwelt.

For even in that hostile territory they would be safer than with their own people.

36

Throughout the next day, Moses separated himself from his fellow fugitives, cloistering himself in prayer within a nook of the barren hills. Knowing that they dare not return to camp, and not wishing to leave their master, Joshua, Caleb, and Aaron kept close together, hoping that the Lord would answer Moses's pleas for guidance.

From experience, Joshua knew that the prophet might be away for days. This was not the first time the servant had been obliged to wait while his mentor sought the word of the Lord. This time, at least, he had company. But this was little solace in such wild country, where their closest neighbors would as soon kill them as speak to them.

It was, therefore, a great relief to the three Hebrews when the prophet reappeared the next morning, assuring them that it was safe to return to camp.

"The glory of the Lord has appeared to the children of Israel," he told them. "They will not harm us, though the word I have for them is dreadful."

Moses's tone confirmed the expression on his face. His struggle with God had been arduous and the outcome disheartening. Lines of stress and sorrow etched his countenance. The man who had always before returned from days of prayer with renewed vigor and with hopeful news, was this time weighted down with grief.

But nothing more did he relay to his three companions. Whatever sad report he would bear to the camp, he would give only when the entire congregation was gathered before him.

Longing to question him, Joshua nevertheless refrained. Moses's silence was foreboding, reinforcing the sense of hopeless resignation which the young Hebrew had experienced when the Israelites set upon them all, stoning the master and driving them into the hills.

Israel had not learned the lessons Yahweh had tried to teach them. Over and over they had bowed to doubt, rebelling against the Lord and his emissaries. And from the look on Moses's face, there was now no hope for their reformation.

When the last mile had been traveled and the camp lay spread out at their feet, they found, just as Moses had predicted, no danger to themselves. The very people who had desired to kill them were today meek as lambs. Rather than calling for a new leader, they heralded Moses's appearance with tears of contrition.

Old men sat upon the ground in sackcloth, their hair and beards full of ashes. Young women and children huddled together, weeping for forgiveness, and the men who had tried to overthrow Moses met him in the wilderness, bowing and seeking his favor.

Still, not a word passed the prophet's lips, until he stood once again upon the slope where Joshua and the eleven spies had given their report.

As he raised his hands, the audience was hushed. Not even a breeze passed over the desert before the master cried like a trumpet, "'How long will these people provoke me? How long will they not believe in me, despite all the signs which I have performed in their midst?'"

Everyone knew it was the Lord's words that he spoke, and not his own. Too many times had they heard him address them thus, for them to mistake that fact.

Without hesitation, Moses continued, though the next utterance would be the most grievous of his prophetic career.

"'Surely all the men who have seen my glory and my miracles, which I performed in Egypt and in the wilderness, yet have put me to the test these ten times and have not listened to my voice...surely they shall by *no means* see the land which I promised to their fathers, nor shall any of those who provoked me see it!'"

Scarcely comprehending the import of this pronouncement, the people stood in stony silence before the preacher. But as the words gradually penetrated their incredulous minds, Moses hit them with more.

"'How long shall I bear with this evil people,'" he shouted, "'who grumble against me? I have heard the complaints of the sons of Israel, which they murmur against me. As I live, just as you have spoken in my hearing, so I will do to you! Your corpses shall fall in this wilderness, even all your numbered men from twenty years old and upward, who have grumbled against me! Surely you shall not come into the land in which I swore to make you dwell, except Caleb, the son of Jephunneh, and Joshua, the son of Nun! And your children, whom you said would become a prey—I will bring them in, and they shall know the land which you have rejected! But as for *you*, your corpses shall fall in this wilderness. And your sons shall be shepherds for forty years in the wilderness, and they shall suffer for your unfaithfulness, until your corpses lie in the wilderness!'"

Awestruck, the people looked to one another, hoping that they had misunderstood. And when they saw only their own desperation mirrored in one another's faces, they began to plead with Moses.

Surely he would retract this edict! Had the Lord not threatened them in the past with total destruction? Surely, Yahweh could not mean what he said. Surely, he would reconsider!

But the prophet was unyielding as rock. When he raised his hands again, it was only to repeat the dreaded word.

"'I the Lord have spoken!'" he cried. "'Surely I will do this to all this evil assembly who are gathered together against me. In this wilderness they shall be destroyed, and here they shall die!'"

Like a twisting knife, the pronouncement severed soul from spirit. Even Joshua and Caleb, who alone of their generation had been spared the evil, slumped to their knees, terrified of the destiny prepared for their people.

Weeping and mourning such as never had been heard in Israel and never would be again, ascended that day to the skies. Would God not repent of this decision? Had he not sworn punishment upon them in the past, yet later changed his mind?

But, indeed, Yahweh had declared himself. Not even Moses, who had pleaded with him for two days, had been able to turn his heart.

And though the people soaked the sand with tears, the prophet could hold out no hope.

Turning with stooped shoulders, Moses left the hill, disappearing into the desert, silent as a shadow.

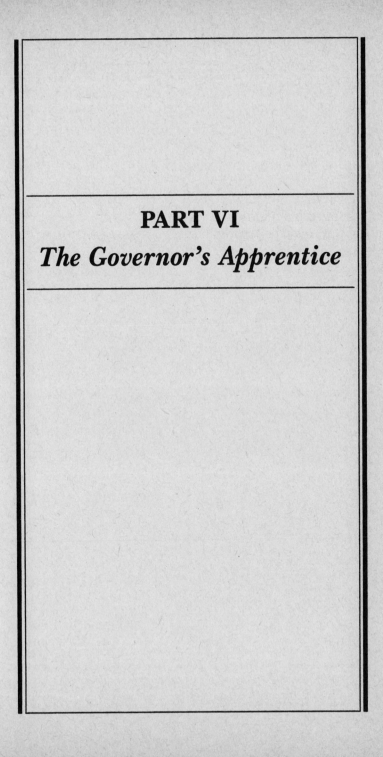

PART VI
The Governor's Apprentice

37

Dirt, sand, and tumbleweeds. Sometimes Joshua felt sure he would go mad from the sight of them.

Twenty years of bedo existence in the wilderness of Zin, following months in the wilderness of Sinai and the wilderness of Paran, should have accustomed him to the taste of grit between his teeth and the feel of desert wind upon his face. But they had not.

He was not a city dweller by nature. Though raised in Raamses, he was of Hebrew lineage, and the love of open spaces ran in his blood. But the land of his forefathers was not desert. It was the land of promise, the land of milk and honey, which he must wait yet *another* twenty years to enter.

Not that life within the wandering camp had been dull. Cohabitation with such a difficult people as Israel presented daily challenges. But those challenges were so bound up with endless sand and the bleak routine of the shepherd's life that he had come to despise the wilderness for more than its dreariness. He had come to despise it because his people would not learn from it. Always they resisted its testing, rather than growing stronger for it.

At least this was true of the older generation. The younger people seemed to be made of better stuff, their spirits more amenable to hardship. As Joshua observed their coming of age, he did from time to time take heart for the future of the nation.

Today, however, he was downcast. He had traveled out from camp toward the north, where eighteen years ago Israel had made one of its most foolish mistakes.

Kicking at the tawny sand as he walked, he had uncovered a vivid memento of that mistake, an Amalekite war helmet. Unearthing it, he was reminded of an incident he wished he could forget.

This helmet undoubtedly remained from the Hebrews' second battle with the sons of Amalek. The first time Israel had confronted the barbarians, Joshua had led them to victory. Their endeavors had been blessed by Yahweh, and the young general's first experience with combat had convinced everyone he should henceforth lead the Israelite army.

But the second time the Hebrews went against Amalek had been a disaster, lacking God's approval from the outset.

Because this helmet bore the symbol of the Amalekites of the Sinai, it was apparently one of the headgear stripped from the southern horde and worn by an Israelite in this second battle. It had been lost in the fracas which saw ten thousand Hebrews slain or routed and sent back to Kadesh in disgrace.

Neither the ark of the covenant, nor the pillar of cloud had left the camp to lead them north that day into battle. The morning after Moses had given his grim pronouncement, telling Israel that none of the elder generation would ever enter the promised land, a host of the people had sought him out in the hill country, resolved to circumvent the edict.

"Here we are!" they had announced, when they found their master. "We have indeed sinned, but we will go up to the place which the Lord has promised!"

Joshua had been present with Moses that day, having followed him into the wilds of the high country, along with Caleb and Aaron. He knew how headstrong the children of Jacob could be, and seeing the determination in their faces, he feared it was worthless to contradict them. But reminding them of the report his men had given, he said, "Brothers, there are Amalekites and

Canaanites in these hills. They have surely seen our encampment at Kadesh, and stand ready to defend their territory."

"But we have fought the Amalekites before!" they rebutted. "You led us to victory against them! Will you not lead us again?"

"Why are you transgressing the commandment of the Lord," Moses intervened, "when it will not succeed? Do not go up, lest you fall before your enemies! For the Lord will *not* be with you!"

But in typical fashion, the people stiffened their necks. "How can God be against us, if we are reclaiming the heritage of Jacob? Is it not ours by promise?" they objected.

Sighing, Moses could only repeat the warning: "The Amalekites and Canaanites will be there in front of you! You shall fall by the sword, for you have turned away from following the Lord! The Lord will *not* be with you!"

The following hours were a horror to recall. With utter disregard for the prophet, the people scorned him, calling him a senile old man and insisting that he was refuting the very promise which he had relayed to them. Surely the land was not meant only for their children! What right did Moses have to put such restrictions on the prophecy?

And wouldn't Joshua come with them? Wouldn't he lead them? He was one of them, was he not, one of their generation? How could he betray them now, when he had been named commanding general by the laying-on of hands and anointing?

Even now, as Joshua relived that moment, his heart pounded as it had that day. Torn between his calling as leader of the Israelite army, and the word of Moses, he had surveyed the faces of the many men he had inspired with courage, the ones who had become, under his instruction, a mighty fighting force. He remembered how they had first gathered before him on the plain of

Rephidim, the most disheveled and cowardly "troops" it had ever been a commander's misfortune to muster. Of course, he had been just as inexperienced as they, when they first took up arms together. But it had been that mutual inexperience and the learning process that had bonded him to his men and his men to him. How *could* he now deny their request, and let them go forth without him—go forth to war...and certain defeat?

Today, as he turned the helmet over and over in his hands, he gently brushed eighteen years of dust and rust from its once-shiny crest. Eyes misting, he remembered how his brave, foolish warriors had headed north, only to be driven back hours later, torn, bloody, and ashamed, more than half of their comrades slain in the briefest battle ever fought. Staggering and falling over one another, they left a trail of corpses half-a-mile wide and littering the hills as far south as Hormah.

Whose helmet was this? he wondered. Which of the thousands he had come to love had died wearing it?

Or perhaps the Hebrew soldier had been hauled away into slavery. That was just as possible. Perhaps he had labored the past eighteen years under whip and rod, just as he had done in Egypt, property of some Canaanite in some Canaanite city.

Clenching his fists, Joshua gazed north toward the folded hills of the promised land. It was alien territory, possessed by heathens. The thought of that nameless soldier in servitude within one of the enemy's walled cities crushed his heart, and the soldier within himself yearned for combat.

Would that God had freed him that long ago day to go against Canaan and all its inhabitants! This very moment Joshua would do so, given the chance.

But just as he savored the desire, the woman of Jericho flashed to mind, and he turned his gaze sadly to the ground.

How many times over the years had she haunted him? And her impact was always the same, softening him, supplanting the desire for revenge.

Tucking the helmet beneath his arm, Joshua turned back toward camp. Bewildered and ashamed of his conflicted feelings, he shook his head.

Someday, he knew, he would lead an army again, and that army would go against Jericho. Surely the Lord would tolerate no softness toward the enemy!

But in eighteen years the memory of the woman had not dimmed. Though Joshua often prayed for release, her memory was as strong today as when he had first watched her in her high window.

38

It was just past sunset when Joshua returned home. Sabbath was beginning, and a hush had fallen over the congregation, which would rest from all work until sunset of the next day.

As Joshua found his tent, ready himself to rest for the night, a scuffle at the edge of the company caught his attention. Someone was being dragged into camp. Half-a-dozen young Israelites, known for their nationalistic zeal, had apprehended the fellow on the desert and were apparently determined to bring him before the council. What his supposed crime might be, Joshua did not know, but one of the arresters carried a heavy sack full of oak twigs, perhaps evidence to be presented.

"He was found gathering wood on the Sabbath!" one of the apprehenders explained, brushing past Joshua on his way to the meeting tent.

Without further word, the accused was hauled through the gathering crowd, and Joshua followed, wondering what Moses's response would be.

Over the years since the sabbath had been instituted as a day of rest, there had been little occasion to test it. The first time people had gone forth upon a sabbath to gather manna, they had found none in the plain, and ever since then they had believed the Lord would not bless any labor attempted on the seventh day. The penalty for deviation from that premise had been expressly stated, and these young men were about to call for execution of justice.

Shaking, and white of face, the wood-gatherer stood before the meeting tent. His hands bound behind him, he was held between two of his captors, and the bag of branches was thrown to the ground before him.

"Moses!" one of the zealots cried. "Come forth! We have brought a man for trial!"

Such a strong word! Joshua thought. Trial? For collecting twigs?

Opening the tent door, Moses stepped forth, surveying the young men and their hapless captive with a furrowed brow.

"This man," the arrester went on, "was caught gathering wood on this holy evening! We think it proper that justice should be served, that Israel may know that the Lord is also holy!"

"Yes!" another added. And quoting the fourth commandment, he cried, "'Remember the sabbath day, to keep it holy. Six days you shall labor and do all your work, but the seventh day is a sabbath of the Lord your God. You shall not do any work in it, you or your son or your daughter, your male or your female servant or your cattle or the traveler who stays with you'!" Then, yet another reminded Moses of God's edict: "'Whoever does any work on the sabbath shall be put to death'!"

This was not the first time these zealots had called for a hearing. Unlike their elders, the men of Israel who forever strained the law, testing the patience of God Almighty, these fellows were among a growing segment of the younger generation who were bent on making Israel into a holy people. Having witnessed the devastations wrought on their fathers' disobedient generation, they had taken it upon themselves to clean up the nation.

How Moses felt about them, Joshua had never been certain. Most of the "cases" which they brought before the prophet had been of little import, and had been easily decided, though they *had* served to remind Israel of its sacred roots.

As for Joshua, his feelings regarding their endeavors were mixed. Almost vigilante in their approach, their fanaticism was worrisome. But he could not fault them overmuch, as their love of the law was a welcome contrast to the rebellions so often staged by their elders, and so often greeted by God's wrath.

For a long moment, Moses stood outside his door, observing the pale-faced suspect, and keeping silent. In his expression, however, Joshua read a conflicted heart. Sympathy for the arrested man, who had been caught in an after-hours attempt to stock his family's fuel bin for the night, and who had probably thought his indiscretion was of little consequence, tugged at Moses's kind soul. Likewise, reverence for the mind of Yahweh prevented him from summarily freeing the fellow.

When at last the prophet spoke, it was to buy time.

"You are right to take seriously the honoring of the sabbath," he told the young zealots. "Your concern for integrity is a virtue. But since this is indeed the sabbath, it is not proper to put a man on trial. Let him be put in custody, and when the sabbath is past, I will hear you."

With this, the prophet turned about and disappeared into his tent, pulling the door closed.

Brought up short, the young men looked at one another in bewilderment. Of course, Moses was right. But was he going soft regarding sin?

Muttering together, they at last turned the accused over to the meeting-house guards, and left with the dispersing crowd.

As the sun descended behind the dark desert hills, Joshua wandered to his own shelter. Amazed at his master's quick wit, he nonetheless knew Moses would struggle with this matter all night long.

He would not have traded places with him, for surely there could be no more difficult demand laid on a man's shoulders than the daily task of seeking a balance between justice and mercy.

* * *

Joshua crept into the dark of Moses's tabernacle, hesitating even though he had been summoned. It was an overcast day, but no burning lamp hung from the rafters of the meeting tent. And from the corner where the prophet kept his bed, the sound of soft weeping met Joshua's ears.

It was the day after sabbath. And what a day it had been! Dismal and horrifying.

It had begun with Moses's pronouncement of the judgment to be meted out upon the wood-gatherer. Though his single, unpretentious crime had been to deviate from the edict of rest, God Almighty had decreed that he must be stoned, taken outside the camp and stoned by the congregation until dead.

Save for a few radicals, it had been a half-hearted crowd that assembled to carry out the command. Even now, Joshua could feel the weight of the solitary rock he had managed to heave in the direction of the crouching victim. And as he tiptoed toward the master's dreary corner, he wiped imagined residue from his palm—wiped it for the hundredth time.

"Master," he whispered through the dark pall, "it is I, Joshua. You called for me?"

At this, the weeping ceased, and he could hear Moses sit up upon his bed.

"Joshua..." the prophet sighed, "I have never felt so alone!"

The servant sat down in respectful silence. Had he known what to say, he would not have spoken, for he sensed that the master's heaviness was beyond lifting.

As Joshua's eyes adjusted to the bleakness, what little light filtered in from the outside told him that Moses's face was raised to the ceiling, and his eyes were closed.

"Oh," the prophet groaned, "I have always longed to know the ways of the Lord, to comprehend his covenant! But his ways are hard, Joshua. What was I to do? I would have spared the man, but God does not allow us to follow our own hearts. When we follow our own hearts and our own eyes, even as the wood-gatherer did, we play the harlot, Joshua. We must remember the commandments, and be holy unto our God!"

Joshua still said nothing, knowing that his purpose just now was to be a listening ear, a grappling post for his master's struggling soul.

But there were others in the camp who were not sympathetic to Moses's plight. There were those who had hung back from the stoning, and who murmured against Moses and his coleader, Aaron.

Even as Joshua sat in the dark tent, trying to console the prophet, the sound of a growing crowd was heard outside. And soon, men began to call for Moses.

Their voices were familiar, for they were leaders of the Levites, members of the priesthood chosen years before at Sinai, and leaders of the Reubenites, foremost tribe of Jacob.

Regardless of the growing number of zealots, the type of which had brought the wood-gatherer for trial, these men were still the acknowledged elite of Israel, and their opinion carried great weight.

"Moses! Aaron!" they cried. "We have had enough of your dictatorship! Come forth and face us!"

Taking a deep breath, Moses wiped the tears from his face, and stood up. Joshua tried to restrain him, but he would face his accusers.

Following the master to the doorway, Joshua stepped with him into the gray daylight. Waiting outside were the most notable members of the Israelite nobility, 250 elected officials. And speaking for them were the Levite, Korah, and Reubenites, Dathan and Abiram.

Aaron, having already arrived on the scene, joined his brother, and together they listened in amazement to the rebels.

"You have gone far enough!" Korah cried, pointing a vicious finger in the prophet's face. "All the congregation are holy, every one of them! And the Lord is in their midst! So why do you and your brother exalt yourselves above the assembly of the Lord?"

Now, this was all that was needed for Moses's spirit to be utterly overwhelmed. For two days he had suffered with the burden of deciding the case of the wood-gatherer. He had come to the decision in great agony, and to be now accused of elevating himself above the people was more than he could bear.

Slumping to his knees, he fell to his face. And with hot tears streaming down his cheeks, he raised himself up again, throwing back his arms and crying, "Hear now, you sons of Levi, is it not enough for you that the God of Israel has separated you from the rest of the congregation of Israel, and has brought you near to himself to do the service of the tabernacle of the Lord and to stand before the congregation to minister to them? And is it not enough, Korah, and all your brothers, sons of Levi, that he has brought you near? Are you seeking for the *high* priesthood also?"

Gaining strength from the sound of his own voice, Moses arose and confronted them boldly. "You and all your company are gathered together against the Lord! But who is Aaron, that you should grumble against him?"

But Korah was not to be dissuaded. "You have exalted yourselves above the entire nation!" he argued. "Already one man has died, and what was his crime? Your power has gone to your heads! Where will your pride take us?"

At this, Aaron took Moses by the arm, lending support. But the prophet sank beneath a broken heart.

"Do you think I love my calling?" he cried, his voice passing over the crowd like rolling thunder. "The hand of the Lord is heavy on my head! I would rather die than bear it another day. You have gone far enough, you sons of Levi! Gladly will I pass my mantle to you!"

Then in strident tones, he shouted, the veins in his neck standing out like purple cords, "Tomorrow morning the Lord will show who is his, and who is holy, and will bring him near to himself! Even the one whom he will choose, he will bring near to himself!"

Then, swirling his robes about him, he turned again for the tent. And closing the door behind him, he retreated once more from the demands of his ungrateful public.

39

The next morning, a scene often staged in the encampment and familiar to every Israelite opened the day. Korah and his two hundred and fifty Levites stood before the tent of meeting chanting and holding before themselves firepans, or censers, of beaten bronze. Within the censers were live coals from off the tabernacle's brazen altar, and from the coals arose the pale smoke of incense, filling the air with heady fragrance.

Thus did Israel always open its holy rituals. But today, the ritual to follow was undetermined, for all Moses had told the men was that they must appear at dawn with their firepans, and that in some undefined way, Yahweh would single out from among them a chosen leader.

Conspicuous for their absence at the head of the congregation were Dathan and Abiram, the outspoken Reubenites who had, with Korah and his company, challenged Moses and Aaron the day before. Though the prophet had invited them to be among the candidates for the lead position, they had refused to appear, accusing Moses of plotting evil against them.

"We will not come up," they had sent word. "Is it not enough that you have brought us up out of a land flowing with milk and honey to kill us in the wilderness, but you would also lord it over us? Indeed, you have not brought us into a land flowing with milk and honey, nor have you given us an inheritance of fields and vineyards. Would you gouge out the eyes of these men? We will not come up!"

It was therefore an angry Moses who stepped forth from the meeting tent. Beside him was Aaron, bearing his own censer, and wearing the miter and vestments of the high priest. When the prophet raised his hands, Korah and his Levites ceased their droning chant, and the entire congregation waited breathlessly to see how God would reveal his chosen man.

Scarcely believing things had come to this, Joshua, who had lain awake all night praying for God's intervention, could not accept that his beloved master should be replaced. Indeed, how *could* anyone ever be found who could lead Israel as Moses had? He had given up the throne of Egypt for these people! He had delivered them from bondage! And yet, they had never appreciated him for the mighty man he was.

Standing by, watching the proceedings with a lump in his throat, Joshua clenched his fists. Israel was not good enough for such a leader! If God did choose to replace him, it would only be to spare him further years of torment.

Passing his eyes anxiously across the skies, Joshua waited for a sign. Would a shaft of divine light come to rest upon somebody's shoulder? Would a voice from heaven speak somebody's name? Would someone's censer flare with white flame, driving back the other candidates?

There might have been as many ways to ordain a new leader as there were people to imagine it. But as Moses had told Joshua, the ways of the Lord were not man's ways. And today, he would single out his chosen, not by pressing the divine finger upon him, but by eliminating all other contenders.

As the congregation waited, a great light did appear, settling over the tabernacle, and a voice did speak from heaven. But rather than an ordination, it gave a fearsome pronouncement.

"Moses! Aaron!" it trumpeted, sending a quake through the earth. "Separate yourselves from among this company, that I may consume them instantly!"

Stunned, the two brothers fell to their faces, and without a thought to their own safety, they began to plead for the lives of the very men who called for their resignation. "O God!" they petitioned. "God of the spirits of all flesh! When one man sins, will you be angry with the entire congregation?"

But Yahweh's wrath would not be curbed. "Tell the people to move back from around the dwellings of Korah, Dathan and Abiram!" came the reply.

Standing shakily, Moses and Aaron passed through the crowd, crying, "Get back now from the tents of these wicked men, and touch nothing that belongs to them, lest you be swept away in all their sin!"

The two hundred and fifty Levites followed the prophet, curious as everyone else to know what would transpire. When they came to the site of the tents of Dathan and Abiram, the tent of Korah nearby, Moses and Aaron stopped, and the families who lived there came forth, trembling.

Dathan and Abiram, standing with their wives and children, were joined by Korah and his kin, all together wondering at the prophet's fearsome countenance.

Turning and facing the congregation, Moses threw his head back, announcing, "What is about to happen is not my doing! It is not in my heart to do it! But by it you shall know that the Lord has sent me to lead you. If these men die the death of all men, or if they suffer the fate of all men, then the Lord has not sent me. But if the Lord brings about something entirely new and the ground opens its mouth and swallows them up with everything that belongs to them, and they descend alive into Sheol, then you will understand that these men have spurned the Lord!"

Falling back in terror, the crowd looked on as Moses's words precipitated one of the most ghastly scenes the nation had ever witnessed.

As though on cue, the ground did indeed open up, directly beneath the homes of the three rebels. Sucked toward the center of the earth, every possession, every soul of the three households fell into the pit. And just as quickly, the earth closed up again, separating them forever from the land of the living.

Terrified, the onlookers stumbled over one another in haste to leave the site, fearing that they, likewise, would be swallowed up. But even as they did make their escape, fire from heaven fell upon the two hundred and fifty Levites, consuming them to ashes upon the desert floor.

And as the people observed the demise of the revolutionaries, no more specific ordination was necesssary: Moses and Aaron were still in command; they were the chosen ones, for there were no contenders.

40

Should this not have been enough? Surely the people would never again question the authority of Moses and Aaron.

But never had there been a more rebellious nation than Israel.

Certainly the sins and injustices of the Gentiles were abhorrent. It was for this reason that God had called Israel out from among them. But the very fact that Israel was so called, the fact that they were the special inheritance of the Lord, made their rebellions more rancorous.

For theirs had been the oracles, the prophets and the patriarchs of truth. Their calling was ancient, going back to Noah, and Shem, and Abraham. And the doctrines of truth had been their special gift from the beginning, tested through generations of bondage, but never lost.

It was therefore most loathsome that they continually doubted the word of God. And despite the deaths of Korah and his men, yet another fourteen thousand and seven hundred died by plague before Aaron, as high priest, interceded.

As if that should not be enough to prove the priest's sanctity, the Lord worked a wonder on his rod, causing it to bud and bring forth ripe almonds, a testimony to Israel that it was a scepter and not only a staff.

Still, the people were obstinate, continually questioning and challenging the Lord's anointed prophets, until one day, Moses himself, in utter frustration, rebelled.

That was a dreadful day for Israel, a dreadful day for Joshua, a dreadful day for the world. For on that day, Moses did relinquish the right to lead the people into the promised land. And on that day, a shadow settled over his soul and over the soul of his servant that would remain for nineteen years.

It seemed an innocent enough transgression. It seemed a forgivable departure, much like the slip the wood-gatherer had made when he went forth upon the sabbath day.

But the consequence would be just as devastating as the punishment brought on that unwitting fellow's head.

It had happened when the children of Israel, in their wanderings, had once more entered the Wilderness of Zin. And it had been precipitated by a personal loss on Moses's part, the death of his beloved sister, Miriam.

Within the past years since leaving Sinai, Moses's father, Amram, and mother, Jochebed, had been taken by death. But this was his sister, kin of his own generation, the one who had watched over his river-cradle and who had safely transferred him to the arms of the Egyptian princess.

Spunky and spirited, she had been a challenge to live with, often butting heads with Zipporah. But she had been loved by all, and her passing left a great hollow in the prophet's heart.

It was this, and the ongoing disrespect manifested by his people, that led to Moses's desperate act.

There was no water in the Wilderness of Zin, at least not where the people were encamped. Always eager to point out their discontent, they descended upon their leader, accusing him once again of neglect.

Conferring with the Lord, Moses came back to the people with orders to lead them to a great rock. There he and Aaron were to speak to the rock, that it might bring forth water.

Given that opportunity to display power, Moses went too far. Bending the command of the Lord, he did not speak to the rock, but to the people, calling them rebels and daring them to observe his feat. Then lifting his rod, he *struck* the rock, not once, but twice.

Indeed, water did come forth, but only because God took pity on the people. "Because you have not believed me," he rebuked his prophet, "to treat me as holy in the sight of the sons of Israel, therefore you shall not bring this assembly into the promised land!"

And so, in a moment of pride and anger, Moses the Deliverer relinquished his chance to complete his original calling.

That had been nineteen years ago. In fact, thirty-nine years had passed since the people had escaped Egypt. Most of Moses's generation and even Joshua and Caleb's generation had by now passed away.

While Moses had not made public the Lord's pronouncement, sharing it only with his servant, its sorrowful impact had rarely lifted.

When his dear brother Aaron, his beloved spokesman, also died, Joshua feared his master's heart would never revive.

That sad event took place at a juncture in time and place that would forever mark a turning point in the lives of Israel and its famous leader. After thirty-nine years of wandering, the nation was ready to make momentous strides toward its geographical destiny. Believing that they should try to enter the promised land from the east side of Jordan, rather than through the Negev, Moses took the people to the border of Edom, the land of Esau's descendants. Good relations had been established with them years before when Jacob and his elder brother had been reconciled. Hoping that this would carry diplomatic weight, Moses sent word to the governors of Edom, asking passage through their territory on the way north.

Much to his surprise, and to the surprise of the disappointed Israelites, their notoriety had squelched all hope for such passage. Though Moses used all his ambassadoric skills, reminding the Edomites of Israel's hard years in Egypt, of the Lord's miraculous and repeated intervention, and assuring them that no harm would come to their country, they refused entrance.

"We will not go through field or vineyard," Moses pleaded. "We will not even drink water from a well. We will go along the King's Highway, not turning to the right or left, until we pass through your territory."

But there was no persuading Edom to make allowances. And when Israel remained encamped at the border, continuing to send messengers, the sons of Esau defended their boundaries, stationing a line of troops, fully armed, along the western front.

It was at this point that the Lord tested Moses more severely than he had ever done before. As they waited at the entrance to Edom, camped at the base of Mount Hor, which stood at the triangular site where the borders of Edom, Canaan, and Zin met, and which overlooked the very land of promise, Moses was reminded once and for all of the fact that he would never lead the people toward their final home.

With that reminder was also the incontrovertible fact that Aaron would likewise be prevented.

In fact, God said, Aaron would be taken to a more heavenly home.

In private conference, the Lord told Moses, "Aaron shall be gathered to his people. He shall not enter the land which I have given to the sons of Israel, because you rebelled against my command at the waters of the rock. Take Aaron and his son Eleazar up to Mount Hor, and strip Aaron of his garments and put them on his son Eleazar. So Aaron will be gathered to his people; he will die there."

It was with feet of lead that Joshua followed his master to a slope of the mountain that misty morning. With them were Aaron and his son Eleazar, a son born to the priest during the wilderness years. Moses had not told his servant what the Lord had said, but Joshua could see from the lines of grief upon the prophet's face that he had wept all night long, and that the cause for this climb up Mount Hor was not one of celebration.

Doubtless, Aaron and his son knew the priest was about to depart this life. In retrospect, Joshua would realize that their plodding walk and the way Aaron leaned upon Eleazar's arm indicated that they had spent the night saying goodbye and preparing for this final hour.

But nothing could have prepared Joshua for what he and the entire congregation of Israel were about to witness.

Once the master, his servant, the priest and his son had reached a level spot, Moses took Aaron's rod and put it in Eleazar's trembling hand. Without preface or formality of any kind, he continued to divest Aaron of his office, lifting his vestment off his shoulders, his mitre off his head, and placing them on his successor.

Then, raising his eyes to heaven, Moses cried, "Into your hands do I place my brother's spirit. Comfort his soul in your palace of eternal rest!"

Falling as softly as a baby into a father's arms, Aaron slumped into the waiting embrace of Moses. Tears streaming down his face, so that he could barely see, Moses called for Eleazar and Joshua to assist him, and tenderly they carried the priest toward the desert floor.

Astonished at this unexpected turn of events, the people stood mute as they took in the reality of Aaron's death. And as they watched him being carried away, the reality of their own emptiness overwhelmed them.

For years they had made Aaron's life miserable, questioning him, doubting him and his brother. Now he was gone, suddenly—without warning taken from them. And his going left a void for which they had no replacement.

Guilt, remorse, grief swept over the crowd as Moses and the little funeral party passed before them. And matching the tears on the prophet's face with their own tardy contrition, they began to mourn.

Loud and long would they bewail the loss of Aaron. Long and loud would they bewail their own sin. For thirty days they would stay at the foot of the mountain, weeping for the one they had abused.

And for thirty days Joshua would stay by Moses's side, his own soul good as dead, and fearful of Yahweh's next move.

41

The next days would forever be a blur in Joshua's memory. He went through the motions of life, but he felt no life within him.

If he felt anything, it was continual fear—fear that Yahweh was an unappeasable tyrant, who could at any moment afflict him or take from him someone he dearly loved.

After thirty-nine years of doing his best to serve God, he knew him less now than when he had started.

Incredibly, it was at this lowest point that he was called upon to lead Israel in battle. Though it had been four decades since he commanded an army, he was still considered Israel's military genius. His victory over the Amalekites at Rephidim, a generation ago, had become legend. And though few of the men who now made up the infantry and cavalry had served in that famous war, they had been raised to honor Joshua as the general who had given the people a military heart.

Therefore, when Edom refused Israel passage through its land, and when they were forced to turn toward the Negev, Joshua was called upon to lead them forth. The Canaanites would be awaiting them, and war was inevitable.

In looking back on that battle, Joshua would wonder how victory had come. He would recall the smell of blood, the cries of friends and enemies, the clash of blade and shield. But he would recall little else.

Depressed of spirit, he was borne through that fray on invisible wings, a strength beyond himself taking him and his men to triumph. And when they were finished, the cities of the Negev were theirs.

But Joshua was unaware of the divine hand. Having mastered protocol through his years under Moses's administration, he received the honors due a victorious, returning general in good form. But he felt none of the glory heaped upon him, and endured the applause only because he had to.

For the Israelites, this was a time of celebration, the first foray near the borders of the promised land in which they had triumphed. But for Joshua, it was a hollow victory, as he had not yet overcome the ambivalence of his faith.

He did not trust this victory. There had been times in the past when he thought he saw the working of God on behalf of Israel. Yet too often miracles had been followed by disappointments, and God's favor now seemed fickle.

Tonight, while the council of elders gathered in the meeting tent, enthusiastically discussing the nation's next moves and plotting how best to overcome pagan neighbors who stood between them and the promised land, Joshua stayed in his own shelter.

He had lost all heart for schemes and strategems. Why the Lord had singled him out from among his generation to go on living, he did not know.

Oh, of course, Caleb had been "privileged," with himself, to remain. He wondered, as he sat in the dim light of his rafter lamp, how his companion-since-youth felt about the honor.

Caleb had been thinking about Joshua at the same moment, seeking him at the council meeting. When he realized that his friend was not in attendance, he came calling for him.

"How can we plot advances into Canaan without our general?" he asked, finding Joshua seated in the dimly lit room. "We need you at the meeting."

"They will do well without me," he replied.

Sitting down, Caleb observed Joshua's glum countenance. "Do I detect in you the doldrums that follow great
conquest?" he guessed.

Joshua shrugged. "Perhaps," he sighed.

"But," Caleb recalled, "you have not been yourself for
a long time...since...the death of Aaron. What troubles
you, friend?"

If there was one person on earth in whom Joshua
could confide his weaknesses, it was Caleb. Even so, he
was ashamed to admit he was afraid.

"Your faith has always been great," he answered, "far
greater than mine. I will never know why Yahweh chose
me, and not you, to lead the army."

At this, Caleb shook his head, his brow furrowed.
"What is it, Joshua?" he prodded. "You are not only a
military hero. You are the man who nobly led twelve spies
to survey Canaan. You are the man who has served Moses
almost forty years, his closest confidant. You are the man
on whom God has laid his hand, and who will surely take
the place of leadership one day! What has become of your
spirit?"

Suddenly, all the pent-up emotion of the past weeks
surged through Joshua like a current. And in a torrent it
came forth.

"*I?*" he cried, jumping to his feet. "*I* take Moses's place?
I would sooner die than betray him like that!"

Confounded, Caleb watched Joshua's frantic reaction.
"Betray?" he stammered. "To succeed Moses would be
betrayal?"

"Yes!" Joshua shouted. "Why should I be privileged to
lead Israel into the promised land, when my beloved
master has been stripped of the honor? I would sooner
die than take that honor to myself!"

There. It had been said. But in the saying, Joshua had
indeed betrayed Moses. For the prophet had told him of
the Lord's restriction in confidence. No one else in Israel

knew that he would not be allowed to take Jacob's children into Canaan.

Amazed, Caleb tried to interpret his friend's raving. "What do you mean?" he asked. "How has Moses been stripped of the honor?"

Pale-faced, Joshua sat down again, holding his head in his hands. "I have kept that secret for nineteen years!" he moaned. "I should not have told you! Promise that my words will not go past this room."

When Caleb sat mute, Joshua reached out an angry hand and grabbed him by the knee. "Promise!" he growled.

"Of course," Caleb winced. "You know your secrets are safe with me."

Withdrawing his hand, Joshua groaned heavily. "Nineteen years ago, my master told me of the Lord's punishment on him and on his brother, Aaron. Do you remember when he struck the rock in the wilderness to bring forth water? Because he and Aaron were presumptuous, they were forever prevented from entering Canaan!"

Eyes wide, Caleb leaned forward. "What?" he marveled. "Were they disobedient?"

Again, Joshua shrugged. "Apparently God had instructed them to speak to the rock. But instead, they took the glory for themselves, using the rod wrongly."

Even this much was hard for the loyal servant to admit. He himself had come to the assessment only after much spiritual wrestling.

"But," he went on, his face etched with resentment, "is not the Lord's way much too hard? I can understand his destruction of Korah and the rebels. But for one small infraction, two of the best and noblest men on earth are put to shame...one already seeing death rather than the holy land!"

With a shudder, Caleb considered these words. Suddenly, Joshua's disillusionment, his agony of spirit, came clear. Who would not have felt as he did, in his place?

Standing, Caleb leaned over his friend respectfully. "These are hard things to understand," he agreed.

Downcast, Joshua looked at the floor, and Caleb placed a hand on his stooped shoulder.

"It is at times like this that we must remember the miracles of God," he offered. "Surely Yahweh loves Moses more than any of us could ever love him. Surely God knows what is best, and in time will lift up your master higher than ever."

Joshua closed his eyes, feeling the sting of tears upon his lashes. "I hope you are right," he whispered. "If you are wrong, there is no hope for any of us."

42

A sweet breeze blew inland from the Gulf of Aqaba, where Israel was camped. Over nearly forty years of wandering, the great company had come to rest here on occasion. When they did, Joshua was always put in mind of the conversation with Moses just before the twelve spies were sent north.

That had been a time of anticipation and excitement for the much younger Joshua. And on the occasion of that talk, Moses had wished for him, not only success on the spying venture, but a future of personal fulfillment.

"May your life be full when we reach Canaan," Moses had said. "May you find life and love, as I did."

Today, Joshua sat in the same place, atop the same dune that commanded a view of the gulf and of the vast northward stretches. As he contemplated the past four decades, he smirked.

Little good the prophet's wish had done! Joshua was now well past middle age, eighty-four to be exact, and they had not reached Canaan. While he was not elderly for his generation, neither was he in the prime of life, and personal fulfillment still eluded him.

Below, on the valley floor, was spread the enormous nation of Israel. More than half of the present population had been born after the flight from Egypt. They had known, in all their lifetime, nothing but wandering and sand. They had seen none of the miracles that had freed their forefathers from Pharaoh's hand. They had not been present at the crossing of the Reed Sea, and had not been part of the victorious war against Amalek. They had not heard the voice of God echo from Mount Sinai, and the covenant of the ten commandments was given to them secondhand.

Realizing this, Joshua ran a veined hand through his hair. Mingled with the dark locks were streaks of silver, and his salt-and-pepper beard was more patriarchal in length than he had worn it years ago.

He was old, he and Caleb and Moses. His father and his grandfather had departed this life long ago, as had most of the men and women who had first heard the liberating voice of Moses ring forth in Raamses square.

But though he wore a patriarch's beard, he was not a patriarch. He had no children of his own, no wife, no family.

Four decades of futile nomadism had brought none of the fulfillment Moses had desired for him. And for a long time he had tasted little more than the gall of life.

A week ago, Moses had announced that the people were to head for the Aqaba, and then turn east, making a circuitous path around Edom. Determined that they should enter Canaan from that side of Jordan, Moses could find no other way to go, seeing that the Edomites had refused them passage up the King's Highway.

This should have been a time of excitement for Israel. They were at last moving on, however obliquely, toward their promised land. In typical fashion, however, the people had thus far spent the journey complaining. They hated the trip through the hot sand. They hated the lack of fresh water, and the dreary manna they had been forced to eat for almost forty years.

As often as possible, Joshua left camp, longing to be free of their continual harping.

He wondered how Moses could go on, day after day, enduring the reproaches of the malcontents. As he rested on the sandy knoll, he ran Caleb's words through his mind for the hundredth time. In a few weeks, barring unforeseen impediments, the nation would be ready to make its first foray into Canaan. If God was indeed planning to restore Moses to a position of honor, he had better do so soon.

As he tried to imagine just how this might transpire, however, his ruminations were interrupted by screams rising from the camp.

Standing up, Joshua headed down the dune toward the sound of the cries.

What met his eyes was scarcely believable. As though the earth itself had grown weary of the griping Israelites, it brought forth from its surface thousands upon thousands of poisonous vipers. Slithering up from nests beneath the sand, and flaring the hoods upon their necks, they struck like flying arrows at the legs and feet of the astonished people.

On every side, men, women and children fell victim to their burning venom, writhing and contorting upon the ground, their faces and limbs swollen and purple, until they expired in feverish torment.

Like helpless infants, those who had avoided the stinging bites or who managed to survive the poisonous fangs wept aloud for deliverance.

"Moses! Moses!" they cried, forgetting the complaints they had against him. "Help us! Or we die!"

Skirting the worst sites of the infestation, Joshua made his way toward the tent of meeting. Despite the grasping hands that clawed at him, begging Moses's servant to lend aid, he managed to reach the front of the encampment.

But to his dismay, when he arrived at the tent, Moses was not to be found.

"Over there," one of the tent guards said, seeing that he sought the prophet. Pointing toward the altar of sacrifice, he directed him to Moses.

There the prophet stood, engrossed in a strange activity, watching the bubbling contents of a cauldron atop the altar.

"Stir, men, stir!" he ordered, as the smiths threw armloads of copper vessels and brass implements into the molten soup. Reaching into the smelter with long poles, the men mixed the shining vessels into the golden stew, until the forms of cups, plates and utensils succumed to the heat, and the soup thickened.

It had been a very long time since the man of God had been so animated, so spurred to action.

"Master!" Joshua hailed him. "What is happening? The people, Master...they are dying!"

But Moses did not look at his servant. Transfixed by the work of the craftsmen, he was absorbed in seeing to it that a peculiar bronze casting was made to order.

"I know," was all he said. "It is the sting of sin that kills my people!"

Oh, no! Joshua thought. Years of stress and disappointment had at last overwhelmed his master's mind. Moses was out of touch with reality, the victim of hopelessness and defeat.

Taking the prophet by the arm, Joshua tried to lead him away from his futile distraction. "They need you, Master!" he pleaded. "Can't you do something?"

But at his touch, Moses turned to him, energy sparking through his black eyes such as Joshua had not seen in twenty years.

"My people perish from the sting of sin!" the prophet repeated. "But the Lord has promised to take their sins upon himself! Go, Joshua! Fetch the standard of the tribe of Judah, the one they bear into battle. Bring it here!"

Utterly bewildered, Joshua nonetheless set out to do as the master said. Running back through the crowd, darting this way and that to avoid the flashing bite of a million serpents, he at last came to the place where the people of Judah camped.

Why Moses had singled them out, and why he wished to have their standard, he had no inkling. But calling for Caleb, their chief representative, he gave him the prophet's command.

Quickly Caleb and a young Judahite, Salmon, brought the standard to him. "We will carry it," they offered, hoisting the pole to their shoulders.

Joshua rolled up the green flag, which bore the symbol of the tribe of Judah, a powerful, striding lion. Securing it to the pole, he headed back to the tent of meeting.

The return trip was not so hasty. Bearing the long standard between them, Caleb and Salmon found it very difficult to weave through the frantic crowd while keeping an eye out for the lethal vipers.

But by the time they reached Moses, the brazen figure he had ordered was cooling in its mold, and while it was still soft, the blacksmiths lifted it from the long pan.

"A brass serpent?" Caleb marveled. "But why..."

"Here," Moses instructed his smiths. "Wrap it around the top of the standard!"

Holding the metal snake with hot tongs, the men complied. Gently unfurling the flag of Judah, they proceeded to artfully coil the brazen viper about the pole.

"Come!" Moses cried, directing Salmon and Caleb to follow him. Taking the pole in his own strong hands, he plodded to the top of a slope overlooking the desperate camp.

There he erected the standard, calling on his two companions to assist him. Steadying its base against the ground, the two Judahites held the top-heavy pole upright, as Moses shouted to the people, "The Lord is our salvation! This very day he takes upon himself the sins of his people—even the very form of their sins he takes upon himself! Look, my children, and live!"

Though they did not understand Moses's words, in despair the Israelites gazed upon the shining image. And as they did, the sound of their weeping was gradually exchanged for shouts of joy.

Everywhere throughout the crowd, people who had been bitten were healed, the venom neutralized and the fever cooled. Mothers held babies aloft, praising God for rescuing them. And men embraced each other, dancing and singing for happiness.

Many others fell to their knees, worshiping and thanking God for his saving hand.

Joshua was among those. And as he knelt at Moses's feet, lifting his hands in praise toward the sky, it was not only the miracle of the brazen serpent he applauded, but the miracle of healing he witnessed in his master's soul.

Caleb's words had come true. The man of God had regained his honored position.

For the first time in nineteen years, Moses stood tall and confident once again, the light of faith and renewed vigor shining from his face.

PART VII
The Giant-Killer

43

As the sun glazed the eastern sky with the pink tints of morning, Joshua stirred restlessly in his saddle. Strange thoughts ran through his mind as he awaited the full light of dawn—thoughts of his youth in Egypt, when he and Caleb had ridden their master's horses through the streets of Raamses, their boyish imaginations full of conquest and glory.

It was hard to believe that today, a lifetime later, he and Caleb once again sat atop husky mounts, eager for the clash of weapons and the cries of battle.

It was also hard to believe that Joshua, who had experienced four decades of debilitating and aimless wandering, who had come of age through great hardship and who now stood within glimpse of his own sunset, should feel so young, so energetic.

But the entire nation had been renewed since the encounter with the serpents, and their sense of covenant with God Almighty had taken on fresh meaning.

Ever since that day, they had marched on toward the east, and had then turned north, with a vigor reminiscent of their flight from Egypt. Except that this time they were not fleeing an enemy. They were on the offense, heading through pagan territory and ready to do battle with any people who stood between them and the land promised to Jacob.

This morning, Joshua and his able assistant, Caleb, sat atop a crest of wilderness between the River Nahaliel and the River Arnon, in the desolate land of the Amorites. Behind them on the wadi-riddled plain spread the Israelite millions, their well-groomed army arrayed in orderly

215

files, and the rest of the nation waiting anxiously beyond them.

Ahead was the Amorite fortress of Jahaz, sprawled like a sleeping lion upon a sheet of sand.

"King Sihon is a clever fellow," Caleb whispered, his voice blending with the constant, arid breeze. "The fort appears to be unmanned."

"It may well be unmanned," Joshua replied. "Sihon may have called his militia back to Heshbon, when he heard we were coming on."

When Caleb evinced disappointment, Joshua was quick to add, "But keep your eyes to the northern horizon. Soon enough you will see Amorites, more than can be numbered!"

Months ago, when the Edomites had refused Moses entrance through their territory, the prophet had turned away from their border, and had lingered south of Canaan. There Joshua had led the successful battle against the natives of the Negev. But neither he nor his master had had much heart for the takeover.

Now, things were different. The Amorite king, Sihon, had also refused permission for the Israelites to pass through his region. But this time Moses had not taken the tuck-head. His army's reputation preceding him, and the inspiring memory of the brazen serpent behind him, he did without incident lead his people straight through Edom and Moab, and then boldly proceeded straight up the King's Highway into Amorite territory. If King Sihon wished to contravene his progress, he would have to meet him in full force.

As rumor had it, Sihon *would* oppose Israel. Though no Amorite was in sight, messengers between the two nations had transferred word to Moses and his general that the king would meet them on the plain of Jahaz.

His pulse pounding with anticipation, Joshua glanced behind him to the troops arranged within the Arnon canyon. The fortress of Jahaz was strategically located

between the two rivers to command a view of the southland. The nation of Israel waited on the field beyond the
Arnon, but the army itself was well-hidden in the enormous wadi. Sihon would not see them until they chose to
rush forward.

Scouts had informed Joshua and his commanders that
there were no Amorites similarly hidden in the Nahaliel
canyon beyond Fort Jahaz. Therefore, they knew they
would have good advance notice of the oncoming horde,
having a clear view across the northward plain.

Still, it was an anxious interval for the Israelite general. He had never led an army in such rugged landscape.
The first war against Amalek had been on flat desert, and
the war in the Negev was amongst rolling hills. This, by
contrast, was precipitous country, and Sihon, knowledgeable of his own terrain, could have many tricks in
mind.

But there was no turning back. For the first time since
leaving Egypt, Joshua was about to engage in a face-off
with neighbors of the promised land that would decide
progress toward its borders.

Just as the rose of dawn gave way to full-blown daylight, the anticipated army of Sihon appeared along the
northern horizon.

Spine-tingling was the sight, and Joshua's breath caught
in his throat.

So vast was the Amorite host that it seemed to spread
from Jordan to the borders of Ammon, straight across
the desert stage. And as it came on, it did so in waves, one
enormous contingency following another, until the landscape was swallowed up with horses and men.

The sound of their marching filled the wilderness like
thunder, until they drew within a mere mile of Jahaz.

At first glimpse of them, Joshua and Caleb dismounted,
leading their horses behind the lip of the wadi, and lying
flat upon their stomachs. Sihon would see neither troop
nor officer of Israel until Joshua gave command.

Doubtless, Sihon and his men thought that Moses had retreated. After crossing miles of uninvaded territory, the Amorites began to run rather than walk, laughing and hooting as they surveyed the unimpeded landscape and the unarmed nation that sat motionless on the southern plain.

In the forefront of the waiting nation, between the army and the general populace, Moses was stationed, flanked by Eleazar and the Levite priests. As always, the ark of the covenant was well-guarded at the head of the congregation, but today, the cloudy pillar, which normally hovered at the head of the traveling nation, had moved back away from the hidden troops. Apparently Yahweh himself was in league with the silent hosts, and would not give away the secret of their presence.

Closing his eyes, Joshua said a silent prayer, trusting that the cloud's retreat did not indicate the removal of God's hand.

Then, when the time was right, when to hesitate might jeopardize the element of surprise, he gave a shout.

Mounting their horses, he and Caleb rushed up the wadi bank, and with an unleashed roar, his army followed, leaping onto the plain of Jahaz like panthers roused from a lair.

Stunned by this unexpected appearance, Sihon and his troops were momentarily disoriented. Spilling around the base of the fortress, they suddenly stopped their march and began to fall over one another in retreat.

But this reversal did not last long. Regaining themselves, they echoed the shout of Israel, and pushed forward, meeting Joshua and his legions hand-to-hand on the Jahaz floor.

Still, they were unprepared for the countless number of men who continued to flood up the wadi bank. Vigorously, Joshua and Caleb led the way, pushing back the enemy, slashing and driving with their swords, until the fortress of Jahaz was even with the front lines of their own army.

At some point in the fray, when his sword was sheened with blood, and his hand slipped on the crimson hilt, Joshua looked above and saw that the pillar had moved forward.

"Caleb!" he shouted to his valorous comrade. "God is with us!"

No longer aloof, the cloud had joined the Israelite forces, and like the rod of Moses, which had lifted the spirits of God's army in the clash of the Amalakites, the pillar maintained its position over the invaders.

"On!" Joshua cried, flashing his scarlet sword in the air. "On to Heshbon!"

Yes—he would take the capital, ten miles to the north! He would not stop on the plain or along the King's Highway until he had overwhelmed the very seat of Amorite power.

All that day and into the night, all the next day and into the next night, Israel would push forth, crushing the troops of Sihon and all his machines of war. Behind them, on the broad road and across miles of desert sand, fallen chariots and slain horses, broken camels and dismembered men would tell the story of Joshua's power.

The land of the Amorites would never be the same.

Nor would Joshua.

He was on his way to the promised land, and behind him he would leave a trail of glory and conquest the likes of which no neighboring nation, or nation of the world, had ever seen.

44

Deliciously weary, Joshua stumbled toward his tent and propped himself against one of the poles. Below him, on the terraced plains of Moab, a festive celebration was in full swing, and he had enjoyed it along with all his victorious troops.

But he had had a bit too much wine, and having been the object of adulation all evening, he wished now to be alone.

The party, and Joshua's fatigue, were the result of one more successful military escapade.

After the battle with Sihon, the Israelites set up headquarters in this green-rimmed swale in the land of the Amorites. From there they had gone forth to subdue the kingdom of Bashan to the north, and it was from this foray that Joshua had returned today.

As a result of that war, the Israelites occupied all the land from the River Arnon, by the Salt Sea, north to the border of Syria, at Damascus. All this they owed to Joshua, and the hand of the Lord upon him.

But being a living legend was exhausting. Joshua was glad for the caressing breeze that blew up from the Jordan River, and for the soothing scent of gum-arabic acacias that thrived in groves along the foothills of Mount Nebo. Should he live out his days in this place, he might be content. Except that its commanding view of Canaan's threshold kept him yearning for the coveted land of promise.

Sliding to the ground, Joshua sat with his back against the pole, tilting his head and breathing deep of the heady air while listening for the rush of the river far below.

Gradually the rhythms of wind and water lulled him asleep. But in an instant he was again awake, jolted by the dream-induced sight of a dreadful giant careening on horseback toward him.

Sitting upright, he wiped cold sweat from his brow. Upon his right palm was still the feel of the spear which he had borne all the way back from Bashan. He had not trusted the weapon to any servant, nor had he trusted it to the sheathe which was part of his saddle. He had carried it by hand all the miles home, because it was proof of the most daring feat of his life.

He had killed a giant! The giant's spear was his souvenir.

Glancing to his side, he saw that the weapon still rested near him upon the ground, and with trembling fingers he stroked it.

"The spear of Og?" Moses greeted him.

Surprised at the prophet's sudden appearance, Joshua jumped to his feet. "Yes, sir," he replied, snapping to attention.

Amazed at the size of the weapon, Moses squatted on the ground and studied it closely. "It is made of iron," he marveled. "I thought only the Philistines had iron."

"I thought so, too," Joshua said, kneeling beside him. "But they say that King Og and his sons are the sole survivors of the race of Rephaim. Perhaps he inherited the spear from his forefathers."

Moses stroked his beard, recalling the legend of the giant race. "Long ago they were a part of Philistia," he agreed. "It is said Og's bedstead is made of iron, as well, and that it is over thirteen feet long!"

Joshua drew his cloak to his chest, all-too-clearly remembering his opponent's gigantic stature.

Over and over, throughout this evening, Joshua's men had told of their commander's exploit, rehearsing the story around the campfires of the celebrating Israelites, telling and retelling how he had met King Og on the misty plain of Bashan, how at dawn of their first warring morning, the black-bearded colossus had thundered forth from the bowels of his stony castle, storming toward the general with fire in his eyes and lightning in his titanic spear.

Like the smoke of a furnace was the pall of his coming, matched as he was on every side by comrades of formidable cunning, all dressed in black armor and heralded by the snorting and stamping of their steeds.

But Joshua, though dwarfed by comparison, had faced him squarely, the story went. And when the King of Bashan charged at him, thrusting his spear toward his chest, Joshua had not dodged it, but had caught it in his own bare hands, and riding it to the ground had turned it about, driving the giant through with his own weapon.

How much of the tale was true, and how much exaggeration, not even Joshua could be certain. But the finale was all that mattered, and the finale was real enough.

Indeed, he *had* speared the giant, and in a deafening fall, his armor crashing with him to the desert floor, Og had met his death.

With that fall, the Bashanites had turned and fled, the Israelites giving chase through the dustclouds of their retreat.

When the war was over, not one remnant of Og was left. His sons and all his family were demolished, and his land overtaken.

All of this Moses had heard from the mouths of Joshua's men. And when he saw, from the shaken look on the general's face, that he had indeed come triumphant through another great test, he placed an arm about his shoulders.

As the two knelt together, before the captive spear, and in the quiet of the breeze which blew up from Jordan, Moses looked deep into his friend's eyes. "My years upon this earth have been many," the prophet said, "and I have not always pleased the Lord. But long ago, when I took you for my servant, I made a wise choice."

Honored by this endorsement, Joshua was nonetheless troubled by his master's wistful tone. "Thank you, sir," he whispered.

But Moses did not hear him. His eyes were closed, and holding Joshua's hand in a firm grip, he was praying aloud.

"O God," he groaned, "may the Lord, the God of the spirits of all flesh, appoint a man over the congregation, who will go out and come in before them, and who will lead them out and bring them in, that the congregation of the Lord may not be like sheep which have no shepherd!"

Now, this made Joshua even more uneasy. But he dare not interrupt his master's meditation. So when Moses left off speaking with the Lord, and looked at him again, the warrior stammered, "Sir, *you* are their shepherd. They need no other."

But Moses disregarded this. "Joshua," he said, "your eyes have seen all that the Lord your God has done to King Sihon and King Og. So the Lord shall do to all the kingdoms into which you are about to go. Do not fear them, for the Lord your God is the one fighting for you."

With a sigh, Joshua looked at the spear. "Yes, sir," he weakly replied. *But can't you go with me, as well?* he longed to cry out.

There would be no answer to this unspoken question. Moses was already making ready to depart for the evening.

Standing, the prophet headed into the darkness toward his own tent.

But calling over his shoulder, he gave one more word. "Meet me at the edge of camp at dawn," he called. "The Lord has told me to climb Mount Nebo, and you are to go with me. Together we are going to view the promised land!"

45

No one came calling for Joshua, to wake him at dawn. The sound of massive movement in camp roused him, and pulling back his tent flap he found that the entire congregation was heading toward the east, in the direction of Mount Nebo, where Moses and he were to make their climb.

Pulling on his cloak, Joshua skirted the crowd and ran for the foothills, finding, to his further surprise, that the tent of meeting had been relocated there in the night.

Apparently an announcement had been made after he left the celebration last night, to the effect that some great event would transpire at Nebo, and Joshua looked desperately for Moses, hoping for an explanation.

When he found him, Master Moses was already halfway up the mountain, and was accompanied by Eleazar, the high priest. Running breathlessly after them, Joshua at last caught up, and took Moses by the arm. "What is happening?" he inquired. "Why didn't you tell me..."

But Moses only gave him a look of grateful relief. "Thank you for coming," he replied, his steps picking up vigor.

Apparently nothing more would be revealed just now, as to the purpose of this gathering.

Helplessly, Joshua glanced over his shoulder. Indeed, the view from this mountain was spectacular, more and more so the higher they climbed.

But as Joshua gazed across Jordan, he stopped short, his breath catching in his throat.

Far out on the distant plain, on the west side of the river, the glimmer of white walls could be seen, topped with turrets and gleaming towers.

"Jericho!" he marveled. "Master, it is directly across from us!"

As quickly as he made this observation, however, his spirit sank within him. He had always known that if he were to lead the hosts of Israel into Canaan, he would have to go against that mighty fortress. Like always, it was not only the strength of the enemy, but the memory of the woman in red, that caused his pulse to trip.

Turning about, he tried to put her from mind. Perhaps she did not even live there any longer.

But he could not fool himself with that notion. She had been a young woman when he saw her, much younger than himself. Doubtless, she still kept her home upon the wall, and lived ... for Astarte.

So, he sighed to himself, plodding behind Moses, *this is the reason for this venture. The master wants to lay before me the plot to overthrow Jericho.*

Just how small-minded such thinking was, he did not begin to realize until Moses, reaching a flat spot visible to the vast company, stopped and addressed the entire nation.

With a face of zeal and glory, he spread his arms wide, and cried, "Hear, O Israel! The Lord our God is one! And you shall love the Lord your God with all your heart and with all your soul and with all your might! And these words, which I command you today, shall be in your heart, and you shall teach them diligently to your sons and shall talk of them when you sit in your house and when you walk by the way and when you lie down and when you rise up! And you shall bind them as a sign on your hand and they shall be bands about your forehead. And you shall write them on the doorposts of your house and on your gates!"

Awestruck, the people listened, sensing that Moses was about to commission them for their future.

Without a pause he went on: "When your son asks you in time to come, 'What do the testimonies and the statutes and the judgments which the Lord commanded you mean?' you shall say to your son, 'We were slaves to Pharaoh in Egypt, and the Lord brought us from Egypt with a mighty hand. The Lord showed great and terrible signs and wonders before our eyes against Pharaoh and all his household. And he brought us out from there in order to bring us in, to give us the land which he swore to our fathers.' So the Lord commanded us to observe all these statutes, to fear the Lord our God for our good always, that he might keep us alive. And it will be our righteousness if we are careful to observe all this commandment before the Lord our God, just as he commanded us!"

Rehearsing the ten commandments, as well a multitude of lesser ordinances, Moses cried, "Remember all the way which the Lord your God has led you in the wilderness these forty years, that he might humble you, testing you, to know what was in your heart! Remember how he fed you with manna, that you might understand that man does not live by bread alone, but by everything that proceeds out of the mouth of the Lord!"

Standing perfectly still beside his beloved master, Joshua felt his own soul quiver. How could he have been so petty as to think this occasion was one of attention for himself? With each passionate word the prophet spoke, it was increasingly obvious that this was his parting speech, that he was about to relinquish his leadership over the people for whom he had given his life.

His eyes riveted on his master's face, his ears tingling with each syllable, Joshua choked back tears, longing to embrace the prophet, to keep him for himself.

But Moses was not finished.

"Hear, O Israel!" he cried again. "You are about to cross over the Jordan to go in to dispossess nations greater and mightier than you, great cities fortified to heaven, and a people great and tall! Know, then, it is not because of your righteousness that the Lord your God is giving you this good land, for you are a stubborn people! You have been rebellious against the Lord from the day I knew you!"

How fatherly were these words, how tender, yet how true! Tears welled in the people's eyes, as they recalled the many times they had turned against this precious man, and against the God of their fathers. Yet he was loving in spite of this, both the prophet and the Lord himself.

"Now, Israel," he went on, "what does the Lord your God require of you, but to fear the Lord your God, to walk in all his ways and love him, and to serve the Lord your God with all your heart and with all your soul, and to keep his commandments and his statutes which I am commanding you today for your good?

"He is your praise and he is your God, who has done these great and awesome things for you. Your fathers went down to Egypt seventy persons in all, and now the Lord your God has made you as numerous as the stars in the sky!

"See, I have set before you today life and prosperity, death and adversity. So choose life in order that you may live, you and your descendants, by loving the Lord your God, by obeying his voice, and by holding fast to him. For this *is* your life and the length of your days, that you may live in the land which the Lord swore to your fathers, to Abraham, Isaac, and Jacob!"

Now, suddenly, the prophet's voice broke, and falling back, he gripped his chest. Reaching for him, Eleazar and Joshua helped him to stand upright, and a great gasp escaped the crowd.

Wishing to deny the obvious, Joshua closed his eyes, and his throat grew tight, as though a cord were wrapped around it. "Lord," he thought, "spare him! Spare my master! I cannot live without him!"

And as if in answer to that thought, Moses spoke again, opening his arms to embrace each one of the millions who stood before him. "I am one hundred and twenty years old today!" he cried. "I am no longer able to come and go, and the Lord has said to me, 'You shall not cross this Jordan.'"

At this revelation of the long-kept secret, the people gasped in horror.

But Moses calmed them. "It is the Lord your God who will cross ahead of you. He will destroy these nations before you, and you shall dispossess them. Joshua is the one who will cross ahead of you," he announced, "just as the Lord has spoken!"

Unprepared for this, Joshua felt his knees buckle, and as Moses turned to him, placing his hands upon his shoulders, the prophet declared, "Be strong and coura-geous, Joshua! For you shall go with all these people into the land which the Lord has sworn to their fathers, and you shall give it to them as an inheritance!"

Now, the servant did not realize it, but he was weeping; large, hot tears coursing down his cheeks. He would have stopped his ears, if it had kept Moses from leaving him.

But there was no circumventing prophecy. And as the master concluded, he plumbed the depths of Joshua's soul.

"The Lord is the one who goes ahead of you," he asserted. "He will be with you. He will not fail you or forsake you. Do not fear, or be dismayed!"

Then, with Joshua hardly knowing it, Moses took him by the hand and led him toward the door of the meeting tent. As they arrived there, the cloudy pillar, which had hovered over the mountain, descended and stood before them, turning this way and that, as though to ward off danger.

Now Eleazar prayed over them, laying his hands first on the head of Moses, then on the head of the servant. And Joshua felt a warmth, as a vibrant stream, course through his body. When Moses likewise placed hands on his head, Joshua felt a tremor pass through him like a quake at Sinai.

"Be strong and courageous!" a voice trumpeted from the cloud. "For you shall bring the sons of Israel into the land which I swore to them, and I will be with you!"

46

Like a dead man, Joshua lay facedown upon the silent mount, his cloak crisp with dew, and his limbs frozen in place where he had lain weeping through the night.

As the light of early dawn found him, he awoke stiff and sore, tears crusted on his cheeks.

The instant he awoke, he wished dearly that he might sleep again, that he might put from mind his master's departure.

Pulling himself erect, he knelt on the ground and peered up the gray morning slope, hoping against hope that Moses might come back again.

But he knew the prophet was gone, forever taken from him, and that although he had similarly disappeared many a time upon Sinai, only to return if Joshua waited long enough, this time it would not be so.

After the glorious speech, in which Moses had commissioned the children of Israel, and after the laying-on of hands, ordaining the general as his successor, the prophet had turned his back to the multitude, and using his sacred staff as a walking stick, had ascended the mountain height. Knowing he must not follow, Joshua had fought the desire. Had it not been for Eleazar's touch upon his shoulder, he might have taken off in a dead run up the mountain trail.

Slowly did Moses climb, but his gaze was lifted high, and there was no hesitation in his aged step. He was going to meet his own Master, the Lord of Heaven. And there was no sorrow in his gait.

His brother, Aaron, had also died upon a mountain. But that had been a terrifying moment, taking place as it did before the eyes of the people, and falling as he did into the arms of son and brother.

It was clear from Moses's demeanor that his death would be a private affair, greeted only by the hosts of heaven. And the arms that caught him would lift him high, away from the gaze of men.

All this Joshua knew, as he watched his beloved's departure. But it did not ease the ache of his heart or fill the vacuum of his soul.

When Moses was no longer visible, having entered the distant folds of the mount, and after the people had remained for a long while upon the plain, the crowd at last dispersed. But Joshua would not turn back. Though Eleazar spoke gently, trying to draw him away, he would not leave the mountain.

Afternoon passed, and dark fell, before Joshua even sat down upon the ground. For hours he had stood, straining his vision up the slope. And only in great fatigue did he at last rest a little.

He did not know when he fell asleep. But all night long he was riven by desperate dreams, crying out like an abandoned child, searching like a wandering son, for his misplaced father.

Now the sun was on the zenith of the mountain, and Joshua knew he could not stay here forever. Hunched with grief, he arose and turned his face to the Jordan breeze, letting it dry the tears that still remained upon his cheeks.

How, he wondered, was he to carry on? How was he to abide life, let alone lead millions of contrary people toward a prophetic destiny?

Afraid to set one foot in front of the other, he stood rooted to the place where he had spent the night. But as he let the breeze pass over him, it seemed to bring solace to his heart.

And in the breeze was a voice. Though it was almost imperceptible, it somehow reached through the turmoil of his soul, and held him for a rapturous moment in the grip of love.

"Moses my servant is dead," it said. "Now, rise up, cross the Jordan with all my people, to the land which I am giving to the sons of Israel. Every place on which the sole of your foot treads, I have given to you, just as I spoke to Moses."

Joshua's chest heaved as the breath of God himself coursed through his lungs, and he fell back, amazed by the courage the words imparted.

"From the wilderness and Lebanon, even as far as the great river, Euphrates, all the land of the Hittites, and to the great sea toward the going down of the sun, will be yours," the voice promised. "No man will be able to stand before you all the days of your life. As I have been with Moses, I will be with you. I will not fail you or forsake you."

How wonderful were those words. If only Joshua might see the one who spoke them!

"Be strong and courageous," the voice came again, echoing the instruction of Moses. "Have I not commanded you? Be strong and courageous! Do not be terrified or discouraged, for the Lord your God is with you wherever you go."

Then, like the breeze that tapered toward noon, the words also died away.

For a while, the successor to Moses waited for further orders, and when none came, he scanned the mountain, not looking, this time, for the departed prophet, but for the face of Yahweh.

His search was vain, but he sensed that he was not alone. Energized, he stepped forward, walking and then running toward camp.

The time had come to move out, and he could not wait to tell the people so.

47

The woman of Jericho sat in her high window, brushing out her long red hair, as was her custom every evening of her life. She was no longer a young woman, but she was still beautiful, perhaps more so than the day Joshua had seen her. For her loveliness had ripened with age, and her womanly qualities were more defined by the wisdom that time had lent to her face.

She did not gaze upon the moon this night, as she had that evening long ago, when, unbeknownst to her, a Hebrew general had admired her. Instead, her eyes traveled across the hills, toward the Jordan River, beyond which the Israelites were camped.

Joshua did not know that she thought of him as often, over the years, as he had thought of her. She had not seen his lingering gaze from her nighttime window, but she had spoken to him, and to his men, in the street next day. And though she did not know his name, or the importance of his office, she had never forgotten the handsome Hebrew with the dark hair and the scrupulous eyes.

It still pained her, all these years later, to remember the look of disapproval that had flashed across his face when his eyes took her in that day. Surely, he was a holy man, like the mighty Moses whose fame had spread from Egypt to Canaan, and to all parts of the world.

Surely, by his standards and the standards of Israel, her profession was lewd and unpardonable.

Still, she often thought of him, wondering what his position might be among the millions who had terrified the nations round about. He was obviously a leader; at least among the small group of men who had entered Jericho, he was the spokesman.

She remembered how he had denounced her group of women at the fountain, and she wondered if he would have looked more kindly on her had she not been marked as a harlot.

He became ever more present in her reveries when the traveling hosts of Israel entered the regions east of Jordan, subduing and occupying the land from Edom to Syria. Perhaps he served under the great general, Joshua, whose military feats were heralded far and wide, equaling the miracles of Moses for legendary value.

Whoever, he was the oft-returning vision of her fantasies. No matter how many men Rahab had known, the one she had seen but once dominated her romantic dreams.

No presence so great as Israel could stay in any one place without its every move being reported among the neighboring lands. Just today, in the Jericho streets, it was reported that the invaders were regrouping, making preparations to push on. Speculations ran wild as to the company's next plans.

Word also had it that Moses had disappeared, that perhaps he had died, and that leadership had been passed to Joshua.

If this was true, Israel's next move would doubtless be to make a definitive advance against Canaan.

No Canaanite, however unschooled, was ignorant of the fact that Israel had long ago been uprooted from the land of its fathers. And no citizen of the world failed to marvel at the flight of the enslaved from four hundred years' bondage in Egypt.

It was widely held that every race and every nation had an overseeing god. Apparently the god of the Hebrews had taken matters in hand to return the people to their homeland. It remained now to be seen whether the god of Israel would prevail.

Rahab shivered with the desert breeze, and drew a scarlet shawl over her shoulders. Israel had thrown terror into the hearts of all people round about, but she, more than most, believed the gods of Canaan would fare ill in any encounter with Yahweh.

It was not only the fate of Egypt that told her this. Everyone knew the story of that defeat, yet most Canaanites held fast to the hope that Baal and Astarte were mightier. Rahab, however, had been influenced from childhood to respect the God of the Hebrews.

Indeed, her personal background was a jumble of environments and mixed training. Her earliest memories were of a caring home, wherein mother and father, simple fabric makers, raised their children to be responsible tradesmen and women. The home was always abustle, in those days, with industrious activity, the coming and going of customers from the front-room shop, and chatty dinners around the evening fire.

Predominant in those memories was the figure of a jolly cook, a Hebrew slave, whom her father had purchased and brought home from Egypt.

Ada was a large woman, as wide as she was high, and she filled the house, from the moment she entered, with songs and happy stories. Most of those songs and stories were of the Hebrews and their history, full of legend and miracles. And as Rahab spent a good deal of time in the kitchen, playing at Ada's skirts and later helping with the chores, she grew up learning to speak Hebrew as fluently as her native tongue.

Along with the language was also imparted a reverence for the God of Jacob, and a wonder at the workings of Yahweh on behalf of those ancient people.

This was a reverence that never entirely passed away, despite the fact that, in time, Rahab's life was radically changed.

The death of her beloved papa, and the introduction of a stepfather, brought with it an new lifestyle, one which would forever sweep away the innocence of her early years, and release a tide of activity that left her helpless in its wake.

Her stepfather maintained the family fabric business, but finding that it did not produce sufficient riches to satisfy his appetites, he began to use his wife's daughters for other purposes.

Selling them for a night or an hour to his male customers, he turned the family home into a den of fleshly indulgence. And when he relocated the residence to the city wall, making it an inn for travelers, the "business" flourished.

Of course, the Hebrew cook had to go. According to the father, she was an undermining influence. After all, he claimed, his daughters' work was a religious activity, done in honor of Astarte, deity of erotic pleasure. While most gods consorted with the love goddess, the god of Israel was much too confining, and the demands he made were not only unrealistic, but contrary to the worship of Baal.

Therefore, when Rahab was only a girl, Ada's influence was removed. And being the oldest sister of the household, Rahab carried the greatest burden of fulfilling her father's goals.

The day Joshua and his men had seen her in the street, she accompanied her sisters and several of the paid women who had come to live in the house. Over the intervening years, she had become head mistress of the brothel.

Despite her attempts to serve the goddess, she had never forgotten Ada, or the stories heard at her knee. Nor had she forgotten the language of the Hebrews, and the chantlike songs that her beloved friend had taught her.

Out of devotion to her family, she tried to suppress the longing they gave rise to. But in her private moments, they returned to haunt her, wooing her heart with wistful phrases and kissing her brow at night like sweet, sad lips.

Placing her brush upon the windowsill, she leaned out toward the east. It was harvesttime in the Jericho Valley. Everywhere the scent of scythed hay and the smoke of stubble fires rose to fill the air. Somewhere beyond the fields the Jordan River swelled, overflowing its banks. And further yet was the camp of Israel.

What did the handsome Hebrew do this evening? she wondered. Would she ever be blessed to see him again?

As she pressed her palms against the sill, rising and leaning out as far as possible, she could see harvesters bedding down for the night outside the city walls. Within the hour, the gates of Jericho would be closed to all traffic, and wealthier people hurried to find lodging inside.

Among the folks entering from the highway, and crossing the great drawbridge, two men especially caught her eye.

In their clothing and general appearance, there was nothing unusual. But as they walked, they seemed to study the walls and the roadway with special care. Now and then, they stopped, conferring together, but scanning the moat, the bridge, and the steep glacis that surrounded the town.

One of them, the elder of the two, especially intrigued Rahab. Something about him was familiar, and when a breeze caught the hood of his mantle, pulling it back from his bearded face, she gasped.

Surely this was one of the men who had, those many years before, entered Jericho! Of course, age had touched him, as it had her, but if he was not the man of her dreams, he might have been his brother, so much did they look alike.

Vainly, she tried to catch a direct look at his eyes. If she could clearly see them, she would know, for no one had such eyes as the man of her fantasies.

But it was too late. The men were moving on, entering the gate, and joining with the multitude who sought sanctuary for the night.

Quickly, Rahab bundled her shawl about her, and headed for the door. If she could descend the stairs of the wall-side house before the men reached the city square, she might see them directly.

Whether or not she had found her long-lost dream, these were surely Israelites. That being so, they were here to spy out the city.

And if they were spies, they were forerunners to an invasion!

48

It was not unusual for Rahab to stand on a street-corner. She had spent a good deal of her life doing so. But the streets of Jericho were not safe at night, especially for a woman. And it was unusual for her to go out after dark.

Nevertheless, it was not fear of danger that made Rahab's heart pound as she stood in the shadows at the foot of her stairs, watching pedestrians pass through the gate.

She stood on tiptoe, waiting for the two Hebrews. If she could spot them, she would try to speak with them. It was this that made her anxious, for if she approached them, they would think she propositioned them. And she had no such intention.

There was no time for strategy. Already they entered the town, observing everything about them with exceptional interest.

Collecting her courage, Rahab stepped in front of them.

"Sirs," she said, just loudly enough to be heard in the moving crowd, "if you seek lodging, I know of a place."

Over the years Rahab had approached hundreds of men with the same suggestion. She did not often blush when she did so. But tonight, her face burned, and her hands trembled.

A mixture of feelings was hers, as her eyes met the eyes of the elder Hebrew. She was embarrassed to intrude herself upon a representative of Yahweh. But she was also disappointed, for she knew instantly that he was not the long-remembered man who had captured her heart.

When she spoke to them, however, the men paid no mind to her feelings, side-stepping her as though she were a leper.

"This is a foul city, Salmon," the elder addressed the younger, as they hastened away. "When I came here with Joshua, such women approached us, and he rebuked them."

At these words, Rahab clutched her shawl to her heart. Remembering how the man of her dreams had denounced her sisters, she reeled at the implication. *Oh, by the gods!* she thought. Could it be that the one she had loved from afar these many years was the Israelite leader himself! Was her beloved *Joshua?*

Falling back against the stairway railing, she drew a sharp breath. Should she go after the men, and try to persuade them to join her? Surely they would need protection in this vile place.

But no. Friends of Joshua would never set foot in a house like hers.

Stoop-shouldered, she turned for home. Tears clouded her eyes as she realized that the very man she had dreamed of was none other than the great general, the holy leader of the chosen people. How he would have laughed, had he known that such a woman longed for his approval!

Lost in dejection, she was halfway up the stairs, before a voice halted her.

"My lady," it called, "psssst...my lady..."

Looking toward the street, she saw that the Hebrews had returned, and stood directly beneath her door, motioning to her.

It was the younger one who hailed her, and she knew they risked detection, calling to her in Hebrew. Hurrying down the stairs, she met them on the landing, and the elder surveyed her up and down.

"Woman," he said, "it occurs to us that when you addressed us in the street, you spoke the Israelite tongue."

Then looking nervously about him, he leaned close and asked, "Are you friend, or foe?"

* * *

Like an anxious housewife, Rahab arranged and rearranged the stalks of flax that lined her rooftop garden. Still engaged in the fabric trade, her family stored the supplies for linen-making on the flat roof, drying the bundled flax in the sun.

"You will be safe here," she said to the two men, as she spread pallets between the stalks, making their beds. "That is, you will be safe if no one heard us in the street."

Standing up, she looked at her new lodgers with a furrowed brow. "You must keep your voices low, for we have...guests...that come and go all night, in the rooms below."

Caleb, the elder Hebrew, cleared his throat. "We will do well, madam. Your generosity is more than we could ask."

Salmon, the younger, smiled broadly. It was apparent that he was infatuated by her beauty, and though he felt awkward in this place, he was eager to please the hostess.

"Do not trouble yourself," he said. "May the Lord bless you for your kindness."

At the reference to Yahweh, Rahab's face colored, and she rubbed her hands together nervously.

"You are servants of Joshua," she sighed. "Did he send you to this city?"

"He did," Caleb answered. "Joshua is now governor of our people."

Rahab blinked back tears. "So I have heard," she replied. "And a fine man he is..."

That she was in awe of the general was obvious. But the two men could not interpret the quaver in her voice when she spoke of him.

For a tense moment, she surveyed their faces. And then, beseeching them, she pleaded, "I know that the Lord has given you this land. Your terror has fallen on us, and the inhabitants of the land have melted away before you! We have heard how the Lord parted the Reed Sea when you came out of Egypt, and how you utterly destroyed the kings of the Amorites, Sihon, and Og. When we heard it, our hearts melted and no courage remained in any man because of you!"

Caleb and Salmon looked at one another, wondering if they should try to console her, so desperate was her tone.

But she went on, as though to hesitate would mean destruction.

"The Lord your God, he is God in heaven above and on earth beneath!" she groaned. "Please swear to me by the Lord, because I have dealt kindly with you, that you will also deal kindly with my father's household! Pledge to me that you will spare my family, my father, my mother, my brothers and my sisters, and save us from death!"

Burying her face in her hands, she wept, the relief of her own testimony sweeping over her, as well as dread of God's holy hand.

But her confession warmed the hearts of her two visitors. Stepping up to her, they embraced her, and Caleb lifted her face in his hands.

"My dear woman," he pledged, "we will give our very lives if any ill befalls you. So long as you keep our secret safe, it shall come about that when the Lord gives us the land, we will deal kindly and faithfully with you and yours."

49

Rahab rested upon her bed, but did not sleep. She had given her servants the word that she would take no clients this evening, yet she lay awake listening to every knock upon the front door, and every voice in the halls of the wall-side inn.

The house where she had served Astarte since girl-hood was a popular stopping-place for men of all nations, not only because its women were practiced in their art, but because of its convenient location near the city gate. Rahab was accustomed to the sound of perpetual comings and goings, day and night, within her house. But tonight she listened for a different kind of caller, for militia or castle guards seeking the two spies.

Sometime toward midnight, she must have dozed, for when a loud rap came at her chamber door, she jolted.

"What is it?" she cried. "Did I not say I wish to be alone this evening?"

Again the knocking came, as though the door would be forced open. Leaping from her bed, she drew on her scarlet robe, and yawning as though she had been wak-ened from a sound sleep, she peered out into the hall.

"What is it?" she snarled, pretending offense when she saw two palace police. "Can't a lady get any rest?"

"Israelites are in the city!" one of them growled back. "Spies, here to search out the land! They were seen entering your brothel. Bring them forth!"

Buying time, Rahab shut the door, and called through it, "I don't know what you are talking about. Give me a moment to dress, and I will be with you."

Running a shaky hand through her red tresses, Rahab

tried to think of a way to cover her tracks. She had, in fact, thought of nothing else all night. Now she must perform.

When the police once more pounded on her door, she stepped into the torchlit hall, and with admirable coolness, confronted them.

"Now, gentlemen," she crooned, "you surely know that men come and go from my place of business day and night. How can you expect me to learn about them all? I know of no Hebrews entertained here this evening."

One of the guards leaned over her, leering into her aqua eyes. "You were reported seen with them, speaking with them in the street and leading them, personally, up your stairs," he said through gritted teeth. "Do you deny this?"

Rahab paused and rubbed her chin, as though trying to remember. "Oh," she gasped, "those two? Why, do you mean to tell me that they were...Oh, it can't be! Israelites? Under my very roof?"

Looking aghast, she glanced up to the roof she spoke of, silently praying for the men who were not *under* it, but *atop* it, this very moment.

Then, focusing again on the guards, she said most persuasively, "I had no idea! I thought they spoke with a peculiar accent. But they seemed innocent enough. Yes, they came to me, but I did not know where they were from. Had I known...why..."

Impatient, the guards pushed past her, ready to rifle the house, but she pulled on their sleeves and continued, "Yes, they were here, but they did not stay long. And when it was time for the city gate to be shut, the men went out. I do not know where they went. But if you go after them, you might catch them on the plain!"

As she spoke, the guards intruded upon several of the brothel rooms, even going so far as to throw back bedcovers, interrupting one lewd scene after another in their quest.

"Perhaps she is telling the truth," one of them growled, as they approached the stairs leading to the roof.

Rahab jumped at this. "Listen!" she cried. "Do you want them to get away? Head for the plain! Pursue them quickly, and you will overtake them!"

By now, the entire house was aware of the search. Men and women in various stages of undress lined the hallways, inquiring into the matter.

Sheathing their swords, which they had carried boldly into the house, the guards turned to go. And when they exited, Rahab soothed her upset patrons.

"Rest easy," she said, turning on a practiced smile. "The police were seeking some vagabonds. But I assured them we take only upper-class clientele here. Go now... my friends...go back to sleep."

* * *

Hurrying up the rooftop stairs, Rahab crept through the flax rows, calling anxiously for Caleb and Salmon.

"Dear men," Rahab stammered, coming upon them, "I suppose you heard the ruckus below?"

"We did," Caleb replied, pulling on his cloak.

"Yes," said Salmon, rolling up his pallet.

"But," Rahab objected, seeing that they made ready to leave, "you are safe now. They will be looking for you everywhere else but here. You cannot mean to go!"

"We will not endanger you further," Caleb insisted. "You are a kind woman, and we do you a disfavor being here."

Fearing for their welfare, the Canaanite woman begged them to stay. But it seemed they were bent on self-destruction, and not even her tears could change their minds.

"Oh," she cried, tugging on their cloaks, "you do me no disfavor! You honor my house! You...bless it!" And holding out her hands to them, she wept, "What will Joshua think of me, if some evil now befalls you?"

Amazed at her persistence, the men might have succumbed to her pleas. But knowing they only jeopardized her safety as well as theirs by further delay, they headed for the rooftop door.

Yet again, she cried to them, "Very well! If you must go, hear me! Slip down by way of the wall. All the city guards will be searching houses and streets, and even the plain beyond. But they will not watch for you upon the wall. You can go down swiftly, and slip through the dark toward the river!"

Curious, Salmon asked, "But how are we to do this? The wall is too high."

Already, Rahab had removed her outer garment, the scarlet robe in which she received her clients. With deft hands she was tearing it seam from seam and length from length, into long strands of blood-red cloth.

"Quick!" she ordered. "Tie these into knots. It is good, strong material! It will make a sturdy rope!"

With a shrug, the two Israelites glanced at one another, and almost laughing, they took up the long shreds, doing just as she instructed.

In moments they had a fine, long tatter of rope. And this Rahab took to the roof's edge.

"Go to the hill country," she directed, "lest those who pursue you happen upon you. Hide yourselves there for three days, until they give up the chase. After that, you may go your way!"

Could any man question such a commanding woman? Why, not even Joshua himself would have withstood her.

But Caleb was still in charge, and was quick to let her know so. "Remember the promise we made to you?" he said, as he threw the rope over an aperture in the ledge. "We shall be free from it unless, when we come into this land, you tie this cord of scarlet in this very opening. And gather your family in the house—your father and your mother and your brothers and all your household."

"Yes," Rahab agreed, securing the top end of the rope to a beam.

"If anyone goes out of the house, into the street," Caleb said firmly, "his blood shall be on his own head, and we shall be guiltless. But if anyone who stays with you is harmed, his blood shall be on our hands!"

"Yes, yes," she nodded. "Now, the two of you be gone!"

Together the men started toward the ledge. But in tandem they returned, embracing her fondly.

Then, composing himself, Caleb cleared his throat.

"Remember," he said in as manly a tone as he could muster, "if you tell this business of ours...we shall be free from the oath."

"So be it," Rahab confirmed, wiping her eyes.

And as the two spies climbed down the wall, she called softly after them, "Bless Joshua for me! Tell him the woman of Jericho prays for him."

50

Up and down the east bank of Jordan, Joshua traipsed on horseback, straining his eyes toward the sunset.

His spies, one of whom was his best friend, had been gone for four days. They were due to return this evening, according to the plan laid out before they left.

The general did not know that they had been in hiding. He did not know that they had almost been discovered their first night in Jericho, or that their "spying of the land" had taken place with the militia of that city scouting the west bank behind them.

When they appeared, true to schedule, the evening of the fourth day, their commander led his horse into the ford to meet them.

"Caleb!" he cried. "Salmon! How did you fare?"

Waving their arms in the air, they greeted him, and Caleb shouted, "Surely the Lord has given all the land into our hands! And all the inhabitants have melted in fear before us!"

* * *

It was a joyous reunion that took place in the general's camp that night. All the leading men of Israel joined about the fire of the meeting tent, which, since the death of Moses, had come to be Joshua's abode.

Eager to hear the story of the spies' adventure, and their military assessment of the region, they sat transfixed as Salmon and Caleb spoke instead of nearly being discovered, of being on the run, and of the woman on the wall who had saved their lives.

The moment they mentioned the "woman in red," Joshua's heart stuttered. No man in the room could have guessed his feelings, or would ever have dreamed that she had been the subject of his thoughts countless times over the past four decades.

"She spoke Hebrew!" Caleb emphasized. And then turning to Joshua, he enthused, "Do you remember that we encountered such a woman in the city square, when we entered Jericho long ago? I am certain as I can be that this is the same lady!"

He need not have suggested this. The general had ascertained as much the moment she was first described.

Nodding weakly, Joshua nudged him to go on. "She is a...prostitute...is she not?" he muttered.

Caleb and Salmon looked sideways at one another, fearing a rebuke.

"Well...yes..." Caleb admitted. "But she seemed to be a friend, and she gave us shelter...nothing more. Master, she is a good woman...for a Canaanite. And I hope we did not overstep our authority when we promised her, by oath, that we would spare her and her family when we take the city."

When the men about the fire whispered in private snickers, the two spies looked at the floor, color rising to their faces.

For a long moment, Joshua was silent, disguising his sense of gratitude, as though the matter deserved careful consideration. "Very well," he replied cryptically. And changing the subject, he asked, "What of the land? Will we have success?"

He knew the answer to that question. Caleb had proclaimed it when they had met upon the Jordan shore.

"Indeed, sir," he repeated, "the land is as good as ours already! The people tremble at news of our every move—not only the people of Jericho, but those of the hill country and the plain, the Jebusites, the Hittites, the Hivites...all of them."

"But what of the walls?" someone challenged. "The land lies open before us, and the smaller towns may be easily taken. But Jericho is the most strongly fortified city in Canaan. How do you suggest we move in?"

"Yes," another jibed, "since you stayed upon the wall, you had a good chance to become familiar with it!"

This allusion to the harlot's house was meant in good spirit, but Joshua bristled at it.

"Enough!" he objected. "Our men did no wrong in entering there. And it seems the woman was kind of heart. Judge her by this alone, and thank Yahweh she was there."

PART VIII
Joshua: God's Warrior

51

It was a misty morning on the banks of the Jordan when the people of Israel began their entrance into the promised land. In the gray of that dawn, Joshua watched as the dream of nearly five centuries was fulfilled, as the people, compassed behind and before with miracles, took their first steps into the homeland.

According to his instructions, the ark of the covenant was borne to the waters first. The instant the priests' feet touched the swollen rapids, the river parted before the eyes of Israel, just as the Reed Sea had parted, and the people crossed over on dry land.

Sitting on horseback, where the tumbling waters gathered in a heap, Joshua watched as the long-sung hope of Israel came to pass, as the longing of enslaved generations was satisfied.

The priests who bore the ark stood still on the river bed, in the very center of the pathway, until all of the Israelites crossed over. And as the people ventured into Canaan, they danced and they sang and they worshiped, for they knew they were the most blessed of the generations who had desired this.

It took several hours for the enormous nation to pass beneath the water-wall. All that time, Joshua prayed for the armed men who led the way, forty thousand warriors ready for combat. Directly behind them went the coffin of Joseph, guarded on every side, and ready for burial, at last, in the land of Jacob.

When everyone had crossed, twelve representatives, one for each tribe, bore on their shoulders twelve great rocks, chosen from the river bed for a memorial to be erected on the western shore.

Spurring his horse, Joshua at last ventured, himself, into the stony bed, and when he had reached the other side, he called to the priests, "Come up from the Jordan!"

Once they had done so, the ark secure upon its poles, the people stood back, awed as the great wall of water tumbled down and a mountain of entrapped rapids swelled through the bed, splashing over the banks and rushing toward the Salt Sea.

Riding to a hill that commanded a view of the Jericho plain, Joshua addressed his people, his throat tight with emotion. "The twelve stones which your leaders have borne from the Jordan are to be a memorial of this great day!" he cried. "Engrave upon each the name of a tribe of Israel, and erect on this shore a monument to the saving hand of the Lord! When your children ask, in time to come, 'What are these stones?' then you shall tell them, 'Israel crossed over this Jordan on dry ground.' For the Lord your God dried up the waters of the Jordan before you until you had crossed, just as the Lord your God did to the Reed Sea, that all the people of the earth may know that the hand of the Lord is mighty, so that you may fear the Lord your God, forever!"

As the nation looked on, the twelve representatives rolled the stones into a high pillar, facing the engraved words outward, so that every morning and every evening of the generations to come, the names would catch the sun and remind the world of Israel's promise-keeping God.

* * *

The days following the Jordan crossing were an active time, not a time to take ease, but a time of preparation and planning. Though the dream of ages had come to pass, there were many trials to be endured, many victories to be achieved, before the people truly *possessed* their heritage.

How Joshua wished Moses were here to talk to!

Much had happened in the few months since the homecoming. The general had commanded that all Hebrew males born since the flight from Egypt be circumcised; the first Passover in the new land had been observed; for the first time in forty years, the Israelites had eaten of the produce of the earth (the rich harvest of Canaan); the manna had ceased; and the pillar of fire and cloud disappeared.

Nothing remained to be done before the long-anticipated assault on Jericho. But how could Joshua make such a bold move without knowing that Moses cheered him from the sidelines?

Sometimes it still seemed terribly unfair that the great prophet had been prevented from enjoying the goal of all his work—that he had died on the east side of Jordan before his dream was realized.

Yet when Joshua remembered the glory of his countenance as he took his final steps up Mount Nebo, disappearing forever into the mists of heaven, he wondered if the prophet had indeed missed anything.

Today, as was his custom, Joshua ventured a way out from camp, to be alone, to meditate on the upcoming days, and to seek help for the responsibilities he shouldered. Tethering his horse to a nearby clump of sage, he sat atop a rock on the Jericho plain and scanned the lush terrain. Fields of chartreuse heather were interrupted everywhere by furrows ready for planting, and the rolling hills leading toward the distant city were thick with budding orchards and tender vineyards.

Truly, this was the promised land, longed after for centuries, the land flowing with milk and honey.

Dominating the landscape was the towered city itself, forebodingly quiet. Here and there a guard could be seen, pacing the walls and gazing toward the east, toward the camp of Israel. There was no coming and going from the gate, no commerce across the moat or in the streets.

The gate was, in fact, closed, and had been since the Israelites were reported entering the land.

Indeed, the city was tightly shut up for fear of the people of Yahweh. But as Joshua surveyed the silent turrets, the sandstone walls, tawny in the evening light, the city put him in mind of a lion, apparently dozing, but ready to pounce.

How much bloodshed, how much devastation would be required for Israel to conquer that mighty fortress? And the question which had plagued the strategy meeting the night the spies returned never ceased to haunt him. Just how was Israel to overcome those walls?

No matter how huge Israel's army, no matter how skilled its bowmen, Israel faced in Jericho its greatest challenge.

The time had come to face that challenge. There could be no delay. Consumed with this reality, the general tried to imagine what wisdom his mentor would have shared.

But he could only recall the smile that had lit the prophet's face the day he ascended Nebo, and he wondered what secret lay behind it.

As Joshua relived that day, he remembered other times when the prophet's face shone with unearthly light. Though sorrow had hounded Moses many years of his life, he had been closer to God than any man, and he seemed to see a future beyond even the conquest of Canaan.

In fact, now that Joshua faced his gravest test, it seemed but one step on a great, tall ladder—a ladder that stretched across the cosmos. And while he had come here to plot maneuvers, it occured to him that all the battles of Israel, every loss and win, all of Israel's worship, her institutions and rituals, were mere shadows of something higher, something deeper than themselves.

The days since the crossing had been full of such shadows: the Passover, the circumcision, the manna, the guiding pillar, the ark which contained the ten commandments, and indeed, the crossing itself. Yet Joshua had no clear understanding of what their deeper meaning might be.

Moses knew. But Moses was not here, and without his instruction, Joshua met a blank wall in his understanding, a wall as high and difficult to scale as the fortress laid out upon the plain.

Laughing sardonically, Joshua shook his head. What was he doing here? How had he come to lead this nation? He had been a prophet's servant, but he was no prophet himself! Because it had been imposed upon him, he had taken the helmet of military leadership. But a man of war was not the same as a prophet!

He regretted that he had not taken fuller advantage of his time with his master. Especially he wished he had asked Moses to expound upon the brass serpent and the healing it represented. For Moses, that emblem, erected by Salmon and Caleb on the standard of Judah, had turned years of heaviness to joy in an afternoon.

"The Lord is our salvation!" Moses had declared, holding the standard high. "This very day he takes upon himself the sins of his people—even the very form of their sins he takes upon himself! Look, my children, and live!"

In desperation the dying people obeyed Moses's command, and they received healing. But none of them understood the symbol, not even the servant of the prophet himself.

Feeling like a spiritual infant, Joshua gazed across the plain to the city of Israel's enemies. Shrugging, he tried to pin his thoughts to the moment. Jericho might be a symbol, but it was also very real. And Joshua might not be a prophet, but he was a soldier. He must be responsible for the duty placed before him.

Had the Lord not spoken to him the day Moses departed? Joshua had not been alone upon Mount Nebo;

the Lord had come to him, promising guidance and insight.

Looking at his hands as they lay open in his lap, Joshua saw the callouses which his spear had worn. Running his hands down his arms, he felt the strong muscles and ligaments that had wielded his sword in combat, and glancing at his thighs, he saw the well-worked sinews that had gripped the flanks of his warhorse.

Joshua was not a prophet, but he was a man of war. And he did not carry a sacred staff, but he bore the spear of the Lord.

This was his calling. This was his duty. And it would serve him well to leave other matters to God.

Ahead, the walls of Jericho deepened to twilight rose. He would find a way to conquer them, he told himself. The Lord had a way, and soon enough he would reveal it. If that was all the prophecy Joshua understood, it was enough.

Standing, he turned for camp. He did not know when the answer would come, but he would be back here to-morrow night, and every night until it did.

Mounting his horse, Joshua drove his spurs into its sides. But suddenly the animal stopped short, snorting at a presence upon the trail.

Through the gloaming, Joshua made out a figure straight ahead, a man dressed in armor, a sword drawn in his hand.

The general's heart leaped, but wheeling in his saddle, he detected no other soldiers in the heather. And charging toward the stranger, he flashed his own sword.

Incredibly, the man stood unmoving on the trail, and Joshua crouched down as he approached, waving his weapon in warning and giving a menacing shout.

"Who are you?" he demanded. "Are you for us or for our adversaries?"

"No," the man replied, his chin raised dauntlessly. "I am the captain of the host of the Lord!"

Gaping, Joshua replaced his sword in its sheath, and with a faltering step, he climbed down from his horse, bowing with his face to the ground.

"What has my lord to say to me?" he cried, stretching his hands along the earth.

"Take off your sandals from your feet!" the mysterious figure replied. "For the place on which you are standing is holy!"

Quickly, Joshua obeyed. Unbuckling his shoes, he flung them aside. Then sitting back, he raised his face to the angel and awaited instructions.

Lifting his sword toward the distant city, the figure said, "See, I have given Jericho into your hand, with its king and its men of valor. You and all the men of war shall march around the city, circling it once. You shall do this for six days, circling it once each day. And seven priests shall carry seven ram's horn trumpets before the ark. Then on the seventh day, you shall march around the city seven times, and the priests shall blow the trumpets. And it shall be that when they make a long blast with the rams' horns, and when you hear the sound of the trumpets, all the people shall shout with a great shout. And the wall of the city will fall down flat, and the people will go up directly to take it."

52

Rahab gripped the sill of her high window, leaning out wide-eyed. The city which had been her home all her life had been quiet as a tomb for days, but just moments ago the shout of a guard had been heard upon the walls, and then another and another, sending an alarm through the streets.

It was the shout every citizen of Jericho had dreaded, the notice of the watchmen that Israel was on the move.

For weeks, ever since word had come of the peoples' Jordan crossing, and of the parting of the waters, no one had left the city. The gate had been pulled shut that night, the drawbridge taken up. It was planting time, but no one went forth to sow the fields. No one went out to prune the orchards and vineyards of the city. All commerce had been cut off, as the king barred entrance to foreigners.

Shut in, the people of Jericho kept close to their homes, speaking in low voices and extinguishing their lights early each evening. The towers of the city were bolted, the doors barred, and all lived in fear of the Israelites' next move.

As for Rahab, the moment she heard of the river-crossing, she had run to her rooftop, securing the scarlet cord to the breach in the ledge, and letting it trail down the wall outside. Such had been the agreement between herself and the spies, that they would be free from their oath of protection if they did not see the cord when they entered the land.

There the scarlet rag remained, a symbol no longer of her profession, but of her dependence on the God of Israel. And her family remained in the house with her,

not because they believed as she did, but because they
had no other hope.

At the sound of the shout upon the wall, Rahab had
gone to her window, throwing back the shutters which
had been closed for days. Just now she craned her neck
as far to the east as possible, knowing that the army of
Joshua approached. All her relations gathered about
her, jostling for a view out the same narrow opening.

"See!" Rahab cried, pointing across the desert. "Toward the river! There they are!"

Forcing the others aside, her stepfather joined her at
the sill, his hardened face animated by fear.

With the glow of the morning sky behind them, the
troops of Israel made a black smudge against the horizon, growing like a cloud of locusts as they moved across
the earth, wave after wave of them emerging from the
wadis and the fields of the west bank and gobbling up the
landscape.

The points of their spears, higher than their heads,
flashed in the dawn light, and the sound of their marching grew like the drone of a gigantic swarm.

In the streets below, could now be heard the scramble
of the king's forces, as they armed themselves, and
prepared for battle. Soon the vibration of chariot wheels
was discerned along the top of the wall, and the clopping
of horses' hooves as the cavalry joined them. Divisions of
Jericho's army would be stationed behind the gate and in
every quarter of the city. But they were also trained to
fight from the towers, and their surefooted horses were
used to maneuvering between the broad battlements.

At first sight of the oncoming horde, the machines of
war, movable nets and banks of spear-throwers, were put
in position.

But as the people of Jericho peered out from their
windows and walls, they saw no such instruments of
battle flanking the army of Israel. While the oncoming
warriors wore helmets and vestplates, while they bore

before them shields and bucklers and carried spears and swords, they were not preceded by battering rams or catapults.

What did precede them was one lone rider, tall and straight upon his horse, but keeping his sword in its sheath.

At the sight of him, Rahab steadied herself against a pounding heart. "Joshua!" she whispered.

Her father did not hear. Nor did her sisters or mother. But they all knew that the dashing figure could be none other, and they exclaimed amongst themselves when they saw him.

"How does he expect to fight, when he has no means to scale the walls?" the stepfather jibed.

But Rahab replied, "They say the God of Israel does the fighting. Shall we mock *him*?"

Snorting, the father turned away, and the others clustered around Rahab, gawking at the dashing general who drew near enough to be clearly described.

"Oh," the sisters marveled, "he is handsome! Is he not, Rahab?"

The woman did not answer, captivated by the ruddy Hebrew as she had been nearly forty years ago.

"How many men does he have?" the brothers gasped, pressing their faces to the opening. "Is there no end to them?"

Indeed, as the city looked on, peering through its closed gates and high windows, it seemed there was no end to the stream of people arising from the Jordan. Two great divisions were interrupted by a small company of men in long robes, bearing a golden box upon poles, and holding beneath their arms ram's horn trumpets.

Then the Canaanites realized it was not just the army of Israel that advanced upon them, but the entire nation. At the fore were the armed men, tens of thousands of them. But taking up the rear, behind the men with the box, were the unarmed hosts, the women and children, the cooks and the tentmakers, the old and the young, the sick and the well, tramping en masse across the desert.

At first the realization was confounding. But then the city began to laugh.

Did Joshua think to intimidate Jericho with numbers alone, when millions of his people were not even soldiers? And where *were* his battering rams, his ladders and catapults? Did he think to demoralize a walled city by the sight of a golden box and seven skinny priests?

As the city scoffed, however, its streets and its battlements resounding with laughter, Joshua came on, reining his horse across the heath until he stood within sprinting distance of the moat.

Directly before him was the place where the drawbridge usually touched down, the bridge from which he had once gazed upon a distant window. Taking his charger to the edge of the moat, he scanned the city wall, until his eyes lit upon a scarlet cord, and tracing it, he found the house of the woman in red.

Raising his right hand, he halted his army and all the nation behind. As the dust of their journey settled around them, he sought the woman of his dreams.

Yes—there she was, leaning out as she had done that long-ago day. This time she did not gaze at the moon, or at the rising sun. She looked instead upon the warrior, the servant of Moses, who had shunned her years before.

And this time, as her eyes met his, he did not disapprove. Smiling, he crossed his arm over his armored breast, saluting her.

Then, with a shout, he hailed his army and his people. "March!" he cried.

Wondering just how the Israelites intended to invade the fortress, the army of Jericho manned its stations. Ten thousand archers stood poised in the parapets, twenty thousand men crouched behind gilded shields, sweaty hands clutching scabbards, hatchets, and razor-fine swords.

If they anticipated a charge across the murky moat, across the jagged, knife-edged glacis—if they expected a thousand ladders against the perpendicular walls and the clawing and grappling of climbers—if they shielded themselves against the sting of arrows and the flight of spears, they need not have done so.

Joshua had other plans.

"March!" he cried again.

And the priests of Israel raised their trumpets to their lips, playing a loud, blasting drone, not once, but over and over, each man's blast overlapping the others' so that they made a perpetual cry.

With them tramped a silent army, their eyes fixed to the top of the wall, and their faces stony.

And behind the army came the nation—men, women, and children, silent as death, their eyes, too, turned toward the turrets and the windows, their expressions grave.

"What is he doing?" Rahab's family marveled.

And the city marveled as well, until, as minutes turned to hours, the Israelites still marched, circling the city in one slow sweep.

By that time, the archers of Jericho had lowered their spears, the soldiers along the wall had seated themselves, as for a show. And word circulated through the city that Joshua was a clown.

By midmorning, every soul of Israel had made one full circuit around the fortress. And as they had come, so they left, crossing the desert toward the Jordan like a dissipating cloud.

Hilarity filled the city streets, as the people congratulated themselves on victory won without a fight.

"When Joshua saw the size of our walls, he lost heart!" they hooted.

But there was a hollow tone in their laughter. Rahab discerned it, and she told her family to stay put within the house.

53

Six million feet which had for forty years tramped through the wilderness, marched for the seventh day around the impregnable fortress of their enemy. Voices which had for decades been lifted in complaint and discontent were silent, obedient to the command of their leader, Joshua. And hearts that had, for generations, doubted that God truly cared, swelled with gratitude and expectation.

Could Israel doubt that the walls of Jericho would collapse, just as Joshua promised? Only recently, the nation had witnessed the parting of the Jordan, and that had been preceded by one victory after another against the kings of the east.

Surely Yahweh was about to reveal himself in another miracle! It remained only for the people to follow his instructions, spoken through their general.

For the past six mornings, those instructions had required one circuit per day about the city. But this day there would be seven full swings about the fortress.

The first few days when they had circled Jericho, the citizens had scoffed. But by the fifth and sixth days, their haunting tread, their steadfast, stony gazes, the bleating of the priests' trumpets and the vibrations of their persistent march had so jangled the nerves of the city dwellers, that even the most mocking soul grew anxious.

Today, when the tramping did not cease with the first circuit, when the Israelites did not vanish again toward the river after one pass, the distress of Jericho increased.

Something, they sensed, was about to happen—something dreadful.

Still, despite the vibrations that shook the city's foundations, despite the eerie wail of the ram's horn trumpets, the Canaanites consoled one another. What, after all, could Joshua do against their invincible walls?

And so they huddled together, wondering how many times the clownish general and his flock of fools would torment them today. Twice? Thrice? Four times?

On and on the marching went, until, for the first time, the city quaked.

Did it only seem that the shutters hung crooked, or that the doors did not swing evenly? Had those large cracks always been in the rafters or the header boards?

When plaster began to flake from the siding, when tiles slipped from the roofs, the people began to congregate in the city square and in the bazaars, hoping for safety in open places.

And on the fifth passage, the citizens called out for their king: "Come forth, O king, from your castle! Come forth nobles and governors, from your sturdy palaces! The streets are cracking, the storm drains are breaking, the monuments and the gates are shattering!"

Then, that which they most greatly feared came upon them. On the sixth passage of Israel, the invincible security of Jericho, the boast and pride of the works of their hands, *the very walls themselves* began to crumble!

They did not fall, they quivered. They did not tumble, but hairline fractures appeared along their joints, and then flakes and chunks plummeted to the streets.

At the witness of this, the king and his governors did come forth from their dark chambers. Standing unceremoniously upon their balconies, they watched, aghast as the commoners at the riddling of the city.

Upon the plain beyond, Joshua and his people also saw the growing damage. The walls appeared to lean a bit, and the jagged shale of the steep glacis was sliding into the moat. Here and there a soldier atop the parapets slipped on a chunk of sandstone, and the warhorses along the wall teetered and skidded, whinnying in fear.

Steadfastly, Joshua kept his face to the wide path before him, the path that had been worn by his nation's six million feet. He was leading his people on the seventh pass around the city, the seventh pass of the seventh sortie, and the thirteenth pass of the "war."

Remembering the promise of the captain of the Lord of Hosts, to be with him in this venture, he closed his eyes and lifted his head to heaven. Then, taking a deep breath, he turned about in his saddle, facing the men of the first division and all the people behind.

Raising his hand, he gave the order for the final trumpet blast. And as the priests blew the long wail upon their bleating horns, he cried, "Shout! For the Lord has given you the city! The city is cursed and all that is in it belongs to the Lord! Only Rahab and all who are in her house shall live!"

With this, such a sound as had never ascended from the earth and never would again, arose from the desert round about Jericho, as three million voices shouted to the skies above.

In an instant, the invincible walls tumbled, crushing the inhabitants, throwing the turreted army to the earth, skiddering down the glacis and burying the moat, toppling outward across the plain and collapsing inward upon the palaces and streets.

The dust of shattered buildings and broken roads ascended to the heavens like a colossal mushroom, and the survivors cried for one another amidst the rubble.

But their cries were overwhelmed by the ongoing shout of Israel, the laughter and the praise of the invading host who ascended from the plain, rushing over the disemboweled city like locusts over a giant's corpse.

Only one fragment of the wall remained intact, the

tiny sliver beside the fallen gate, upon which was perched the house of Rahab. From its rooftop still waved the scarlet cord, and within, the family remained alive.

54

Joshua waited on horseback as the people of Israel spilled past him, shouting and dancing and making their way toward the vanquished city. As the millions crawled over the fallen walls, ready to take the booty, they pushed through the rubbled streets, completing the task of destruction.

Men and women, young and old, oxen, sheep, and donkeys they killed with the sword; and any remaining husk of a building they demolished.

Bearing sacks full of silver, gold, bronze, and iron upon their shoulders they emerged from the cataclysm, depositing the booty in a stash which would go into the priests' treasury. This they would do for the next several hours, returning over and over, hauling out whatever was of value to the nation, until the city was utterly stripped.

As Joshua observed all this from the field, Caleb and Salmon joined him. "Did I not say the Lord has given us the land?" Caleb cried, running up to the general. Spreading his arms wide and turning round and round, he laughed, "All the inhabitants of Canaan will melt away before us!"

"Yes," Joshua replied with a broad smile, thinking that Caleb looked as young as he had the day they left Egypt. "So you said! But let us not forget the promise to the lady who saved you."

"Indeed not!" Caleb enthused.

And Salmon jumped to comply. "Shall we fetch her?" he offered.

Joshua glanced toward the tiny pinnacle of wall that still stood, teetering beside the crumbled gate. A lump rose to his throat as he traced the scarlet cord toward the shuttered window.

"Yes," he answered. "Fetch her."

* * *

Evening was coming on over the fallen city of Jericho. The legendary fortress was no more, its only marker a titanic mound. And into the darkening sky flames leapt from its midst, as the children of Israel set it ablaze.

By morning it would be a nothing more than a funeral pyre.

But there were a handful of souls left alive who had called it home, and these Joshua watched as they emerged from the rubble.

Approaching him upon the plain, they were at first nothing more than silhouettes, hunched and tiny against the orange stage. But as they became more distinct, he saw that a woman led the way, supported by Caleb and Salmon, her family trailing behind.

Now Joshua had led mighty armies, he had conquered kingdoms. He, who had begun as a hesitant warrior, had become accustomed to the feel of weapons in his hand, and to the weight of armor upon his breast.

He was a mighty general, unafraid of anything.

But as the woman became distinct before him, walking toward him on the plain, his hands trembled and his pulse fluttered.

He was used to the drama of war, but unused to dramas of the heart. He had often thought of this lady, tracing her face in his mind. But he had never had to trace the lines of his own feelings.

A man in a man's world, he had been able to put her aside when he wished, taking her out at night, when he slept beside his fire, or placing her upon the saddle behind him when he daydreamed along the trail. She could be whatever he wished at those times, say what he wished, and leave when he wished. For she did not live in flesh and blood before him.

Now, this very moment, that was changed. And so the fearless one trembled, the valiant one slipped from his saddle, clinging to it upon knees of jelly.

Bright-eyed Caleb and Salmon did not know what a war their general fought as they presented Rahab to him.

Bowing respectfully, they gently ushered her forth.

"The woman who saved our lives, sir," they said. "If you greet her, she will understand, for she speaks our language."

But Joshua did not hear them. He did not see them, nor did he see the star-struck family clustered at her back.

All he saw was Rahab, dressed not in scarlet, but white linen. Upon the linen and upon her radiant face were traces of smoke and ash. But beyond this she was perfect, her crimson hair a halo, and her aqua eyes transparent as a virgin's.

He could not know that she thought him also perfect, the savior of her people, the captain of her heart. But as she gazed upon him, he read volumes in her worshipful eyes.

Before he could say a word, she fell to her knees before him, grasping his feet and kissing them. Then pulling back, she surveyed his handsome face, and clung to his hand.

"Master!" she wept. "You have kept your promise!"

Overcome, Joshua choked back tears. "Dear lady!" he groaned, lifting her to her feet. "You once told me your house was my house. Now your house and your city have fallen. But you are welcome to live with us. *Our* house is *your* house, for as long as you wish to stay."

EPILOGUE

The Lord your God is He who has been fighting for you.

—Joshua 23:3 NASB

Joshua sat outside his tent in the camp of Gilgal, where the children of Israel had dwelt since entering the land almost seven years before. From inside his shelter, a new tent erected alongside the tent of meeting, came the sounds of soft singing and childish chatter. And those sounds blended on the air with the aroma of good home cooking.

Though the woman who bustled about the cookfire was not Hebrew, the songs she sang were of the Hebrew tongue and to the Hebrew God. They were songs she had learned at the knee of a slave, the family maid who had taught her the love of Yahweh when she was a child.

Now she had children of her own, the offspring of her love for a Hebrew man. Though such fulfillment had come to this couple later than to most, it was all the sweeter for it. And it was all the sweeter because of the miracle it represented.

For the union of Joshua and Rahab symbolized more poignantly than most the grace of God.

Men generally stayed away from the house when their wives were cooking. But Joshua had gone without the comfort of wife and children, and had endured the blandness of solitary meals all his life. It was now his chief joy to linger over Rahab's shoulder when she puttered in the tent.

Moments ago she had shooed him away. But just now, he drew the tent flap back again, and seeing her bent over the fire, a baby on one hip and another playing at her feet, he could not resist the urge to sneak inside.

Standing, he tiptoed in, lingering in the shadows just

beyond the door. No matter how many times he had let his eyes feast upon the beauty of his wife, she never failed to please him. Right now, she was unaware of his presence. Had she known he looked on, she would have brushed the hair back from her face, she would have disentangled the baby's sticky fingers from her long red curls. But Joshua loved the effect, just as it was.

Drawn like a moth to a pulsating ember, he crossed the room, and bent over her, breathing on her neck.

With a soft giggle, Rahab turned to him, and Joshua lifted the babe from her arms, placing him on the floor to play with his brother.

Then taking the ladle from her hand, he dropped it in the pot and encircled her small waist with his arms.

For a long while he gazed into her aqua eyes, recalling how his master, Moses, had desired for him fulfillment and happiness once they entered Canaan.

Only days later Joshua had seen this woman for the first time. Though forty years had intervened between that glimpse and their union, thoughts of Rahab had kept the spark of hope alive through many trials, and ultimately the prophet's desire had been fulfilled.

"I love you," Joshua whispered, drawing her to his chest.

To these simple words, so often spoken, Rahab thrilled, for they represented the approval she had so long craved.

Reaching up, she ran a soft hand down Joshua's bearded cheek, and he grasped it in his own, pressing the palm to his lips.

As he did, his kiss traveled to her mouth, and a surge of ecstasy passed through him like always.

But the baby was crying now, and its brother tugged on mother's skirt.

To the door came visitors, and Joshua reluctantly released Rahab from his embrace.

"Papa," yet another son called, "Caleb and Salmon are here to see you."

The general stepped outside, greeting his tousle-headed firstborn, and joining his Judahite friends about the outside fire.

"Sit," he offered, prodding the embers with a stick. "Will you stay for supper?"

Glad to do so, the two companions, one as old as Joshua and the other much younger, reclined upon the ground. Joshua pulled his eldest son onto his lap, and Caleb chuckled, patting the little boy on the knee.

"Has your papa ever told you the story of the day the sun stood still?" he asked, stirring the fire with a stick of his own.

"Many times!" Joshua interjected.

"Tell me again, Papa!" the lad begged. "It is a good story!"

Shaking his head, Joshua sighed, "Oh, son, not now..."

But already Caleb was rehearsing the account. "The kings of the Amorites came out against your papa," he recalled, "after the defeat of Jericho. And all the people of the hill country assembled against him! 'Do not fear them,'" Caleb quoted, throwing his chest out and mimicking Joshua, "'for I have given them into your hands! Not one of them shall stand before you!'"

At this, the boy's eyes grew wide, as though he had not heard it a hundred times, and he looked up at his father proudly.

"So your papa and the hosts of Israel came upon them suddenly, by marching all night from Gilgal and surprising them! And we struck them as far as the cities of Azekah and Makkedah. And it came about as they fled from before us, that the Lord threw large stones from heaven upon them, and they died. More of them died from the hailstones than those we had killed with the sword!"

The lad stirred excitedly in his father's lap, and Joshua smiled, remembering that day well.

"Then your papa spoke to the Lord before the entire congregation," Caleb went on, "and he prayed,

'O sun, stand still at Gibeon,
And, O moon, in the valley of Aijalon!'

"So," Caleb said, leaning forward and pointing a finger at the boy's nose, "do you know what happened
then?"

"Yes!" the boy laughed. And then he chanted, joined
by Caleb and Salmon and his father:

The sun stood still,
And the moon stopped,
Until the people avenged themselves on their
    enemies!
And the sun stopped in the middle of the sky,
And did not hasten to go down for about a
    whole day!
And there was no day like that,
Before it or after it,
When the Lord listened to the voice of a man!
For the Lord fought for Israel!"

Thrilling to the oft-recited tale, the three men and the
boy laughed together, and Joshua held his son tight to his
chest.

But supper was about ready. Rahab called through the
door that she needed help, and Joshua, gazing across the
fire, saw the light leap in Salmon's eyes at the sound of her
voice.

Nodding toward the tent, Joshua said, "Would you
mind?" And Salmon eagerly complied, jumping to do
Rahab's bidding.

Sending the boy into the house, as well, Joshua stared
into the flames of the campfire, and Caleb studied his
mellow face.

"I have been greatly blessed," Joshua said wistfully.

"Yes . . . you have," Caleb agreed. "And there are many
more blessings yet to come."

Joshua nodded. "Rahab is a young woman," he mused. "She deserves the best."

"And she has it!" Caleb declared.

Joshua knew he had the loyalest of friends in Caleb. He also knew that Caleb read his heart. Leaning near the fire, he looked soberly into the Judahite's face.

"I am not so young," he reminded him.

"Nor I," Caleb deflected.

But Joshua would not abide sidetracking. "If the time comes..." he said, "when she is alone..." At this, he cleared his throat, his eyes misting, "...if the time comes... Salmon is a good man."

Caleb looked at the tent, listening to the friendly voices inside. Then, casting his gaze to the ground, he nodded.

For a long while, silence hung between them. But at last, Caleb shook himself and clapped Joshua on the back.

"My general," he said, "there is much yet to be done! The land must be colonized, the government established! We were in our forties when Moses sent us to spy out Canaan. We are now twice that age, yet look at *me*! I am still as strong today as I was the day Moses sent me! As my strength was then, so my strength is now, for war and for going out and coming in!"

Then, grabbing Joshua by the knee, he declared, "So is yours! You are as strong today as ever!"

The general smiled openly, leaning back with a laugh.

"You are good medicine!" he chuckled. "My dear friend, Caleb, you have always been a joy to my soul."

"And you to mine," Caleb affirmed. "We have neither of us been prophets. But we have done well in the role we play!"

Huddling together, the two men prodded the fire with their sticks. As they did so, the sticks became swords in their hands, and they dreamed together, as they had as children, of wars yet to be won and worlds to be conquered.

So many were the battles won by Joshua, and so numerous the territories conquered, no single book could do them justice. They are recorded in the chronicles of the Jews.

And he had yet more years of vigor and productivity. Eight prophets were descended from him and Rahab, so say the Jews. And when he left her to Salmon, a descendant of Judah, she bore the line of Christ.

So Joshua, the reluctant soldier, had become the warrior of God. And when he spoke to the people, he always reminded them, "One man can put to flight a thousand, for the Lord our God is he who fights for us...just as he promised."

People Making A Difference

Family Bookshelf offers the finest in good wholesome Christian literature, written by best-selling authors. All books are recommended by an Advisory Board of distinguished writers and editors.

We are also a vital part of a compassionate outreach called **Bowery Mission Ministries**. Our evangelical mission is devoted to helping the destitute of the inner city.

Our ministries date back more than a century and began by aiding homeless men lost in alcoholism. Now we also offer hope and Gospel strength to homeless, inner-city women and children. Our goal, in fact, is to end homelessness by teaching these deprived people how to be independent with the Lord by their side.

Downtrodden, homeless men are fed and clothed and may enter a discipleship program of one-on-one professional counseling, nutrition therapy and Bible study. This same Christian care is provided at our women and children's shelter.

We also welcome nearly 1,000 underprivileged children each summer at our Mont Lawn Camp located in Pennsylvania's beautiful Poconos. Here, impoverished youngsters enjoy the serenity of nature and an opportunity to receive the teachings of Jesus Christ. We also provide year-round assistance through teen activities, tutoring in reading and writing, Bible study, family counseling, college scholarships and vocational training.

During the spring, fall and winter months, our children's camp becomes a lovely retreat for religious gatherings of up to 200. Excellent accommodations include heated cabins, chapel, country-style meals and recreational facilities. Write to Paradise Lake Retreat Center, Box 252, Bushkill, PA 18324 or call: (717) 588-6067.

Still another vital part of our ministry is **Christian Herald magazine**. Our dynamic, bimonthly publication focuses on the true personal stories of men and women who, as "doers of the Word," are making a difference in their lives and the lives of others.

Bowery Mission Ministries are supported by voluntary contributions of individuals and bequests. Contributions are tax deductible. Checks should be made payable to Bowery Mission.

 Fully accredited Member of the Evangelical Council for Financial Accountability

Every Monday morning, our ministries staff joins together in prayer. If you have a prayer request for yourself or a loved one, simply write to us.

Administrative Office:
40 Overlook Drive, Chappaqua,
New York 10514 Telephone: (914) 769-9000